Monongahela Dusk

Monongahela Dusk

JOHN HOERR

illustrated by Bill Yund

Autumn House Press

PITTSBURGH

Autumn House Press Staff
Editor-in-Chief and Founder: Michael Simms
Executive Director: Richard St. John
Community Outreach Director: Michael Wurster
Co-Director: Eva-Maria Simms
Fiction Editor: Sharon Dilworth
Coal Hill Founder and Technical Editor: Joshua Storey
Coal Hill Poetry Editors: Anna Catone, Philip Terman
Associate Editors: Rebecca Clever, Laurie Mansell Reich
Fulfillment Manager: Bernadette James
Assistant Editor: Carolyne Whelan
Media Consultant: Jan Beatty
Editorial Consultant: Ziggy Edwards
Publishing Consultant: Peter Oresick
Tech Crew Chief: Michael Milberger
Intern: Laura Vrcek

ISBN: 978-1-932870-31-2
Library of Congress Control Number: 2009924718

All Autumn House books are printed on acid-free paper and meet the international standards of permanent books intended for purchase by libraries.

This project was supported by the Pennsylvania Council on the Arts, a state agency, through its regional arts funding partnership, Pennsylvania Partners in the Arts (PPA). State government funding comes through an annual appropriation by Pennsylvania's General Assembly. PPA is administered in Allegheny County by Greater Pittsburgh Arts Council.

In memory of my mother and father,

Alyce J. and John P. Hoerr

Acknowledgments

This novel was in the making (and remaking) for some years, and many people assisted in its birthing. My wife Joanne and son Peter read, reread and edited many versions. Several people commented on various parts of the novel, including Nancy Russell Washburn, Roy Weiskircher, Ruth Ann and Bill Molloy, Dorothy Varnavas, Russell Gibbons, Ronald and Lynn McKay, and free-lance editors Jim Wade and Julie Albright. Polish expressions used in the novel were suggested by Dorothy Lillig. For advice and encouragement provided at critical times, I owe special thanks to David Demarest, an authority on industrial history and literature in western Pennsylvania, and Peter Oresick, a writing teacher and poet deeply versed in Monongahela history.

I appreciate the support of friends and associates at the Battle of Homestead Foundation and its president, Charles McCollester. The foundation, which encourages research in western Pennsylvania's rich trove of labor and industrial history, was instrumental in seeing this novel to publication. Through this group I met my collaborator, Bill Yund, whose drawings give depth and feeling to scenes in this novel. Finally, I owe a debt of gratitude to Autumn House Press and its editor-in-chief Michael Simms and fiction editor Sharon Dilworth for undertaking this project.

Monongahela Dusk, like many historical novels, contains fictional scenes based on or suggested by real events. My short description of the 1948 smog that killed more than 20 people in Donora owes much to Lynne Page Snyder's 1994 doctoral dissertation, "The Death-Dealing Smog Over Donora, Pennsylvania: Industrial Air Pollution, Public Health Policy and the Politics of Expertise, 1948-1949." The chronology of the 1949 pension strike in the steel industry is based on *Collective Bargaining in the Basic Steel Industry*, published by the U.S. Department of Labor in 1961. In writing about the 1948 convention of the United Steelworkers of America, I consulted convention proceedings published by the union. Eric Leif Davin's study of 1930s mill town politics provided useful background.

Disclaimer

This novel is a work of historical fiction set in my hometown, McKeesport, Pennsylvania, during the 1930s–'40s. While the city pictured in this novel has many of the attributes of the real McKeesport, I have populated it with imaginary people. City officials named here did not really exist. There was no Mayor D.R. Shoaf or Councilman McPhee. The mayoral election that I have taking place in 1945, in which a longtime Republican mayor is defeated by a Democrat, actually happened in 1941, when Mayor George S. Lysle was defeated after serving 28 years. The city's main traffic thoroughfare, Lysle Boulevard, was later named for him. A neighboring community, White Oak, did not become a political entity until 1948, but to simplify references I refer to it as existing in 1945.

Readers who know the real McKeesport will note that I use a fictional company, the Watts Tube Works, in place of the National Tube Co., a subsidiary of U.S. Steel Corp. and once the world's largest producer of steel pipe. I grew up with National Tube, even worked briefly in the mill, but in writing this novel I needed an imaginary plant in which I could place fictional scenes that capture the spirit of my story. The Watts's production equipment and product lines differ somewhat from those of the old National Works. None of the officials at the Watts Tube Works or the Watts Steelworkers local union existed in real life, and in fact no character in this book was based on a real person alive or dead. I use fictitious names for other places and institutions, including banks and churches.

PROLOGUE

From the rear of the storeroom a thick-shouldered man stripped to his undershirt pushes a line of beer cases on a clattering roll conveyor. It's a hot, sticky June day in 1938, stale air thick with the odor of fermenting hops in stacks of cases containing not-quite-empty bottles. In this dark, old storeroom, Bonner imagines, the last pre-Depression owners went bust more than ten years ago, leaving shreds of dreams curled up in dust balls. The place was unoccupied so long that the warped floorboards still resonate with footsteps from a week ago when Bonner moved in.

The front door opens. Bonner watches two men enter and walk slowly toward him. He knows they have not come to celebrate the store-opening.

The first man, short, stumpy and snazzily overdressed in a double-breasted suit of tropical plaid, glances about the mostly empty storeroom. "Like I always say, the best inventory is a slim inventory. Glad to see you're back in business, Pete."

Bonner mops his face and neck with a handkerchief. "Nice of you to stop in, Sal."

"Listen, when Pete Bonner starts a business, it behooves the rest of us to pay attention." Almond-shaped eyes, fixed on Bonner, hang momentarily, either dreamy or threatening. "Truth is, though, I'm disappointed you didn't take me up on that loan. We could've been partners, you know?"

Bonner pulls two full cases off the conveyor, one in each hand, and carries them a few steps to a stack. "Can I get you anything, Sal. A case of beer?"

"Never drink the stuff. But Pixie, here..." He nods at his companion, who stands behind him, arms folded, a great bear resembling a man. "Give Pixie a case of Tube City." Grotto shows a five dollar bill.

Bonner throws a case of Tube City on the conveyor. "It's on the house."

Grotto jerks his head and Pixie drapes a red handkerchief over the conveyor for his boss to lean on. "You got trouble with some people, Pete. You and your helper, that coal miner whatzisname." Grotto looks around. "Where is he, out with the truck?"

A trembling Chesterfield clamped in Bonner's mouth seeks out the flame of a shaking match. "What people," he says, finally inhaling, "are we talking about?"

"All I can say is, it's people...an outfit we cooperate with. Political and business matters. Keep the valley safe for business, keep the commies out, keep business conditions stable. Stability, that's the key. Stability is good for my interests and their interests. I prosper, they prosper...hell, Pete, you prosper, too."

As he speaks, Grotto checks his natty get-up, brushing off lint and invisible dust. "This organization wants to know if you and the miner happen to have some...proprietary information of theirs. Know what I mean?"

"Still in the dark, Sal."

Grotto grows impatient. "They think you know something, you and that coal miner. Something you heard or saw on a trip to West Virginia. These people want to know what you told the cops. It's sort of like their right, you know? Due process." He takes two paces, turns back. "When they first come to me, I figured it was you they wanted. But I said, 'No capisce.' Wouldn't rat on my pal Pete Bonner. But opening this store, you may as well hollered to the world, 'Here I am.' Now they know."

Bonner has listened closely. It will do no good to feign total innocence. "What you're saying is, they don't know what we might know, but if we don't tell them—" He briefly closes his eyes.

"Shit, you can make anything sound ridiculous." Grotto calms down. "There's an easy way out, see. Give them what they want. It's like this Hitler in Germany, he wants part of Czechoslovakia. Give it to him, what the hell! They're nothing to us." His eyes narrow. "Give them the miner and tell them what they want to know."

"Set him up? Why him?"

"He's a union man, and they don't like union. They do things to make a point, see. I'll give you a minute to think it over." Grotto glances at his watch.

Bonner hefts a case from the conveyor onto his shoulder. He walks unsteadily to the rear of the storeroom, thinking it over. Finally it has come.

Grotto calls after him, "What's he to you? Just a piece'a shit coal miner. How'd you ever hook up with that bird?"

Bonner dumps the case unceremoniously on a stack where it doesn't belong. He steps outside, and the brightness makes him blink. Cars are creeping by on the four-lane boulevard behind his parking lot. Beyond the street, across several pairs of railroad tracks, the Watts Tube Works fills the skyline, its great iron-and-steelmaking furnaces standing idle in these hard times. A thin curl of smoke dribbles from one open hearth stack, the final breath of an expiring ash. Catching Bonner's vacant stare, it puffs itself into an illusory plume of black smoke, very much like the real smoke he saw hovering in the sky as he drove south toward Uniontown a year ago—on the day he met "that bird."

PART 1: 1937–1938

CHAPTER 1: June 1937

Since early morning the outcast has walked hard across the wooded foot-hills, avoiding highways, towns and occasional hikers. Glimpsing open sky to the east, he plunges through a thicket of mountain laurel and stumbles into a small clearing littered with burnt shards of bark torn from a lightning-downed beech. A blasted place of random violence that has drawn him there, he thinks, like a church attracts the righteous. Foolish young tree, standing exposed near a knobby outcropping of rock, it toppled down hill, branches spread wide, smashing everything below. Through the gash in the foliage he sees, at the foot of the ridge in the east, a row of clapboard houses jammed into a dark hollow. Just another mine patch: coal dust in the bacon fat and shit in the creek.

Strapped to his back are a blanket roll and a makeshift rucksack stuffed with a change of clothing, a few provisions, and makings for his work. He unfolds a homemade map and traces his route through low hills approaching Chestnut Ridge, the westernmost hump of the Alleghenies in southwestern Pennsylvania. Another one or two days' hike, he figures, grinding a coal-blackened thumb into a dark "X" marking his destination. Right now, though, with lightning flickering atop Chestnut's summit, he needs to find shelter. He looks out across the rolling hills and sees high country in the north and south. To the west, stretch farmlands, ranging in color from shaggy green to velvety tan, a beautiful quilt to the innocent eye. But this is his country, and he sees something else. He sees five hundred feet of earth and rock stripped back like skin and fat from a bear carcass, revealing thousands of soot-faced men with Slavic and Italian names grubbing for coal in the massive Pittsburgh and Connellsville coal seams that underlie this region. In that hidden world, men swarm like maggots enslaved to almighty owners who crush the spirit from all living things. He shakes a fist at the offending countryside.

The man walks down hill toward the east, moving at a half-trot, half-walk. He descends a quarter-mile or so and suddenly steps off into nothing. "Yo!" he cries, sliding down a grassy slope on his rump and landing finally in a ditch beside a sunken dirt road. Rising on wobbly legs, he sees that the mountain dropped him at the edge of the scabby mine patch. A wood-slat sign identifies the place as "Goose Neck Hollow, Property of H.L. Myers Coal

& Coking Co." A dozen shacks line the road, leading to a mine at the head of the hollow with a great dark blotch where an explosion blew out the mine mouth. Women bending over wash tubs in the back yards, frayed blankets and miners' blackened long johns hanging out to dry, barefoot children with the pasty faces of potato eaters, a few old men standing around with their hats on. No young men in sight. Across the road, a small cemetery tells him all he needs to know about Goose Neck Hollow: six mounds of dirt, each sprinkled with wildflowers and headed by a newly-hewn wooden cross, and one large, unmarked mound. Six miners and their mule killed in the explosion.

When the stranger appears at the foot of camp, mothers call in their children and front doors slam one after another going up the line. You don't trust anyone in this seventh year of the Great Depression, with strikes breaking out all over and bands of armed company men patrolling the hills. Standing in the middle of the road, the man raises his arms in peace. "This here's a friend," he calls out, addressing the empty, falling-down porches. He waits for an answer, head averted. Hearing no response, he tips his cap and settles into an abandoned Model-T sitting on rusty axles in roadside weeds. He spreads out his bedroll in the rear seat well and collects a couple armloads of firewood. The storm appears to have meandered southward, occasionally flickering and growling down toward the Mason-Dixon Line. When he begins heating his last can of stew over a small fire, two boys suddenly appear in the road. Their bare legs look like slivers of shaved pinewood in the pulsing firelight. The stranger tells them to get their own pot, and when they return with an iron kettle, he scrapes three-quarters of his stew into the kettle. "Where's your paps?" he asks.

"Gawn to find work..." says the boy who holds the kettle. "Or..." He nods toward the burial plot.

"You should of ate the mule instead of burying her."

"We did. Them's just bones in the dirt."

The boys hurry back up the road with the kettle. After pissing out the fire, the man lies down in the Model-T with knees drawn up to his stomach. Some hours later, heavy rain rattles on the Model-T's roof and drips through its many cavities. At dawn, or what should be dawn according to his reckoning, he glances out his open bay window—into an oily, opaque nothingness. Fog lies as still as stagnant water in a strip-mine cut. He climbs out of the Model-T and gathers up his rucksack and walking stick. Wetness everywhere, water dripping from tree branches, waist-high weeds glistening like knife edges. He scatters the ash-muck of last night's fire and strikes eastward. The mist takes on a yellowish tint and smells faintly of sulfur.

A sudden woman's shriek pierces the stillness and continues, rising and falling, mournful as death itself. Shouting voices, boots pounding on porch boards, followed by a continuous keening. He splashes across a narrow creek tumbling alongside a row of outhouses. On the other side he stops briefly and looks back but sees only the malevolent mist closing around the property of H.L. Myers. He wheels in fury and crashes through the woods. The screams follow him, resounding over the hills... through the countryside... across the nation. Hear America screaming?

At dawn next day an explosion blows apart a tipple and coal preparation plant at the Bridgett #2 mine owned by H.L. Myers, west of Uniontown. The blast shatters windows, and an orange glow balloons in the night sky. No one is hurt because the mine is on strike, and the nearest people are three union pickets stationed a hundred yards down the road. Acrid smoke fills the air as two tons of coal burn in the smoldering ruins.

■

Shortly after dawn, in the town of McKeesport, fifty miles northwest of Bridgett #2, Albert P. Bonner prepares for his monthly sales trip. He tosses a valise, straw hat and double-breasted blue suit coat on the back seat of his car beside cartons of bar coasters and placards advertising Fort Pitt beer. He closes the door and looks at the sky. A stranger might think the sun rises over the Monongahela Valley on two fronts. In the east, atop the slanting rows of shingled roofs and telephone wires, the horizon is a vivid red band heralding the sun fresh from a quarreling Europe blundering toward war. In the west, a paler reddish-orange glow from Bessemer steel furnaces flushes the valley sky. Between the two dawns, on the hill where the Bonners live, a few day-turn workers are walking downhill to the trolley stop.

Bonner's second-hand 1934 La Salle, shabby and road-weary now but once a beautiful machine with distinctive pontoon fenders and portholes in the hood, kicks to life with a gasp and a rattle. He turns to the house and waves to Mae, standing on the back porch in her pale blue robe, hugging herself against the morning chill, too cold to bare her hands. She never wants him to go on these trips. Sometimes he drinks too much, falls in with a rough crowd, stays away a day or two longer than he planned, gets involved in strange deals. The country is full of trouble these days, and she worries that he will drive right into the middle of some violent labor dispute. God knows, there are enough of them going on, wherever you have a steel mill or coal mine, it seems, and people are being killed. Only two weeks ago in South Chicago, ten demonstrators were shot dead by police near a Republic Steel plant. The "Memorial Day Massacre," they call it.

Bonner descends a series of steep streets lined with modest brick and frame homes. He breathes deeply, savoring a brief smell of summer dampness before it dissipates in a stew of industrial fumes near the valley floor. There he eases along in thickening traffic as he passes the Watts Tube Works stretching along the Monongahela. A thin trickle of workers with lunch pails crosses in front of him at a traffic light. It's the same everywhere, factories working at a reduced level, jobless lines growing again. The country is stuck halfway in the Depression and halfway out. The bear came out of his den seven years ago and began gorging on hard times. Now, groggy and fat, he can't squeeze back in. Not even President Roosevelt has enough energy to give a final heave on the bear's rump.

Driving south on Market Street, he halts abruptly at the curb in front of City Hall. In a splash of early morning sunlight, men carrying placards are shuffling in a circle, chanting "Go, C-I-O! Go, C-I-O!" Everybody is talking these days about this CIO, a conglomeration of unions the very mention of which induces businessmen to froth at the mouth as they goddamn its president, the mine union leader John L. Lewis. But a labor demonstration in McKeesport! Mayor D.R. Shoaf, famed for his antipathy to unions, banned public assemblies twenty years ago. And yet a dozen policemen, lined up across the entrance to City Hall, seem uncertain what to do.

Someone shouts "Pete!" A man detaches himself from the knot of spectators and hurries toward the car with a peculiar combination of limp and waddle that identifies him as Tommy McPhee. Councilman Thomas McPhee, that is, one of Bonner's old poker pals, a retired fireman who injured his leg when he fell through a burning staircase. Now he treats the withered limb with contempt, dragging it behind, foot spragging sideways, as if to say, "Keep up or drop off, miserable, useless thing!"

McPhee sticks his head through the open window. "Haven't seen you for months, Pete. Let me hitch a ride up the street, get some breakfast." At Bonner's nod, he opens the door, still talking as he hauls in his right leg with two hands. "I got up early this morning, wouldn't miss this demonstration for nothing."

Bonner pulls into the line of traffic. "What's going on, Tommy? Who're they striking?" The chanting fades in the rear.

"Not striking, Pete, just showing support for the steel strike in Youngstown. Maybe also spittin' in the face of old high mucky-muck, Donald R. Shoaf. See, we got this Wagner Act now, and we're free to organize and that means free to assemble in public and say anything we want. And the police bullies don't know how to handle it." McPhee is fiftyish, still lean and vigorous, and with his ill-matching gray suit coat and brown trousers, his ankle-length black boots, he might be a countryman lounging in an Irish country pub. For years, as the only Democratic member of the city council, he has been a New Deal, pro-labor thorn in Republican Mayor Shoaf's royal backside. He votes so often in his minority of one, he is known as "Opposer" McPhee.

Bonner turns left at an intersection in the waning life of an amber light, then right and continues south on Walnut Street. Traffic is thinning as they move farther from the Watts Works. "Any chance the strike'll spread down here to U.S. Steel?"

"Nope! Old Myron Taylor," McPhee says, referring to the chairman of U.S. Steel, "was scared out of his pants by the sitdown strikes in Michigan. So he says to John L. Lewis, 'Okay, we'll recognize the steel union if you promise not to strike U.S. Steel.'"

"Sounds sensible," Bonner says.

"Sure it is, but you ought to hear your old businessmen pals at the Elks Club. Calling Taylor a coward and traitor as they sip manhattans and snack on pickled pigs' feet." McPhee spits out the window. "Speaking of which, all the guys're wondering why Pete Bonner hasn't been around the club in ages." He gives Bonner a Depression kind of look. "How are Mae and the boys?"

"They're okay. Mae's nervous because I'm on the road a lot. I'm heading out right now, in fact. Going south through Uniontown and down to Cumberland."

"Uniontown?" McPhee flashes a worried glance. "I'll get off up here at Hubble's. Can I buy you a coffee... or something?"

"No thanks, Tommy." Bonner stops in front of a stone-front dive where, it's said, day-turn workers can have a pre-whistle belt or two with ham and eggs.

McPhee throws his bad leg out of the car and slides along with it. He closes the door and leans back in the window. "Dangerous times on the road, Pete. This crazy fear of unions has the owners quaking in their wing-tips. Company thugs are roaming the hills, wildcat strikers shutting down mines, commies fomenting revolution..." He limps sideways with the car as Bonner begins inching forward. "Anything can happen."

"Okay, Tommy. I'll be careful." McPhee's hands finally slide off the window frame. "Tell the fellows I said hello."

The seven o'clock mill whistle goes off as Bonner pulls away. Cars scuttle off the street. Crossing the Youghiogheny River, he leaves the city and

14

picks up speed on a two-lane highway twisting through low hills. It's all so new, this union invasion. "Goddamned anarchy!" his business friends call it, branding John L. Lewis a "thug and dictator." Bonner frowns and nods, but Lewis's villainy troubles him less than the sad state of business: nobody buying, nobody selling, and FDR still retreating from the activism that shook up the nation in his first term.

Descending to a flat stretch of Route 51, he sees far to the south, probably near Uniontown, a column of smoke drifting upward, luring him on. He lights a Chesterfield and settles in with his thoughts and plans, seeking a way to get back into business on his own. Ruddy-faced with a brush mustache, he is forty years old, six feet tall, and chunkier than during his ball-playing days. Growing up in a rural river town where his father ran a general store, Pete played semi-pro baseball with the sons of miners and farmers on remote and dusty fields, with mile-long coal trains chugging by and air horns blasting up from sternwheelers on the river. After serving on a battleship patrolling the North Sea in World War I, he made a lot of money in the real estate business with his father. But they lost everything in the chaos following the 1929 Crash. Now Pete has thinning brown hair, an addiction to Chesterfield cigarettes, and plenty of ideas—but no money.

He drives into Uniontown around eight-thirty. Vacant brick factories line both sides of the street. Sirens are wailing. The smoke Bonner first saw miles back has expanded into a dense black cloud west of the city. He turns onto U.S. Route 40, rising steeply to the south. It cuts across the rump end of the Alleghenies, bounds over a series of low mountains and crosses the Mason-Dixon Line into Maryland. Roadside markers call it "Historic Route 40," America's first "national" toll road, hacked out of a wilderness trail soaked in the blood of Indians and frontiersmen and British and French soldiers. After dozens of trips, Bonner knows its hills like the lumps in his old leather armchair.

He accelerates for the three-mile climb up the face of Chestnut Ridge. It's a slow, grinding ascent, the La Salle laboring in second gear. Rounding a curve, he plunges abruptly into writhing, swirling wraiths dashing against the windshield. Chunks of mist form and reform in yet more ghastly shapes. It's like driving into a mob of faceless men. He swerves the car leftward, shocking himself back to reality. It's fog, of course, "upslope fog," as they call it, created by warm air cooling and expanding as it flows up the mountain, always present in this area but especially aggressive today.

Leaning out the window, he sees that he has crossed into the left lane. He veers hard to the right and feels a thump on the right front fender, and a real face comes flying over the hood of the car, shouting at him, then slipping away to the right. "God almighty," Bonner whispers and halts the car on the road shoulder.

He walks down the roadside, squinting into the mist. Five yards, ten yards. A truck grinds up hill in the distance, shifting into a lower gear. Hearing a groan, he sees a man lying face down in a ditch. He wears a thin jacket over a gray denim shirt, faded trousers, and black work boots with the heels worn down to nothing. A cloth cap with a turned-up peak lies nearby. One hand clutches the shoulder strap of a ratty, brown knapsack attached to a blanket roll. Bonner tugs on the man's shoulder to turn him over. "Hey, fella, you hurt?" The man is young, probably in his mid-twenties, though his swarthy face is already hard-set, his high forehead a washboard of wrinkles.

The man opens one eye. It registers shock, then pain, then suspicion. "You the dumb bastard that hit me?" The man pushes himself to a sitting position and looks around, instantly alert. He feels his rear end and grimaces. "You got me square in the ass. What's your fender look like?"

"I'll get you to a doctor." Bonner extends a hand.

"No doctor!" He rises stiffly. "You feel guilty, give me a lift up the hill."

Bonner hesitates. The other man, toughened by work, is lean and hard. There is a scar on his left temple with the stitch marks still showing. His hands are horny as shells, embedded with dirt, and the right one has only four fingers and a stump where the little finger was. Tough, mean hands that have seen hard work and are capable of anything.

The man grins at Bonner. "Don't worry, bud. Maybe I got designs but not on you." He limps up the road and tosses his pack through an open rear window.

Bonner pulls into traffic. A stream of lights moves slowly down the left lane, cars becoming more and more visible as the fog thins. The passenger sits with his back against the door, half facing Bonner, studying him. "So you're a salesman, huh? Beer, I'll bet, with them Fort Pitt beer signs in the back seat." Bonner says nothing, and the man continues. "Me, I'm a coal miner. Going south to look for work. Goddamn companies hereabouts blacklisted me for pushing the union."

Bonner notices sweat stains in the armpits of the man's jacket. He has been walking hard, perhaps running. Bonner says, "I've never seen anybody hike up this hill."

The rider stares back at him. "Maybe I ain't no ordinary bird." Fearlessness tinged with bravado. Accusing eyes: *You look at me and see a coal-digging hunky slob.*

Bonner decides to ignore the challenge. He speeds up, Route 40 rising and falling rhythmically from one forested ridge to the next. The passenger soon falls into a deep sleep, his head rolling back and forth on the back of his seat. At nine o'clock Bonner begins making calls at taverns along the highway, handing out placards and coasters as a reminder that Fort Pitt provides the "zest and heft" missing in all other beers. Sleepy bartenders listen to his sales pitch and tell him, sure, they'll push Fort Pitt—if they ever get any customers.

Bonner crosses the Pennsylvania-Maryland border and pulls into a Gulf station, where a man is leaning against a faded orange pump. Bleached planks and beams, the cobwebbed detritus of a never built addition, lie stacked against the ramshackle station hut. In response to Bonner's breezy "Fill 'er up," the proprietor fiddles with the hose and bangs on the pump to get it started. Bonner checks the radiator, then closes the hood and pays the attendant. Finally awake, the miner stands at the edge of the station driveway, looking up and down the road. Birds twitter in the trees.

A sudden screeching of tires. Bonner looks up and sees a two-door green Ford with a bashed-in front fender sliding down the highway with locked wheels, leaving a trail of burning rubber. It comes to a halt some fifty yards beyond the station. Within seconds, it is rocketing back towards them in reverse, weaving across the centerline.

The miner now is running toward the La Salle. "Let's get out of here!"

It is too late. The Ford swerves backwards into the driveway and comes to a crunching stop beside him. Two men jump out of the car. Both are large and heavyset, wearing cheap suits and battered fedoras. The driver pulls a blackjack out of a back pocket as he strides up to the miner. "Hold up, pal."

The second man walks toward Bonner. "This guy hitchhiking with you?" He opens a rear door of the La Salle, and the miner's rucksack falls out. "Look-a here, Tom," he says, holding up the pack, "a regular old coal-patch suitcase."

Tom slams the heels of both hands against the miner. "Even going forty I could spot him standing there. Must of been the smell."

"Are you cops?" Bonner says finally. The question sounds foolish.

The proprietor runs into the station and slams the door.

"No, they ain't cops," the miner shouts. Backing up under Tom's pushing, he knocks his assailant's hands away. "They're goddamn company dicks, Coal and Iron Police. Paid whores and murderers! They ain't even human, just scum in a cesspool."

"You just bought yourself a beating, hunky," Tom says. He takes a vicious swipe with the blackjack, misses.

The miner tries to reach into his trousers pocket. "You come near me, I kill you, fat prick."

The second detective says to Bonner, "Stay put and maybe you won't get hurt." He pokes Bonner in his soft belly, then quickly circles to the rear of the hitchhiker.

When the miner half turns to face the second man, Tom leaps at him, and pulls his jacket up from the bottom, locking his arms. The man in the rear delivers two hard blows to the kidneys. Their victim cries out but continues to squirm and kick about with his legs. Tom knees him in the stomach.

Bonner wants to jump into the car and drive away. But his legs take him, unwillingly, in the other direction. The detectives are smashing their man up against the wall of the hut, punching him in the back. From behind, Bonner wraps his arm around Tom and heaves him aside. He reaches into the wood-pile and picks up a four-by-four swathed in spider's silk. Calmly, as if swinging in the batter's cage, he whacks the other man across the back of the shoulders. The man straightens up with a yell. Bonner swings again, swatting him just under the knees. He goes down with a loud groan.

When Tom turns to see what happened to his partner, the miner snatches the four-by-four from Bonner and, batting at only half strength, clouts Tom on the side of the head. Blood spurts out of his left ear.

With the two mine dicks writhing on the ground, the miner drops to his knees coughing bloody phlegm into the dirt. But he is up in a moment, pulling from his pocket a switchblade knife. "We got to get out of here," he says. He limps to the green Ford and punctures the thin-walled tires. The car sinks, corner to corner, four hissing sounds meshing into one.

Before he knows it, Bonner is back at the wheel of the La Salle, speeding south. The miner is pounding his knees like tom-toms, intoning, "Oh shit, oh shit! We knocked those sons-'a-bitches into kingdom come. It'll be a cold day before they kick a coal miner again." He extends his right hand to Bonner. "Thanks, brother. Joe Miravich thanks you."

Carried along on this joyous tide, Bonner introduces himself. He grins, mimicking Miravich, forming a manly bond with the young miner. It seems only right: we thumped the bad guys. How good it felt to smash the four-by-four against Tom's back. Then he thinks, Oh, Jesus, what have I got myself into?

They start up the long hill to Keyser's Ridge, but their flight is slowed by a rattletrap pickup carrying a bureau, a bed with a brass headstand, and three children peering over the tailgate. Migrant family heading south. To what?

Unable to pass the pickup, Bonner crawls along at fifteen. At this speed, cops on foot could catch up. "Wait a minute," he says. "Who are we running from?" Reflexively, he turns on the Delco, affirming his unconscious belief that all knowledge is wafted about on air waves. The radio pours out static and the faint strains of hillbilly music. He twirls the dial through broad bands of atmospheric noise and returns to hillbilly.

"You want news?" Miravich says. "I'll give you news. Wars, revolution, killing, starvation, disease, earthquakes, mine cave-ins, the rich growing richer and making the rest of us pay for it. There's your news, buddy." He reaches to turn the radio off.

"Leave it on!"

Finally, barely audible, a newscaster tells of war, revolution, starvation...a mine explosion near Uniontown, Pennsylvania. The Bridgett #2 mine owned by H.L. Myers...firemen still sifting through the rubble...no injuries reported, but heavy property damage...authorities questioning officials of the Mine Workers union. Police also are searching for an unidentified man seen in the vicinity.

Bonner turns it off. "It was you, wasn't it? That's why those guys were after you."

"I shouldn't of stood next to the goddamn highway. Yeah, it was me, and I'm glad I done it. But don't worry. Nobody seen me. All them company dicks knew was, I was a miner out on the highway. To them, all miners is the same."

"Coal and Iron Police? I thought the state outlawed that outfit."

"Yeah, they passed a law couple of years ago. But a lot of them still hire out to operators like H.L. Myers. I never worked that mine, but I know all about that operator, a curse on the human race. Worse even than Frick Coal and Coke. He was going to bring in scabs to break the strike. I could of blown the whole goddamn mine and all the coal in it. But I just sent a message, took the tipple only, when no one was around." He gives Bonner a quizzical look. "Wait a minute! Here you are, calm as ice, letting me brag on about something that ought to get me twenty years."

Bonner stops on the road shoulder and looks straight ahead, considering his choices. He slowly turns to his passenger.

Miravich is chuckling. "A bad day, huh, brother? You set out to sell a little beer and you wind up fighting mine dicks and running from the cops. You got a criminal in your car, and you can't give him up without sticking yourself in jail." He shrugs. "Go ahead, dump me. I ain't going to fight you."

Bonner has heard how union men address one another as "brother," implying some sort of familial relationship among good men who look out for one another. A deeply embarrassing notion, he thinks, having been around and seen plenty of men doing just the opposite. Nonetheless, making up his mind, he says, "We've got to get off this road. Every saloon owner from here to Cumberland knows me and my car."

At Keyser's Ridge, Bonner turns off on a country road leading through Accident, Maryland and into West Virginia. The ease of their escape pleases Bonner until, ten miles inside West Virginia, a road sign denouncing Demon Rum reminds him that he, a beer salesman, is driving ever deeper into what may be the driest state in the union. His euphoria evaporates and, as always when stuck in a place that offers no business opportunities, he feels somehow less than a man, an occupational cripple denied a purpose in life. But wait! Abruptly grinding to a halt on the roadside, he snatches a road map from under the visor and runs a finger from here to there. Yes! He pulls back onto the blacktopped highway and heads southwest, aiming for Charleston, the state capital, figuring that wherever politicians and people of influence are gathering to plot raids on taxpayers' money—there, booze is being sold and consumed.

■

Enchanted country, West Virginia. Grim forests, jagged peaks and ridges, un-expected swoops of treeless green with solitary white or gray houses nestling in a far-off field. Hill after hill, up one side and down the other, the old LaSalle struggling and clanking on the way up, then descending in wind-whistling dives. Hawks soar over hidden meadows, and ravens sit brooding on phone lines that seem to lead nowhere. Bonner has a sensation of plunging ever deeper into a dream.

After a while the spectacular turns to ordinary and he finds himself alone in the car with a wanted bomber. Bonner studies him again. A young man no longer young. His angular face, all knocked out with raw scars and ugly knowledge, looks as if it has been hammered out of tin. That grin—is it cun-ning, mischievous, or both?

Upon being told their destination Miravich laughs. "So we're speeding down to Charleston for no good reason, huh? You're making it up as we go. Like me."

"Bombing coal mines? You get a kick out of that?"

"Same kick as profiteering on booze." Anger sets him off. "My mom and pap come over from Croatia, thought they'd find a better life, them and lots of others. So where'd they go?" The man looks at Bonner, demanding his attention. "Ever see one of them giant induction fans that draw air into the mines?"

"Uhhh," Bonner mutters, concentrating on the road.

"Well, see, it was like one of them fans, operating on a great vasty scale, sucked whole boatloads of them unskilled immigrants right off dockside in New York and hurled them down all these mine shafts out here. Before they know it, they're spending a lifetime hacking at the coal face with their women holed up in miserable mine patches. It was like the bosses kept them locked up underground till they kicked the bucket in a roof fall or mine fire. Slaughtered like pigs in a rendering house, up to a thousand miners killed every year in those days..."

His left knee pumps to a furious beat, a piston driving this calliope of anger. He himself was born, he says, in Galded Crossing, Pennsylvania, but you'll not find her on any map. The company spied a coal outcropping and tore into it with a steam shovel. Stripped the vein right down the main street, like pulling on a thread in a sweater till there was nothing left but a pile of woolen fluff. The family had to move, and then move again and again, coal patch to coal patch, outhouses, no running water, disease, early death. The bottom dropped out of the coal market in the twenties, and there was price-cutting, followed by wage-cutting and war with the union.

"My pap," he says, shaking his head. "All this turned him inside out. He got drunk and beat us kids and lit out on his own now and then. His whole life he spent as a peasant, the first half in Croatia and the last half in America. He stood up for his rights when he had to, and lost a lot of jobs doing it."

Bonner stops for lunch at a roadside shack where the Missus sells home-smoked sausages, goat cheese, and hard black bread. The travelers sit in the shade of a grapeless grape arbor, gnawing on chunks of bread and sausage and slices of tangy cheese. One day, Miravich continues, his pap failed to come home from work, probably on one of his benders, young Joe figured. But his mother suddenly dropped the baby in the bathwater and straightened up like somebody lashed her to a board. No! she said, her black eyes bulging. They ran up to the mine portal as the whistle went off and, sure enough, a man-trip presently came up out of the darkness, pulling a haulage car with bodies stacked like cordwood. A flash fire had caught them by surprise, trapped them in their section with no bricks to build a safety chamber, no brattice cloth to redirect the flow of air, and no breathing devices. "They might as well stood them up against a wall and shot them," Miravich says.

The cheese leaves a lingering taste that suggests the inside of a beehive oven after the coking. The remedy: a few swigs apiece from a flask of rye that Bonner pulls out of a woman's high-heeled galosh in the trunk of his car. That hits the spot, and they're off again, racing across the western flank of the Cacapon range.

At the age of fifteen, Miravich confides, he quit school and went into the mines, lying about his age. Over the next several years, he suffered a couple of broken bones, lost a finger, and was trapped for thirty-seven hours by a slate fall, six hundred feet underground. Things began looking up in 1934, when FDR endorsed unions, and the UMW exploded with new members. But it wasn't long before the operators began cheating on the contract and getting rid of union firebrands like Joe Miravich. "I wound up like Pap, on the blacklist, getting angrier and meaner. Started wildcat strikes, smashed windows, beat up a couple foremen, knocked a scab over the head with a fence post..."

■

They drive into Charleston in late afternoon. Caught in a westering sun, the statehouse dome is a brilliant golden blur gently pulsing with glorious notions for the uplifting of mankind. Heat waves float in the dusty air. Corpulent men in suspenders lean panting against telephone poles, and strolling women fan themselves with fake palm leaves. By all indications, it is a city of rare thirst. Liberally dispensing dime tips to sidewalk news hawkers, Bonner obtains the names of various "private clubs" where alcohol is served. It is time to work.

When Bonner parks the car, the miner shoulders his pack and hands Bonner a handwritten promissory note, guaranteeing payment some day for the ride. "Why not pay now?" Bonner says. "Watch my back when I go into these places."

The miner combs his hair and changes into his best shirt, a fuzzy brown flannel that looks as if it has been scrubbed with sand. Bonner takes another long swig of rye whiskey, straightens his tie and puts on his straw hat.

It is like entering a speakeasy: a knock on a metal-sheathed door, suspicious eyes peering through a peephole. Bonner tries the "I'm-a-friend-of-Vinnie's" gambit, and the door opens on a dim taproom where a few couples hold hands at small tables and men with graying hair huddle in close conversation. Bonner unerringly makes his way to the manager, hands him a business card, and starts talking. He talks about the light, dazzling quality of the elegant Fort Pitt Pale Ale, so fitting for people sharing a quiet rendezvous in a dark place. If he finds enough demand at "clubs" in the Charleston area, he'll gladly arrange for a Pennsylvania distributor to make a discreet shipment of Pale Ale to Charleston in an unmarked truck. Bonner has a hearty man's way of drawing people into his orbit, as well as a hearty man's way of downing liquor. At the third club, he stands a drink for the house, courtesy of Fort Pitt

Beer. He carries a lot of cash on these trips for just such situations. Evening slides into night. Singing with a group at a piano, he feels people crowding in, jostling him.

The next thing he knows he is walking unsteadily down a dark street with Miravich clutching his arm. Bonner pulls angrily away.

"Your new pals," Miravich says, "had their hands in your pockets all the way down to the crotch."

Disputing this charge, Bonner stumbles backward off balance as a blazing whiteness pins them against a store window. A car pulls up to the curb, and large men in uniforms shove them rudely into the back seat. Miravich protests, "I ain't drunk," and is whacked across the head. A lofty voice intones, "You are being arrested for public drunkenness in the city of Charleston, West Virginia."

CHAPTER 2: June 1937

Cell doors clang, someone shouts, "Git up! Git up!"

Bonner discovers the early morning pleasures of incarceration in a drunk tank. Although his trousers are torn at one knee, his suit jacket is stained and crumpled, and his hat and tie are missing, it is a relief to note that he has survived the night in one piece. He and Miravich and about thirty other men have slept on thin mats laid side by side on the battleship-gray cement floor around the perimeter of the cell. Awakened by jailers, they are stretching, yawning, and moaning. Alkies with sagging jowls shuffle dazedly about. A single black man stands stiffly in a corner. There is a toilet to flush away the night's juices, cold tap water to rinse off grime, and even a glimmer of sun through a tiny, half-moon shaped window near the ceiling of the basement cell.

The prisoners are marched to a serving line, then back to the cell, each bearing two pieces of white bread, a tin of gravy, and a cup of hot, black coffee. Everybody eats ravenously, sopping up gravy with bread. The men begin banging their mess tins, calling for more bread. But the din peters out when nobody comes.

"Most of these guys ain't real drunks," Miravich whispers in Bonner's ear, "just hungry tramps off the road."

Scruffy, hard-eyed fellows gather in small groups and automatically extend their hands, palms down, as if warming themselves over a fire in Hobo Jungle. They split into factions of trashy vagrants and classier hoboes, and everyone seems to know his place. After a while, the inmates are led out to the prison yard to wait for arraignment. But not Bonner and Miravich. A guard and two burly trusties push them back into the lockup, jabbing them with mop handles. "That's for giving us trouble last night," explains the guard. What trouble? Loudly protesting their innocence. Swearing at the jailer. Demanding the right to make a phone call. "You ain't going to get out of here so easy," says one of the trusties. He has short hair, hollow eyes, and taut gray skin makes his face a dead man's mask. The other trusty, a barrel-chested man, wears a filthy red and white checkered shirt.

Now Bonner and Miravich are alone. The miner lies down. Bonner paces the cell, muttering to himself, overcome by feelings of guilt, humiliation, anger. His head is pounding. Hope for the immediate future, fueled by the hot coffee and starchy meal, has receded. Worry about his job and family fills the void. Will he never learn? Tommy McPhee was right: In times like this, anything might happen.

Bonner stands on a bench under the half-moon window and tries to get a whiff of fresh air. He hears shoes scuffling on the prison-yard bricks. Conversation, ribald laughter, a shout or two, the crack of bat meeting ball, running footsteps. Two voices distinguish themselves from the general noise. The speakers must be standing close by, apparently right over the window. One man is urging the second to join him in a plot to "kill..." Bonner almost topples off the bench when he hears the word. "...kill this bigwig union boss...at a rally in Youngstown... next Saturday."

Bonner snaps his fingers, summoning Miravich. The two flatten themselves against the wall, ears upturned to the window.

The voices fade in and out. It seems that the speaker is one of the trusties who drew a three-day sentence for either "loudness" or "lewdness" and will be released today. "Lucky you come in last night," he says. "I was looking for a partner." The other man's response indicates that the two have worked together in the past.

"It's a good deal," the trusty says. "That CIO union outfit's got a big steel strike going on up in Youngstown. That's where I knock off the Steelworker union boss. Phil Murray's his name."

"Who pays off?"

"This guy. Says he deals with Mr. Buck, a big company man."

"Who?"

"Buck! Buck! I worked for him before, breaking heads on picket lines out at the mines. Five hundred smackers, and you get two." The reply is drowned by a guard's whistle. "Got to go now...wait for you after court." Scraping sounds.

A hoarse whisper chases the trusty: "Hey, Whitey, slip me a couple pieces of bread when we get back in."

When the prisoners shuffle back to the cell, Bonner and Miravich covertly scrutinize each man. But the clues heard at the window prove to be no help. Neither Gray Face nor Checkered Shirt, the two trusties, has white hair or other characteristics deserving of "Whitey." The hungry sidekick could be any of seven or eight men who stand at the cell bars, demanding this or that—but getting nothing.

In late afternoon Bonner and Miravich are the last two prisoners to go before the magistrate, whose morning round of golf has delayed the arraignments. Bonner wants to argue his case. Miravich says, "Keep your mouth shut, or he'll clamp you back in that tank for a week." His tone indicates a significant maturing from the bluster of yesterday, and Bonner hears in it an intimate acquaintance with the ways of petty despots. Both plead guilty to public drunkenness. The judge fines them ten dollars apiece and gives them an hour to get out of town. "We don't take kindly to drunks in Charleston."

At the prison check-out desk, Miravich turns his pockets inside out and finds less than a dollar in change. Bonner pays both fines and emerges from jail in a foul mood. The diversion of the past twenty-four hours has cost him untold sales opportunities, new customers, commissions. How could he have been so foolish? He wants to turn the clock back to yesterday morning, and resume his trip to Maryland. They find the La Salle on a side street where Bonner parked it. As he starts the engine, Miravich pulls his rucksack and blanket roll out of the back seat. "Ain't you forgetting something?" he says, standing at the front passenger window.

"All right, get in. I'll drop you outside town."

"Okay, but there's something else."

Miravich has barely settled in his seat when Bonner guns out with screeching tires. He drives in silence, radiating anger. He stops at a used car lot and trades in the La Salle for an old Pierce-Arrow with two bald tires and a new license plate. He loses fifty dollars in the deal and trades dullness for style to boot. But he must go with the odds. The fracas at the gas station occurred in Maryland, and the odds are that Maryland state police have put out a bulletin for a '34 La Salle carrying two dangerous men.

They drive ten miles toward Maryland before either man utters a word. "We have to talk about that murder," Miravich finally says. "Can't just leave it back at the jail."

The salesman says nothing.

"Those boys're going to drill Phil Murray. We've got to go up to Pittsburgh and warn him."

Bonner struggles with the gear shift. The clutch is slipping. "Not me. I'm going to Cumberland. Wasted enough time already. I'll give you a nickel for a phone call, or you can hitchhike to Pittsburgh."

"I know. You got beer to sell." Miravich spits out the window. "You want murder on your head?"

"Look who's asking."

"Whatever I done, I never murdered." Miravich tries again, taking it very slowly, the way he does when instructing new miners going underground for the first time. "We got to go up to Pittsburgh...and tell Phil Murray...that he's going to be shot dead on Sunday. Three days from now. You got to come with me because he ain't going to believe me. I'm just a hotheaded coal digger and troublemaker."

Miravich pauses for a moment, holding on to the door handle as Bonner wheels tightly around a curve. West Virginia races by, faster going than coming. "He's a no-account union man, that it?" No answer. "Don't it make your piss boil? To think some company boss can order a guy shot full of holes? Any guy, union or no union?"

Bonner drives on for a mile or so. At the next intersection he halts on the side of the road and fumbles in a shirt pocket for cigarettes. The pack is empty. "Damn!" he says, crumpling the package and tossing it out the window. He jams the gear shift into first, turns north and heads toward Pittsburgh. Hundreds of starlings burst out of a nearby tree.

■

Bonner stands at a window in an anteroom of the CIO's suite of offices in Pittsburgh. It is early Friday afternoon. Haze and particulates, bonding glutinously, have made the usual thick soup of what otherwise would be a beautiful day. Looking westward from the 36th floor of the Grant Building, you should be able to view the point where the Monongahela and Allegheny join to form the Ohio. But Bonner can see no farther than a poor lost pigeon bobbing in the gloom.

Miravich told him that Phil Murray chose this location for the offices of the Steel Workers Organizing Committee, known as SWOC, "rhymes with squawk," because several major steel companies are headquartered here. It is John L. Lewis's belief (and thus Murray's) that when your enemies travel first class, you must do the same. So the story goes, according to Joe Miravich. He related it on their long drive up from West Virginia, giving details, names, personal histories of labor leaders like Lewis and Murray, the progress of the steel organizing campaign, the origins of the CIO, astonishing Bonner with his knowledge of the subject. Bonner listened carefully because he was, reluctantly and only temporarily, he hopes, getting mixed up in it. Gradually his picture of Miravich changed. He had first represented himself as an uneducated radical who speaks a strange coalfields dialect, the kind of anarchical fiend that Bonner's business friends see in all unionists. He may be all of this and more, but he apparently reads newspapers and keeps up on the CIO business through some kind of underground network.

Having seen his fill of suspended dust, Bonner turns from the window and glances around the crowded waiting room. A half-dozen men—CIO organizers, Miravich says—sit on hardbacked chairs and a couch lining the walls, gabbing in a mixture of Southern drawls. Miravich sits apart, his nose deep in a CIO pamphlet, wallowing in one of Bonner's old suit coats. They have been waiting for two hours to tell their supposedly urgent story. When they arrived, Miravich demanded to speak to Murray himself. A man at the reception desk asked them to sit down and then seemed to forget them.

Ten phones, it seems, ring at once. Shirt-sleeved aides dash from room to room, newspaper reporters with notebooks in their coat pockets amble in and out. Miravich has identified a couple of important SWOC officials, whispering to Bonner as they stride through. Lee Pressman, stocky and pin-striped, with slicked-back hair, general counsel of both the CIO and SWOC; David J. McDonald, secretary-treasurer of SWOC, square-jawed and self-regarding. SWOC has three hundred organizers in the field, trying to sign up workers at every steel mill in the country. Meanwhile, thousands of workers are on strike at Youngstown, Bethlehem, and other Little Steel companies in a half-dozen states. The rumor is, the strike is going badly.

Bonner sits next to Miravich and opens a folded newspaper with a huge banner headline: "Strikers Killed in Youngstown Riot." He foresees the paper's afternoon banner: "Businessman Caught Spying in CIO Headquarters." He leans forward, rolling an imaginary straw hat on two fingers. He lost the last one in Charleston.

Bonner and Miravich finally are led into the inner corridor and questioned by a hierarchy of aides, leading up to Dave McDonald. They refuse to tell him why they must speak personally to Murray, will say only that it is a matter of life and death. "I see," McDonald says, and walks away, muttering, "Crackpots."

Murray steps out of his office to summon an aide. Miravich rushes forward, and several large men converge on him. "Goddammit, Murray!" he shouts. "You sprung me from jail in Brownsville, nineteen-thirty-three, after I pulled that trooper from his horse. I owe you one, and you got to let me pay up."

"Let him go," Murray says.

"We got something urgent to tell you, me and Mr. Bonner of McKeesport."

Reluctant as he is to become involved, Bonner rises to the occasion. "There's not much time left, Mr. Murray. More people could be killed." He holds up the newspaper and taps the headline.

Murray invites them into his office, along with some aides.

They tell the whole story, starting with the beating of the mine dicks. As planned, Bonner handles the narrative, Miravich embellishes with descriptions, Bonner brings it back to reality. McDonald and the others ask probing questions.

When they finish, Murray leans toward Miravich. "Do I remember you?" he says. "Yes, the Brownsville jail. A young hothead, right?" He stares vacantly at the ceiling. "I see more and more like you these days, in the cities, in the coalfields—"

Bonner watches this man Murray, whose notoriety in McKeesport is second only to John L. Lewis's. He is tall and paunchy under his buttoned vest. In profile his face has a soft, almost rubbery look, suggesting vulnerability. Large brown eyes focus carefully on each speaker. He is fifty-one years old, a former miner himself who has served for many years as a vice president of the UMW under Lewis, but Miravich says there is a growing rift between the two. Lewis negotiated the U.S. Steel agreement without Murray knowing about it, and Murray then called the Little Steel strike on his own.

Murray's staff shifts restlessly. They want to get on with the struggle, make decisions, dispatch organizers, schedule rallies, set up soup kitchens, check with the South, check with the West, pin needles in the organizational map. Just when activity should be at a peak, Murray invariably sinks into a coma of indecision.

"...young guys like you," Murray is saying. "You think revolution means getting beat up by the police. I don't know whether you're really serious about winning this fight, or just showing off?"

"You stop holding us by the tail, maybe you'll find out," Miravich says. "Anyway, my pap always spoke well of you. He was killed at Rusty Fork, nineteen twenty-seven."

"Rusty Fork," Murray repeats. "A bad day. Ten or eleven dead. Yes." He looks at Bonner. "You sell beer, do you?"

"Can we check with your employer?" McDonald interjects with dry sarcasm.

"Sure," Bonner replies, "if you swear that I'm not involved in any effort to organize Fort Pitt salesmen." He thinks for a moment. "I'm just a businessman, retail and wholesale businesses, real estate. No connection with the steel industry. If you don't believe me..." He rises.

"Please sit down, Mr. Bonner," Murray says wearily. "You'll have to excuse us. When businessmen come to us, they usually want some kind of sweetheart deal." Murray leans forward. "You heard what those thugs said. What do you suggest we do next?"

Everything Bonner has learned up to now about societal order inclines him to say, "Call off the strike and let America get on with its business." But that belief began to change, he now realizes, when those wraiths beat against his windshield on Route 40. Stifling his first impulse, he says instead, "I don't have any doubt, Mr. Murray, that what I heard at that jail window was two thugs planning to murder you for a few bucks."

Murray nods slowly, considering, then decides. "I think we ought to lay a trap at the rally and prove to the world it's the companies who're instigating violence. We'll need the police for this." He looks to his staff for opinions.

"I disagree, Mr. Murray," says a Youngstown expert. "Telling the Youngstown cops is the same as telling the company. Come out of the same gob pile, thick as damp ashes. I say do it ourselves."

"But we have an alternative in Ohio," Pressman says. "Governor Davey wants to avert violence. With an assassination threat, he would surely call in the state police."

"Martin Davey," Murray says, nodding. "Yes. He's a Roosevelt man, sympathetic, though he can't take our side publicly." He smiles. "Get him on the phone."

A personal call from Murray to Governor Martin L. Davey in Columbus brings a quick response. Davey immediately dispatches a team of state police investigators to Pittsburgh. When they finally arrive two hours later, Bonner and Miravich repeat their story. And then it is decided: SWOC will go ahead with the rally, flooding it with CIO organizers and state cops in plainclothes. They'll keep the local cops out of it. Miravich volunteers to tag along to help identify the gunmen. Bonner goes home at last.

■

Newspapers mention that the Little Steel strike is coming to a climax, but the Sunday rally receives barely a comment. On Tuesday night Miravich calls Bonner and reports that the Ohio state cops blanketed the rally and prevented anyone from getting near enough to fire a shot at Murray. They caught one gunman, whom Miravich later identified in a lineup. "Remember the guy I called Mush Nose in the drunk tank?" Miravich says. "They found him in his cell this morning with a homemade file in his back. But his pal, Whitey the trusty, escaped from the rally. And the cops couldn't find any company man named Mr. Buck. If there is a Mr. Buck, the cops said, he's a pretty dangerous character and you and me, we'd better watch out."

Miravich tells how Murray thanked him and Bonner for saving his life and said he'd hire Miravich as an organizer if he wasn't such a hothead. Miravich bummed a ride from Youngstown to Pittsburgh with one of Murray's aides, and from there took a streetcar to his sister's home in Duquesne.

"Duquesne!" Bonner breaks in. "That's right across the river from McKeesport."

"I didn't come here to be close to you," Miravich says. "My sister lives here. Her husband's a steel worker, Eddie Cramczak. I can stay with them, but I got to find a job to pay for my upkeep. Meanwhile, them mine dicks are looking for me, and Mr. Buck's goons are probably sniffing around. Meeting you, Bonner, put the whole world on my tail."

"Is that so?" Bonner says dryly. "For both our sakes, stay out of trouble."

"Trouble's what I do best. You know any employers looking for a trouble-maker?"

Bonner switches the receiver from ear to ear. "How'd you like to drive for me?"

"You mean drive you on your trips?"

"The state suspended my license for six months... that speeding ticket we got on the run up from Charleston. I couldn't pay much, but we could keep an eye out for each other."

"So you figure four eyes'll keep us safe when the hawk is circling? Suppose there's more than one hawk?" A pause. "Okay, I'll do it."

CHAPTER 3: September 1937

Everybody calls it the mill. Once upon a time, in the 1870s, a single mill—the Watts Tube Works, founded by the Watts brothers—sat on the riverbank here in McKeesport, banging iron into useful shapes. Expanding into steel products, the plant was caught up in a succession of ever-larger mergers that took place around the turn of the century and eventually became part of U.S. Steel Corp., what most people call "the Corporation." The Watts Works now is a two-mile-long agglomeration of furnaces, hangar-shaped mill buildings, sheds, trestles, piles of ore and coal, fire, and smoke. Now there are mills galore: primary mills, slab mills, blooming mills, billet mills, and tube mills that produce all sizes of pipe. But the plant is still known by everybody in town as the Watts Works, Tube Works, the Watts, or simpler still, the mill.

Mae Bonner knows only one thing about the mill: it is either working or laying off. It has been that way ever since she can remember. Today, in September 1937, the Watts is laying off, which is bad for everybody. But her current personal predicament may be even worse. She is sitting rigidly in the passenger seat of the Pierce-Arrow as it bumps along Fifth Avenue in McKeesport. The Joe-person, as she refers to Joe Miravich, is driving, and she is plain scared. She has it fixed in her mind that coal miners are violent people who knock down whatever is in their way, and she expects a collision momentarily. He is an invader in her world, alien both in ethnic origin and appearance. She has never known anyone with a stub where the little finger ought to be, and she tries not to look at the horrid thing, sticking out at a right angle as he grips the steering wheel.

Becoming aware of her interest, he raises his hand to provide Mrs. Bonner a closer look at the stub. "Lost this pinky in thirty-three at Barking Ridge," he says. "Had my hand spread out on the seam, just leaning there, see…" He demonstrates, reaching across his body and pressing the right palm against the window pane. "… and a cross-eyed old geezer sunk a pick in her."

"Ohhh!" Her involuntary shudder is cut short by a sharp warning, "Joe!" as the car momentarily veers to the right. Two hands on the wheel, he regains control. She says, "Will you please not drive so fast."

"Fifteen ain't fast where I come from."

"Will you please stop saying 'ain't' with the children in the car?" Her young sons are in the back seat. "Then why is it so bumpy?"

Miravich sighs and slows to ten. The problem is, the Pierce-Arrow's tires keep slipping in and out of the street car tracks and bouncing over patches of bricks warped upward. The city, county, and state lack money to repair normal wear and tear on the streets, or sewers, or—indeed—the sewage plant itself, which now and then quietly discharges a few thousand gallons of raw sewage overflow into the Monongahela. The city is broke. Everyone is broke.

Mae is generally aware of this situation. The Bonners' landlord calls every other week to demand payment of two months' back rent owed on their home. A hundred dollars. She manages to put him off, telling one fib or another. Everybody lies to get through the Depression. Often she pretends to be a flighty housewife whose husband handles all financial matters but happens to be away on a sales trip. This excuse involves only moderate fibbing because Pete usually is traveling—in the company, unfortunately, of this four-fingered Joe-person. After dropping her and the kids off downtown to shop for clothing, Miravich will pick up Bonner at his office and set off on another jaunt. Instead of traveling south to Maryland, they'll head north toward Oil City, a new sales territory assigned to Pete at his request. Why he asked for the change has not been revealed to her. How could there be more demand for … beverage (she dislikes the word "beer") in that cold climate up north than in the hot and thirsty south? No, something very peculiar is going on in her husband's life, of that she is certain.

"Stop that!" she says to the boys in the backseat, who are quarreling over a toy rubber airplane. Albert and Paul, a bundle of pure energy masquerading as individual offspring. One says the airplane should go "vroom!" and the other insists on "puttaputta." She mediates: "Sometimes it goes 'vroom' and sometimes 'puttaputta.'"

Miravich says, "Now that we're downtown, where are we going?"

"Just go straight until we come to the alley." She ignores his quizzical look. "There's the alley. Turn right and let us off."

Miravich turns right into a narrow brick lane and pulls up at a loading platform of the Union Credit Clothing Store. Empty cardboard boxes and other debris are scattered about. As he gets out of the car, a large black car turns into the alley. It halts abruptly, and, changing its mind, backs out, and glides away. Was it following them? Miravich takes a step toward the street, but Mrs. Bonner is calling. She has let the boys out of the back seat and is placing an empty wooden crate in front of the loading platform. She steps on the crate, puts her hands on the four-foot-high platform, and boosts herself up. Flash of calves at work under the swirling skirt. The lady in Mae blushes as she stands on the platform, dusting off her hands. "Will you help the boys up, please?"

The boys already are scrambling up, whooping and pawing one another. They think it's a game. Miravich is astonished. This is the first time he has had a chance to study first-hand the behavior of city dwellers. "Mrs. Bonner," he says, "ain't you supposed to go in the front door?"

She smoothes out her skirt and shrinks him with a cool stare.

"Okay, it ain't...isn't my business. Look, I know you don't like me, but I am not your enemy, see. Your husband helped me out of a jam, and I'm just helping him."

Mae notices that his nose is crooked. "All right...Joe. Leave the box there for when we come out. You may go now." She looks quickly up and down the alley and escorts the boys through the rear door.

It is a most delicate time in Mae Bonner's life. Everybody knows that people shop at Union Credit Clothing because they can't pay cash. "$1 a day down for any item," the store's ads proclaim. Mae refuses to have the world see her walk in the front door. She believes in keeping up appearances. Her father, a merchant, drummed into his children that there must be standards in life. He was a tough father in a high, stiff collar who set a nine o'clock weekend curfew for Mae and her sisters, forbade their dancing in public, and refused to allow them to drive a car. He dallied with women other than his wife, but he was never a day in debt.

Lined with racks of clothing, the store smells of wet wool and fresh leather left over from a mild winter. Mae goes immediately to the knickers rack.

"Aw, Mom," Albert says, "I hate knickers. The big kids don't wear them."

"Me, too," says Paul. He leans against a row of overcoats, which give way, burying him under wool and fur. Muffled laughter.

"Daddy and I decided," Mae says, picking up the fallen coats. "You'll wear knickers and like it."

She plows brusquely through the knickers, looking for the right sizes. Mae Bonner, thirty years old, a brunette with a part on the left side and curls rolling around the back of her head from ear to ear. She doesn't consider herself beautiful, but full red lips give her a dazzling smile when she feels warm and secure, or a stone-like contempt when confronted by someone or something she dislikes. Her blue eyes regard the world with continuing amazement because, in fact, there is so much she doesn't know. She lived at home and taught first graders until she turned twenty-three and met man-about-town Pete Bonner, ten years her senior. He swept her off her feet with his bigness, his generosity, his competence. She sees now that she was naïve about the world of men. She knew that he liked to do business, make deals, drink with his friends, play poker, go to the race track. She didn't go into marriage blind. But she thought that everything she could offer—including her dazzling smile, ha!—would easily turn him away from those pursuits. But his latest escapade has convinced her that he won't change. All she can do is curb his worst impulses. She wonders if this will leave room for love.

Still looking for a size 15 waist for Albert, she sends the hangers flying down the rack, one after the other. Too large...too large...too large...Sometimes she has no one to talk to except her Irish imp, and now she poses a question: Exactly what part of her husband can she claim, after all, for her own?

The imp responds instantly. Startled, Mae replies, Oh, that part? She squeezes the crotch in a pair of corduroy knickers. The corduroy whistles back.

■

The Bonner home is a six-room red brick house with basement and back-to-back fruit and coal cellars in the residential belly of a plateau that rises from McKeesport's river flats. Every room bespeaks Mae's industriousness with dust rags and hand sweeper. The living room is furnished with modest pieces acquired randomly, as finances permitted, after the Bonners' wedding set was forcibly removed in 1931 when they couldn't keep up payments. There are a camel-back davenport, Pete's armchair with hassock, a gleaming, mahogany rocking chair for Mae's mother and Pete's mother when they visit, separately, end tables with lemon-colored lampshades, and a Victrola on a small stand. Prints of farm and hunting scenes hang about the walls. A bookcase with glass doors contains several nonfiction works, novels acquired by Mae during her brief membership in a book club, and large pictorial histories of the Great War in English and German. On the bookcase mantel sit a Philco radio and framed family photographs.

It is a warm Sunday afternoon in the middle of September. Bonner has returned from a long trip north. He plays catch with his sons in the back yard. Paul, the younger one, stiffly holds out his glove, closes his eyes, and gets bonked on the head. It was an easy lob, no damage. The child holds back his tears and tries again. Bonner is proud.

Mae watches her husband from the kitchen window, trying to understand why he has enclosed himself in a shell ever since returning from that aborted trip to Cumberland. She calls them to dinner. "Albert and Paul, come in and wash up while Daddy—" she tries to sound jocular, "scrapes all the wet grass off his shoes." She holds the screen door open as the boys dash in. Bonner stands alone in the middle of the yard, gazing to the west where a pall of red smoke obscures the sinking sun.

In the evening, Bonner takes the family for a drive south along the Monongahela and up Dravosburg Hill. "Depression Entertainment," he calls the outing, the only kind the Bonners can afford. He goes a half-mile past the Allegheny County Airport on Lebanon Church Road and parks on the roadside behind other sightseers. "Look, kids," he says. Off to the left rises what must be the largest slag dump in the world, a two-hundred-foot high, mile-square mound of partly smoldering clinkers. The surface is pitted with tiny eruptions of molten ash which spill down the hillside in narrow streams of reddish-orange, creating a glow that has guided many an aviator through dark and stormy nights to a safe landing on the hilltop runway.

"What is that, Daddy?" Albert asks.

"That's red-hot slag," he explains, half-turning to face his sons in the back seat. "You've seen Daddy shovel out ashes from the bottom of our furnace at home. Well, slag is what they shovel out of the bottom of the blast furnaces in the mills. They load the slag onto railroad cars and haul it up here and dump it on top of that hill." He omits the finer points of the story, namely that slag, the silicon residue of iron-smelting, a rock-hard, ugly, valueless material, is too bulky to be discharged into the river like chemicals and sewage. So, decades ago, the Corporation began dumping the slag into natural ravines and hollows. When Bonner was a boy, Lebanon Church Road ran alongside a deep hollow tangled in undergrowth. Now, heaped with daily dross from blast furnaces at several U.S. Steel mills in the valley, the hollow has been transformed into a great heap of slag that cools and settles into a concrete-like hardness.

A switching engine chugs across the heap, pulling a dozen hot cars loaded with slag. A brilliant splash of red cascades down the side of the hill as the first car is tipped. An audible *oohing* and *aahing* floats out the windows of parked cars. A second rail car goes belly up, then a third...and soon the hillside is aflame with rivers of clinker-lava.

"As good as a movie," Bonner says as the fire dies down, "and it's free."

When they get home, Mae hustles the boys upstairs and to bed. Bonner twirls the dial on the Philco, but stops when a flicker of lightning glows in a side window. A chill starts in his bowels. Bloated from eating too much dinner, he sees himself growing larger and larger in Mr. Buck's spyglass.

The questioning starts within seconds after Mae returns to the living room. "I want you to tell me truthfully. There's something wrong, isn't there? And it has to do with that Joe-person. Who is he?"

"I told you, Mae, I hired him as a driver because my license was suspended. I'm paying him out of my expense account, and it's not much, believe me." Bonner sits in the easy chair and picks up the newspaper.

"You said he's a coal miner?"

"He *was* a coal miner. All the mines blacklisted him." Bonner talks loudly, his temper besting him. "People shouldn't deny a fella the right to work just because...he's a union man." He blinks and looks away.

She sits on the edge of the davenport, hands in her lap, legs together. "I've never heard you talk like that, Pete. Like that John L. Lewis. You didn't tell me there was union trouble. What does he mean to you, this...Morvich, or whatever his name is?"

Bonner throws the paper to the floor. "It's 'Miravich.' *Mir-a-vich.* You can't pretend people don't exist by mispronouncing their names."

"That's really mean." She hates feeling guilty. "I just worry," she says, getting up and checking if the screen door is tightly closed, "that you're in some kind of trouble."

"That's what you do, Mae. You worry. There's no trouble. Let's talk about more important things." He goes into the dining room and returns with a yellow legal pad.

Oh, no! she thinks. When he comes to her with a yellow pad filled with calculations, he means business—that is, he means to start one and wants her approval. Every six months or so he comes up with a new proposition...a new way to go broke! There are business cycles, and there are Bonner cycles, and from what she's observed, the two seldom converge. She stares uncomprehendingly at the columns of numbers. Written at the bottom of the sheet in capital letters and underlined, like a conclusion that flows irrevocably from the data, are the words "Bonner Beer Distributing Co.!"

Before she can utter a doubt or two, he rushes on, explaining the need to be self-sufficient in a roiling economy and citing the benefits of bringing Dad in from the road. Making arrangements, of course, would take time. He must find a vacant storefront at a suitable rent, apply and pay for a distributor's license, buy a third-hand pickup, hire a driver-helper (Joe Miravich, of course, she notes), and acquire a sizable amount of startup cash. "It'll be a narrow squeeze, but we can do it," he says triumphantly.

There is a long silence while Mae gazes thoughtfully at her polished fingernails. "I just don't understand," she finally says, "why it must always be beer."

Taken aback, he declares, "For God's sake, Mae. The choices are pretty limited at a time like this. Beer is what I know. What do you want me to sell, pants?"

"It's just that beer is so—" Her body stiffens. "You know how I feel."

"Then why bring it up? That was over long before we were married."

"Not that I knew about it *when* we were married."

"Mae, honey, I asked you to marry me, not hear my confession." He holds out a hand to her. "A long time ago. No one got hurt. We just sold a little beer." In fact, he and his father bootlegged quite a lot of Canadian beer during Prohibition in the early twenties. They quit in 1926 when gangsters threatened to move in.

"Beer is just temporary anyway," he continues. "When times are better, I'll take our money out of beer, get back into real estate and build homes and apartment buildings." He is pacing now, more excited than usual.

"And where will we get that 'startup cash?'"

"I'll think of something." A flash of light in the south makes Mae flinch.

Thunder rumbles continuously, and a sharp breeze sets the porch rocker to swinging and squeaking. Passing behind Pete, Mae shuts the front door. When she turns, he is leaning on the mantel, ear to the radio loudspeaker, listening to what sounds like a throaty soprano ascending to a high note. Actually, Mae thinks, he is composing his own music for a new financial plan which in due time he will present to her in finished form. Meanwhile, as usual, she will have no idea what is coming next. She often wishes she could withhold a vital piece of information from him, one that could have a profound impact on their lives. Such as…well, such as whether Oxydol or Rinso produces a whiter, brighter wash. On that, of course, she first must make up her own mind.

CHAPTER 4:
October 1937–March 1938

A nasty Saturday morning, overcast sky bellying down, grinding the mill's sooty effluvia into every inch of street and sidewalk, every building, every dwelling place, and every creature out and about at the dawning of this unusually cold October day. Numbed hands cupped to his mouth, Miravich turns his back on a gust of wind that bursts through the narrow passageway from the millyards, preceding what will be a similar explosion of night turn workers out of the main gate when the 7 o'clock whistle sounds. He and a half-dozen other organizers will circulate among them and ask for contributions to a CIO organizing fund ("Spare a dime, buddy, for the good of all working-men?")

His gaze falls randomly on a black-clad figure on the opposite corner, who retreats around the corner. He has seen her often before, the loony lady hanger-on at the fringe of CIO activities, who always seems to have her eye on him, observing him—spying on him?—at rallies, meetings, and on picket lines. He hurries across the street and turns the corner. But she has disappeared, possibly concealing herself in one of several doorways. At that moment the mill whistle begins its monotonal bleat, and Miravich must abandon his search or be swallowed in the flood of men surging through the mill gate. "Hey, buddy," he says, approaching the first man out. Intent on catching a bus, or belting down a shot and beer, the man knocks aside Miravich's cannister and hurries on his way.

Miravich collects only $1.45 by the time the last night-turn worker straggles out of the Watts. He's been vaguely aware of the mystery woman for the past month or so, ever since he began working as a volunteer CIO organizer on days off from his job as Bonner's driver. The CIO is recruiting members at small industrial plants throughout the valley. Management at these factories, unlike executives at U.S. Steel, are still fighting the union, and company spies lurk everywhere. Why not in a woman's dress? That would be as good a reason as any why "Dowdy Dottie," as everybody calls the loony lady, hangs around, though curiously, only on weekends. She always wears the same outfit, an ankle-length, seedy overcoat buttoned securely around a considerable girth, lumpy muslin stockings, low-heeled shoes, babushkas of varying colors and floral designs that obscure much of her face. On the picket line, marching around with a "Go, CIO" sign, she sometimes bawls obscenities in a hoarse, throaty voice at the plant guards. Everybody tolerates her because she knows the right curse words.

A sales trip to Oil City takes Miravich out of town for five days. On the following Saturday, back in McKeesport, he joins a flying squad of CIO dues pickets who cram themselves into several cars and race up the valley to a tin-plate mill on the Youghiogheny. Although organized recently, the tin workers have been shirking their dues payments (dues checkoff on pay checks is still a gleam in the union's eyes). When they arrive at the plant, Miravich sees Dowdy Dottie disembark from one of the cars. As afternoon-turn workers approach from a parking lot, the picket captain orders his squad to line up across a narrow road leading to the mill gate. "Visual education," the CIO calls it. If the workers refuse to fork over fifty cents and have their names checked off, they'll not get into the plant. Most oblige, grudgingly, but a few, asserting their right to get a free ride on the backs of dues-payers, try to push through the line. Minor scuffles break out. Glancing down the line, Miravich sees Dottie retreating before a large, snarling man. Reaching her in a bound, Miravich throws himself in front of the resister as a lunch pail swings toward him at the end of a roundhouse right. His head seems to explode; pain, blackness, then a piercing, harsh light. He stumbles forward, but rubbery legs take him in the opposite direction. Now he is looking up into a whirlpool of faces, tree tops, the sky, a blinding sun. Whistles blow. Men run and shout. Somebody wraps a bandage around his head. In the midst of this tumult he vaguely hears a woman's cool voice, quite close to his left ear, saying, "Come to the Dandy Hotel, Room 303, seven o'clock tonight."

At seven on the dot, Miravich ascends two stone steps and enters the lobby of the Dandy. An old man snoozes in the lobby's one armchair, and a bald clerk leaning on the counter at the front desk gives Miravich an incurious once-over. "Rooms $1.50 & Up," says a sign on the wall behind him. "Kindly Furnish Yr Own Spittoon," says another. Miravich gropes his way up a dark staircase. On the second floor he hears a rhythmic banging on the wall and guesses it's a headboard celebrating an ardent coupling. The Dandy has this reputation. It's a three-story brick and stone building just off Fifth Avenue, one of the city's two-dozen or so room-to-lets that started out as boarding houses for immigrant steel workers and now call themselves hotels. The clientele includes construction workers, railroaders, and a few old pensioners.

Miravich climbs to the third floor and knocks on 303.

"Come in." Full-throated woman's voice, rising invitingly on the "in."

He hesitates with his hand on the knob. It could be a setup. "Who's in there and how many?"

"Just me," she says. "Are you coming or not?"

He takes off his cap, steps quickly inside, and checks left and right before focusing on a figure on the bed. It is Dowdy Dottie. "Shit!" he mutters.

Plump and frumpy, still bundled up in her babushka and coat, she sits with her back against the headboard and legs crossed on the bed, smoking a cigarette. "I wanted to thank you for what you did this afternoon," she says. "How's your head?"

Miravich touches the bandage on the side of his head. "Got a couple of stitches. Still ringing." He could swear her voice belongs to another person. The words come out brisk and clipped at the ends, like the way society dames talk in the movies. His eyes again sweep the poorly-lit room: a bureau, a couple of chairs, and a bedstand holding a bottle of whiskey and two glasses.

"Don't worry. We're alone." She swings her legs over the bed and stands up. "I've been watching you for some time, Joseph Miravich." She begins unbuttoning her coat. "I like your spirit. You're a fighter."

"I hope you ain't got a gun under that coat," he says, backing against the door.

"I also think you can be trusted. You see, I have a secret, and I want to share it." She pulls the coat off and undoes a pillow that is strapped around her waist. When it falls to the floor, Dottie loses twenty inches around the middle.

"Wait a minute," he says, not meaning it.

Now she is down to a skirt and pullover sweater and the figure of a full-bodied, but decidedly not fat, woman. Shapely legs show through the lumpy stockings. "Jesus, it's good to get out of that contraption," she says, making her arms work like wings. She stops and stares at him. "You *can* be trusted, can't you, Joseph?"

"Ain't there supposed to be music to this?" he says weakly, practically holding his breath, wondering what comes next.

"That's one thing," she says, shaking her finger at him. "Your grammar is atrocious. But we can fix that." Next, she unties her babushka and flings it aside. Reddish hair tumbles down in a stringy page boy. She peels off an astonishingly life-like rubber beak, revealing a nose of routine dimensions. "You may wonder why I've gone to all this trouble, Joseph." She produces a damp rag and wipes thick makeup off her face. It's like scraping packing grease off a new motor. "The answer is," she adds, peering at him over the top of the rag, "I cannot afford to be identified for what I am." More rubbing.

"I ain't sure what that is," he says.

She extracts a set of massive tooth braces that puff up her cheeks and lips, then applies a bit of lipstick. "There!" she says, facing him. Liberated from the gadgets and grease, she emerges a woman of about thirty-five, Miravich guesses, with a precociously hard-bitten face. Her forehead is a clutch of wrinkles, and her mouth droops to one side in a perpetual frown. Miravich sees a still-attractive woman who has let an even greater beauty fade through neglect or dissatisfaction.

She takes a short drag on her cigarette and blows smoke upward and to one side, the way Bette Davis does it. "This is the real me, Joseph. Not Dowdy Dottie, the syphilitic old camp follower. My name is Dorothy Klangensmith, and I teach Latin at McKeesport High School. That's the reason for the disguise. I'd lose my job in a moment if the superintendent knows I'm pro-union." She repeats the Bette Davis act with the cigarette. "So, tell me, what do you think?"

Miravich takes a tour around her. "I think maybe you're a little crazy. You teach Latin? Say me some Latin."

"*Veni, vidi, vici.*"

"Sounds Greek to me. But it don't matter." He inspects her again and shakes his head. "It's like a groundhog come out of his hole."

"Her hole, Joseph. Why must all important activity be characterized as 'his'?"

"Never thought much about it. But if there's girl groundhogs, I guess there's girl Pinkertons, too."

"Joseph, I am not a spy. I am one of you. I am a female worker who happens to be a teacher. I'm one of you, believe me." She stubs out the cigarette. "The trouble is, I'm not with you. I want to be more involved in the most important revolution in American history. How can I do that as a woman and a teacher? If I were Mother Jones...but I'm not. So I pretend to be Dottie." She takes him by the hand. "I want to be with you, Joseph. I want to feel like you do, suffer like you do."

"That ain't all it's cracked up to be." He takes his hand back.

"We're all part of the exploited masses. I want to be your friend, to share things with you. It won't be one-sided. I can help you, Joseph." She sits on the bed and her skirt rides up over her knees. "Come and sit here."

He believes, too, that the masses are exploited, but it doesn't sound right coming out of her mouth. "Look, lady, I ain't your pupil, and I still don't know who you are or what you are." He puts on his cap and goes to the door.

"I guess you're right to be suspicious. But you needn't be frightened of me."

"Me frightened of a woman? Hah!" He reaches for the door knob.

"Can we talk again? Talk at least?"

"I'll be around. But no more conks on the noggin." He backs out the door.

He thinks about her over the next week as he drives Bonner to and from Oil City. A phone call to the high school reveals that there is indeed a Latin teacher named Dorothy Klangensmith. The next two weekends, he observes her around CIO headquarters. She hovers on the edge of conversations, sneaks a cigarette when no one is looking, and spends a lot of time hitching up her false belly. She appears to be lonely, but hardly a spy. Recalling what is underneath that ridiculous overcoat, he begins edging closer to her, mumbling a few words. "How's it going?" and so forth. Anybody who'd undergo such discomfort to be part of the working-class has to have some good points.

One weekend he goes again to her room at the Dandy Hotel. This time Dottie has disappeared before he arrives. He is greeted by Dorothy, wearing high-heeled pumps, silk stockings, a V-necked white blouse, every red hair in its proper place. One thing leads to another and before long they are stuck together and moving sideways in lockstep and crashing down on the bed. They do a quick one, so tangled in clothing that neither feels certain that everything is in its proper place. They undress and go at it next with a measured ferocity. Dorothy demands more than the simple mechanics. He is a quick learner and soon has her nipples peaking taut and red. When she arches up, it's like entering a covered bridge and meeting a landslide coming from the opposite direction.

After this tryst, they begin spending entire weekends at Dorothy's apartment near the high school. One day, after they've exhausted her list of sexual variations, she pours each a considerable portion of Scotch, lights a cigarette, and tells her story.

"I was born into a plump German family in Milwaukee," she says, exhaling smoke. "Plump and wealthy and stodgy, and of course we looked down on the proletariat. My dad sold musical instruments, my mom was a hausfrau, and I was pretty and smart enough to be a rebellious bourgeoise." The family tradition was that girls should be educated to get married, run a well-ordered household full of fashionable furniture, and produce two sons, one for the family business and one for the professions. Dorothy fled from such a future, landing first in New York City, where she taught in a private high school. She joined radical political and literary groups. She tried acting, she tried writing. She traveled to Europe.

Along came Roosevelt, the NRA, the Wagner Act, and the revolt of the working-class. Wishing to become more politically active, Dorothy dabbled in activities organized by—she studies him for a moment, decides to trust him—Communist-front organizations. Later, she attended several Party meetings, but the men assigned her menial duties "befitting" a woman. She read about the CIO and longed to be a part of the movement. She applied for teaching jobs in Flint, Detroit, and Pittsburgh, where the walls of capitalism (she thought) must be tumbling down. Finally, a year ago, she landed a job in McKeesport, mostly because all other applicants fled the valley upon first exposure to the smoke and grime and masses of people whose last names ended in "ski" or "czyk." Dorothy, in contrast, was attracted to these "beacon lights of the proletariat."

In her travels, Dorothy has left behind a few lovers and more than one marriage proposition. "Only the dull ones proposed," she says, drawing on her cigarette, "and I didn't want to be tied down with them. So I moved on." She laughs. "Now I've got myself in a real fix. I'm too young to give up sex but too old to get married."

Miravich sometimes feels cooped up during the weekends at Dorothy's apartment. He is raring to go when he gets there, but flopping around in bed consumes only so many hours. When that's done, he'd like to hang around with the guys. That's the way they did it any place he's ever been: wham, bam, and a beer with the boys. But there's some compensation in Dorothy's cooking. He is still living with his sister and brother-in-law across the river in Duquesne, and food is not all that plentiful in a laid-off steel worker's home. Miravich contributes most of his meager driver's pay to his sister but still feels badly when the Cramczak kids watch with doleful eyes as he devours half a baked potato. Under Dorothy's care, he can save up his hunger for weekends and chomp his way through a procession of pork chops and lamb chops in the intervals between lovemaking. Sometimes he sneaks a chop off her table to feed his nephews.

Along about the third weekend, he notices that her apartment is filled with books, and she seems to have read them all. She sets him to reading. It is painful work; he hasn't had his nose in a book since he dropped out of school at fifteen and took up mining. Getting through a novel, connecting thoughts from paragraph to paragraph, is especially difficult when the words don't excite his sense of smell or touch. *The Red Badge of Courage* and *Of Mice and Men* are relatively easy because he understands fear and violence. But when Dorothy gives him a book called *The Portrait of a Lady*—to sharpen his sensibilities, she says—Miravich revolts. Trying to diagnose his reading problem, Dorothy persuades him to read a passage aloud. He gives it a go, stumbles badly, and flings the book into the kitchen. "My God, Joseph," she says, "you can barely read at the third grade level. What kind of schooling did you get?"

"I learnt to run when I saw sparks flying at the coal face."

"Don't take it personally. You're just a symptom of a larger problem." She teaches Latin to the children of doctors, lawyers, and businessmen because these kids are on the road to college. But the workers' sons and daughters are shoved down "vocational" or "commercial" tracks and handled as if "they're fodder for the mills and mines." They learn barely enough of the three Rs to get along in modern society. But when she complains to school officials, she is met with indifference and hostility.

Miravich must learn to talk correctly if he wants to fight the bosses, Dorothy says. "They use speech to suppress workers. Newspapers parrot their speeches and press releases. Publishers print their books. The picture they give of your life is their picture, drawn to their benefit. They are stealing your life from you, Joseph. You must learn to communicate effectively, and you cannot do that by grunting, cursing, and 'ain'ting'."

He takes lessons in talking. Put the subject here, verb there, object at the end, leave out the "ain'ts," put "gs" on the ends of "ing" words, don't mix up the tenses. He is surprised to find this helps him say things he only thought before. She introduces him to books about the Civil War, and he discovers the joy of reading history, studying all the ways that men have oppressed other men—and women, as Dorothy insists.

She chain-smokes, drinks a lot of Scotch, and talks endlessly about "workers' movements." She gently berates him for working as a driver for a beer salesman. Then comes the day when she asks if he knows any communists.

"Maybe I do and maybe I don't," he says guardedly. "Nobody talks about it. Right now, organizing the union is what's important."

Her lower lip ducks skeptically into its corner. "There must be planning going on. What are the next steps, how to nationalize industry, and so forth. Political action, social action...where do we begin?" Furrows deepen in her forehead. "I want you to introduce me to your party contacts. Where can I meet them?"

When he denies knowing any such persons, she becomes annoyed. "What are you so suspicious of? Can't you ask around, find out where they meet?"

"What should I do, walk down the street and shout, 'Anybody know where the Reds are meeting tonight?' Like that?"

When she drops him off late that night in downtown McKeesport, Miravich goes to a meeting. They have asked him to join, but he hasn't made up his mind.

By March of 1938 their affair has lasted five months. It's as if he has fallen headfirst into a honey-trove: every weekend thrashing around in bed with an uninhibited woman, eating decent food, learning how to read and speak the right way. Meanwhile, there has been no hint of pursuit by Mr. Buck or the mine dicks, excepting of course the black car that followed Miravich briefly into the alley behind the clothing store. He had a sense then that the hounds had found the scent. Why did they back off?

Miravich and Bonner seldom talk about these various threats during their long drives, but one or the other is always glancing around to see who might be sneaking up behind. Bonner calls home every evening from the road, and Miravich once overheard him urging his wife to check the padlock he installed on the cellar storm doors.

This fear and intrigue fades from Miravich's thoughts when he crosses the threshhold of Dorothy Klangensmith's secluded world and settles into a round of reading, eating, and lovemaking. She, however, is becoming restless. "Let's go away together," she says one weekend. "Another city where the movement is strong. Detroit or Akron. We can live together openly, not hide like this."

"Nope," he says. "I got to stick around here."

"Why?" For a guy who lives moment to moment, the finality in his words startles her. "Why?" she repeats, rising on an elbow. "What're you keeping from me, Joe? You're so secretive. I don't keep secrets from you."

He looks at her, lying half-covered by a sheet after sweaty doings. She, in fact, is telling the truth, he thinks. The only secrets she has are the political kind that you withhold from school officials. For all her learning and education, she is a far simpler, probably more honest, person than he would ever be, even if he read all the books in her apartment three times over. Dottie has a truly simple view of the world. Join a movement and obliterate poverty, misery, disease, the ruling class, private property...The Dowdy Dottie disguise is merely a uniform in her movement of one.

"Why are you looking at me that way?" Her small green eyes grow large with uncertainty, and the sharp point of her nose quivers, pulling the upper lip into an unintended and unattractive sneer.

He reaches over and gently draws the lip down with thumb and forefinger. "You don't want to be looking down on yourself...Dorothy. You're a good woman."

She does not understand. "There's something in your life you're not telling me."

He gropes for his socks on the floor. "I promised to have dinner at my sister's. Big celebration. Eddie's got a job painting some rich guy's home, and I'm going to help."

"But I roasted a chicken just the way you like it."

"Sorry." A toe pops through a hole in his sock. "Can I take some for the kids?"

CHAPTER 5:
March 1938–June 1938

Repetitive winter: the valley thaws and freezes, thaws and freezes. A mid-March storm has left patches of smoke-blackened snow on the open hills and cliffs along the Monongahela. From high points in McKeesport, you can see drivers zig-zagging on the highway under the bluff across the river, trying to outguess the timing of huge icicles crashing down from promontory ledges. Catching a glimpse of that game on his drive into town, Bonner sets up a similar contest between himself and the overhanging Depression. He decides to act as if the business climate will break for the better. First, he will consult the best barometer of economic activity that he knows.

He parks the car on Fifth Avenue and walks a block or so to Louie's Confectionery on Ringgold Sreet, across from the downtown bus stop. A black Packard two-seater, motor idling, sits in a no-parking zone in front of the store. Inside, Bonner squeezes between cases and shelves crammed with newspapers, comic books, magazines, cigarettes, candy, perfume, soda pop, Tum-Tums for the queasy stomach, heart-shaped boxes of chocolates for the little lady, and condoms for the asking. Louie is reciting numbers on the phone as he leafs through a tiny white note pad. "...nine-nine-eight, one-six-four..." On and on. Louie is bored. He sighs; he scratches his butt; he yawns. Numbers writers are unhappy in their work, Bonner thinks. Even the illicit thrill of beating the law eludes them in McKeesport, where the numbers racket is regarded as a beneficial illegitimate business.

He finally hangs up. "'Jesus, what a day!" Louie Grotto is short and exceptionally round, and he stands all day, wedged between the soda fountain with its ice cream cooler and a shelf with the cash register. "Not on the road this week, eh?" Louie adds, warming to his customer. "How's tricks?"

"Not bad." Bonner pulls a small wad of bills out of his pocket and begins counting them off. "How's business holding up, Louie? Any gain over last week?"

"I'd say so. Damn phone is ringing off the hook." Puffy cheeks force his mouth into an irritable pucker. "What'll you have?"

"Three-five-six boxed for fifty cents, six-five-three straight for fifty, and a pack of Chesterfields." He watches Louie scribble on the pad.

Shadows shift at the rear of the store. "Well, I'll be damned, Pete Bonner, big as life," says a husky voice, emerging from a rear room.

Bonner first sees glossy satin collars on a dark overcoat, then a fedora pulled low over the eyes. Into the light steps Salvatore Grotto, Louie's older brother. He is trimmer and taller than Louie, but still short, five-seven or so. Sal comes out from behind the counter. Smiling, sharp-eyed, he stops and looks Bonner over. "I haven't seen you, geez, in seven or eight years. Heard you went west."

"Hello, Sal. Yeah, I tried California for a year or so. But it was bad there, too."

"Who would've thought it could happen in America?" Sal Grotto steps back a few paces to reduce his angle of vision. This is the way of short people who have achieved high station in life: never look up at people you should be looking down on. And Sal has gone up in the world. He is a kingpin of the numbers racket in lower Allegheny County. He also, reputedly, controls prostitution, loan-sharking, pinball machines, and sordid, unnamed vices. Charities solicit him, women seduce him, politicians cater to him, and police avoid him.

"I hear you're peddling beer on the road, Pete. Quite a change. huh?"

"I make a living."

"Takes guts," he nods approvingly. "You lose one, you adjust, you go on. It's what makes this country great," Sal says.

Bonner pays Louie and picks up his numbers slip. "How're things with you, Sal?"

"So-so, so-so." A despairing shrug. "You know, the small businessman, always scratching against bad times. You've been there, Pete." A shake of the head. "But," he adds, hauling himself out of economic funk, "you beat the odds for quite a while, Pete. Geez, remember that Palmer deal, the first time we met?" Sal turns to Louie, continuing the story. "Pete here bluffs the jerk right out of his knickers. What was that property worth, Pete, five thousand, maybe?"

"About that, I guess."

"More maybe. A business bluff, clean as a whistle, and I still don't know how you did it. You know, Pete, me and you, we could've made a go of it. I always said that, didn't I, Louie? You were a helluva businessman. But you needed breadth, see, that was your problem. I was wide and you were deep. Deep needs a hedge, see. Didn't I warn you? Uninsured real estate was too volatile, too risky. My breadth and your depth, I thought we could make it work." As he talks, Grotto takes Bonner by the arm and starts to walk out. "Maybe some day."

Emerging from the store, they see a police officer standing behind the Packard, writing a ticket. It is Officer Rafferty, the city's only motorcycle cop, clad in leather coat, Sam Browne belt, and knee-length leather puttees. "Rhi-no" Rafferty, everybody calls him, both for his size and because he carries a .30-.30 hunting rifle in a boot on his bike. He is frequently seen blasting shore rats down on the river bank.

Seeing Grotto approach the car, Rafferty reflects a moment on his future, and snaps shut the ticket book. He flings a leg over his motorcycle and kick-starts it. The machine bursts to life and Rhino, looking straight ahead, roars away.

Grotto ignores the performance. "By the way, Pete," he says, standing beside his open door, "do I hear you're in trouble?"

"Me? What kind of trouble?"

"Could you be on somebody's list you don't want to be on?" Grotto briefly studies Bonner's pale face. "What I heard is somebody's looking for a beer salesman who maybe overheard something." He shrugs. "But then I hear a lot of rumors. I'm like a priest in the confession box, see, people come and mutter things."

Bonner's hand freezes on a coat button, but he laughs. "I wouldn't know about that. I was brought up Episcopalian."

"That's a good religion, too. But listen, anybody bothers you, I want to be the first to know. You need a loan to start a business…anything. Reach me through Louie."

Watching Grotto drive up the street, Bonner shivers and turns up his coat collar against the snow. He had only a fleeting acquaintance with Grotto in the old days, but he knows this much: whatever Grotto hears in his confes-sional, someone usually suffers as a result. Bonner turns sharply and strides into the wind. Flurries of wet snow fly up his nostrils, melt on his cheeks, trickle down his neck.

At Jefferson First Federal, McKeesport's second largest bank, two immense Doric columns frame the narrowest entranceway in town, an architectural statement about frugality, signalling to depositors that this marble clam will snap shut on money leaking out. Bonner once owned enough stock in Jef-ferson to be nominated for the board of directors, an honor he declined for reasons of time. You don't make money sitting in board meetings. He shakes the snow off his hat, announces himself, and is immediately led to the bank president.

Henry Parsimmons is sitting behind a temple of pale hands at his walnut desk. "Pete Bonner! It's been ages." About fifty years old with thinning blond hair, he still wears a stiff, high collar with a gold stick pin. "Remember those bridge nights, Lydia and me and you and Mae? We ought to start up again."

He means not a word of it, of course, considering that they parted on quite unfriendly terms during Roosevelt's election campaign in 1932. "Henry," Bonner says, "I want to offer Jefferson first crack at a really good business deal." He needs a $1,000 loan, he says, to start a new business. "It's a really good plan, Henry." He pulls out a much-creased sheet of yellow legal paper with figures running down one side and lays it in front of Parsimmons.

The banker smiles, ignoring the paper. "Another year, another plan, eh, Pete? What kind of collateral are we talking about?"

"I own a couple of undeveloped lots in Maude Township—"

"Hillside lots? Taxes paid up?"

"Well, yes, and...no. But it'll be prime real estate some day. And I'll give the bank part ownership in the new business until the loan's paid off." At Parsimmons's skeptical look, Bonner rushes on. "Look, Henry, you and all the other banks have cash stashed in the vault. You're hoarding it, worried about getting caught again with bad loans. But we need that money in circulation. You can take a chance on businessmen with a proven record. Like me."

Parsimmons twirls a pen in its holder. "You know what I hear, Pete? I hear you've had dealings with this Phil Murray union character."

Bonner takes a deep breath. "Where'd you hear that, Henry?"

"Around...you know." He leans forward and puts on his perspicacious look. "Pete Bonner's always been a loner. But that's dangerous business."

"Why in God's name would I get involved with the union?"

"Why in God's name did Myron Taylor recognize the goddamned union in the first place? Now we have men marching around town with those goddamned CIO signs. Murray, Lewis, Roosevelt—what a bunch! Socialism with a capital 'S'." He jams the pen back in its holder. "But I forgot. You're a Roosevelt man, aren't you? Spend, spend, spend, and if that doesn't work, pack the Supreme Court." Parsimmons pauses, pulls back a little, composes himself.

Bonner rises, pockets his jottings, and puts on his hat. "I'll see you around, Henry."

■

The Elks Club and City Hall grew up side by side on Market Street, Belgian block twins blackened by mill soot. Back in the old days Bonner served as a club trustee, golfed on the golf team, and played bridge on the bridge team. But he refused to march in Armistice Day parades, having had his fill of the military in 1918. The men's-only bar and grill is a large, comfortable room with a thirty-foot-long bar and two dozen tables with leather-upholstered chairs. It exudes a distinctive odor of maleness and commerce, the combined fragrances of cigar smoke, aged whiskey exposed to air, wintergreen after-shave lotion used by the downstairs Elks barber, and woolen pinstripe suits reeking of sweat and fear.

Bonner steps into the past. Elderly bartenders shake his hand. A half-dozen old pals and poker cronies come over and slap his back. First up is Parker Stowe, still handsome and rugged with wavy black hair and the sun-leathered face of a one-time wildcatter. "Gas" Stowe, as he's known, made a fortune during a natural gas boom in the early twenties. He invested wisely and now lives the life of a gentleman farmer on a large estate up the Youghiogheny. Bonner is truly glad to see him.

Opposer McPhee is there, of course, and Fat Charlie Pritchard, the salesman, amateur comedian, and sometime confidence man, still on parole after a two-year prison term for embezzlement. They gather in a circle and tell tales on one another. "Remember when…" The best story is about the time Bonner and McPhee, then Hook & Ladderman McPhee, drank all night in a speakeasy outside town. "The old No Cork Inn, remember that joint?" McPhee says, taking up the story. Well, he and Pete tumble out of the place at five-thirty in the morning. They see a trolley car across the road—you know, on the old 68 line coming up the valley from Pittsburgh. In those days, a system of trolley lines linked Pittsburgh with many towns in the valley. The motorman, McPhee continues, is taking a leak in the weeds. Every boy's dream, growing up in McKeesport, was to just once in his life take a streetcar for a spin. So they hop aboard and take off toward town, Pete in the motorman's seat and Opposer dinging the bell. When they get her up to speed, on that straightaway where the mill starts, she's swaying like the rear end of a ladder truck going around a corner. McPhee pitches from side to side, eyes rolling. They go barreling up Fifth Avenue, whooping and dinging, buzzing the business district. Cars screech to a halt, blowing horns. On they go, running red lights, all the way through town to Trolleys End where motormen have to stop and reverse direction.

"We figured we'd head back downriver to Pittsburgh," McPhee says. "So we got out and lowered the front trolley boom and tried to raise the bugger on the other end. But we was too drunk to groove it on the wire." He pantomimes thrusting up the boom with a trolley hook while staggering in a circle. "Some old lady come up and says, 'Is this the 68 to Pittsburgh?' Pete lets go the boom to take off his hat and says, 'Sorry, Ma'am, but this here's the smoker to Chicago.' But the boom comes down on my head. Flattened me out on the tracks. Then the cops showed up."

The old gang laughs long and hard. Bonner buys a round of drinks, though he himself is on the wagon. As the group breaks up, he invites Stowe and Ed Crabtree, who owns a bus line, to lunch. Crabtree, however, wants to eat in the banquet hall where a business group has scheduled a "luncheon" with a speaker from Pittsburgh. "We got to hear this guy," he insists. "Lays out the whole thing, how Roosevelt and the unions are strangling free enterprise."

Bonner dislikes this kind of thing. He never goes to the weekly Rotary Club luncheon to munch on Swiss steak and gripe about Rooseveltian socialism. Stowe feels the same way. But he shrugs and tugs at Bonner. "Let's go, Pete. It's like taking medicine when you're a kid. Pinch your nose."

The hall is packed and close, not enough ventilation, and cigarette smoke hangs in the air. They find the last empty table in the rear. It is very good company to be seen in, indeed. At every table the cream of McKeesport business—merchants, foundry owners, lawyers, the managers of Murphy's Five-and-Ten and the Penn McKee Hotel, Mayor D.R. Shoaf, and Martin Dinsmore, general superintendent of the Watts Works.

As waiters serve the Elks' specialty, rare steak sandwiches on poppyseed rolls, Stowe and Crabtree inquire into Bonner's welfare. What brings him into town on a weekday when he's normally on the road or doing paperwork at his office?

"Thought I'd look around," Bonner says.

His friends exchange glances. "Yep," Stowe says, "I thought so when I first saw you across the room with that far-away look. I thought, 'Pete wants to start a business.' I was right, wasn't I?"

"Well, maybe..." He hesitates. But these are old friends. "Well, yes. Nothing fancy. Just...beer. A beer distributorship."

"Oh, hell, Pete," Crabtree says, "your timing is lousy. Remember that bar and grill you opened when soup lines were first forming? And that trucking business a couple years later. The Depression's worse than ever now. Nobody's buying anything."

"I think we're at the bottom," Bonner says. "We're coming out of it."

Stowe shakes his head. "The market's still dropping like a rock. Don't hurry it, Pete. There's no hall of fame for starting the most businesses."

"Well, then, I'm ahead of the market," Bonner says. "Mill-town people like beer, and when the mills start up and money starts flowing...summertime...baseball, heat, thirst. Put it all together, it adds up to beer." He halts abruptly, embarrassed to find himself making a pitch to these fellows. His crotch is sweating.

Crabtree is shaking his head. "Save your money. You have kids now, Pete. Besides, where will you get the capital?"

Bonner is not prepared for this reaction. But he always has been defenseless with friends. He gives each a frank look.

"Oh, no!" Stowe declares. "For your own good, for Mae's good, nosiree."

Bonner remembers how Stowe came to him for money after he'd drilled twelve wells that came in dry. With Bonner's loan, he drilled a thirteenth well, which tapped one of the biggest natural gas pockets ever discovered in Allegheny County. Stowe paid him off, dollar for dollar, period. Bonner remembers this but says nothing.

"It's just not a prudent thing to do," Crabtree says. "You invest, make money, and the government taxes it away to prop up relief payments. That goddamned cripple in the White House, he'll turn around and give it to all the fakers on relief."

And Bonner remembers the founding of Crabtree Bus Co., with the first bus underwritten by a loan from Bonner Real Estate. In those days, McKeesport real estate was a cash conveyor running right into Bonner's office. He allowed Crabtree to dissolve the loan in one eighteen-hole match. Gambling on his skill, Bonner tried to slice around a lake with a three iron. He lost by two strokes and killed a duck dozing in the shallows. So it went in those days. Crabtree and Stowe at least were honest about it. He can see a half-dozen others in the dining room who won't return his gaze. Loaning money became addictive for him, like eating peanuts.

Waiters serve chocolate parfait as the meeting chairman introduces the speaker of the day, Dr. Robert S. DuBray, executive director of the Greater Ohio Industrial Propagation Association. Two minutes into his speech, he issues a call to arms against all forces that threaten the stability of industrial capitalism, including relief programs, unions, the welfare state, corporate taxes, the Democratic Congress, and FDR.

Bonner lets his mind wander, and when it circles back to the present, the speaker is talking about the current state of labor relations. "A few years ago," he says, "as you and I concentrated our energies on battling this Depression, the duplicitous little men in Washington passed a labor law. It decrees that you who invest capital and produce the goods of the world must expose your businesses, open up your books, to this creature called collective bargaining." He pauses and explodes sibilantly into the microphone, "I call it 'collective extortion,' and you will know it by its practitioners—these stumbling Frankensteins plucked from the shop floor and mine depths, wearing baggy suits and snap-on ties bought on credit—these are the men appointed to relieve you of profit and honor....John L. Lewis and Phil Murray..."

From his table in the rear, Bonner has trouble assembling a firm outline of DuBray the man. Where the face ought to be, a pale blotch drifts in and out of the smoky haze. But his voice rolls through the fog on melodious waves. Bonner thinks of a spirit floating out of the flaring RCA Victrola horn, mesmerizing an audience of dogs. A clapping and stamping of feet greet each felicitous phrase. Bonner feels his pulse pounding and his head splitting, one part unable to escape the barren realm of personal poverty while the other tumbles down a black pit toward a writhing mass of faceless men, like those who flew at his windshield in the fog on Route 40.

When he finishes, Crabtree claps loudly and marvels, "Great, huh?"

"They ought to put him and Lewis in a small room, naked," Gas Stowe says.

Bonner mumbles goodbyes before the applause ends and slips out of the hall, angry at himself for having violated his own cardinal rule: Never put the arm on people you once staked in friendship; it is best not to know how time dims gratitude.

At home that evening, telling Mae about his day, he passes lightly over the morning and noon events and focuses instead on his afternoon search for a vacant storeroom on Lower Fifth Avenue. "I found one, honey," he says excitedly. "It's just right—old building, low rent, office and warehouse space, loading platform in the rear. With a little start-up money, we could make a go of it."

He stops pacing and turns to look at her with a broad smile. "Do you realize, by midsummer we could be in business?"

■

Young Albert Bonner, clad only in pajama pants, sits on the top step of his front porch, savoring the smell and feel of morning freshness. Bees hover over a burst of dewy red azaleas, then dive into pistilsful of nectar. The rhododendrons glisten with a frosty topping. A brown and white cat slinks into the front yard and sucks wet grass, drawing its mouth across the blades with a dreamy look. Sparrows chirp overhead on telephone wires; there are no trees along McKeesport's functional brick streets. The boy hears alarm clocks ringing through open bedroom windows. Along comes a rubber-tired milk wagon, drawn by a blinkered horse with canvas bags muffling the hooves. The milkman jumps out with a case of clinking quart bottles and hurries from porch to porch, depositing fulls and picking up empties. Back in the cab, he whistles softly and the horse steps off, leaving a gift steaming on the bricks.

The boy laughs and twitches his nose. His mother calls him to breakfast, and he stands with a yawn, expanding his little bare chest. Just then an old green car rattles slowly up the hill and stops momentarily in front of the Bonners'.

As Albert steps inside, his father pounds down the staircase from the second floor. "Who was in that green car, son?"

"There were two men, and they looked pretty mean." Albert goes to breakfast and asks his mom for an extra big helping of Wheaties, Jack Armstrong's Breakfast of Champions, because it builds muscles.

Leaving the boys in the care of Mae's mother, Bonner drives his wife downtown to have her first look at "our new business," as he puts it. Two days ago, on Wednesday, June 15, he officially opened the Bonner Beer Distributing Co. in a storefront-warehouse on lower Fifth Avenue, in a secondary business district that died even before the Depression. The meandering brick street walled in by rows of three-story brick buildings with mostly abandoned storefronts. Death in Brick: Mae notices that unlived-in brick seems to wither and crack like a chunk of red Jello left out overnight.

The office is separated from the rear warehouse section by a half-glass partition, so that a person sitting in the office can watch workmen dealing with beer in its various packages, bottles, cases, kegs. As they walk through the warehouse, puffs of dirt spout up with every step. She spots huge dust webs in the corners of the pressed tin ceiling. Bonner's entire stock of beer, three cases, takes up a pitifully small space in an area that, he assures her, will eventually hold five hundred. A rusty roll conveyor resting on rickety sawhorses runs down the middle of the storeroom and out a rear window. Backed up to the loading platform stands a pickup truck with flaking red paint and Joe Miravich, stretched over a front fender, banging on something under the raised hood. The lot fronts on a four-lane boulevard beyond which, across a half–dozen railroad tracks, the Watts Works fizzes, clanks, and steams.

"So?" he says, beaming, with a gesture that takes in the whole sorry enterprise.

"Wonderful," she says, choking back a sob. Can this be their future?

"Ah, Mae." He puts an arm around her shoulders. "We'll make it. Trust me."

A half hour later, she boards an uptown streetcar to do the banking requested by Pete. She wedges herself apologetically between two people on the wicker seat that extends along one side of the car. The trolley jerks along Fifth Avenue, starting and stopping, as the motorman tugs on a bell cord to clear the tracks. Here, at the lower end of town and on the adjacent hillside live the newer immigrant families in tiny apartments, boarding hotels, and narrow frame houses that cling precariously to the slopes. Most of the trolley riders are women and old men with heavy Slavic faces, dressed in threadbare clothing and mumbling in their native tongues.

It is like traveling in a foreign country. She has lived in McKeesport all her life, has smelled the smoke and swept the soot and breathed the pollutants and regulated her life to the three-times-a-day mill whistle. She went to school with the sons and daughters of "mill men," as her father referred to them, disdainfully, and later taught them at a Catholic grade school. Her heart aches for the old women who, lugging stout paper bags filled with groceries, must climb wooden staircases, a hundred or more steps, up from Fifth Avenue to their hillside homes. Mae now realizes that she has not the faintest idea who these people are, or how they think, or what they talk about. She feels miserably out of place in her gay spring getup, linen coat, white hat—all old and somewhat worn but well preserved. She smiles across the aisle at a woman with a purple and mauve babushka knotted tightly under her chin, accentuating the extraordinary power of large, walnut-shaped eyes. The woman fixes a belligerent stare on Mae's open-toed pumps.

Mae feels uncomfortable about taking on this new commercial role, doing the banking for Bonner Beer Co. Since getting married, she has never been anything more, or wanted to be anything more, than a mother, housewife, and volunteer worker at the hospital. A month ago, Pete announced they'd saved almost enough money to start the beer business. He still needed cash to make monthly payments on the truck, warehouse, electricity, telephone, and other "miscellaneous" items, and to buy an initial load of beer. Fortunately, he had a plan to raise this trifling piece of cash, one that involves a series of banking transactions which he has asked her to carry out.

Mae steps off the streetcar on upper Fifth Avenue and goes immediately to Second National Bank, where their joint account contains $10. She deposits $100 in cash, representing the remains of Pete's last pay from Fort Pitt and money he raised by selling his Spaulding golf clubs. Mae carefully places the deposit slip in her purse, feeling wealthy, if only momentarily. Unfortunately, it is all spoken for. A batch of checks mailed by Pete last week, covering all his monthly business expenses and exceeding the amount just deposited, will probably arrive at the bank for payment within a day or so. And Pete still lacks about $30 needed to buy a load of beer to fill orders already on hand. Now comes the crucial next step in Mae's mission. Per Pete's instructions, she walks three blocks east on Fifth and enters Jefferson First Federal, where the Bonners maintain a joint account with a $3 balance. She sees Henry Parsimmons, sitting at his desk behind a railing, where Pete said he would be. She strolls to the center of the lobby, directly across from him, and pretends—though given her knowledge of banking, no acting is needed—to twirl in confusion, tiny housewife lost in this great institution of commerce.

"My God, Mae Bonner!"

She turns and sees a tall, elegant man striding across the lobby, hands extended.

"Henry Parsimmons, what are you doing here?"

"I'm the president."

"Good for you, Henry."

He steps closer and speaks confidentially. "I hear Pete is opening a beer business."

"Oh, yes, and it's going so well. The orders are flowing in, and the beer is... pouring out."

Parsimmons refocuses his gaze. "But in times such as these, money so tight..."

"Oh, Henry!" she says with a teasing look. "Tight money, loose money, bull market...wolf market—what do I know about business? Pete takes care of all that."

He takes off his glasses and roughly wipes the lenses with a red silk handkerchief from the breast pocket of his three-piece suit. "Is there some way I can help you, Mae?"

"I'm in such a hurry, Henry. I have this check on our account at..." She glances at the check. "...Second National. But that's way up the street, isn't it, and this is my Junior Committee day at the hospital, and first I've got to go to the hairdresser, and I need to cash this check so Mother can pay her back rent. She's been ill, you know."

"Mae, Mae." He casually inspects the check. "You do have an account at National, don't you?"

She fumbles in her purse, pulls out a National monthly statement, folded so that only the name and address shows. "I brought this along to help me find the place, but time is just flying..."

He raises a hand, the gentleman's say-no-more sign, and takes the check to a teller's cage. Returning, he counts out thirty dollars, places it in an envelope, and folds her two gloved hands around it. "Remember those bridge games at the country club? Lydia was always so fond of you." His hands linger on hers.

She'd known that at some point there would be touching: Henry Parsimmons was a toucher. He had an eye for married women other than his wife, and particularly for Mae, as the Bonners had discovered at bridge, when she felt a hand groping for her knee under the table. Pete has assigned the banking job to Mae partly for this reason, and partly so that Pete, freed from banking chores, could travel around and drum up new orders. But Mae now must extricate herself from the banker's all-too friendly grasp. Forcefully, but not so forcefully that bystanders would notice, she withdraws her hands, observing during the brief struggle that he has, either for fun or practice, stamped a red "LOAN REJECTED" on the back of his left hand. Mae says pointedly, "Lydia is such a wonderful, loving person. Give her my regards." She turns and hurries out.

Miravich is waiting outside, as planned, in the pickup. He stows the cash in his sweaty cap and rushes off to Pittsburgh, a forty-minute drive, to buy a load of beer. He'll return to McKeesport, pick up Pete at the store, and the two will deliver the beer, on order, to several taverns. Over the next few hours she eats a sandwich at G.C. Murphy's lunch counter, strolls up and down the avenue, and shops in several stores, though not intending to purchase anything, for she has no money. At two-forty-five, she stands at the curb in front of Second National. Ten minutes later, Bonner's pickup rattles to a halt in front of her, and Pete leans out the passenger-side window with an envelope stuffed with money collected from the taverns. She dashes into the bank just before closing time and deposits $31, easily enough to cover the check cashed by Henry Parsimmons.

A business is born.

■

Bonner enjoys working alone, thinking as he works, doubling as boss and warehouseman. Miravich is out with the truck, and Mae has a day off to clean house. Two weeks of business has left the storeroom in a mess. Bonner is reorganizing the place, stacking full cases in one place, empties in another. The cases fall neatly into place with a heavy wooden clatter, the din of business in the making. Although he has taken off his shirt, sweat trickles down the insides of his arms. But it's a pleasure to perspire in the service of money-making, running his own business, beating down the Depression.

When the phone rings, he hurries to the office. People have been calling all morning, responding to an ad he placed in *The Daily News*. "Bonner's Beverages/All Brands to Slake Your Thirst." No mention of "beer" because the newspaper refuses to accept ads for alcoholic beverages. Not that it matters. In this city, "beverage" means beer. He paid extra for two lines of agate type at the bottom of the front page, and by chance chose a day when melting-pot

McKeesport is much interested in news from Europe about Hitler's demand that Czechoslovakians chop off a piece of their country and hand it over to him.

Relatives, friends and potential customers, relatives have called, as well as Charlie Pritchard, Gas Stowe, and Ed Crabtree, the last two reminding him, not so incidentally, that if his business failed, he knew where he had heard it first. Bonner has barely hung up the phone for the tenth time when Opposer McPhee shows up in person.

He brings greetings from City Hall, he says. A flask springs to hand, and he sprinkles a few drops on Bonner's conveyor to christen the venture. "Here's to beverage."

Bonner politely declines to drink and resumes shoving a line of empties down the conveyor. McPhee trails behind, swigging and talking, which is what he does best these days, shooting the breeze with the boys in the fire-houses and down at the Water Works. He walks with that curious dip to the left on his withered leg.

"That sonofabitch stuff-shirt Presbyterian is the biggest hypocrite north of the equator," McPhee says, referring to his favorite conversation piece, Mayor D.R. Shoaf. "But when shit comes to shove, he'll break a law quicker than anybody. That's why we had to flush 'er two nights ago."

"Flush 'er?" Bonner says, unwillingly caught up in the story.

McPhee, nodding, pivots at the end of the conveyor and follows him back. "Two in the morning he calls and he tells me to get down to the sewage plant, there's an overflow situation and we got to flush 'er out. The crew chief won't open the damn valve without someone in authority on the premises. 'Yeah, but why me?' I ask. 'Because,' he says, 'you are the commissioner of Water and Sewage, and it's your responsibility.' 'Since when?' I says. 'Since now,' he says. 'I just appointed you. It'll be in the paper tomorrow.' So I remind his divinity that I happen to be the fire commissioner and I don't go for doubling up to get his Republican ass out of trouble. Then he gets angry and he says, 'This is not the time for partisan politics, Tommie. The shit is backing up, and you got to get down there and flush 'er out.'"

Bonner throws two cases on the conveyor and leans over them, puffing. "For Christ's sake, Tommie, what's wrong with...flushing 'er?"

"What's wrong is, it's against the law to flush sewage into the river. But old Shoaf, he says, 'We got a fast-flowing river, we'll send it down to Pittsburgh and let them handle it." He pauses, takes a swig. "So it was either us or Pittsburgh. All shit goes to Pittsburgh, Peter. I heard they resell it."

Publicity is like warm spring rain: it brings out all forms of life. As a late afternoon shadow creeps down the front of the store, a man in a gray suit introduces himself as Walter Grubmann, local representative of the Greater Ohio Industrial Propagation Association. "We are a nonprofit organization providing counsel to Mr. Businessman on tax and employment matters," Grubmann says, handing Bonner a business card. "We represent his interests before legislative bodies. We're his eyes and ears on the world at a time of growing hostility to free enterprise. A deadly disease is eating at the guts of capitalism, Mr. Bonner, the insidious disease of unionism..."

As he talks, Grubmann surveys the storeroom, turning this way and that. His ponderous head seems to require that he swing his entire body to glance right or left. When he turns to the front of the store, Bonner points the way out.

Two more visitors show up, Sal Grotto and a large man with disheveled features on a fleshy face, wearing a baggy black suit. Grotto calls him Pixie. Bonner offers a propitiatory case of Tube City to Pixie and listens with fluttering heart as Grotto talks of "certain people" that have been looking for him and Miravich. Feigning innocence, Bonner realizes, will not put Grotto off the track.

"Give them what they want," he tells Bonner. "It's like this Hitler in Germany, he wants part of Czechoslovakia. Give it to him, what the hell! They're nothing to us." He lowers his voice. "Give them the miner, and tell them what they want to know."

Bonner has a minute to think it over: either agree to set up Miravich for some kind of catastrophic event and tell Grotto's associates what they want to know, or...or he himself will fall victim to a catastrophic event. He finds himself walking numbly to the rear of the storeroom with a case of beer on his shoulder.

"What's he to you?" Grotto calls after him. "Just a piece'a shit coal miner. How'd you ever hook up with that bird?"

Bonner walks out the door to the loading platform. He sees cars passing on the boulevard, the Watts's furnaces in the distance, a ribbon of smoke tailing from an open hearth stack...Joe Miravich lurching out of the fog on Route 40...

He walks back to his visitors, picking up his shirt and tie on the way.

Grotto looks at his watch. "That's two minutes. What's it to be?"

Bonner tries to button his shirt, but two holes at the top elude their buttons. He gives up, and the shirt hangs partly open. He feels more naked than before. "I can't do that, Sal. But what if—"

Grotto cuts him off with a laugh. "Don't say I didn't try." With a flick of a finger he sets a roller to spinning. "Hope you got insurance this time, Pete."

Pixie moves toward the case of Tube City but veers away to follow the boss.

"Take it!" Grotto growls over his shoulder. "Pete Bonner's no Indian giver."

CHAPTER 6: July 1938

Miravich carries Dottie's suitcases onto the train and heaves them into the overhead rack. She stands in the aisle like a little girl, wearing a green Alpine cap with a feather in it. He puts an arm around her. Close up, he sees the traces of tear streaks on her heavily powdered cheeks. People are moving back and forth, knocking them off balance. They fall together into a double seat, both laughing awkwardly.

"I'm sorry," he says, meaning sorry that things did not turn out as she wished. But he is not at all sorry about refusing to move to Detroit with her. When, the day before her departure, she asked why he wanted to stay in Mc-Keesport, he could not explain himself. Did he have obligations here that she didn't know about? "I've just got things to do here," he said. What things? He shrugged.

"I'm sorry, too," Dottie now says, affectionately patting his hand, as they say their last goodbyes. "But don't worry about me. At least I gave them a piece of my mind." She is referring to the city school board, which summarily fired her after receiving reports that she was engaged in radical activity. They refused to provide evidence or name her accuser, beyond making veiled references to a powerful organization, based in Pittsburgh, which exposes communist infiltrators in the working-class.

She selected Detroit with a hope of becoming involved somehow with the auto workers' union. "It's a very progressive union," she says. "There's so much to do for the workingman." Her eyes, shiny with optimism, turn to the dirt-streaked window.

Still the idealistic prattle, Miravich thinks, groaning inwardly. Nonetheless, he likes her more at the end of the affair than he did at the beginning. He kisses her on the cheek and stands in the aisle. "If you need anything—"

She pulls a book from under her arm and gives it to him. It's John Steinbeck's *In Dubious Battle*. "For you, Joe. Solidarity forever."

It has not occurred to him to give her a gift. When he raises his eyes from the book, she is staring again out the window. For her the train has already left the station.

■

By mid-July, Bonner Beer Distributing Co. has survived an entire month, God knows how. Scraping along, scrimping, sticking to it, Bonner and his hard-working colleagues, Mae and Joe, have created a new enterprise dedicated to serving the community. It is still a hand-to-mouth operation, barely growing, delivering beer to a few saloons, rewarding new customers—one or two every week—with a free calendar, grudgingly paying bills by means that Mae still does not fully comprehend.

On the morning of the first monthly anniversary, the phone is ringing as Pete and Mae arrive from home. Bonner hurries into his office and answers. "Sure, sure, right away," he says. He scribbles on an order pad. The Victory Bar & Grill, a new place just opening, wants a half-barrel of Duquesne pilsner. Two men will be needed to put the keg in the basement, soon as possible. "You're first on the list," Bonner says.

Exuberant, he plops into in his revolving desk chair and does a quick three-sixty, doffing his hat as he flashes past Mae. "I told you business would pick up. A new place, way out on East Fifth Avenue."

Bonner takes off his suit jacket and begins preparing deposit and with-drawal slips for Mae's round of the banks. She, meanwhile, is doing her morning cleaning. Wearing a yellow, saucer-shaped summer hat and her best beige pumps, she attacks the floor with an old straw broom. She detests dirt and believes that profit is earned through cleanliness.

The office contains a desk, two chairs and a filing cabinet. A twenty-year-old ribbonless Underwood and a paperless adding machine are stored in one corner, awaiting a time when letters must be typed and long columns of fig-ures totted up. The desk faces the partition window through which Bonner can watch the warehouse area, where cases of beer are stacked neatly against one wall. A small pile here, a small pile there—Fort Pitt, Duquesne, Iron City, Tube City, Rolling Rock, Tech, Stonys. The refrigeration system consists of what last night was a block of ice, now a puddle of water, sitting atop a single keg of Duquesne in a wash tub. Bonner envisions the day when a refrigerated cooling room is crammed with cooperage. He can hear the clatter of the con-veyor as case after case rolls out to the loading platform to be carried away by a fleet of trucks.

Miravich reports for work. "She's getting hot out there," he says. "By after-noon, you won't be able to spit a good hawker. Oops, sorry, Mrs. Bonner."

"Good morning, Joe," she says, giving her famous pained smile. In her eyes, he still has plenty of crude edges, but now she regards him as a real person, not just a Joe-person. Once a week or so they play their roles in the "prospective banking" game introduced by Pete. Joe meets her uptown with the day's cash receipts for deposit before three o'clock in order to cover funds that Jefferson First Federal has involuntarily "loaned" to Bonner Beer Distributing for a few hours, or a day, or a weekend.

Miravich picks up the order spike. "Victory Bar and Grill? A new place?"

"Some fool has decided," Bonner says, pitching his voice toward Mae in the corridor, "that the demand for beer is taking off." He winks at Miravich and adds, "But we'd better get there before he goes out of business. Roll out that half of Duquesne, Joe. We'll both have to go on this one."

"Sure thing, boss." The mocking tone signifies that Miravich has not forgotten that even in this small firm a yawning gap separates labor and capital.

Bonner is used to the mockery, but he senses that labor is trying to communicate some urgency with a variety of hand signals. "Why don't you freshen up, honey?" Bonner says to Mae. "I'll have the bank stuff ready when you get back."

When she leaves for the downstairs bathroom, Miravich takes a quick look out the storefront window. "You know that green car that showed up at your house? I been keeping my eyes peeled ever since, and on my way in, guess what I saw?"

"What?" Bonner hears a crashing sound in his inner ear, like waves breaking on a shore, or the roar of an approaching mob.

"A green Ford parked up the street and around the corner, like it was hiding. Two blocks from here. The mine dicks found us. I'll never forget that bashed-in fender."

Both rush to the front door and glance up and down the street. They see only a little white dog peeing on the corner telephone pole. Back inside, Bonner says, "I've got to get her out of here." He shouts: "Mae, are you ready?" No answer.

"And there's more," Miravich says. "Last night when I was out back locking up the pickup, a big black car come down the street moving real slow and stopping at the curb and starting up again. When I walked out to the street, she disappeared around the corner and I put it out of mind. But how many big black cars are there in McKeesport? We'd better get out and come back with guns."

"That'll be too late. No! After she goes, we'll barricade the doors. Damned if I'll let them destroy my business!"

"Your business? Bonner, you crazy? People want to kill you—and me too. Forget the business. It isn't your money anyway."

Desk drawers bang open and shut as Bonner searches for weapons.

"What're you talking about? Here!" He tosses a small paperweight to Miravich.

"I couldn't knock out a squirrel with this. I'm talking about how you're using the banks' money." Miravich scans the street again through the window, then turns to Bonner. "You even got your wife involved. What happens to her if she gets caught?"

"She won't get caught. Where is she? Mae!" Bonner knocks aside a chair as he leaps across to the window facing the storeroom. "Go ahead, leave if you want to—" He stops, startled momentarily by his own image. Sunlight pouring through the storefront window has made a mirror of the inner window. Looking for Mae, Bonner sees a paunchy man with rolled up sleeves, still wearing his hat as if he has places to go and things to do, the big-deal, small-town entrepreneur, caught in the act of being himself. A fraction of a second of self-loathing gives way to sensations of fright and panic. But this is no time for reflections. Adjusting his gaze, he stares through the man in the window. "Mae," he says with relief as she strolls toward the office.

"Joe and I have a lot of work to do," he says, escorting her outside. His hand shakes as he gives her a manila envelope.

Mae runs to catch a trolley. She turns while boarding, as if guessing he might be watching, and waves gaily, off on another adventure.

"Well?" he says, holding the door open for Miravich. "Are you leaving?"

"Locking the door won't keep them out," Miravich says. "But we can even the odds. Should be plenty of boys hanging around the CIO office." He goes to the phone.

"Wait, wait! The CIO?" Bonner is thinking in terms of cost, the price that must be paid for all things, good and bad, all products, all services, all seemingly selfless proffers of assistance. In an instant, he envisions an entire cycle of union-management relations: in return for CIO protection, he grants union recognition, which is followed by extortionate contract demands, a long strike, loss of customers, bankruptcy.

"What do you think, I'm trying to organize the place?" Miravich dials a number. "The CIO doesn't want a minnow like you, Bonner. A lot of these boys used to be miners, and they hate the Coal and Iron Police."

"Okay, okay." Bonner hesitates, letting the foolish feeling drain from his face, then adds, "I'll see if those other guys damaged the pickup." It has been sitting outside all night at the loading dock. He grabs the ignition keys off a hook and runs to the rear.

Miravich reaches a friend at CIO headquarters and asks him to send a flying squad. Fortunately, a meeting has just broken up, and the CIO man promises to send a car load. A matter of ten minutes…Miravich suddenly exclaims, "The pickup!"

He drops the phone and races to the loading dock. The rear of Bonner's head is visible in the cab. "No! Don't start it!" Miravich leaps far off the dock, landing next to the truck. "Get out!" He lunges at the handle of the driver's door and pulls it open.

Bonner stares at him. Across a gap of space and time, their eyes meet and weld, metal to metal. Bonner already has depressed the starter pedal half way to the floor. Miravich clutches his left wrist and yanks as if he intends to rip the arm from its socket. Bonner topples heavily out of the cab, and the two fall in a heap. Miravich closes his eyes, waiting for the explosion.

Nothing happens.

They lie beside the truck, dazed and scared, for what seems several minutes. Finally, Bonner sits up with a grimace and shakes out his left arm. "You think the truck's wired?" he says. His voice is high and unsteady.

"What else?" Miravich says. "That black car didn't come down here for the view." He slowly gets up and opens the truck hood. "Yep, it's here all right. Here's your message from Mr. Buck, I guess."

Bonner takes a peek. He sees a packet of red and white sticks wrapped in black tape. Feeling dizzy, he gulps mouthfuls of air to keep from fainting, then sits on the running-board, mops his face with a handkerchief, and lights a Chesterfield.

Miravich reaches tentatively toward the bomb, then pulls back and closes the hood as if to put the device out of mind. "Not sure how to disconnect a car bomb," he says. "Maybe it'll come to me." He settles beside Bonner on the running-board.

They stare into the dirt.

"Joe—" Bonner pauses not knowing how to say it.

"Forget it," Miravich says. "You saved me, then I saved you. Your turn next time, then my turn. I think it'll go on like this. You ever see vines catch hold of one another in the woods? Neither of them can let go and they grow all their lives that way, getting twisted and tangled. To chop one down, you got to chop both down."

"Both!" Bonner exclaims. "That's right. They wanted to get both of us in the truck. That order from the new saloon was a phony, a setup. I thought there was something fishy about opening a bar way out on East Fifth Avenue."

"So business isn't growing so fast after all."

They sit a while longer, calming down, trying to decide what to do next.

A loud, crashing noise comes from the front of the store, the sound of shattering glass. Miravich jumps up. "The mine dicks!"

They run inside and grab whatever they can find for protection. Miravich picks up an old iron stave from a wooden keg. It curves round on itself, and Miravich guesses he'll have to lasso them with it. Bonner hefts a couple of heavy quart beer bottles.

Two dark figures stand in the front doorway. They walk slowly to the rear, one man carrying a pistol.

"Are your friends coming?" Bonner whispers.

"They'd better be," Miravich says.

The detectives stop ten feet away. "We've been looking for you, boys," says the one they remember as Tom. "It took some time, but it's going to be worth it."

"Throw down those things," the second dick orders. He comes forward and picks up Miravich's stave. "You guys are pretty popular birds, got lots of people on your tail. But we got here first. We're going to take you for a ride—after I beat in your brains." He turns the stave over and over, examining it. "What's this for?"

Shouts fill the front of the store. Men rush through the front door. There are half a dozen, all hardy fellows carrying bats and clubs. The dicks wheel to face them. When the men see Tom's gun, they stop and fan out in a line. A standoff.

The CIO picket captain steps forward. He is a tall man with a large gut, dressed in suit and hat like the dicks. "Okay, you bastards," he announces. "You can't shoot all of us. Maybe fire once, but the rest of us are going to catch you and rip your hearts out."

"Stay put!" Tom says. He half turns to his partner. "What the hell we do now?"

"Out the back door. I seen a pickup." He leads the way, edging past Miravich. "Ignition keys in the truck?" he says to Bonner.

"If you step on the starter you're dead. The truck is wired."

"Bullshit!" The two dicks back out of the rear door, then turn and run.

Bonner and Miravich go cautiously to the door. The CIO men sound like a thundering herd coming up behind. When Bonner gets to the doorway, he sees that the dicks already are in the cab. "No! No!" he shouts.

The man on the passenger side leans out and points the pistol. Bonner and Miravich fall to the platform. They hear the gun crack once, twice. Splinters fly off the door frame behind them.

With a cough and a sputter, the truck engine starts. The pickup lurches out from the dock, waits for one car to pass, then turns into the street. The

CIO men pour through the doorway, too late, as the truck pulls away, shifting into second.

"It was a goddamned dud," Miravich says.

Then it comes, an explosion that makes the boulevard ripple like a ribbon in the breeze. The pickup dissolves in a fiery ball that unaccountably veers left, jumps a curb, and rolls end over end toward the mill, throwing off bits of metal, seat fabric, rubber, and flesh.

Stunned silence, then Bonner says quietly, "There's the message from Mr. Buck."

Fortunately, the street and sidewalks are empty. Few pedestrians walk here at any time, and cars going both east and west are stopped at traffic lights. But on the other side of the boulevard, across the railroad tracks, a siren wails in the Bessemer shop, and men pour out of the building. They think the explosion was theirs.

Fire trucks scream down the boulevard. By the time police arrive, the CIO men have cleared out. Bonner and Miravich volunteer as little information as possible, given that they do not know much to begin with and considering that it might be dangerous to share what they do know with a police force rumored to be infiltrated by the mob.

As a half-dozen cops search the storeroom, Miravich nudges Bonner into the office and closes the door. "I think I got it figured out," he whispers. "Mr. Buck is no dummy. He knows them old Coal and Iron cops are morons who usually screw up. When he heard the mine dicks was on our tail, he put his own killers on the job to make sure it got done. But they couldn't even wire a bomb right."

A crowd gathers outside the store, and the phone rings constantly. The fourth caller has a familiar husky voice. "Don't know how you escaped that one, Pete. An explosion like that should've blown you into a million bits. But I want you to know, see, I didn't have anything to do with it. I hate violence like that, see. Who they think they are, bombing people...in my fucking town!"

"Okay, Sal. So tell me, was Mr. Buck behind this?"

"Mr. Buck...Chiang Kai-shek, what's the difference? You blow up a beer truck, who do you think gets blamed? We do, that's who. People think we control beer. But I passed the word, one more stunt like this and kablooie goes cooperation from us. As of now, you're off the hook, my sayso."

"I appreciate this, Sal, but a little more information would help..."

"Help who? You know nothing, you can't say nothing to the cops. Which is the best way for you to look at this. You're a know-nothing." He hangs up.

The evening *Daily News* carries a hastily-assembled story about the incident, reporting that two unidentified thugs stole the truck and accidentally blew themselves up. According to reliable police sources, the men were union organizers who intended to carry out a bomb threat received earlier at a non-union trucking outfit located a few blocks from Bonner's store. It is the only explanation that makes instant sense and fits in with what people generally believe to be true about unions: cross them and you get bombed.

■

When Mae returns from uptown, Bonner closes for the day and drives her home. She is bursting with questions, why this and why that. He reassures rather than explains, summarizing all that has happened in the vaguest possible way.

"But someone must know something. An explosion...men killed...our truck blown up....Somebody must know something."

He shakes his head, it's a mystery. She begins sobbing. "God," she says, her shoulders heaving, "what have we got into?"

Receiving no response, she says firmly, "I want you to get out of this business."

Stubborn defiance pulls his face into a taut mask. In this mood his silence has ended many a conversation.

Several hours later, when the boys are in bed, Bonner says, almost casually around the edge of a newspaper, "We can't get out without losing everything."

"For heaven's sake, if you can start a business with nothing, why can't you end it with nothing?"

He crunches the newspaper in his lap. "We will get through this, I promise."

They barely speak the rest of the evening. She takes particular note of the obstinate set of his chin and mustache, recalling that he displayed such a grim determination most memorably the time he helped a brother-in-law repair a broken sewer pipe in his back yard and had to stand ankle-deep in the discharged...uhmm...as they shoveled it into a barrel. By the time they finished Pete's mood had darkened into one of ferocious tenacity—finish the job or die trying. And so it is tonight, except that she happens to be on the receiving end of the...uhmm...he is shoveling.

By mutual though unspoken agreement, husband and wife sleep in different beds. As Mae crawls in with Paul, their younger son, he asks sleepily, "Is Daddy coming, too?"

"No, darling, Daddy won't be coming..." and almost adds, "now or ever."

Although only five years old, Paul has an active night life. He wriggles, moans, flips from side to side, smacks his lips, flaps his arms, and jams an elbow into her stomach. She feels the pulsing warmth of the child's body as it thrashes about, striving to make room for itself in a hostile world. She falls into a fevered half-sleep and dreams that after Pete wins the argument, as she assumed he would, she and the boys leave him. They move into a squalid tenement downtown, and she earns a meager living as a washerwoman. Lacking money for college, Paul and Alfred go to work in the mill while Pete languishes in prison for bouncing checks (they actually bounce like tennis balls in her dream). On this harrowing vision she weeps herself to sleep.

Mae awakes resolved to do what is right for Paul and Albert. Given Pete's obstinacy, only she can save the marriage. Seeing that he is already up, she sits at her vanity table and applies a bit of lipstick, a smear of rouge, and a couple of streaks of eye shadow. Dressed in her pink robe and slippers with white fluff on the toes, she goes downstairs, pauses at the kitchen door for a last-minute check on her intentions, then steps lightly into the room. Pete sits at the table with his back to her, reading the morning paper as he pierces the eye of a fried egg with a corner of crusty rye toast.

Over his shoulder she reads headlines: Hitler has annexed Czechoslovakia, Japan is rampaging through Nanking, and Roosevelt has returned to priming the pump—in consequence of which a resentful but opportunistic Dow-Jones is rising day by day.

"Good morning," she says cheerily.

"Mae—" he says, half-turning to her with a look that she might construe as contrite if she paused to study it.

Instead, wanting no obstacles between her and her sacrifice, she goes directly to the sinktop and pours a cup of coffee. After taking a sip, she says, matter of factly, "Do you want me to do any banking today?"

Coming to her side in a bound, he throws an arm around her waist. "That's my girl." He mashes a kiss against her cheek. "And I was just beginning to wonder—"

"Wonder what?"

"Whether Fort Pitt would take me back as a salesman."

PART 2: 1943–1944

CHAPTER 1: July 1943

Joe Miravich squints up the line through goggles filmed over with dust and sweat from three hours' hot work in the War Effort at the Watts. Steamy orange mist, hovering over the blooming mill, bathes everything in a soft glare that sometimes makes him see double. Hissing steam jets and the roar of massive rolling machinery pound his thoughts to powder. He is standing on a rickety metal platform, waiting for the next freshly-rolled "bloom"—a 16-foot-long block of near-molten steel with 20-inch square ends—to come banging down the conveyor run-out table. Sixty yards up the line, the rolling mechanism resembles a giant washing machine wringer, two hard-steel rolls set horizontally in the conveyor table, one above and one below. Fed into these whirling jaws, relatively softer steel ingots are squashed into elongated blooms. Above and to the rear of the rolls, in the control pulpit straddling the table, roller Harry "Rooster" Wooster controls the action of the rolls with levers, knobs and foot pedals. He is slamming ingots through at a fast rate, as if any slackening in steel output would endanger his two airmen sons who are flying bombing missions over Germany.

It is the middle of July, six o'clock in the evening, three hours into the afternoon turn at the Watts Works. One-time coal digger Miravich is now steelworker Miravich, afternoon-turn shearman on the Watts's 46" blooming mill. Standing at his control console, peering into the orange mist, he sees another bloom passing through the hot-scarfing machine where Mike Rizzo skins off a thin, fiery layer of bad surface metal. Then it smashes to a halt at the shear position, snapping and cracking as the skin oxidizes. Superheated waves of air beat against Miravich's face. He pulls a lever, causing a rotating blade to cut up through the bloom, cropping waste steel off the front or "top" end. With another lever, he moves the bloom forward, slices off the bottom end and sends it on its way to the billet mill where it will be rolled into a smaller shape.

He hears a shout from below. Mickey Totten, the spellhand, climbs onto the shearman's platform. "Tough day, huh, Joe?" he shouts over the noise.

"Nah. In the mines we rested harder'n this."

Totten grins and sticks his middle finger in Miravich's face. "Go eat your cabbage sandwich, Tonto. You got thirty minutes."

Miravich removes his goggles and gloves and, lunch bucket in hand, jumps down from the shearman's platform. He goes out a side door of the building and crosses the mill road. Dozens of semifinished steel slabs, awaiting shipment, lie across wooden eight-by-eights placed flat on the ground. He chooses a slab for his lunch table and grabs the first object that comes to hand in the lunch bucket, a ham and cheese on pumpernickel. Chewing steadily, hungrily, he turns his gaze across three sets of railroad tracks and up an embankment toward the city. On the far side of Lysle Boulevard, "Bonner Beer Distributing" is painted in black letters near the top of a brick building. Four trucks are backed up to the loading dock, indicating that Bonner is four times more prosperous than he was in '38. One truck, carrying a pyramid of beer cases, pulls out of the lot. Miravich closes his eyes and sees the red pickup hurtling down the street in a ball of flame.

He shakes his head, rattling out the ghosts, and peels an orange. He hired into the Watts Works in 1939 when business began to pick up, a little later than Bonner had predicted but better late than never. Phil Murray, not one to forget a favor, passed the word down to a local union officer at the Watts, who saw to it that Miravich was hired.

"I got bigger aims than driving a beer truck," Miravich said to Bonner on the day he told him he would leave to work in the mill.

"Sure, you want to join the union, cut the bosses down to size, get elected, organize the world." Bonner, not one to display emotion, surprisingly squeezed his shoulder. "Stay with me, Joe. There's a future here. I'll teach you business."

Miravich laughed. "You already taught me business. You bilk the banks, and charge all she'll bear."

"I'll tell you what," Bonner said, drawing himself up to face labor squarely. "It's time you got a raise. I'll raise you—" He looked upward, calculating. "I'll raise you to fifty-five cents an hour."

Miravich shook his head. "I can get seventy in the mill."

Bonner looked steadily at him and finally nodded. "Just give me a week to find another driver."

Miravich went to work in a labor gang in the Watts open hearth shop. A year later, as War Preparedness got under way, better jobs began opening up. He wangled a transfer to the blooming mill, joined Rooster Wooster's crew and worked up to the shear position. Now he's slotted in a line-of-progression that could take him all the way up to the prestigious job of roller in about twenty-five years, if he keeps his nose clean and plays his cards right and if enough guys retire or die in the meantime. When the war started, he tried to enlist, figuring he may as well vent his anger on Tojo and der Führer as on the mill bosses. But he was rejected and classified 4-F, unable to fight on account of, apparently, there was no device of war that could be operated with only nine fingers. He cursed the miner who severed his pinky finger with a pick. Denied the opportunity to travel and see the world for the lack of one lousy digit! Miravich displayed his mutilated hand wherever he went so people wouldn't think he was hiding behind a 3-A deferment for defense work. And yet, someone had to make steel for the boys overseas; you couldn't get it all done with old men and women. As the soldier on the poster said, sticking his finger in the chest of a worker in overalls: "Those overalls are your uniform, bud."

Miravich moved out of the Cramczak home and into a one-room, upstairs flat near the Watts Works. He threw himself into union business, spoke up at meetings, studied the labor contract with the intensity his mother had wanted him to devote to the Catechism. He took high school courses in night school and learned how much he didn't know about geography, history, and the English language. Eternal thanks to Dowdy Dottie—no, to Dorothy Klangensmith—who had advised him to go back to school. Poor Dorothy! Sometimes he thought about her. Where did single, female, middle-aged, sex-loving, radical Latin teachers go to find fulfillment?

At work he made friends everywhere he could, roaming around the mill during breaks and acquainting himself with different operations and workers in all nationality groups—Irish, Slovak, Polish, Czech, Lithuanian, Hungarian, German, Swedish, English, Scots, Italian, Ruthenian, Greek, and even the small band of colored men mostly confined to labor gangs. When he felt he had apprenticed long enough, Miravich ran for blooming-mill committeeman and narrowly defeated the aging incumbent. Now he serves on the local's six-member grievance committee, each member representing a roughly equal number of workers in one of six departments in the Watts.

Miravich finishes the orange and wraps up his garbage. He lies back for a moment to contemplate a heavy, grayish-blue sky, sitting on the Watts's spiky bed of smokestacks and furnace tops. The tallest structures are the iron-making giants, four blast furnaces, with small blowoff pipes occasionally spurting jets of blue flame. Pig iron produced in these furnaces is converted into steel in open hearths and Bessemers. Lined up side by side in one huge shop, the Watts's eight open hearths are the primary steelmaking furnaces. There are also three oldtime Bessemers used to produce specialty steel.

Rolling on his side, Miravich can see the open-air Bessemer shop, framed by trestles and stairways. Workers there are just beginning a "blow" in a cast iron vessel which is mounted on trunnions and can be moved from a horizontal to a vertical position. They feed the furnace with steel scrap, ore and molten pig iron as it lies with its mouth tilted to one side. Swinging the loaded vessel by means of hydraulic machinery to a vertical position, they blow jets of air up through her innards to purge the iron of carbon and other impurities. As cold air hits a molten bath of 3000 degrees F., a great stream of flame shoots thirty feet into the sky, lengthening and widening, shading from golden yellow to a brilliant orange or red. Henry Bessemer's wonderful roaring enema! After five to ten minutes, as carbon is burned off, the flame gradually shortens in length and is sucked back into the vessel, leaving an inflamed wound in the sky.

When the blow is over, Miravich gets to his feet and hitches his overalls. A train approaches on the middle track, gathering speed for the trip down the valley. Gondola cars loaded with triangular piles of pipe stretch far to the rear. Headed for the oil fields of the southwest. The great Steel for Victory Drive is going full blast. In the Monongahela Valley, every man who wants work is working, and thousands of women have entered the mills to replace men gone to war. Great quantities of steel are pouring out—sheet steel for airplanes, ships, guns, trucks, and jeeps; armor plate; steel construction shapes; tinplate for K-ration cans and all sizes of shells and bombs. From Pittsburgh south to Allenport, forty-five miles of river windings, the valley is a living, writhing organism. Twelve major steel plants, scores of related factories, 75,000 hourly workers and thousands more foremen and managers. Trains rush up and down the valley, strings of coal barges clog the river bends, trucks and trolleys and cars and people choke the mill town streets. You don't have to be stupidly patriotic to see that making steel, here in the Monongahela Valley, with fire and smoke dominating even in the heavens, puts you as close to the center of things as a man could want. The owners and bosses still control the life and destiny of every last person in the valley, but this too can be changed.

Miravich waves to a fireman in the locomotive cab. The man raises his shovel overhead. Labor united.

Six hours into the shift, waiting for the next bloom, Miravich stretches and raises the goggles to wipe sweat from his eyes. A loud crashing sound from one end of the mill building makes him jump. He still feels uncomfortable in these surroundings. Going from a coal mine to a steel mill is like moving from a closed pot to a skillet over an open fire. The blooming mill is located in a big old barn of a building that seems to vibrate with the violent action of ingots being fed into the roll stand and the whirring of two 3000-

horsepower motors that power the rolls. Above the continuous background roar of giant machines and crashing ingots there is a loud hissing as jets of water hit the hot steel at various points, sending up clouds of steam, and the shouts of puny-voiced men trying to make themselves heard. A mixture of sweet and acrid odors has your nose in a constant state of confusion. When you work in a coal mine, he thinks, death has two options: It could crush or suffocate you. Here, in the mill, death has an arsenal of weapons in addition to those two. You might be melted into soup by a splash of molten metal, rolled into hamburger on the roll tables, fried to a crisp by falling power lines, knocked flat by a load swinging from a crane hook, or run over by a slag truck on your way out of the plant. Figuring that his job gave death too much of a chance as it was, Miravich even quit smoking cigarettes.

As a committeeman, he has made safety his first order of business, filing three dozen grievances in the past two weeks alone, reflecting the arrival of a new department superintendent, Phil Shumly. "Hotshot" Shumly, transferred in from another department to give blooming a shot in the arm, likes to set production records. Knowing little about rolling steel, he nevertheless decrees all kinds of shortcuts, often against the advice of his foremen. His shortcuts usually create hazards for the men.

Miravich hasn't had much time today to look for safety violations because Rooster Wooster has been banging the ingots through at a record rate. But a delay of some sort has stretched into ten minutes. Miravich looks up the line and sees that Rooster has left the pulpit and is talking to Skip Tucker, the turn foreman. Miravich jumps down from his platform and heads in that direction. Rooster is a scrappy old guy, in his fifties, lean and wiry and smart, a good crew leader. He could slow down the torrid production pace with all kinds of tricks learned over thirty years, but he doesn't want to let his sons down.

From a distance, Miravich sees Shumly burst into the discussion. Within seconds, Rooster is gesturing angrily. He takes off his cap and flings it to the floor, a typical gesture by Rooster when the bosses issue foolish orders. Shumly points to the pulpit, commanding him to return to his post. Rooster takes the chaw out of his mouth and dashes that to the floor, too.

When Miravich comes up on the group, Shumly is screaming at Rooster in a hoarse voice, telling him to "get this mill going again." Skip Tucker is standing by, hands in hip pockets, looking embarrassed by his boss's tantrum.

"Bullshit!" Rooster exclaims. "I'm not rolling another piece of green steel."

Miravich understands. Ingots are described as "green" when they have not been heated to the proper temperature in furnaces called soaking pits. Rooster can tell from the color of the ingots as they pass beneath the pulpit whether they are too cold, too hot, or just right for the ultimate use the blooms will be put to.

"You'll roll what I tell you to roll," Shumly says. Shumly is only in his thirties, a relatively young man for a department superintendent. He has a turtle-like face, with a sloping forehead and bulging eyes, and he snaps at people rather than talks to them. "I say what's green and what's not green, and I say they're not green."

Miravich butts in. "Maybe you're too green to know what's green. A smart boss listens to his men."

"Keep out of this, Miravich. This is an operational decision, not a union matter."

"It matters to us what kind of stuff we're producing for the soldiers."

Noticing that the rest of the mill crew has gathered to watch the argument, the superintendent raises his shoulders. "Wooster," he says, "I'm telling you for the last time, get up there and get this mill going."

Rooster stands looking at him with arms folded.

"You do what I say or go home." Shumly glances at the foreman. "Anybody else in this crew can roll steel?"

Tucker points out Gabinski, who works in the pulpit with Rooster, and Totten, the spellhand. Gabinski grabs his crotch and hurries stiff-legged toward the wash room.

Shumly turns to Totten. "You! Into the pulpit."

"Busted hand," Totten says, showing a hand he's just wrapped in an oil cloth.

"You damn jackass!" Rooster says to Shumly. Agitated, he pats his pockets, looking for something else to throw down. Miravich hands him his hardcover notebook. The roller winds up and slams it down right between the superintendent's feet. A puff of soot spouts up around Shumly, turning his shirt gray.

"That does it, mister, you're suspended," Shumly says. He adds, shouting after Rooster on his way to the locker room, "And take three days off while you're at it."

"That makes it a union matter," Miravich says, raising his voice. "If Rooster goes home, everybody goes home." He walks off slowly, not looking around but setting his shoulders, defiant and sure of his following.

He hears nothing behind him except the throbbing motors. Then Shumly's voice: "You men, come back here. This is an illegal work stoppage."

Miravich counts them as they enter the locker room. All ten men in the blooming mill crew, plus two millwrights, a pipefitter, and a laborer named Billy Pyle. "One more coming," says Billy, the last man in.

"Who is he?" Miravich asks.

"It's a she, Joe."

"What!" Miravich darts into the corridor and catches her before she goes into the women's locker room. It's Drubiszewski, the girl who sweeps up on the afternoon turn, a new hire. He has seen her name on the roster. "Hey, wotsyourname," he calls.

She swings around, and in the dim overhead light he sees only bright lips on a dirty face. "My name's Droo-beh-*shev*-skee, Mitzie. Got it?" she says tartly.

"Okay, okay. Thanks for coming out."

"That's what the union's for, isn't it?"

■

Pete Bonner often walks next door around noon to the Saboulovich Hotel & Cafe for a quick sandwich and the latest gossip while Mae watches the store. Entering Saboulovich's is like stepping into an old pair of work clothes—tattered and redolent of stale sweat, but scrubbed clean daily. Bonner has seen the two daughters, hefty young women, walking along the bar top, rousting spiders and popping paint bubbles in the ceiling with broom handles. Narrow tables on gimpy legs line one wall, and a sagging wooden cornice, with ends rolled up like papyrus paper, overshadows the back-bar mirror. At lunchtime, men wearing peaked hats and caps line the bar, elbow to elbow, drinking and gabbing. Bonner enjoys the sight of a thirsty man drowning his nose in a glass of draft beer, then turn to look at him with a foam-flecked mustache. He also enjoys the sounds of foreign tongues wrestling with English.

John Saboulovich, corpulent and arthritic, with a droopy, white mustache, shuffles up and down behind the bar, serving customers and chatting about the war, local politics, baseball, and happenings in the mill. In the dining room, five boarders, who live upstairs in tiny rooms, sit at a big round table, eating steamy, pungent stews. They came over from Hungary, Slovenia, and Serbia intending to return to their families in the old country with a pocketful of American dollars. But they are stuck here for the duration of the war. Meanwhile, the Nazis are wiping out their villages and hanging their kinfolk.

The place reeks of onion, garlic, and boiled cabbage, odors of which Bonner is particularly fond. He opens a jar rimmed in brine and pulls out a pickled pig's foot to snack on. He orders his usual shot of rye with a soda water chaser.

Saboulovich skitters a shot glass across the polished wood and leans stiff-armed against the bar to pour whiskey into the glass, twisting his wrist to end the pour. At lunchtime, laborers and maintenance men, who aren't tied to production jobs, come up from the mill for a beer and a hot meal. Today, two men are talking about last night's walkout in the blooming mill, led by Committeeman Miravich. Bonner's hand pauses over the open pig's feet jar. "Miravich?" He orders drinks for his informants and asks a few questions. Opinion at the bar is divided about the propriety of the walkout. Some say it's wrong to strike in wartime, but others say it's about time the men stick up for their rights. "Joe Miravich, he sonna m'beech tough union man," sums up an oldtimer.

When Bonner returns to the office, Mae is working at the adding machine. To demonstrate her displeasure with his too-long absence, she pounds the keys and pulls the lever harder than necessary—*tit-tit-tit-kachit*! Saboulovich's is altogether too chummy and comfortable for a man with Bonner's weakness. One of the reasons she works two or three hours a day, answering the phone and doing the books, is to exercise some restraint over him. What she really needs for him is a straitjacket. *Tit-tit-tit-kachit*!

Bonner laughs as he studies his wife, crisp and neat in a blue and white pinafore with square shoulders and a short, hemless skirt—wartime's "hard silhouette," as the fashion magazines call it. At the age of thirty-six, she has lost the youthful fuzz that once gave her face a springtime glow, but her pale blue eyes still peer out with an unworldly innocence. He loves this about her, trying though it sometimes is, and he hopes those naked eyes of youth never turn glassy.

The front door opens and two men enter, one large and the other short and dumpy. Bonner first recognizes the big fellow by the length of hairy, bare wrist sticking out of his suit sleeves. Pixie. Sure enough, the tubby one—boy, has he been spooning up spaghetti!—is Sal Grotto, twenty pounds heavier than when Bonner last saw him two years ago at the $50 window at Wheeling Downs. He is natty as all get-out in a a double-breasted cotton seersucker suit, mid-'30s style, with a blue yachtsman's tie.

When Bonner introduces him to Mae, Grotto removes his white Panama hat and holds it over his heart. "Mrs. Bonner. What a pleasure! Your husband speaks often of you, and now I can see why."

"How do you do?" she says formally. Her eyes turn hard and mean.

The two men leave Mae in the office and walk down the aisle of the storeroom, followed by Pixie. Hundreds of cases now line the walls, in columns that reach to the ceiling. A new conveyor system with gleaming rollers has retractable spurs, like railroad sidings, that reach back into the beer stacks. The walls and ceiling are painted canary yellow, and overhead lamps flood the place with light. Outside, a helper is banking cases on the sloping flanges of the truck bed to form a pyramid, while two empty trucks wait to feed at the dock.

"Ver-ry impressive!" Grotto exclaims. He sucks in a low whistle and re-volves slowly, taking it all in. "A lot different from the last time I was here. Remember? I said I'd be back some day? Looks like the war's good for beer."

"People are thirsty and have money to spend." Feeling a rush of nastiness, he says, "And how are your new businesses, Sal?"

"New businesses?" The sentence ends with a warning question mark.

Bonner rashly pushes on. "You know, meat, sugar, coffee..." The Grotto empire, everyone knows, has expanded into the black market for all sorts of commodities made scarce by war—the aforementioned staples, along with liquor, tires, cigarettes, butter, used cars, gasoline rationing stamps, food ra-tioning stamps.

Grotto wheels and walks back into the storeroom. He halts and faces Bon-ner. "Whatever I am in, Pete, I am doing well in. It's what I'm not in that bothers me." He pauses. "Which is why I'm here. I am *not* in beer. Know what I mean? I believe in an old principle. It's called tit for tat. I got you off the hook five years ago, Pete. That was tat. Now it's time for tit." Grotto pats Bonner's arm. "No handout expected. I got money to invest in a partnership."

"Beer has its problems, Sal."

"I don't see problems here. I see beer stacked to the ceiling here."

"The cost-price ratios are bad, low profit margins. You know." Bonner tries to gauge the depth of business knowledge behind those sharp eyes. "It takes a lot of labor to move beer around."

"Labor? I can get labor dirt cheap. Manure costs more. Am I hearing some-thing disturbing here?" He turns slowly with a sideways glance at Pixie.

"If you like what we've done," Bonner says, trying a different strategy, "let me show off my new cooler." He leads them into an alcove and opens a heavy door. They enter a low-ceilinged room about thirty feet long and half as wide. When Bonner shuts the door, they are enveloped in frigid air. Double-decked rows of wooden and aluminum kegs line one wall. At the far end of the room a waist-high door that slides upward on a weight-and-pulley mechanism leads to the loading dock.

"Ahhhh!" Pixie says, luxuriating in the coolness. He takes a bottle of beer offered by Bonner and sits on a keg near the dock door.

"Ver-ry impressive!" Grotto says, shivering slightly. He looks for a place to sit.

"I've got a thousand bucks tied up in this, Sal. Insulated walls and the very latest refrigeration equipment." Bonner picks up a dutchhead, a burlap sack filled with cork for dropping kegs on, and lays it on top of an aluminum half. "Have a seat, Sal."

Grotto crunches down on the dutchhead. "That's a pretty penny for an ice box."

"Yep, and I'll have the loan paid off in ten years at three percent."

"Myself, I prefer paying cash. Cash in, cash out."

"In this business you have to keep ahead of the competition," Bonner says. "I took another loan to buy the building next door and knock out the adjoining wall. Then I had to build the garage out back, buy the new conveyor, new office furniture, new bathroom for the men so they could have a urinal...." At a grimace from his guest, Bonner gives a helpless gesture. "It was either that or deal with a union."

"A urinal for beer slingers!" Grotto exclaims. "Most of these guys was raised on a one-hole crapper. I could of told you that." He stands up, rubbing his sore butt. "You do own this building, don't you?"

"Oh, sure, bought it last year. Of course, I took out a second mortgage to buy two new trucks. I'll be ready for the boom after the war."

Grotto expels a mouthful of mist. "Boom!" he exclaims. "Haven't you heard, Pete? The boom goes off the rose when the last shot's fired. Mother of Mary! Talk about mortgaging the future—you've mortgaged two or three futures." He reaches for the door handle. "Pixie, finish that goddamned beer! I'm freezing my butt off."

Outside the cooler, Grotto faces Bonner. "You're banking on the come, just like you did in the twenties. You're in five miles over your head, Pete. I put money in here, it'd be like sticking my feet in concrete." He shivers again. "I hate the cold like I hate debt...like I hate competition."

Grotto walks quickly to the front door, tipping his hat as he passes Mae in the office. "Just one more thing," he adds, his hand on the knob. "All you told me...all these loans and mortgages—it's all copacetic, yes?"

"It's all in my books, Sal. PLCB regulations. A distributor has to record all transactions, give full information on partners—"

"What? The Liquor Control Board? Who said we got free enterprise?" He scowls at Pixie, who opens the door for him. "You want my advice, Pete, dig yourself out of that hole. Cash in, cash out." Turning to leave, he throws back over his shoulder, "And you still owe me that tit."

In the evening Bonner stays late at the office, working on a false set of books.

■

Sunday afternoon, the boys out of the house, Pete and Mae make love. Three fans play on them, for Bonner tends to sweat when exerting himself. He leans over and draws his mustache lightly across her chin.

Usually these are quiet events; only the furniture talks. Today, Mae is nervous. "The boys," she says. "Did you send them far enough?"

"Uh-huh." Kneeling beside her, he forms a goose head of his right hand and gently nips her breasts. "While you were taking a bath," he says, pausing to nuzzle the navel, "I drove them to Shoaf Field. We took balls and bats and picked up two of their friends." He gently eases her shoulders back. "Even if they get tired of playing ball, they've got to walk home. Do you know how long it takes young boys to walk half a mile on a hot day?"

"Just one thing," she says, her Irish Imp taking over.

"What?"

"Did you take all the bats to the field?"

"Not all," he says triumphantly.

Later, he puts on his shorts and one sock and sits on the edge of the bed, thinking. She knows that look: he is planning another move on the chessboard of beer.

CHAPTER 2: August 1943

Committeeman Miravich arrives early for his first meeting of the Watts Works Management-Labor Committee. Located on the second floor of the office building, the meeting room contains a large oaken table with pencils and pads lined up in front of six chairs on one side, seven on the other, and one at the head. On the west wall hang black and white photographs of the Watts's blast furnaces, Betty, Irma, Martha, and Matilda, named for Corporation executives' wives with a tendency to rotundity. The opposite wall presents three color pictures of globs of orange smoke in the sky, representing the three greatest-ever Bessemer blows, and a large group shot of Martin Dinsmore, general superintendent of the Watts, with his six department superintendents. Attired in yellow asbestos suits and cradling asbestos headgear in their arms, they pose in front of Blast Furnace Irma on the day she won the "E for Excellence" flag for record-setting production. The first line of the caption reads simply, "THE WATTS TEAM."

Miravich stands on tiptoes and inspects the photograph. "What's that black blob in the background?" he asks.

Pat McNally, the local president, peers over his shoulder. "That's where they blacked out all the guys who do the work."

Promptly at nine o'clock that same "Watts Team" files into the room. Dinsmore, a heavyset man of about fifty with thinning brown hair and impatience scribbled all over his face, takes his self-appointed place at the head of the table. "Let's get this over with. I've got steel to make." He leads the group in reciting the Pledge of Allegiance and gets briskly to business. "No need to read the minutes of the last meeting since there was no new business. Agreed?"

"Aye," say the six superintendents as they drop to their seats in unison on the right side of the table.

"I object to omission of proposals made by the union," McNally says. He sits on the left side along with six union committeemen.

"They were ruled out of order, and therefore are not part of the record. Objection overruled."

Dinsmore's every move signals his distaste for the notion that management and labor should sit at the same table, let alone negotiate on any matter.

He and his superintendents are present only because corporate management has ordered its plant managers to form "joint management-labor committees" to promote the War Effort, as recommended by the federal War Production Board. The committees are supposed to solicit ideas from ordinary workers on how to increase production in order to defeat the fascist powers. Now, at this seventh monthly meeting, Dinsmore moves swiftly through a list of announcements. Under new business, Phil Shumly gives a report on war bond sales at the Watts, and Dinsmore entertains a motion to adjourn.

"The union," McNally interjects, "has new business."

"State your new business, Mr. McNally."

"The union has some ideas on raising output in the Watts." McNally passes a stack of papers to the head of the table. "Mr. Chairman," he says, "I submit these employee suggestions on improving efficiency."

Dinsmore pushes the papers away. "Your motion is out of order. Plant efficiency is an operational matter under management authority and therefore is not within the scope of this joint committee."

"The union disputes the chair's ruling," McNally says.

"You dispute? Being disputatious, Mr. McNally, is contrary to the cooperative nature of this undertaking. Out of order."

McNally has been through this before. Now he reads a declaration. "The union has a continuing objection to this committee in that the refusal of the company to discuss matters pertinent to the war effort is contrary to the wishes of the president of the United States." He sits down, looking tired and defeated. He is one of those emaciated Irishmen, deep lines troweled out from the corners of his eyes, who makes a daily trip to hell by way of the pub.

"Out of order! Do I hear a second to a motion to adjourn?"

"Hold on!" Miravich blurts out. "I thought management was supposed to listen to our ideas." His union cohorts stare at him and shake their heads. Such an innocent!

Dinsmore sits glowering, gripping the edges of the table as if prepared to up-end it. "The management of this plant will not engage in a discussion of operational matters with any so-called representatives of any employees. And, therefore, Mr...." the chairman consults a sheet of paper. "...Mr. Miravich, you are out of order."

"If the union can't make suggestions, what the hell can we do?"

Dinsmore points to a big carton box in the corner. "Five thousand Win the War buttons. The union can pass out those buttons. Good for morale."

"I got new business," Miravich says.

"What is your business regarding?" Dinsmore asks.

"Regarding the use of bad steel in the blooming mill."

Dinsmore bristles. "You are out of order, not within the scope—" He stops because Miravich is bending over and reaching under the table. "What's this?"

Miravich brings up his lunch bucket and opens it. He pulls out a six-inch long chunk of semi-finished steel and slams it on the table. Everybody jumps. "This is a piece of one of those green blooms that we was forced to roll a week ago. Until Rooster Wooster and the whole crew walked off the job and got our asses spanked with a suspension. You take this piece down to the forge and heat it and do a chemical test on it. The carbon content will prove we were running green steel. Is this the kind of steel we want to send to our GIs fighting overseas?"

"Absurd!" says Phil Shumly. He stares at the piece of scrap as if trying to perform spectroanalysis in his head.

The other superintendents seem to edge away from Shumly, and even Dinsmore flicks a glance at him. Then the chairman bends forward, still gripping the edge of the table, and everybody rocks back in his chair in case the table topples over. "You are way, way out of order, Mr. Miravich!"

Miravich ignores him. "Our people are angry. If there aren't changes made by Monday, giving us a say and stopping the safety violations, we're hitting the bricks."

"Motion denied!"

"That wasn't a motion," Miravich says. "It was a threat."

"Meeting adjourned."

When the union people get outside, McNally turns furiously on Miravich. "What the hell, Joe. You had no authority to do that. We don't talk strike unless the committee votes on it."

"Well, we weren't getting anyplace acting like gentlemen. Yes sir, no sir, and if we're good boys we get to pass out those buttons.'"

"You got to admit, Pat," says a committeeman named Terhune, "Joe got their attention." Two other committeemen, Coyle and Burke, nod in agreement.

"There's not going to be a strike," McNally says firmly. "Phil Murray signed a no-strike pledge for the duration of the war, and we're going to abide by it."

"Yeah, well, Phil Murray don't have to face the heat in the mill every day," Miravich says. "I say we put it up to the members this Sunday at the picnic." He raises the lunch box in front of the three committeemen who seem to be on his side and rattles the chunk of steel. "How about it, fellows?"

McNally's protest comes too late. Miravich carries the day, four ayes to three nays, just before a plant guard tells them to get moving, they're blocking access to Mr. Dinsmore's office.

■

A glorious day for the union's annual picnic, all-blue sky, green hills soaking up the blazing sun, but scores of cars are swimming in a metallic glare as they idle in stalled traffic waiting to enter the park. Eddie Cramczak's old Chevy, with a "B" sticker on the windshield, is allowed only three gallons a week, and most of that is probably going up in smoke, joining a cloud of exhaust vapor hovering above the cars. He taps his fuel gauge as if this will reduce consumption, then barks a cranky "Stop it!"to his two young children who are wrestling with Uncle Joe Miravich in the back seat.

"See!" Miravich admonishes the kids. "Now you'll have to get out and push." He threatens to open the door, and they scream "No, no!"

Also crammed into the car are Anna Cramzcak, old Mrs. Miravich, and Joe's date, Mitzie Drubiszewski. They ran into this traffic jam on a two-lane road leading to a park named Rainbow Gardens. Affixed to the park when it opened in the 1920s, the name's suggestive charm was born of the same belief in a fantasy world that powered the concurrent stock market run-up late in that decade. The park contains a swimming pool, kids' playground, amusement arcade, dance pavilion, and picnic groves—everything except easy access for cars of the industrial *hoi polloi* it was designed to serve.

Finally Cramczak finds a place in a crowded lot. Miravich grabs a food hamper and sets off with Mitzie. This is the first time he has seen her in something other than pants and work shirt. In shorts and white cotton blouse, she is a pretty full dish, almost as tall as he and all legs and sparkling hazel eyes that see a joke in everything. Her cheeks are slightly drawn in, as if she is always sucking on hard candy.

Hundreds of people crowd the small midway area, throwing balls and darts, eating ice cream cones and pretzel sticks, weaving back and forth, a muttering sea of people, girls in shorts and halters, women in pinafores that end above the knees. The war has done wonders for women's legs, even when they're dyed or painted to resemble stockings.

Attracted by a crowd swirling around the swimming pool entrance, Miravich and Mitzie push forward to see what's going on. A half-dozen Negro men are marching in a small circle. The leader carries a large sign which says: "WE CAN SERVE IN THE WHITE MAN'S ARMY, BUT WE CAN'T SWIM IN HIS

POOLS." A squad of policemen stand at the ready, but the Negroes are not attempting to block the gate. Some whites dismiss them with a wave, some spit on the ground, a few shout, "Go home, niggers!" But most walk silently past.

Miravich raises a hand in greeting to Walt Tyrell, the protest leader, who nods ever so slightly in return. Solemn and compact, he has a blunt nose and wide, thick lips spread across a dark caramel face. He and Miravich shoveled slag side by side in the open hearth pit for several months in 1939, swapping jokes and stories, these two fugitives, one from a coal mine and the other from an Alabama sharecropper's farm. Then Miravich got promoted on a whites-only bid list, and Tyrell stayed in the pit.

Miravich senses Mitzie's questioning look. "They have a point," he says. "I guess I won't be swimming today."

"Oh?" she says, adding mischievously, "Do you swim a lot?"

He eyes her sharply, catching a hint of entrapment. "The truth is, you put me in water, I'd sink like a week-old cow pie. But if I did swim, I wouldn't now because I need the coloreds' support in the local."

"But you need the whites' support, too, don't you?" She affects an innocent look. "Which is why you're not going to join the protest? Is that how politics works?"

"Something like that. Let's get a beer."

They find the grove staked out by the Cramzcak clan. Eddie has two brothers, both steelworkers, and two sisters married to steelworkers, and they all have families. What with all the little Cramczaks, there must be two dozen people buzzing around. He introduces Mitzie to all the Cramczaks and leads her to his mother who sits in a camp chair, staring blankly across the clearing. She wears a sack dress that goes down to her ankles. Her feet, encased in thick black shoes with square heels, are lined up at attention, and her hands are clasped in her lap. He kneels in front of her. "Having a good day, Mama? This here is my friend Mitzie."

Mrs. Miravich nods and smiles vaguely. Her worldly work is finished, all eight children grown now, and she lives with the Cramczaks. She is only about seventy—nobody knows for sure because they didn't keep records in the peasant village where she was born—but life in the patches wore her down, and death is closing in.

"Where've you been with that hamper?" his sister chides Miravich. She and other women are laying out food on two picnic tables shoved together, platters of cold cuts, German potato salad, cold sauerkraut, sausages, pastries. They chatter, meanwhile, about shortages of coffee, tea, sugar, butter, meat, candy, even chewing gum. The rampaging black market is enriching crooks, they agree, the gasoline-rationing system is unfair, and the wartime freeze on wages is squeezing everybody.

The men have been sitting around nursing their beers, listening to the women complain. Sonny Cramczak, the youngest of Eddie's brothers, speaks up first. "Jeez, who says we got nothing to strike about?" He turns to Miravich. "I'm with you, Joe. The women said it all. Let's shut 'em down."

"No, no!" breaks in Eddie Cramczak. "Striking won't get us more gas. It's a dumb thing to do. Besides, the union pledged not to strike during the war."

"Joe's right about safety," says Eddie's brother Mike. He stands with one foot on a bench and holds a bottle of beer. "In the pipe mill, they're pushing so hard to raise the pipe count, oil's lying in puddles on the floor and everybody's slipping and falling. Like me." He holds up his free hand with two splinted fingers.

Dodo Cramczak, always at humorous odds with her husband, says, "You boys can't go on strike every time Mike falls down. He does that all the time at home."

A third Cramczak brother throws in. "Look at the miners. Every time you turn around John L. Lewis has them on strike, and people are coming to hate all unions."

Miravich can't restrain himself. "Yeah, we have that no-strike pledge," he says. addressing Eddie, "but while we're turning the other cheek, U.S. Steel's turning a huge profit. Last year, they tore down the whole First Ward in Homestead to put in a new rolling mill. It cost fifty million bucks of taxpayers' money, thousands of people lost their homes. Sure, more steel for the war effort, but who'll get all the profits? The owners, not the people who sacrificed."

"Come on, Joe," DoDo says, "you're balancing out some big score sheet, but the rest of us're just trying to live day by day."

As the debate peters out, Miravich's opinion tally indicates something less than unanimity in the working-class. He invites Mitzie to take a stroll in the woods. They stop in the shade of a white oak tree. His arm slips inside hers and around her waist. She bends her elbow and locks it there. "What're you laughing at?" he says.

"How come you never noticed me before that day we walked out?"

"I was working on it slow and deliberate. Why? You in a hurry to get somewhere?"

"I don't know yet. Where are you going?"

"I'm just beginning to see my way." He puts his other arm around her. She steps back against the tree trunk, pulling him with her. His lips crush an eyebrow. Heat radiates from her, pulses from her, like a hot bloom passing close. He presses up against her and tries to suck the hard candy out of her mouth.

She says, "I thought it would feel this way."

"You thought? You mean you never did this before?"

"It's been a while. I'd just about forgotten."

"A looker like you? No dates?"

"Like the song says, they're either too gray or too grassy green." She runs her finger lightly across the scar on his forehead and the scar on his chin and the stubble of a pinky finger. As if she owns him.

The old oak supports them for a while, until they slide off into the underbrush. And then she says NO! When he tells her that people don't say NO these days, she says I DO, and only SHE—no one else—will decide when the time is right.

"Well, you are something!" He had had designs on her, and trying to carry them out he had seriously injured himself on a twig.

"Yes, I am something," she says. "You'll get over it."

Late in the afternoon, back in the picnic area, Miravich announces he is going to the main pavilion to talk to some union people before the meeting. Mitzie gets up to accompany him. "Where're you going?" he says.

"To the pavilion with you."

"Not now. There won't be any women, just a bunch of guys."

"I pay dues too, remember?"

Miravich laughs. "Okay, I'll put you down as a good union member. I'll see you later at the big meeting." Holding her arm, he tries to turn her around. She resists. Fire shoots to his head. "You're acting like a mine mule. What's got into you?"

"You didn't buy me like a dog. 'Stay when I say stay.' We're just on a date." Her fierce gaze burns right through his eyes and out the back of his head. Then she twists away. An earring, catching the sun, flares in his face.

He walks rapidly out of the grove.

The pavilion is filled with men, standing around, sitting at tables, drinking beer out of milkshake-size paper cups. A crowd huddles around one table where six or seven guys hunch over a poker game, tossing dimes and quarters into the pot with a steady clink-clink. Only a few years ago it would have been pennies and nickels. Men call to him as he makes his way across the floor. "Give 'em hell, Joe!" "Bust their balls, Joe!"

Two men, converging on him from each side, take his arms and draw him back against a log pillar. "Just a minute of your time, Joe." He recognizes John and Carl from years ago when he attended a couple of CP meetings. He never knew their last names and doesn't want to know them now. They urge him to stop this strike talk. The union should store up its militancy for after the war and concentrate on turning out planes, tanks, and guns to supply the Soviet Union in its struggle against Hitler. "Think of the big picture, Joe," says the man named John.

Miravich thinks of the big picture all right, the picture of these guys switching back and forth, war to peace to war, in step with the Soviets. "Tell you what," Miravich says, breaking away from them, "why don't you speak up later at the meeting?"

Pat McNally, who is rallying his group against the strike, approaches Miravich. Instead of launching an angry tirade, the local president puts on the mask of an Irish father saddened by the feuding among his sons. "Don't you know you're splitting the local, Joe? We're obligated to abide by the no-strike pledge."

"Yeah, well what's management obligated to do? Talk with us, right? Do you see them talking? Everybody's fed up with all kinds of things."

"Sure, lots of complaints, gripes, some real issues, some not so real." He lights a cigarette. "Look here, Joe, you may feel like you're running with some radical wind. But the people in this valley, see, they're stem to stern conservative. You get yourself out too far, they'll pull the plank out."

Miravich feels sorry for McNally. A decent man, and once a strong leader, he seems to be wasting away from the inside. Something that nibbles at your testicles, leaving an empty sack. For a moment after McNally leaves, Miravich considers going after him to see if they can work out a deal. But no! What's right is right.

The meeting starts at five o'clock, a few hundred people gathering on the lawn outside the dance pavilion. After bland speeches by local politicians, people in the crowd begin to chant, "Vote! Vote! Shut 'em down!" McNally tries to take charge, arguing that no official action can be taken at a rally. A man from the union's district office warns, "Mr. Murray isn't going to like this..." Shouted down, he retires stiffbacked to the rear.

Miravich and other pro-strike committeemen introduce militants from various mill departments who describe unsafe practices caused by the rush to produce more, faster. Rooster Wooster puts in an appearance to wide applause—rollers are highly respected—and retells the story of the green steel. Miravich does his bit with the chunk of steel, holding it up, shouting, "This is what management is putting in the hands of our poor servicemen overseas. It's so brittle," he says, turning it on end to show a shear point, "I accidentally broke it in half this morning when I dropped it in my bathroom." He takes another piece out of his pocket; it fits neatly against the first.

The mood of the crowd, roiled by high spirits and beery anger at the corporation, clearly is pro-strike. "All in favor," someone calls out, and the crowd roars. They don't even get around to calling for the no vote.

Miravich jumps down from the bandstand and dives into the dispersing crowd, looking for Mitzie. She and Eddie are walking to the grove. "Congratulations!" she says in a mocking way. "You were pretty good up there."

Eddie says, "Hey, Joe, is that really a piece of green steel you have there?" Miravich laughs. "It's just a hunk of metal I picked up on the mill floor." He asks Eddie to drive Mitzie home because he has to meet the boys and plan the strike. Turning to Mitzie, he says, "Am I going to see you again?" He tries to look contrite for whatever she thinks he did wrong. He's big enough to do that.

"Sure. I'll be on the picket line...sir?" She goes up the path with Eddie.

Why is it, he wonders, that you can't win anything free and clear?

The rebels decide to strike this very night, starting with the night turn at eleven. "We hit them fast and hard in the dead of night," Miravich decrees, remembering the coal wildcats he took part in. Nothing more nourishing for a newborn strike than five or six solid hours of nighttime, the blacker the better. If the moon is out, you stand at the edge of the road and piss upwards, intoning, "Drown the moon, drown the moon." Puts you in the right frame of mind, and sometimes it even works. Some of his best memories are of nights he and his buddies sped around the countryside on dirt roads, shutting down all the mines in the district. All you had to do was post one picket on the entry road. God, what a feeling! The power of the workingman! If you could get your arms around it and do it every night, it'd rank up there with sex.

Miravich and his lieutenants work furiously for the next three hours, phoning key men on the night shift, rounding up the staunchest militants, then swooping into town at ten o'clock and setting up picket lines at the Watts's three gates. By the time the night turn begins showing up, all gates are blocked and guards are running around inside like headless chickens. The afternoon turn floods out of the mill at eleven o'clock, hurrahing when they see the pickets. Only skeleton crews remain at work to keep the furnaces on heat, and the mill sinks silently into the night.

Daylight brings an avalanche of cops and out-of-town visitors. By nine o'clock, pickets at the main gate of the Watts are far outnumbered by local, county, and state police, federal marshals, and a company of the National Guard. By ten, representatives of the War Production Board, War Labor Board, National Wage Stabilization Board, Office of Price Administration, and the Justice Department are wandering around. Labor experts from the Greater Ohio Industrial Propagation Association offer their assistance to management. Dozens of newspaper reporters clamor for information. Ambulances are lined up outside the plant; firemen stand by with hoses hooked up to hydrants; Rhino Rafferty, the motorcycle cop, races up and down Lysle Boulevard.

"You'd think we were starting a revolution," Miravich observes.

At eleven o'clock, emissaries from Phil Murray show up with a signed note inviting the strike leaders to visit him in his office, forthwith. Murray's burly men hustle Miravich and three others into two cars and speed off to Pittsburgh.

■

Stashed in a stuffy boardroom near Murray's office, the four committeemen are kept waiting long enough to repent their misdeeds. The union now occupies several floors in the Commonwealth Building in Pittsburgh, having moved from the Grant Building suite that Miravich first visited in 1937. In the boardroom, he goes from wall to wall, studying official portraits of union officials, pondering the breathtaking changes that have occurred in those six years. The Little Steel companies finally capitulated under government pressure as war approached, and SWOC was converted into the United Steelworkers of America with more than a half-million members. Murray was elected president and Dave McDonald, secretary-treasurer, along with two vice presidents. Their portraits hang side by side, but there's an empty space where John L. Lewis's once hung. What a strange turn of events! The man who started it all, toppled from power by his own excessive pride, expecting the workers of America to mass behind him and defeat FDR in 1940. When they did just the opposite, voting overwhelmingly for Roosevelt, Lewis resigned as CIO president. He retreated to the United Mine Workers and began vilifying Murray, his former protégé and new CIO chief. Miravich murmurs aloud the once fearsome name, "John L. Lewis," now an empty patch of wall.

They are escorted into Murray's office. Wasting no time on pleasantries, the president scolds the Watts committeemen and threatens to take over the local if they refuse to call off the strike. He dismisses all except Miravich.

Murray takes off his suit jacket, unbuttons his vest, and rolls backward in his chair, bracing his feet against the edge of the desk. "It's been a long time since you walked into my office, Joe, you and...the beer salesman... Bonner, right?" With a nod from Miravich, he continues, "Strange, or maybe not so strange, the police never got to the bottom of that plot. Did you and Bonner ever have any trouble?"

"Once, years ago, but some nice fellows volunteered to take our place."

Murray momentarily looks puzzled, but he has other things on his mind. "Joe, I owe you a lot, but I can't ignore what happened at the Watts. When we signed a no-strike pledge to see us through this war, we made an absolute guarantee. No exceptions. There's nothing in that document that exempts Joe Miravich and the Watts Works."

"I'm a loyal union man, Mr. Murray, but I don't want to be a slave to the company. Look at Lewis. If the miners need something, he doesn't fall down on his knees and beg. He takes them out on strike and to hell with the no-strike pledge."

Murray pops forward in his chair. "Forget Lewis!" He pauses, thinking better of the tongue-lashing he was about to launch. "Tell me, Joe, do you want to win this war?"

"Damn right! Why don't you ask guys like Dinsmore and Shumly and all those bosses if they want to win? We can show management things they've been doing wrong for thirty years. But they sit there like tree stumps, refuse to listen. 'Plant efficiency is an operational matter,' they say. But who gets blamed for bad steel? We do! Who gets blamed for interruptions due to breakdowns and accidents? We've had enough of that shit! I thought we was fighting for 'industrial democracy,' like you say in your speeches."

Murray nods and looks down at a paper clip he's bent out of shape. "It's the way of their class, the capitalists and their factotums, arrogant, dictatorial. It hasn't changed one scintilla since the day I first went down a mine shaft." He stands and buttons his vest. "Industrial democracy is a goal, Joe, a goal on the horizon. We'll have to tear up society to get to it, but we can't do that in the middle of a war, can we?" He glances at his watch. "So, Joe, you're going back and put an end to this strike."

"We haven't got anything out of it yet."

A scary change comes over Murray's face; his mouth hardens into a thin sliver, his eyebrows arch, and his cheeks collapse. "If you and your friends don't take down the picket lines before the afternoon turn, I'll impose a trusteeship on the local for the duration of the war. And if the company fires you, I won't raise an eyebrow, and you'll be finished in the steel industry and the United Steelworkers of America."

He flicks a switch on his intercom. "What's next?"

∎

Miravich and his friends give in. The pickets disappear, and people begin trickling back to work. Under orders from the Corporation, the Watts management makes one concession. A memo goes up on bulletin boards, declaring that all superintendents will "review" safety procedures in their departments.

On the first day back in the plant, the four renegade committeemen are transferred to labor gangs as punishment for leading the wildcat strike. Miravich draws the worst assignment, digging a ditch to nowhere outside the blooming mill. He is standing on the bottom with a pick in his hands when Rooster Wooster visits him on a break.

"We won something out of it," Rooster says, looking down from the edge of the ditch. "No more cold steel coming out of the soaking pits."

"They'll still do whatever they damn please and we don't have a say."

"Listen, Joe, the guys like the way you stood up for what's right."

Miravich is stuck for words. He brandishes the pick. "I'm not as good with one of these as I used to be."

On his third day in the ditch, Mitzie appears above him. "What're you digging?"

"You got me. They just told me to go down six feet and dig towards the river."

She looks in that direction. "That's a hundred yards away."

"I better get moving, then."

"Are you going to take this lying down?"

"Do I look like I'm lying down?" But her nagging gives him an idea.

The next day he reports to work in a rented tuxedo, frilly shirt, clip-on bow tie, top hat, and all. Dozens of workers see him as he walks the quarter mile from the gate to the blooming-mill shop. By the time he has descended into the ditch, still wearing the tux, a small crowd has gathered. He starts slopping mud out of the hole with his shovel, then takes up the pick. He finds the old rhythm and makes the pick rise and fall in blurry arcs, showing these steelworkers how a coal miner can make the earth move. The men yell encouragement.

When Mitzie arrives, he tips his hat. "How's this for taking it lying down?"

She grins down at him. "You're crazy, Miravich."

"Will you go to the movies with me Saturday night?"

She thinks for a moment. "Ask me again on Friday."

The labor gang foreman comes along. "What the hell you doing, Miravich? You can't wear them clothes."

"The rules say only to wear hard toes, and I'm wearing them." He turns a foot up to display his metatarsals, then gets back to digging. "Look at all I got done today."

From afar, workers at windows and doors jeer the foreman. He fusses and fumes but can't think of what to say, and so he walks off as if nothing untoward is happening. Word spreads through the plant. Production workers leave their mills and furnaces for a few minutes, take a quick gander at Miravich digging in his tux, and hurry back to work.

After lunch break, the foreman returns and tells Miravich to clean his tools and report to the blooming mill.

"You telling me to quit?" Miravich looks over the lip of the ditch, shading his eyes against the sun. "I'm nowheres near the river yet." He hauls himself out of the hole and, shouldering pick and shovel, saunters up the roadway in the mud-spattered tux. A huge cheer arises, and he doffs the hat and bows to all sides.

Later, the true story of his liberation comes out. When Martin Dinsmore went out to lunch that day, he found that the story had leaked out over the saloon society's news network. Everybody in town was laughing over Miravich's stunt, which only added to the popularity of this dangerous radical. Dinsmore rushed back to the plant and gave the order to get Miravich out of sight—and out of top hat and tails.

The best thing that comes out of this episode is his reunion with Mitzie. On Saturday night they see *Casablanca*, and her shoulder touches his when Sam sings "As Time Goes By." Later, they have ice cream sodas at a dairy place called Isaly's on Fifth Avenue. Miravich apologizes, though he's not sure what for. He'll say practically anything because he wants this woman to be his wife.

CHAPTER 3:
September 1943–December 1943

On a warm September day, one of their days off, Miravich and Mitzie set off on a scenic tour of the valley, rattling along in his brother-in-law's Chevy. Sunlight tries to skinny through narrow openings in a ragged cloud cover, but smoky bursts from the mills keep closing the gaps. A sticky breeze whips through the open windows, mussing Mitzie's hair, and the air is so gritty you could sharpen a pencil on it. Miravich hopes to find a secluded spot on a Monongahela riverbank for a picnic and perhaps to rent a boat. Neither he nor Mitzie has ever been on a river, or in a river, or even near a river—driving over bridges doesn't count—despite the fact that there are rivers all around. "Doesn't it make you wonder," he said, "why we got all this water and never use it?"

But where to consummate this dream? If you drive north from McKeesport, mills and railroad tracks crowd the shorelines all the way to Pittsburgh—in Duquesne, Braddock, Munhall, Homestead, Rankin, Hazelwood, and South Side Pittsburgh—leaving no room even for a standup picnic. The woodsy solitude he craves is more likely to be found upriver, or to the south, Miravich decides, and he heads in that direction after picking up Mitzie. Almost immediately they get stuck at a train crossing on Lysle Boulevard as a Baltimore & Ohio freight lumbers through the middle of town. In preindustrial days a century ago, the city, then a sleepy hamlet seeking fame and fortune, paid the B&O to establish a right-of-way across the edge of the village. The plan worked. Now, nearly four-score trains a day pass through the center of a city swollen in size, bringing traffic and commerce to a standstill.

Slow-moving boxcars glide ka-bump-ka-bump over the grade crossing. Heat waves dance above idling engines. A few drivers get out of their cars and tug at shirts sticking to damp chests. From a pipe mill at the nearby Watts Works comes a hollow clanging of pipe against pipe. Someone turns up a car radio, and a serenade by the Andrews Sisters floats down the line:

> I'll be with you
> in aap-ple blossom time...

Mitzie fans herself with a highway map.

Patti Andrews breaks into a solo:

> I'll be with you
> to change your name to mine.

Miravich glances covertly across the seat, but Mitzie is looking out the window.

The box cars are still going ka-bump ka-bump. A faint whistle sounds from the locomotive, probably in the next county by now. At last the caboose comes into view, and people scramble back into their cars. Exhaust plumes from dozens of tailpipes as drivers gun their engines. The caboose sways through the crossing, gates go up, and cars surge across the tracks from both directions.

Miravich drives across the Youghiogheny and a few minutes later crosses the Monongahela to Dravosburg dozing on a hillside. He turns south on a road that parallels the shoreline. Mitzie swivels her head to take in all the sights, railroad tracks on the left and a steep bluff rearing up on the right. "This is the farthest I've ever been away from home," she says,

"Five miles!" he says, pitying her. "I've been lots of places, down to Charleston and up to Youngstown. I helped organize mills in this valley, like the Irvin Works way up on this hill, out of sight."

Her view blocked by the bluff, she nods and says, "We never had enough money to go anyplace, and my father never learned to drive. Never wanted to. We never even took a streetcar to Pittsburgh."

"That's our next date," he says. "We'll take a streetcar to Pittsburgh."

She laughs. "The only trip he's ever wanted to make is back to the old country. We would have gone long ago if it hadn't been for my mother."

A reverential look always transforms Mitzie's face when she speaks of her mother. She has told Miravich about her. Sonya was an exceptional woman who developed a love of books and music from her father, an outspoken school teacher who was banished to a remote village during the long Russian domination of Poland. Sonya emigrated to America with her husband Stanley, a carpenter by trade, after World War I. She taught in a Polish Catholic school in McKeesport and cherished the hope of sending her children to college. Mitzie was brought up to be proud and independent and to think for herself. Stanley, known as "Stosh," did not compromise much with the new world. He learned only enough English to get along, never filed for citizenship, and for all these years he has worked and saved with one thought in mind—to return to the old country. Sonya died of cancer in 1940. Her loss gave Stanley a further reason to reject the country where she died. After finishing high school, Mitzie gave up thoughts of further education in order to take care of her father.

"I wish I'd known your mother," Miravich says. "Good people like her, they don't have a chance to bloom in a mill town."

"She put it all into me," Mitzie says matter-of-factly.

He drives slowly, looking for a picnic grove near the river. But railroad tracks monopolize the narrow space between river and highway. "We'll find us a place upstream," he says confidently.

A few miles farther on, rounding a curve, they abruptly drive out of the solid green hills and enter Clairton on State Street. The film projectionist switches from monochrome to vivid technicolor, and they blink at the change. Two- and three-story buildings pack both sides of the street, squeezing together, thrusting garish neon signs out over the sidewalks; dozens of retail stores selling candy, furniture, appliances, groceries; plate-glass storefronts filled with all types of bric-a-brac; dark doorways of saloons; and people everywhere, walking, standing in bunches, sitting on wooden chairs on the sidewalks, leaning out of second-story windows—and all of them are Negroes.

Noting Mitzie's astonishment, Miravich says, "There's a lot more colored here than we got in McKeesport. The Corporation brought them in years ago to work the coke batteries." He points out the Coke Works on the left, a long string of hundred-foot-high, flat-topped structures. "One of the dirtiest jobs there is, working on top of the ovens, with gas and smoke pouring out."

"What are those...tower things?" Mitzie asks.

"Quenching towers. That's where they spray water on the hot coke after it's baked in the ovens. That's steam you see gushing out."

They move slowly in a line of traffic. "I can see sort of a gentle mist settling down over the city," she says.

"Yeah. A gentle mist that dissolves the paint on cars and homes. Look over there." Across the river is a horrid, grassless knob, the remains of a lush green hillside. "God knows what it does to your lungs. Over here in Clairton, some of the mist drifts over the white homes up on the hill. But the coloreds get a lot more of it, living in the bottoms. Only way they ever get to climb that hill is to clean house for the bosses' wives."

A half mile up State Street, they pass the steelmaking end of the Clairton Works, blast furnaces and open hearths and rolling mills. Clairton falls behind, and the two-lane road winds with the river. He keeps looking for a "boats for rent" sign but sees none. The river remains inaccessible. Small factories, storage tanks, transmission towers, and power stations line the shore. Ungainly coal preparation plants stand on stilts straddling railroad tracks. A haulage belt soars above the highway and plunges into the cliffside to gorge on coal. Instinct makes them duck their heads as they drive under it. A long train heaped with coal glides slowly down the valley without apparent beginning or end—it might circle the globe, endlessly revolving, dropping off coal somewhere down-Earth and coming around to feed again at the prep-plant hoppers.

"We do a lot of work in this valley," Miravich says, "and someone's taking out lots of money."

"Making money but not reddin' up," she adds, staring at an enormous black pile of mine gob sitting by the roadside. On windy days, the mound generates an evil gray cloud of clinkers and dust that sweeps down on all living things. Mitzie shakes her head. "My mother used to say, you hurt Nature, she'll always take revenge."

"Yep," Miravich says. "Lots of work and lots of money. But where's the water?"

He drives on through villages with wide-porched frame homes and a glimpse of the river at the end of sloping lawns. On and on he drives, thinking he'll find a path to the river around each curve. Instead, impenetrable thickets or small factories or railroad tracks. And then they arrive at Donora. According to the map, the river bends itself into a horseshoe curve, and Donora sits on the inside (the part that spins around the peg when you throw a ringer). Industry occupies the riverbank: a zinc works as well as a steel mill, both operated by a U.S. Steel subsidiary. The town sprawls across a steep slope above the plant, nearly surrounded by prematurely balding hills on three sides. Driving downhill from the north, the tourists see a thickening in the air below, with fog lingering on the river and a gauzy veil drawn across the downtown.

"I was through here once before," he says, "and it still reminds me of a sump at the bottom of a shaft."

Donora is a busy little place with trains gouting steam, sternwheelers inching through the river fog, old men wheezing on street corners. Open hearth stacks give off smoky streams that seem to dash against a low gray ceiling and spill back earthward. Miravich slows to let a woman cross the street pushing a baby carriage with a frilly pink canopy. She waves a "thank you" and disappears in the mist with the next generation.

A mile or so south of Donora, he pulls off the road where a thick patch of woods obscures the river. "Doesn't anybody think to cut a path down to the water?" Miravich says crankily.

"We could try the other side."

He shades his eyes and squints in that direction. "Looks like more of the same to me. Damn steel companies! Damn railroads! They hog all the good land in the valley. People were here first, but coal operators bought the mineral rights out from under them. Then the railroads bought right-of-way along the shoreline from here to the Mississippi. Then the steel owners gobbled up what's left on the river banks. Maybe that was okay a hundred years ago, but we're the ones got to live with this dirt and crap in the river. See, I figure there ought to be a law that every so often we get to review who owns what, especially if the 'what' is land and water we all need."

She nods thoughtfully. "The companies did bring jobs, though."

"Okay, they brought jobs. I say, since the jobs are on what ought to be public property, the people who work the jobs should have a stake in the jobs."

"Is that socialism?"

"More like common sense."

They sit quietly. The sky bellies lower and darker, threatening rain. "Fact is," he says, "we're not going to get close to the river before it shrinks to a little-bitty crik down in West Virginia." He proposes turning back rather than going on and depleting Eddie's precious gasoline. "I'm sorry, Mitz. Break me out a sandwich, will you."

She unwraps one of the sandwiches she had brought. "Don't worry. It's been an education for me."

Miravich takes a bite and chews with distaste. "Spam!" he growls, and thrusts the uneaten portion into the bag.

"There's a war on, Joe."

"Yeah. A war on my stomach." He laughs. "You got an education, and I got indigestion."

As he wheels the Chevy around and heads back down river, she continues, musing, "When you live in McKeesport, you think nobody lives anyplace else."

"There's a lot like you," says Miravich, world traveler. "It's like the company captured you people, and put you to work in the mill, and said, 'We'll give you jobs. But you stay put, see, and don't talk or meet with nobody else in any of the mill towns because they're your enemies.' The coal operators tried the same thing with us."

"That's a strange way of thinking." She looks at him, black hair blowing across her forehead.

He says, "See, I got this theory. Long time ago the companies came up with a plan to build all these mills on the river close to the coal. They separated them by patches of woods and bad roads so's the men in one mill didn't know what was going on in the next mill round the bend. That way there was no solidarity. Well, we finally got the union into all the mills. Next step is to get the union into all the men."

"And the women."

"Right, women, too. And when the war's over, we'll get rid of this no-strike pledge and take on these fat cats."

She runs her eyes across his hard profile, dark, handsome but for the scars, and most of all, tense. She turns away, thinking. They have been dating once or twice a week for about a month, going to movies, kissing and squeezing on her porch, talking about the union and the people they know. She finds him honest and funny and—always—angry, a man who stands up to the bosses and fights for the workingman. But what else?

"So this is what it's to be," she says, "taking on the fat cats? This is Joe Miravich now and forever?"

The suddenness of it draws a sharp glance, then a slow grin. "I think my pick's struck a vein," he says. He thinks for a few moments, leaning to the left as he negotiates a bend. "I wish I could say it better, but here goes." He takes a deep breath. "It doesn't look like I'm going to discover a new medicine or play the piano in a monkey suit..."

He stops abruptly. "What a load of BS! I'll tell you honest, Mitz, I used to think my mission in life was to hurt people. I mean evil people, like the coal operators who squashed the life out of my pap and others like him. I won't make any bones about it, I still want to cut those bastards down to size. That's the only thing I ever wanted to do, get power for us workers. Why should management run everything? Why should they make all the decisions, produce so much here, lay off those bums there? Do like this, do like that. We should tell them how to make steel."

"You want to run the company?"

"I want to run the union with a say-so in running the company. See, I had a little part in forming this union, and I'd like to see it do some good things for our people."

"What else?" she says, as if she's a teacher, leading him.

"The union has got to be more than just a wage machine. We got to get equal rights for us hunkies and the coloreds, too. And we have to clean up this valley. It's disgraceful living like this, dumping sewage in the rivers, drowning in soot, breathing coal smoke, playing the numbers." He shakes his head. "Maybe that's the worst thing, the numbers racket. They take our money, and the company takes our lives."

What with all his halting starts and stops, they are approaching Clairton by the time he finishes. A thunderhead looms in the west, and rain sprinkles the windshield. They chuckle. Water at last. Mitzie lets up on him, for the time being.

■

Being in love gives Miravich thoughts he's never had before. The rhythm of life, for example. The subject preoccupied his father, who had a reputation in the mine camps as a brooding thinker. If someone made the mistake of asking him, routinely, "How's it going, Mike?" he would raise one hand straight out in front of him, palm down, and move it slowly from left to right, describing a series of valleys and peaks, the ups and downs of life over an unspecified, but obviously lengthy, period of time. Mike had developed his rhythm-of-life theory in the old country, Croatia, but there were some parallels in America. As Mike explained to all who would listen, Croatian barons resembled America's mine foremen, the king or emperor was the mine superintendent, and God was the "boss man," the absentee owner. It was He who organized the whole shebang so that peoples' lives flowed with the seasons—sowing in spring, cultivating in summer, harvesting in fall, and consuming in winter.

Miravich has just read a short history of Croatia. How simple it must have been, he thinks, to know always what came next, not only this year but also the following year, even twenty years from now. A centuries-long rhythm of seasonal waves, broken occasionally, of course, by the outbreak of plagues and baronial feuds and the Turks and French marching through and the Hungarians finally taking over, but essentially remaining the same, decade after decade, season after season.

He seldom got along with his father, but he recognizes that the old man bequeathed him, if nothing else, a point of reference. In the Monongahela Valley, God shares power with the industrialists. The gentle, straight flow of His changing seasons is forced out of its channels by powerful surges of economic cycles—the booms and busts, ups and downs, of steelmaking. People get to thinking that long layoffs are inevitable, why worry when they come? The mills will always start back up, they say. The mills will never close for good. As if Someone Up There had put them on a list of protected things. Miravich disagrees with the general view in the valley. The Depression, it's clear now, never would have ended without the war.

The war forces Miravich to conduct his courtship of Mitzie in herky-jerky, sporadic bursts of fervor, interspersed with numbing hours of overtime work and sleepless sleep. The two of them work the same shift, rotating together through the three turns, changing every week. They are equally uncertain whether day is night or night is day, but they are never far apart. Neither can hide much from the other.

In late November, Mitzie introduces him to a custom of utmost importance in the valley. Football has never excited Miravich. He played some as a kid and has unpleasant memories of end-over-end punts bouncing sharply off his chest. Then he went into the mines and forgot about football. His indifference to the game puts him decidedly out of step with ninety percent of men in the mills. If you can't talk passionately about McKeesport High "killing" Clairton or "murdering" Monessen, you're considered lacking in town spirit and wanting as a union politician.

One Saturday afternoon Mitzie takes him to a McKeesport-Duquesne game. She has to show him which side of the field to sit on, how to stumble across twenty pairs of blanketed legs to get to their seats, and when to jump up and cheer. The ball flies back and forth, young men fling themselves at each other, and he has never spent such a boring three hours. Nor does Mitzie give herself body and soul to the game.

"That reminds me," she says at halftime, "I'm going to keep working if we get married."

"What reminds you?" he says.

"I remembered we go in on night turn. And that started me to thinking. I hope you can pull some strings and keep us working the same turn."

"You mean if we get married?"

"That's what I said."

"Not in my book, you don't."

"Don't what?" She has to shout to make herself heard over the noise made by a high school band highstepping down the field.

"You don't work after we're married. No wife of mine's going to work."

"Joe, it's good money."

"I wasn't going to marry you for your money."

She sits stiffly beside him, refusing even to cheer, in consequence of which the discouraged Tigers fumble behind their own goal line in the final minute. The Dukes recover for a touchdown, score an extra point, and emerge with a 20–14 victory. The two lovers, though still at silent odds, escape the stadium as mounted police gallop into the melee. Walking down Huey Street, Joe and Mitzie ward off objects hurled from cars by hateful Dukes fans. "Boy, this sure is a lot of fun," Miravich says.

Finally, sipping strawberry sodas in Isaly's, Miravich looks into her hazel eyes, and feels as if a spirit is being sucked out of him. "I'm sorry, Mitz, first that we lost to them Duquesne bums..." He pauses. "Do I sound like a Tiger fan? Second, I'm sorry for arguing with you because I love you and am asking you to marry me."

Mitzie's eyes bulge as she draws on a strawful of soda. "Are you sure?"

"As sure as I hate Duquesne. And you can work for a while after we get married."

"I can, can I?" she says, and they both laugh. "Yes, Joe, I will."

But they have avoided a fundamental issue. It's like skipping winter to get to springtime.

■

A few weeks later, in December, Miravich makes another big decision: he will run for president of the Watts Works Steelworkers local next spring. Since last summer's strike and his ordeal in the ditch, "Tuxedo Joe" Miravich has ridden a high wave of popularity. The time is ripe. Pat McNally has decided to call it quits, and there is no heir apparent in the local's Irish hierarchy. It will be difficult to overcome the contempt that many of the old-guard Irish, German and English have for anyone, union "brother" or not, whose name ends in "vich." He needs large numbers of voters to overcome this bias, and his association with Mitzie might provide that political dividend.

Slovaks and Poles, two of McKeesport's largest ethnic groups, tend to vote for their own in municipal and union elections, banding together to fight against discrimination by old-stock Americans. Slovak society accepted Miravich when he became part of the Cramczak family. Now Mitzie has drawn him into the Polish community, and the Poles have welcomed him with open arms. All, that is, except Mitzie's father, Stosh.

Stosh is an odd old duck. Always a loner, he felt betrayed when Sonya died, betrayed by her and by America whose doctors allowed her to die. When Hitler invaded Poland, postponing Stosh's return to his homeland, he turned even more bitterly against the States, arguing that Roosevelt somehow should have stopped Hitler. Deprived of wifely love and affection, he dotes on his daughter. In return, she cooks and keeps house for him as he grows increasingly remote from old friends and family. Mitzie dreads introducing Miravich to him but can put it off no longer.

They sit in her kitchen one day in the middle of December when Stosh comes home from work. He bangs through the door, shaking snow off his clothing. Dropping his lunch bucket and jacket and hat on the floor, he turns and sees Miravich. He has short arms which dangle pincer-like from broad shoulders, and his thick chest bulges under a set of red suspenders.

"Papa," Mitzie says nervously, "this is Joe Miravich, the one I told you about."

"Hello, Mr. Duba..." Miravich had practiced for this day, but still his tongue gets twisted in his teeth. "Druba-shev-ski," he says elaborately.

Stosh scowls at him from pale blue, angry eyes. "Yuxy-mush," he says, sarcastically Americanizing the Polish phrase *yok sie masz*, meaning 'how are you?' He speaks sharply in Polish, then translates. "Funcy punts union man, huh? Union, shit! Hamerica, shit! Rosafelt, shit!" He sits at the table, ignoring Miravich and begins pulling off his boots.

"Papa, that isn't nice," Mitzie scolds.

"Nice, shit!"

"Mr. Drubiszewski, I want to marry your daughter," Miravich blurts out.

Stosh continues to ignore him and barks at Mitzie in Polish. She shakes her head and argues with him but eventually appears to give in. She leads Miravich out of the kitchen. "This isn't a good day for it," she says. "Wait for me here."

Miravich hears her opening and closing a cabinet door. Glasses clink. A chair scrapes on the floor. Stosh, meanwhile, pounds the table and talks in a loud, angry voice. Worried, Miravich goes to the doorway and peeps in. A fifth of whiskey sits on the table between father and daughter, and each holds a shot glass full of amber liquid.

"*Nostrovia!*" Stosh says in his harsh bass, elaborately rolling the "r." He tosses down the shot.

"*Nostrovia!*" she repeats, and does the same.

Stosh pours two more shots and resumes his ranting. Mitzie keeps nodding and agreeing with him. He stops abruptly and holds up the shot glass. "*Nostrovia!*" he says mournfully. She replies in kind. Down goes the whiskey. More vehement monologue by Stosh as he refills the glasses. He waves his arms and flashes his eyes, giving splenetic vent to some deep vein of anger. He rages on for five minutes, reverting to English only to refer frequently to a particular "bustard" in the mill. At his signal, they again raise their glasses, and wish good health. Stosh bolts his whiskey, but Mitzie pantomimes drinking with one hand and empties the shot glass in her tea cup.

The ceremony is finished. The old man stuffs a cork in the bottle, gets up unsteadily, and brushes past Miravich without looking at him.

"What about it, Mr. Drubiszewski? I want to marry your daughter."

Stosh staggers up the stairs. "Union, shit! Hamerica, shit!" floats down the stairwell.

Mitzie briskly puts the bottle away and wipes up puddles of liquor on the table. She keeps her face averted from Miravich.

"Two straight knockers in five minutes!" Miravich says with a whistle. "I thought you didn't like the stuff."

"Do I look like I enjoyed it? I told you to stay in the living room."

"I know, but I thought—" He pauses and goes closer to her. There are tears in her eyes. "What was that all about?"

It has been going on for years, she says. When Stosh has a bad day in the mill, he wants to drink whiskey and talk. The ritual, he believes, flushes the soot and smoke and bad feelings that have accumulated. The role of drinking partner and mother confessor fell to Mitzie when her mother died. She gets through the ordeal by pretending it is as harmless, and evil-tasting, as castor oil.

"He's a bitter old man," Miravich observes. "What good's it do to work all your life and wind up so bitter? There ought to be more to it than that. Who was the SOB he kept talking about?"

"The carpenter foreman. He's an Irishman who's been giving Papa a hard time. You know, 'Come here, hunky! Go there, hunky.' His name is McCaffrey. A real bastard."

"Why doesn't your dad talk to his committeeman?"

"Papa doesn't think that way. That's the way America is, he says, full of hate and prejudice. He's too proud to ask someone to fight his battles for him."

"Oh, yeah? I'll take care of this McCaffrey bird. But you've got to convince your dad to let us get married."

"He won't stop me," Mitzie says. "He loves me too much to hurt me."

"He's got some funny way of showing it."

Miravich learns another thing about her. One day in December she leads him to her bedroom, saying she wants to show him something. He takes the first six stairs two at a time, then slows down. "Hold on, Mitz," he says, thinking about her father. He is due home from the mill any time now.

But she disappears in the room and reappears a minute or so later carrying a shoe box filled with wooden objects, some lacquered to a high gloss, some raw wood.

"Just so you'll know, I do this in my spare time. I'm not very good at it yet." She picks out a finely-shaved pyramid topped by a sphere and raises it critically to the light. "But I intend to be."

"I think it's good. Whatever you do is good. What is it?"

"A woodcarving, of course." She drops the object into the box and tosses the box on her bed. "We'd better get downstairs before Papa comes home."

She is a woodcarver, not a whittler with a knife but a carver, one who uses chisels and gouges. It has never occurred to him that a woman might have a pursuit in life other than cleaning house and bringing up children. Mystery deepens his love for this female Polish woodcarver.

CHAPTER 4:
March 1944–May 1944

The wedding is set for a Saturday in May 1944. But Miravich first must make his peace with the Pope. Though brought up a Catholic, he bowed out of the church at the age of fifteen, his fall from grace coinciding with his descent into the mines. Since Mitzie wants to be married in the church, Miravich agrees to talk to her priest. Father Miroslav Strunka is known far and wide as the "Polish labor priest." A thick man in black garb with stubby facial features, he speaks highly of the dignity of work and the right of the laboring man to join organizations of his own choosing.

Miravich goes to confession for the first time in about twenty years. Kneeling in the darkened cubicle, awaiting his turn, he hears the priest mumble words to the sinner on the other side of the box. At length, the shutter on that side slides shut with a soft shuuuk, and his shutter slides open on one of the more violent lives in western Pennsylvania. "Bless me, Father, for I have sinned," Miravich says, adding, "a lot!" thinking this honesty will earn him a check mark on the credit side of the ledger. This is agony for him, all the things he has done, like purposely hurting people. He pours it all out, or as much of it as he can remember, give or take a split head or two.

"...and after that," Miravich says, five minutes into his recital, pausing to recall what comes next, "...after that—"

"Yes, yes," Strunka says impatiently.

"Now I forget my place. What year was I up to?"

"Nevermind. I take it there was more of the same."

"More of the same, and some different, too."

"Was any of it done maliciously?"

"It wouldn't of made an impression if I did it for fun."

"Are you truly sorry for your sins?"

"To the extent what I did was sinful, I am truly sorry. To the extent they got what they deserved—" Better left unsaid.

"To receive absolution you must renounce your sins against Jesus Christ."

He thinks for a few moments. "Okay, I admit hurting people was wrong. And I promise no more of that unless... well, look, turning the other cheek don't always work so well."

The priest sighs. "We'll take it one step at a time, Joseph. Now say a good Act of Contrition while I work out a penance for you."

That penance calls for Miravich to say many "Our Fathers" and "Hail Marys," along with two or three other prayers he has never heard of. He is still kneeling at the communion rail, reciting prayers and counting them off on his fingers, when people start arriving for evening Mass.

■

Mitzie and Joe say their "I do's" on a radiant spring day at the altar of St. Stanislaus Kostka Polish Catholic Church. Brightly-hued plaster of Paris statues of Sts. Peter, Paul, Cecilia, and Rita look sternly down on Miravich and Mitzie as they kneel on a prie-dieu. A twenty-foot high painting of the benevolent St. Stanislaus, patron of the poor, hangs above the tabernacle. Organ music periodically erupts, filling the church with sound waves that rebound from pillar to marble pillar. One thing about the Poles, their ice boxes may be empty, their kids may run around with shoe soles flapping, but their tithes support magnificent churches. In return, it is said, He provides for His parishioners in mysterious ways.

The miner in Miravich makes him flinch at each thunderous noise made by the congregation moving at the priest's command. They kneel in unison; sit in unison; stand at the reading of the Gospel—and far back in the church someone accidentally kicks over a kneeler. Half the congregation turns to see what happened. Five ushers in coal-black suits converge on the offending pew.

Father Strunka sings the wedding Mass in a ringing, nasal voice. *"Kyrie eleison, christe eleison, kyrie eleison..."* Miravich shudders and wants to hold his ears, but he considers himself honored. That the pastor of the city's largest Polish Catholic parish, a man committed both to God and to labor, who officiates only at the most important weddings, has assigned himself to marry Miravich should convey an important message to all Polish steelworkers: cast your vote for Joe Miravich.

He steals a glance at Mitzie. She wears a Polish-style bonnet of flowers from ear to ear instead of a bride's crown, and her head blazes with color. She is breathtaking in a flowing satin gown, the same one worn by her dear mother thirty years ago in Poland. As she bows her head to make a sign of the cross, the topmost daisy on her head gives him a wary wink. He wears the much-scrubbed, painfully-paid-for tux that he wore to dig the ditch outside the blooming mill. Mitzie urged him to wear it for sentimental reasons. As he walked into the church, men standing outside gave a shout for "Tuxedo Joe."

The Mass is over. As they float down the aisle, now man and wife, organ booming and people singing, Miravich wonders who is picking up and setting down his feet, because he knows he isn't. Mitzie beams left and right and practically drags him down the aisle, as if she can't wait to start cooking sausage and sauerkraut, make babies, and see them off to college. Life is reeling by quicker than Miravich means it to.

As they near the end of the aisle, someone bolts from the last pew and hurries out of the church just as the ushers throw open the big oaken doors. It is Billy Pyle, the blooming-mill laborer, a chubby little man with a receding forehead and a chin that slopes into his neck. Billy is a good-hearted fellow, though not over-endowed mentally. At work he follows Miravich, offering to run errands for him, forever grateful to the committeeman for rescuing him from a bullying foreman. Miravich smiles, knowing now who kicked over the kneeler. Outside, they see Billy across the street, leaning against the hood of a gleaming red car, a third-hand, '42 Ford, the last new model built before the war. A wide grin seems to extend around Billy's neck. Now all the world can see how prosperous he is.

"Billy finally got his car," Mitzie says.

"Yeah." Miravich waves to him. "The mill's a wonderful provider. Let's hope he can drive."

Standing in the receiving line, the Miraviches shake scores of hands of well wishers, including his mother, all the Cramczaks, the Drubiszewskis' relatives and friends, Rooster Wooster and his wife Jenny, and the rest of the blooming mill crew and their wives. Marple, the union's district director, shows up and gives Miravich a paternalistic pat on the back. Even Pat McNally, eyes glassy already at noon, idealist to the end, hoping to keep unity in the local, wishes them luck.

Stosh still hasn't given his formal approval to the marriage. Nor has he thanked Miravich for getting the carpenter foreman off his back. But no one can say he is a cheapskate. He insisted on throwing a big reception for the newly married couple. Miravich would have settled for simply getting hitched. He wants to try out the furniture in the two-room apartment he's rented over Maroni's Butcher Shop at the corner of Tenth and Walnut. A kitchen table, two chairs, and a sturdy pine-paneled bed in the living room-bedroom with a view of Bortolo's Bar & Grill across the street. He has stocked the cupboards with enough canned food to see them through a two-day, indoors honeymoon, and Mitzie is eager to set up house. But she defers to the wishes of her father.

The reception starts at five o'clock, and immediately Polish Hall is inundated with people. As the guests arrive, the cavernous old place seems to quiver with a sound like a dozen spoons stirring an empty saucepan. Johnny and His Polka Dots, a five-piece band, is banging out brassy versions of swing tunes. Wives and sweethearts rush to claim tables encircling the dance floor while the men line up at bars in three corners of the hall. By 5:10 p.m., the bartenders are slopping out free booze, two bottles at a time. Carrying highballs in their hands and bottles of beer sticking out of their armpits, the men crisscross on the dance floor as they hunt for ther wives and girlfriends. The evening explodes with a fierce elation. It's Saturday night in a mill town, in wartime, and this is the spring's major social event for the working-class of McKeesport. Except for the wives and mothers who weep in honor of men far away, the war is far away. It is going as well as can be expected: D-Day approaching in Europe, Americans in the Pacific island-hopping ever closer to Japan, men on the Home Front putting in fifty hours a week. Pity the poor guys who work the afternoon turn and can't be here and, even more, the unfortunates in the crowd who must hold their liquor, morosely awaiting the night turn.

Bride and groom hold court near the head table. Miravich feels a prickly sensation on the back of his neck, turns quickly, and sees Pete Bonner approaching. Bonner tries to hide his growing paunch under a double-breasted suit. When he grins, his mustache opens in the middle like a black valise and spreads across his face. They shake hands. Miravich introduces him to Mitzie, describing Bonner with sudden inspiration as "the guy who introduced me all at once to beer and banking."

"Mrs. Bonner sends her best," Mr. Bonner says. "She...ah, couldn't come..." Even a self-possessed man like Bonner is unable to hide his embarassment. "Wouldn't come" would be nearer the truth. Mae believes that people ought to stick to their own social world. He and Miravich stroll to one of the bars, and Bonner orders a double rye for himself and a shot of vodka for Miravich. Drinks are free, but he slaps down a dollar tip. "Best of luck, Joe," he says. "*Nostrovia!*" says the proud adopted Pole. They drink. Bonner orders another round, but Miravich upends his shot glass: no more for him.

Miravich inquires of Bonner's business. "You can hardly walk through town these days without seeing a different Bonner Beer truck," he says. "You must have a dozen."

"Only six," Bonner says modestly, "but we're just getting started."

"You're going to wind up owning the whole valley. When you do, just remember, the working-man drunk you to power."

Bonner the beer man and Miravich the steelworker stand in the middle of the dance floor, heavy in conversation. From a distance, Father Strunka studies the pair as he sips a glass of red wine. He asks District Director Marple if the big man with a mustache is a union man. "He doesn't look union to me," Marple says with finality.

"One thing, Joe," Bonner says, turning serious. "You're campaign's getting a lot of publicity. Newspaper stories, handbills on telephone poles. Maybe somebody from the old days is still trying to add two and two? Maybe Mr. You Know Who is still out there."

Miravich is staring across the dance floor, watching Mitzie in profile as she talks to her bridesmaids. He feels the inside of his stomach being sucked out. Turning back to Bonner, he says, "I'm not the Joe Miravich I was in thirty-seven. All the stuff that happened back then, that day on the road and everything that come later, it all seems like something I dreamt after eating bad pork."

Mitzie comes and whisks her husband away. The crowd divides, subdivides. An announcement from the bandstand starts a mass movement to the tables. Father Strunka says grace, urging God to protect "this newly-married couple and all our heroic boys overseas." White-shirted waiters serve dinner. Chicken noodle soup, cucumbers and sour cream, roast chicken, kielbasa, sauerkraut, fat and chewy homemade noodles, boiled potatoes, rye and pumperknickel bread. When the waiters bring platters of cookies, cakes, and peach-filled tarts, people groan and jiggle their distended stomachs.

Johnny and His Polka Dots return to the bandstand after plundering a small buffet table and strike loudly into "The Beer Barrel Polka." They follow with a half-dozen other polkas. Couples whirl around the dance floor, knees pumping high, the men whooping "hoo, hoo, hoo," spectators clapping to the beat of the music. They stop between tunes, wipe their foreheads with handkerchiefs, start up again. Faster and faster they go. Men fling off their suit coats and women toss high-heeled shoes into the crowd. Body heat raises the room temperature, and tiny showers of sweat spray into the already humid air.

The Polka Dots take a break, and dancers limp to their seats, fanning themselves, breathing heavily. Bridesmaids escort Mitzie to the center of the cleared floor, where a single chair has been placed. They take off her veil and tie around her waist an apron bedecked with ribbons and lace. The theme color is baby-boy blue, signifying the Polish priority in offspring. Mitzie sits gravely, symbolically now a housewife owing domestic duties to God, husband and community. Everybody applauds and joins in singing "I Wish I Were Single Again." Women dab their eyes, and men shake their heads. One chorus of this song is enough for everybody, and the band eases into a slow, lingering "Sentimental Me," with Johnny himself crooning.

> *...so in love with you*
> *don't know what to do,*
> *senti-mental me.*

Miravich and Mitzie do a slow turn around the floor, eyes riveted on each other. They finish to rousing applause and visit Stosh, who is sitting alone, staring drunkenly at nothing. "Bye, Papa," Mitzie says. "Keep the house clean. I'll come see you next week."

He gives her a fierce look. She kisses his cheek. "Mitzie, Mitzie!" he cries despairingly, *"Dovidzenia moja Kochana."* Goodbye, my love.

Borne on wings of desire and hope, soaring with angels and the patron of the poor, Joseph and Mitzie Miravich escape into the brightly-lit streets. Air raid blackouts were halted some time ago.

CHAPTER 5: May 1944

A week passes. It is Sunday afternoon at the Watts. Miravich works on the shear-knife platform. Incessant booming, hissing, pounding. Hot steel crackles and spits fiery flakes on the mill roll-out table as he chops the bottom end off a bloom. The sizzling slice collapses and crumbles down the scale chute. He relaxes, waiting for the next bloom. The westering sun breaks through dirt-caked windows high on the river side of the building, throwing patches of pale light on the shop floor. From his balcony he watches grotesque shadows sail across this stage to be swallowed in the dark void beyond. Workers emerge from the mill's dark recesses, bathe unknowingly in the pallid glare, and disappear. Billy Pyle, carrying a push broom under one arm, plods through with the gait of a plow horse. Phil Shumly enters from the left, halts, gazes around for malingerers and, finding none, exits right. Two old millwrights, each carrying a long-spouted oil can, meet solemnly in the center. Without speaking, they exchange cans and saunter off in opposite directions. And finally Mitzie appears, wearing a hard hat and lugging a shovel on her shoulder. "Oh, shit!" Miravich says to himself. This means she's been assigned the miserable job of cleaning out the scale he's been flushing down the chute. Mitzie stops and slowly pirouettes, sunning herself before descending into the scale pit under the blooming mill. She waves gaily in his direction, knowing he'll be watching from his perch.

Fifteen minutes later, Miravich takes his break, relieved at the shear-knife by a new spellhand because Mickey Totten has gone to war. He eats the last half of his cheese and banana sandwich and looks around for Mitzie. Probably still in the scale pit. He fights off the temptation to give her a hand, knowing it would only annoy her. She has a funny attitude about things like that. Many men assigned to the pit come out begging for help. But the one time he went to help her, she said angrily, "They're paying me to do it, not you." Thinking about her, Miravich hops over a low pile of timbers and heads toward the control pulpit to chat with Wooster. A week married, and he's still learning about women. He figures he'll know it all by the end of the second week, but in the meantime revelations are piling up. One is, she's as good at making love as he is.

Climbing the stairs to the control pulpit, he hears laughter inside. It's a loose and easy day. Nothing has gone wrong, no breakdowns, no fulminating foremen, no arguments. The pulpit serves as the social center of the blooming mill. Everybody stops there, men on breaks, workers from other departments who are passing through. When Miravich arrives, it's already well stocked with visitors, including a millwright, a pipefitter, and Tucker the turn foreman. Everybody stands or leans against the reinforced plate-glass windows. Rooster stands at the front window, like a captain on the bridge, looking down at the roll stand about twenty yards away. He controls the conveyor and roll stand with levers mounted on a console in front of him and foot pedals under the console. As ingots pass beneath the pulpit, he halts them briefly for an inspection, then sends them churning into the rolls. To his right, Gabby Gabinski works the manipulator controls that flip the ingot from side to side after each pass through the rolls. Blam-blam-blam! He and Wooster coordinate their movements with near-perfect timing, manhandling the ingot as if they were two chiropractors working a patient on a stretch-table. The constant banging sends tremors through the mill, making the pulpit rattle and shake. But the noise is muted when the door is closed. You can hear yourself talk and think.

Rooster half turns when Miravich enters. "What's new, Prez," he says, jamming a lever forward.

"Not yet. Everyone here plan to vote Tuesday?" Miravich looks from face to face.

"I would if I could," Tucker says. "I like this guy Dowd from the billet mill. He agrees with us foremen. The men should be required to salute us. "

The men guffaw and give him the finger. "You know where you'll get your salute," Rooster says.

Tucker, a short man with powerful, hunched shoulders, feigns shock. Like most turn foremen, he was promoted from the work force. Unlike many, he didn't acquire boss's spots with the change and is generally well-liked.

"The true fact is," Miravich says, "there's good bosses and bad bosses."

"I guess so," Tucker says agreeably.

"The difference is," Miravich continues, "the bad bosses are shitheads, and the good bosses let the shitheads like Phil Shumly and Marty Dinsmore run over them."

Something flickers over Tucker's face. The conversation has crossed the line between banter and real hostility. He takes a step and faces Miravich. "I didn't know you were going to turn this into a union meeting, Joe. You hate who you want to hate, but leave me out of it." He goes out the door.

"Fucking foreman," says Jack Hamrick, the pipefitter. "Nobody invited him in here anyway. He's like all the rest of 'em."

"You're wrong, sonny, he ain't like the rest of them," Rooster throws over his shoulder. "He's as fair and honest as they come."

Humiliation is eating away Hamrick's face. No one wants a tongue lashing by Rooster. "You old rogue," Miravich says. "You hurt this poor boy's feelings."

"Feelings without facts don't rate high in my book." Rooster blasts a bloom through the rolls on its fourth pass, using a little body English to get it just right. He glances sideways at Miravich. "Like you said, Joe, you ain't the Prez yet."

"Okay, Rooster, maybe I went too far. I'm still young and learning."

The millwright, one of the men involved in the oil-can transfer witnessed by Miravich, is leaning against a side window with his arms folded, an empty oil can dangling from one fist. "I got something to ask you, Miravich," he says. His name is Andy Lovedale. White-haired and fat, seventy years old if a day, he was working at the Watts the day church bells chimed the turn of the century.

"I read in the paper," he continues, "where you said the union's going to bring democracy to the mill. Does that mean we vote on everything... whether to put in a new mill, or what price to charge for steel?"

"C'mon, Andy, I never said 'vote.' What I mean is, when they want to know how to run a mill the right way, they ask us. When Rooster here says the steel is green, management listens to him and stops sending green steel from the soaking pits. This means we don't come to work just to be jerked around on a string. It means we get something more out of work than dirty hands and a pay envelope. That answer your question?"

"Not altogether." The old man ruminates. "I can show them how to install a new rolling mill because I've put in a lot in my time. But if I tell them how to do it, then it's only a small step to telling them when to do it, which crosses me over into telling them whether to do it, and pretty soon I'm the boss and the worker, too. See what I mean?

"You just climbed the management ladder faster'n Carnegie himself." Miravich tries to laugh it off. "Well, okay, yeah, I think maybe we should tell them whether. Some day, yeah. I haven't worked out how yet. One way I heard about is like they do in some automobile plants in Detroit. The union steward has equal power with the foreman over most matters. Now, that's just one idea. First, we have to get pensions and longer vacations and better wages and more safety."

"I heard some management guys say you're a commie."

"Andy, I thought you stopped listening to stupid people when they said Orville and Wilbur would never get off the ground."

Lovedale lifts his oil can to make another point, but Hamrick interrupts. "Hey, Miravich, get an eyeful of your old lady." He points to the floor below.

Everybody looks out the window on the right side. Mitzie is leaning on a shovel and blowing hard from the climb up out of the scale pit. She's coated in red grime from forehead to metatarsals. Her eyes are dark sockets in a sea of ocher. One shirt sleeve is missing from the shoulder down.

They hear laughter rising from the mill floor. Miravich starts to go to her aid but thinks better of it. She picks up the shovel and slowly walks towards the locker rooms. She doesn't seem injured, just tired.

"The mill ain't no goddamn place for a woman," Hamrick says.

"First time I heard you make sense," Rooster adds.

The door opens. It's Larry Meach the rigger and numbers writer, making his daily rounds. "You should of seen what I just seen heading for the showers," he says.

"We seen it," Hamrick says.

"Izzat bitch yours?" Meach says to Miravich. "Still putting your old lady out to work?" He pulls a little white pad out of a shirt pocket and licks a finger to turn a page.

The punch knocks two fingers half way down his throat. Meach bends over, gagging. A churning of bodies makes the pulpit shudder. Spitting blood and cursing, Meach starts a roundhouse right from a crouching position.

Miravich parries the blow and knocks Meach to the floor. "You ever say another word about my wife, I shove that pad up your ass!"

Gabinski and Hamrick pull Miravich away. Rooster bounds back from the console and pulls Meach to his feet. "Get out of here and take that foul mouth with you."

"He don't scare me," Meach says, straining toward Miravich. But Rooster pushes him out the door.

Miravich shouts, "I told you before, Leech, I don't like you or what you do."

"It ain't the union's business what I do, fucker. You better watch yourself."

Rooster and Gabinski hurry back to the controls and maneuver quickly to make up for lost time. Blam-blam-blam!

"Well, hell, Joe!" Hamrick says. "Nothing wrong with playing a dime on a number now and then. Everybody does it."

"Not me," Miravich growls. "I learned too much about the value of a dime when I was a kid. I wouldn't give a penny to them bloodsuckers even if they guaranteed me a million-dollar hit."

"Who made you a priest?"

"Listen, those numbers guys got you by the balls," Miravich says. "What do you think they do with that money? It doesn't go to an orphan's home or to widows of workers killed on the job. It doesn't go to the USO. It goes to loan-sharking and prostitution. It goes to politicians who live off our backs. The whole business stinks. Go ahead, run after him," he says to Hamrick. "That quarter's burning a hole in your pocket. Did you vote against that fund for war widows?"

Rooster laughs as he jerks a lever. "I'm with you, Prez. But you better decide whether you're going to be a preacher or a street fighter."

Break over, Miravich goes back to work. At seven o'clock he is spelled again. Mitzie is nowhere in sight. As he steps down from the shear stand, Billy Pyle is hurrying toward him. "I got a message, Joe. Some guy wants to see you in the motor shed. Union business, he says."

The orange mist closes in around them, hissing and blasting as if alive. "Who is it?" Miravich shouts.

"I don't know him, Joe. Never seen him before."

"Why doesn't he come here?"

"Said he got to talk in a quiet place." A siren sounds as an overhead crane moves down the bay with a load. Billy plods along beside him, talking a blue streak. As they approach the end of the mill building, he asks, "You want me to come with you, Joe?"

"No, Billy. Thanks."

The motor shed is an old brick building, located between the blooming mill and open hearths. Decades ago, it housed a rolling mill, but now it's used as a storage area for motors, mill rolls and other gear stacked in large wooden crates. No one works full-time here. When a foreman needs a piece of equipment, he sends in a couple of riggers and a crane operator to pick off a crate with the overhead crane and load it on a forklift.

The high windows, black with grime, admit little light, and the place is dark and drab. Miravich walks across one end of the building, looking down each of three aisles formed by crates piled five or six high. He can see only half the length of the gloomy bays. No one in sight, no movement. Cupping his mouth, he hollers, "Anybody here?" No answer. "Who wants Miravich?" he calls out. Did he hear a scraping noise? He hesitates a moment, then starts down the center aisle.

Stupid management has laid in five times more equipment than the plant can possibly use, and the crates rise ten feet above his head on both sides. He shouts again. No answer. He continues down the boxed-in aisle, heavy with the smell of packing grease. A sudden yawping and flutter of pigeons' wings in the eaves where they nest. Do they know something? Feeling a tremor pass through the crates on his right side, he stops and gropes for a pick-hammer on his belt to tap the roof and see if she's solid—and comes up empty-handed, of course, because he is not back in the mines. He might as well be, he thinks, enclosed as he is by unevenly stacked crates filled with ton upon ton of engines, mounts, shafts, generators, and pumps. Man Crushed by Obsolete Machinery, he thinks, reading his own obituary. Realizing he's made a bad mistake, he breaks into a run.

He hears footsteps behind him, and someone shouting, "Joe, Joe!"

He wheels and sees Billy rushing toward him in a half-run, half-waddle. "Up there, it's him!"

Miravich looks up, sees a shadowy leg in a crevice between boxes, hears the crunch and creak of wood leveraged against wood. And then crates are crashing down. He dives the other way. A great numbing blow on his left leg. He is on his back. For a few seconds, wonderful clarity. He pushes himself up on an elbow, looks around the box pinning his leg and sees a jumble of other crates in the aisle. An arm is sticking out. "Billy!" he cries. "Billy boy!" He hears someone clambering across the top of the stack. An object strikes the concrete floor with a clanging sound and bounces in front of him. A heavy-duty crowbar. Now he feels a crushing wheel with spikes running straight up his leg, digging into ankle, calf, knee, thigh, moving toward his groin—

When he awakes, Mitzie and several men are kneeling beside him. She brushes his long hair off his forehead. People are shouting. He hears the overhead crane start up and glide toward him. "Billy?" he says. "How's Billy?"

Now tears well up in her eyes. Men are hollering. Shoes shuffle around him. A puddle of oil draws him in.

■

Mae Bonner has never had so many people in her home at one time. It is Sunday afternoon, May 21, 1944, and the Bonners are giving a family party to celebrate their fifteenth wedding anniversary. Voices, laughter, men trooping in and out of the kitchen to get a beer or highball, children scampering all over the place. Irritable and fidgety, she floats between living room and kitchen, trying to do everything at once: encourage mingling, empty ashtrays, prepare snacks, watch for drinks teetering on the edge of tables, and listen for the sound of children getting into trouble.

"Never again!" she whispers to her sister Irene, who has entered the kitchen with her. "Never again so many kids."

Thirteen children, aged nine to fifteen, cavort in and around the Bonner home. They have come with their parents, seven pair in number, the sisters and brothers of Mae and Pete Bonner, along with their spouses, and one unescorted wife with husband at war. Also attending are Grandma Dempsey and Grandma Bonner, Mae's and Pete's mothers who have long been widowed. Men tend to die young in McKeesport.

Bonner had wanted a large family get-together. Mae, with her fine sense of social proportion, had argued against having both families at the same time. Mixing the plump, earthy German-English burghers of Bonner's family with the thin, moody Scots-Irish tipplers on her side would be like making a pudding of sausage and Guinness. "You worry too much about these things," he said. As usual, he prevailed. But come the morning of the party, this day of all days, he went to the office to work on his precious books and was not yet home when his guests arrived.

Mae is furious with him. She throws up her hands, seeking solace from Irene. "How did I ever let Pete talk me into this?"

"Don't kid yourself," Irene says flatly. "You let him talk you into it because he's the husband and you're the wife." Angular and bony, Irene has assumed her battle stance. Arms ringed with bracelets cross her bony chest like bejewelled bandoleers: one hand grips the opposite shoulder and the other holds a tumbler of whiskey and ginger-ale to her thin lips. "Men always get what they want," she adds. "They may not like it when they get it, but they always get it."

"You're getting tipsy, Irene."

"No, I just hate men."

"It can't be that bad."

"Try my life sometime."

A chorus of cheers swells in the backyard, and a minute or so later Irene's son Bobby bursts through the kitchen screen door. "Mom, I just hit a home run."

"Through whose window?" she says, but she runs adoring fingers through his mud-colored hair.

Mae goes into the living room. Members of the two families have all met at one time or another but only on occasions like weddings and funerals. The party started a half-hour ago, but still they are arrayed on opposite sides of the room. She imagines the area between them as a conversational junk yard filled with discarded beginnings and limp endings. "Awfully warm weather for May...business picking up...Pirates off to losing season..." Women of both families are sitting bolt upright, careful not to rumple Mae's decorative pillows and doilies. Bonner's four sisters, all husky women with a stubborn Saxon streak, like Pete, are polite as always, but Mae detects coolness in the way they act toward her. She suspects they think that she holds herself aloof. The men of both clans, meanwhile, look uncomfortable and awkward in their Sunday suits and ties. Most are standing, and the beer-drinkers are encumbered with coasters, napkins, and thin-stemmed pilsner glasses provided by Mae (she hates to see men guzzling straight out of the bottle) and have no hands left to gesture with.

Not a thing out of place, for which she is thankful. But God, what a painful scene! Guilty feelings overwhelm her. As Pete always says, she sets the bar too high. "Come on, everyone," she says, "enjoy yourselves...please." Grim smiles. She passes among them, offering pretzels and cocktail peanuts. "Pete'll be home soon."

Talk fades away. Another lull in the conversation, barely distinguishable from the conversation itself. Women smooth out their dresses and men hold their glasses to the light and study bubbles in their beer. And then!—the sound of a car pulling up outside. All heads turn to the rear of the house where the ball-playing bedlam has momentarily ceased. A man's voice, faintly: "Hiya, fellas. Toss it here." Crash! A broken basement window. "I said here, not there." Laughter. The screen door creaks open and bangs shut. Footfalls coming through the kitchen, and Pete blows in, big as life. First thing, he tells the men to take off their suit coats and loosen their ties, which they all do except Irene's husband, Fred the haberdasher, who is never seen outside his home without a coat and tie. Bonner goes round the room kissing all the womenfolk in turn. His very presence animates people, and the center of the party shifts with him. Mae watches from the sidelines. The man who saved the day, so ruddy and handsome in an open-necked white shirt. She envies his easy familiarity. But he possesses more than that. His sisters love him and look up to him as the big brother. Everyone in the Dempsey family also loves Pete, and he, therefore, has two families to her one.

Talk now begins to flow between the families; it needed only someone to start the bung. There is broad common ground in war's prosperity. Many of the men are proprietors of small shops, including a grocery, a butcher shop, a clothing store. One sells life insurance; another manages a hardware store; one is a mill foreman. All but the last were on the verge of failure during the thirties. Now they can't get enough help to run their businesses.

"You can't hire delivery boys old enough to drive," exclaims a Bonner sister whose husband owns a grocery. "The draft's snapping them up soon's they get out of high school."

"Seems like half the city was on relief five years ago," says the hardware man. "Now we got men putting in sixty-hour weeks at the Watts. They're paying down on Frigidaires that won't even be made till after the war."

The conversation turns to everybody's favorite topic, the daily struggle with ration cards and shortages of meat, butter, cigarettes, gasoline, tires, razors, silk stockings. Even sliced bread is unavailable because bakeries can't buy slicing machines.

"That's what I miss most," says Charlie Muhlenkampf, the mill foreman, who is married to one of Bonner's sisters. "My Liz is all thumbs with a knife, which means I get knuckle sandwiches for lunch."

"How would you like my entire fist in your mouth?" Liz retorts.

"I miss zippers most," says Andy the butcher, leaning against the mantel. A laconic, dreamy man, it doesn't occur to him that he has invited attention to his crotch until several sets of eyes focus there. "I didn't mean—" he says and turns sideways to inspect whether he has buttoned up. This, in fact, is a grave problem for men. Since all zipper production is dedicated to military uniforms, civilians can't buy clothing with zippers. Men have had to learn all over again how to button up the fly.

One of Bonner's sisters remarks that rationing apparently causes no hardships for the Bonners. "How do you do it, Mae?"

"It's not me," she says briskly, turning to her husband. "How do you do it, Pete?"

He shrugs, trying to cover up his irritation at her tone.

"Let's be truthful," says Sadie, his oldest sister. "He gets extra butter for me."

"If it wasn't for Pete, I'd run out of smokes," says a brother-in-law.

"I'd run out of whiskey," says Irene.

It turns out that Bonner has helped them all, on both sides of the family, in one way or another. "Doesn't surprise me," says Sadie. "He knows everybody in town. He always was that way, always found a way to get what he wanted."

"Saint Peter," Mae sums up dryly.

The tone changes. No one wants to feel too good about the good times when servicemen are making the ultimate sacrifice on New Guinea and in Italy. An Allied invasion of Europe is rumored to be near. Tears spring to the eyes of the Bonner girls when they talk about their baby brother, Tug, who left his wife, Mary, and infant daughter when he went to war. Mary tells of receiving a letter from the Pacific Theater. Tug's cruiser was in a name-censored battle. The only thing he wrote about it was—and she breathlessly repeats his words—"Honey, I saw things I never want to talk about."

The three o'clock mill whistle brings the conversation around to the Watts. Someone asks Charlie, the foreman, if he has had any trouble with the union. Charlie is a sandy-haired, big-chested man with the straightfaced expression of a perennial jokester and story-teller. He keeps a storehouse of anecdotes about life in the mill.

"What's all this talk about a radical named Miravich who's running for president?"

"Yeah, Joe Miravich, a Croatian guy." Charlie turns to Bonner. "Isn't he the fellow used to drive for you?"

Bonner nods. "A good man. What's he like in the mill?"

"Only met him once, some months ago," Charlie says. "They called me in on emergency to run a turn in the blooming mill. This fellow Miravich comes up to me soon as I step out of the wash room. 'I'm the grievanceman here,' he says, 'You going to give me trouble today?' I say, 'I don't have too much trouble to spare, but if you want some maybe I can oblige.' He says, 'I just wanted to warn you, I'm a tomcat when trouble comes.' Well, I hold out my hand and say, 'Meet your big brother, the lion.'"

"So what happened then?" someone asks.

"We shook hands and went to work. And we set a tonnage record on that turn."

Pete and Charlie seem to have bridged the gap between the families, at least for now. Feeling better, Mae goes out on the back porch to check on the children. The older boys have left off baseball and are shooting marbles in the alley. Three younger children, the Muhlenkampfs' two and Mary Bonner's one, are swinging around the cast iron clothes pole that Pete implanted in a corner of the yard.

As the falling sun sets the pole top ablaze, she returns to the living room. The conversation has turned to presidential politics. Irene's husband, Fred the haberdasher, utters his first words of the day. "Roosevelt's a sick man and won't last through the war." He has been drinking steadily from a tumbler of straight whiskey; brackish fluids building up on the inside now come bursting through in a flood of words. "And when FDR goes, all his rich Jew friends and Eleanor's nigger lackeys'll take over."

A momentary halt in the tirade is greeted by shocked silence. Irene is glaring at her husband and forming the words "Shut up!" with her lips. Hunched over in Bonner's armchair, Fred appears to have shrunk inside his double-breasted suit coat. "It's already started here," he continues, looking down at his shoes. "The kikes already own half the shops on Fifth Avenue, marking everything down to drive the rest of us out."

Mae throws a pleading look at Pete who is chatting with Betsy. Do something, for God's sake! Fred lurches recklessly on, naming his commercial nemeses, "...your Kleins...your Rosenbergs...your Kaplans..." Bonner goes to his side and urges him to come into the kitchen and have another drink. Fred pulls away and continues ranting.

Bonner dislikes being rebuffed. "Who needs a drink?" he says, going to the kitchen. Charlie, Betsy and Irene follow him. But the exodus is too little, too late.

Mae feels isolated. She hears ice clinking in a glass and realizes that her hand is shaking with anger. She does not care if some think Jews should be held accountable for the Crucifixion, nor if some think coloreds should not mix with whites. What matters is, this house, her home, has been defiled by outrageous words of hate.

"Hey, everybody!" Mae says loudly, stepping to the middle of the room and interrupting Fred. Her comic impulse taking over, she does a two-step shuffle and a bow in Fred's direction. "Ta-da! Let's hear it for Fred the haberdasher."

He takes a deep gulp of his highball as if to reward himself.

■

By eight o'clock most of the guests have gone home, tomorrow being a work day.

When the phone rings, Mae answers, guessing it is Irene. Before she can speak, she hears a man's voice, sounding weak and far away.

"It's Joe," says the caller, closer up but still phlegmy. "I think I got one."

"Joe who? Got one what?"

"A message from Mr. Buck. Isn't Pete? Oh, shhh..." The beginning of a foul word cut short she suspects. The voice returns. "Miz Bonner..." Labored breathing. "It's Joe Miravich. Let me speak to him." A loud rustling noise on the other end. More labored breathing, and then "...please."

She calls Pete. "It's Joe Miravich, and something's wrong."

Bonner talks on the phone only a minute or two. He hangs up and walks past her and out to the back porch. She finds him leaning on the banister, gazing westward. A spectacular burst of orange billows over the mill.

He glances at her. "Joe's at St. Ann's. A mill accident, bad leg injury."

"Who is Mr. Buck?"

He jerks his head, dismissing the question.

But she senses, as keenly as she feels a sudden breeze on her bare arms, that a profound chill passed through him. She shivers, and he automatically puts an arm around her—for the wrong reason. No matter. It is comforting and warm, and she snuggles closer. A sulfurous scent rises from the mill. The glow in the valley spreads and fades into night. Soon there comes spewing up the smoky soul of another furnace (what kind of furnace she could not say), racing across the face of the older glow, a revolving, whirling, mixture of cloud and smoke receding into yesterday and the day before, and further backward yet, like a deep sorrow rolling backward, no longer easily understood or consoled, but unfathomable in depth.

CHAPTER 6:
May 1944–June 1944

After waiting for two days, Bonner receives Mitzie's approval to visit her husband at St. Ann's Hospital. She is standing in the doorway of Room 622 when he arrives. Miravich lies sleeping behind her. Her black hair is pulled severely back over her ears and clasped behind her head, setting off high cheekbones and pursed mouth. A formidable young woman, Bonner thinks. The surgeons, she explains, managed to save Joe's right leg but amputated three toes when gangrene threatened. Mitzie sags a bit, suddenly appearing very tired. Bonner persuades her to go to the cafeteria for a bite of lunch while he watches over the patient. She studies him a moment, but hunger wins out.

For five minutes Bonner sits at bedside, studying a softly snoring Miravich. He appears to have frozen in place, lying on his back with his right leg canted stiffly upward at a ten degree angle and suspended in a sling. His milky face is contorted in a final, pre-sleep grimace. Bonner grows impatient. He wants to question Miravich before Mitzie returns. Trying to will him into wakefulness, Bonner stares at him, and staring, comes to see that this is not the Miravich that he picked up on Route 40 in '37. That Miravich was a half-wild, unpredictable cur, ferocious or playful, always shrewd, sometimes open and friendly, other times hostile and defensive. At the center of those mood swings there seemed to be a half-formed creature engaged in continuous change, as if a new one were growing out of the old. And so came to be this new, older Miravich, whoever he is.

A little old nun interrupts Bonner's deliberations. Attired in a white nurse's habit, she sweeps into the room with a clacking of beads at her waist and goes straight to the foot of Miravich's bed. As if drawing a stuck drape, she roughly tugs a rope on the trapeze-sling mechanism.

"Yohhh!" cries Miravich, snapping to a sitting position, suddenly and fully awake.

"Your leg was too low," says the nun. Her look implies that his pain is just punishment for his complicity in lowering the sling. Then she sizes up Bonner, who has jumped to his feet. "Well," she says, "is this the Mr. Buck you've been talking so much about in your sleep?"

Both men seem struck dumb.

"Apparently not," she says, and departs.

Bonner shuts the door. "Why didn't you just page Mr. Buck over the loud-speaker?" He laughs uneasily. "How do you feel?"

"I should of stayed in the mines. Dirt doesn't weigh as much as crates filled with motors." He blinks with pain. "They keep lopping things off my right side. First the finger, then the toes. No wonder I'm tilting to the left." He looks quickly at Bonner. "You get a message from Mr. Buck, too?"

"No, no. What makes you think it was him? Mitzie said you didn't see who did it."

"No, but who else could it be?"

"That was years ago, Joe. The investigation never got anywhere. Why would Mr. Buck suddenly show up again?"

"Do rattlesnakes stop rattling?"

"We don't even know if there was a Mr. Buck. Like you said, maybe it was all a…" He shakes his head.

"A bad dream? Was that bomb in the truck a dream? That bird in the Youngstown jail with a shiv in his back—was he a dream?"

Bonner suggests other possibilities: an angry foreman or a worker with a grievance against the union. Miravich presses his lips together and says nothing. "You have the election coming up," Bonner says. "You've said a lot of things, got people angry at you. Could it be a political feud in the union?"

Miravich grimaces. "Jesus, Bonner, you too? That's what the cops think. Everybody figures we settle elections by murdering one another. Sure, I got political opponents, but no enemies like that. If it was a union man that called me to the motor shed, Billy would have known him. Christ, Billy!"

Miravich closes his eyes. From a nearby room they hear Rosy Rosewell, the Pirates' radio announcer, despondent over another losing game. Miravich makes an effort to push himself up in bed and Bonner pulls his chair closer. They sit conspiratorially close, gathering in what little warmth is left after the sun burns through the clouds, the smoke emanating from the Watts, and the dirty windows of St. Ann's.

"What is it? You've thought of something?"

"Yeah. I'm thinking of a rat, name of Meach. A parasite, runs numbers in the mill for Sal Grotto. Maybe he's a company spy, too."

Bonner considers the idea. "I doubt it, Joe. You're no threat to Grotto. You may be a helluva union leader, but you're not going to stop the numbers racket in the mill."

Miravich is still surmising. "They could of brought someone in to do the job. Outside contractors. There were three or four construction crews work-ing overtime on a new boiler house."

Bonner shrugs. "Maybe. But who sicced them on you?"

Neither man talks for a while. Miravich looks out the window. "Is that the sunset or a Bessemer blow, that flaming red?"

Bonner looks over his shoulder. "What red? I see orange."

"Looks red to me. We can't agree on anything. I still think Mr. Buck was behind it. Or Whitey. Remember Whitey, the one we never saw, the one that got away? He's still out there someplace."

Bonner pulls out his Chesterfields. "Do you mind?" He lights one, and blows smoke at the floor. "Did Billy say anything about this fellow that might give us a clue?"

"Billy tells me, this guy wants to see you in the motor shed about union business. I ask who is it, and Billy says he's never seen him before. I should have known right then—" Miravich rises on his right elbow, excited, pushing himself through the pain. "Billy says the guy has a blue face. Yeah, a blue face! I says, 'What do you mean, blue face?' He says, 'Joe, I ain't kidding, this guy has a blue face.' I says, 'Was he colored?' He says, 'No, he has a blue face but his hands're white all over.'" Miravich flops back on the bed, breathing hard.

"A blue face?"

"Yeah, blue. You know blue, don't you?"

The conversation ends inconclusively. Bonner goes to work and tries to put Mr. Buck out of his mind. He has a business to run. But it will not leave him alone. During odd moments he finds himself reviewing excerpts from that day in 1937 on Route 40. The fight with the mine detectives...the drive to Charleston...the morning in the drunk tank...the conversation in the prison yard...the name "Whitey" which did not seem to suit any of the men who returned to the cell from the prison yard...was it a dream? By nightfall he is scrutinizing each face in memory, as if he were flipping cards and memorizing their place in the deck. He awakens at five in the morning, shivering in a clammy pajama shirt. He sees dozens of writhing bodies, all tangled as if in a snake pit. Their faces come forward and recede, featureless faces, blank faces. He sits on the edge of the bed and pulls off the shirt, wondering if he has the flu. Suddenly, one face comes up enlarged, with a nose, eyes, ears and... strange-colored skin. The skin is gray, battleship gray, gray as a cadaver's skin. One of the trusties; Bonner remembers him because his peculiar gray skin reminded him of a boyhood friend who was gassed in France during the first war and later died in a seizure. Billy said the man who wanted to meet Miravich had a blue face. Blue! He visualizes a blue face, or is it gray? Of course! Many people see gray where others see blue. What Billy saw as blue, in the dim light of that mill building, really was…gray, and the trusty with a gray face really was…Whitey!

He goes into the bathroom and smokes a cigarette. He ponders what to do with his lead, slim as it is. He is in the dark and does not know which way to turn. He can think of only one thing to do, which is to strike a match. At the office a few hours later, he calls Sal Grotto and asks for a meeting.

They meet in the back room of Louie Grotto's confectionery. Surprisingly, Pixie is with Sal. Why, Bonner wonders, would Sal bring a bodyguard into his brother's store? Are there hidden tensions in Grottodom? At Sal's signal, Pixie draws a curtain across the doorway, shutting out Louie at the cash register. Pixie turns on a small radio and dials up Grotto's favorite music, Dixieland jazz.

"What's on your mind, Pete?" Grotto says abruptly. "A consolidating loan maybe to reduce all that debt?"

"It has to do with Mr. Buck. Remember Mr. Buck? Before the war, when I was starting my business. He tried to…get Joe Miravich and me?"

"So?"

"You made a phone call, got us off the hook. Do you still have connections with that outfit?"

Grotto sits sideways at a roll top desk, gently massaging cruel lines in his forehead. He seems distracted, irritated. "What is this, a quiz program?" he says, throwing up his hands. "I ask a question, you answer with a question. Nobody's got answers these days, just questions. You go home at night, the wife asks questions. You get up in the morning, the kids ask questions. You go to work, the employees…" He raises his voice on "employees," and Bonner guesses this is meant for Louie on the other side of the curtain. "…the employees ask stupid questions. You turn on the radio to listen to jazz, you get a quiz show. Like Doctor I.Q.," he adds, referring to a popular radio program. "What do you think I am, some turd in the balcony who needs fifty bucks?"

Pixie, who rarely laughs, gives out a snicker.

Bonner chooses to ignore the obvious decline in Grotto's regard for him. "If you're still involved with that outfit, I have some information. Might give you a leg up. Consider this a favor. You helped me once and now I give you tit for tat."

"Oh?" The forehead lines vanish. Grotto likes to receive favors. "Okay, what?"

He listens with interest as Bonner relates the attempt on Miravich's life. Has Grotto heard about it?

"Sure, I got informants in the Watts. But I don't give a rat's ass what happens in the mill. On the public streets is a different matter." He shifts impatiently. "Come on, Pete. It's a busy day."

Bonner tells of his and Miravich's suspicion that Mr. Buck hired someone to murder Miravich. The culprit, Bonner continues, is apparently a thug with a gray face named, oddly enough, Whitey, and he probably has an arrest record as long as your arm. Grotto's men should have no trouble locating him and confirming the story.

"Yeah. Then what?"

"Then you'll have something to hold over them."

"Yeah. Tell me again, why is this guy with gray skin called 'Whitey?'"

"I got the idea from Pixie. Would you mind standing up, Pixie?"

Grotto nods to him, and Pixie rises, hulking over them in the tiny room.

"Why do you call Pixie, 'Pixie?'"

"I see what you mean." Grotto is not amused. "So what do you get out of this?"

"Like I said, I owe you a favor. If you find out something, let me know."

The phone rings. "Salvatore!" comes the mocking voice of Louie through the curtain. "It's Mama."

Grotto picks up the receiver, dismissing Bonner with a curt nod. As he leaves the store, Sal and Louie are shouting at each other.

Three days later Bonner receives a hand-delivered envelope containing a clipping from the Pittsburgh Press pasted on a sheet of notebook paper. It's a one-paragraph story about a man known to the police as Robin "Whitey" Lark, with an arrest record as long as your arm. He was killed in a car bombing in Northside Pittsburgh. Scrawled in the margin is the message, "Whitey had a skin disease. Not any more. Mr. Buck cured him."

■

"What in hell did you tell him for?" Miravich says. Bonner has shown him the clipping and told him about the meeting with Grotto.

Bonner gazes out the hospital room window. The Bessemer cloud is clearly, unambiguously, reddish-orange this morning. "What else was there to do?" he says glumly. "Maybe it wasn't too smart. But at least I flushed out the bird."

"Yeah. You flushed him right into the fox's den. What'd you think Grotto was going to do, give him a free hit on the numbers and turn him over to us? Now we're back where we started from."

"At least we know for a fact there is a Mr. Buck. Grotto says so."

"Praise the Lord, a message from Mr. Grotto!" Miravich waves his hands like a Holy Roller. "Why are you dealing with this hoodlum? You'll hook up with anybody, won't you?" Miravich throws off a sheet and slides his bandaged foot over the side of the bed. "I'm the one Whitey tried to kill. I should get a sayso in what to do with him."

"Damn it, Joe, you didn't ask my permission to run for union office."

Miravich hops to the foot of the bed, hospital gown billowing around him. He stops and faces Bonner. "What's that supposed to mean?"

"Your campaign for president. You're making headlines, attracting attention. People call you 'strike-happy,' a 'rabble-rouser.' Maybe you're a threat to this Mr. Buck, just like Phil Murray was years ago. Whatever involves you and Mr. Buck involves me, too. My advice is, drop out of the race."

Miravich lurches toward the bathroom door. "Just like you gave up your business when Mr. Buck threatened you." He pushes the door open and again faces Bonner. "You know what? We're stuck together like dogs doing it wrong."

■

When Miravich comes home from the hospital, Mitzie plies him with food, gives him sponge baths, and makes love to him on the roll-out bed in their apartment. Later, lying side by side, they listen to jukebox music wafting out of Bartolo's Bar & Grill across the street. *Praise the Lord and pass the ammunition.*…She haltingly raises the question, should he withdraw from the union election.

"I'm staying in, dammit," he says. "The union wasn't involved in what happened. I think somebody mistook me for someone else. But in any case we'll be well protected." He nods at a shadow outside a blind drawn on the rear window. Johnny Chubb, one of a pair of Chubb brothers hired by the local union to guard Miravich and Mitzie round the clock, stands on the fire escape landing. Johnny and his brother Ernie, steelworkers themselves, perform locally as a mud-wrestling tag team. Joe's friend Red Terhune, Miravich's campaign manager, persuaded the local to pay the Chubbs' wages while they take temporary leaves of absence from the Watts.

"But who do we need protecting from?" Mitzie asks. "Somebody from your past? From your coal-mining days?" He shakes his head. "Your union-organizing days?"

"Leave it alone, please, Mitz." He falls back on the bed and wraps his arms around her waist. "Trust me on this. I won't let anybody hurt you."

Abdominal muscles rippling, she sits up. Putting a hand under his chin, she raises his head. "Now listen to me, Joe." She squeezes his face. "I don't like to be patronized. I get enough of that in the mill, and I had a girlhood full of it with my father. So please spare me the 'I'll take care of you, little girl' crap."

He wrenches free and rotates his aching jaw. "Where'd that come from?" How did they go from intense passion and pleasure to anger and rejection in only fifteen minutes? Mitzie the wonder girl must have inner struggles of her own.

On June 8, D-Day plus two, Miravich sits on the stage of the local union hall, listening to a reading of election results. He looks out at the scores of union members and guests in the audience and feels oddly embarrassed. Thousands of young Allied soldiers have just died courageously on the bloody beaches of Normandy, and here's Joe Miravich hobbling around with a foot in a cast because the evil Mr. Buck ordered his murder. But separate investigations by the police and the company have produced no leads. A report on the "accident" issued by the Watts's security department declares, in its entirety: "Laborer Wm. Pyle killed and Shearman Jos. Miravich injured by falling crates in motor shed. Cause: faulty stacking of said crates by work force."

The audience breaks into resounding shouts for "Tuxedo Joe!" when the election teller announces his victory, 4,000-plus votes to 1,000 for two other candidates. His entire slate, including six committeemen and other officers, carried the day, validating his multiethnic approach. The old Irish-English hierarchy led by Pat McNally has been replaced by a porridge of nationalities represented in Miravich's coalition, excepting only the colored race, which nonetheless supported him. McNally, promoted to the district staff, is not unhappy. Handing Miravich a gavel, he says, "Tomorrow the world, huh, Joe?"

PART 3: 1945–1946

CHAPTER 1:
January 1945–April 1945

On a clear, frosty evening in January 1945, a middle-aged man with a boxy, mustached face and powerful shoulders, sloping toward fifty, steps out the front door of his newly-purchased two-and-a-half story brick home in White Oak just outside McKeesport. Standing on the top porch step, Pete Bonner takes a long drag of a cigarette and surveys his new neighborhood, or what he can see of it in darkness illuminated by the Bessemer glow. An hour ago, in the final dribble of daylight, moving-men carried the last piece of furniture up the front steps and into the house, Mae supervising. Only now does it occur to him that fifteen years have passed since he and his father defaulted on lines of credit totaling $5,000, an amount—quite large for those days—that Pete had urged on his father to make investments that would enable them to recoup earlier losses. But prices fell, values vanished, banks collapsed, and the Bonners failed to make one miserable loan payment and thereby lost three dozen properties, their real estate firm, and the Bonner family home in White Oak. The elder Bonner suffered a heart seizure and died within a year. Now, Pete Bonner has returned, perhaps not in triumph but certainly on a commercial upswing. The Great Depression has finally ended for the Bonners.

Mae joins him on the porch, her small body drowning in Pete's overcoat. "They left it in decent condition," she says, having finished a minute inspection of the house, "except for the basement sink, which will not drain, and we need a load of coal. Otherwise…" She holds out an ashtray. "Don't flick ashes on the porch."

"Yes, dear." He crushes the cigarette in the ashtray, puts an arm around her, and inhales deeply. "The air's fresher out here, don't you think?"

Mae samples the air. "It's certainly different." She sniffs again. "I smell manure."

"You would," he says, laughing. "There's a small farm about a half-mile over there at the foot of that hill—" he points vaguely northward, "with cows and horses. In the twenties, there were at least a dozen farms. It's more like a suburb now."

Mae is trembling, despite the overcoat, but she stays on, rotating slowly, absorbing the shapes and profiles of a new neighborhood. Trees are everywhere, bare branches clutching at the sky, and the roofs of houses present a different pattern than in the city, where the roofs march up and down hills in perfect procession, each chimneyed peak a little higher (or lower) than the preceding one. Out here, houses sprawl across a valley floor, and from ground level you can never see more than a few roofs at a time. The new home is only a mile farther from the Watts than the old one, but the distance seems to have diminished the significance of the mill, along with the inevitability that her sons will be somehow forced to work there.

It is so cold that the stars seem to quiver—a possible effect, Bonner thinks, of viewing them through a thick film of dust overlying the valley. Nonetheless, he has no trouble finding Orion the Hunter in the southern sky and points it out to Mae.

"During all those nights on watch aboard ship," he says, "we learned how to identify the constellations. But I've forgotten most." He is silent for a while. "I haven't even looked at the stars for more than twenty years. Too busy, I guess."

"Busy making all that money with your dad," Mae adds, "and then losing all that money."

He makes a murmuring sound that could signify assent or annoyance. "You might say that."

The leap back to White Oak gives Bonner a sense of having finally gotten the best of "*them*," as he sometimes puts it to Mae. "*Them*" refers to the whole conglomeration of things and people—the national economy, local economy, laws, banks, steel mills, unions, buyers and sellers, politicians and racketeers—everything that bears on Pete Bonner and his business. After being down and nearly out, he has struggled back, despite all that *they* have thrown at him. Now, with plenty of cash in the bank and his business growing day by day, the wage-driven demand for beer being what it is, he is planning new ventures. That long fallow decade of the Depression has drowned in its own misery.

Paul comes running out the front door, shouting, "Hey, Dad, the marines took another island in the Pacific." Paul follows the war closely and has begun talking about when he'll be old enough to join up, only six years from now.

"There's good news," Bonner says. He guides Mae toward the door. "What's for dinner, dear?"

Steak, baked potatoes, and green beans. Over coffee and dessert, Bonner announces his plans for the entire family. "After the war," he says to his sons, "we're going to expand into construction and real estate. We'll build apartment and office buildings and homes. After college, you boys will come into business with me. Albert will be the architect and Paul the lawyer. How does that sound?"

His wife and sons are stupefied. "That reminds me so much of your dad," Mae finally says. She declines to elaborate in front of her sons.

Later, in the bedroom, he opens a window. White Oak flows in on a thin stream of cold air, carrying not the smell of manure—despite Mae's insistence, Bonner knows that the odor of manure does not travel in cold weather—but the smell of triumph. He has beaten *them*, for now. Occasionally, he still dreams about a horde of faceless men charging toward him out of the fog, a brief but irrevocable vision, repeating over and over his introduction to the crazy cycle of violence and fear which started that day in 1937 on Route 40. Although he tells himself that Mr. Buck has disappeared for good, it's hard to believe his own soothing counsel.

■

In the pitch black of midnight a winking red dawn flashes on and off below the horizon of the window sill: "Bortolo's Bar & Grill" in blinking neon script. The calf of her leg presses on his shoulder, powerful leverage for enterprising hips. He clutches the pommel atop the headboard, riding it out, his insteps spragging across mattress buttons bared when the sheet pulled out. Her arms flung up and lightly pincering his neck, lips illuminated in the neon glow silently laughing with the sheer joy of it. *My wild Polish bride.* She sucks out his breath, his very spirit. *Bor-to-lo*, he thinks, timing the syllables to conform to the flashes. *Bor-to-lo, Bortol-o...*The darkness inflates, floating them up and out with the rising pace. *Bortolo Bortolo, Borto-Borto-Borto, oh...*

Laughter in the street below. Car doors slam and engines start. The flickering red winks out for good, Bortolo closing for the night, going home, his pockets bulging with payday money.

Miravich rolls over and switches on a lamp. "You sure I didn't kick the cradle too hard?"

Her muffled voice: "I don't hear any screaming." She turns on her back and caresses her two-month pregnancy. "Speaking of which, I guess we ought to start looking for a bigger apartment."

"Hell, that'll mean more rent."

"Joe, that's the way it goes? You get older, have babies, move into bigger homes, pay more rent. Life."

He arranges items on the bureau top for when he goes to work in the morning—billfold, change, notebook, clip-on lead pencil, pen knife, pocket-size union contract. Mitzie watches with unconcealed envy. She quit work at the end of her first month of pregnancy but would probably lose her job anyway when the men come home from war. The union has made it clear that returning servicemen will displace women even if they have longer seniority. "Interesting day tomorrow?" she asks.

"More grievance meetings. A big incentive-pay problem in the open hearth. Complaints about wage inequities every place." He sits beside her on the bed. "The company won't settle anything till we snarl and get ugly about it."

"I think maybe they're scared of you, Joe."

"When you're scared of somebody, you're supposed to do what they want. They don't do anything I want. Remember that management-labor committee set up early in the war? We were supposed to work together on increasing production. Management said no to everything we put on the table. They didn't want ideas, not from wage workers for God's sake. It was a waste of time. So a couple days ago I sent them a letter saying we've had enough. They castrated that committee, and I killed the peckerless thing."

He goes to the window. The sky is high and clear with stars spread across the top and a pulsing redness in the west. A wind is blowing hard, and he feels little puffs of moist coolness coming through cracked putty in the window frame. The mill is seeping in, destroying the intimacy of their bedroom. "Arrogant sons-of-bitches!" he mutters.

"Joe, darling." She comes up behind him. "They are not worth doing something you'll regret."

He turns around and kisses her forehead. "I told you a long time ago, I quit that. Besides—" He sits down, holding both her hands as if what he is about to tell her can only be transmitted by touch. "This is a lot bigger than scaring the shit out of a mine owner. This calls for a political solution. We have to get the union to where we have some power outside the company. That means putting a pro-labor man in office."

"We already have Roosevelt."

"It's a good question as to who's got who there. No, I mean right here in the city. The local's going to run somebody for mayor. We decided today, me and the—" He pauses, puffs out his chest, and issues a correction. "The union committee and I have decided."

"Well," she says, sounding dubious, "if you think that's wise…"

Later, waking up in the middle of the night, he reflects on how he pushed the committee to reach out and seize the political power they need and not consider the union confined to the mill. He turns restlessly in bed and lightly places a hand on Mitzie's shoulder to confirm that she is still breathing. He tells himself that this is one of many acts of love he performs, unknown to her. Calmer now, he is ready to sleep, his nose hooked on the curve of her neck. If he can't force the meek oldtimers in the local to act like free men, he thinks drowsily, he can always retire to the best bed in McKeesport.

■

To prepare for the union debate, Miravich does some research at the public library. How did it come to pass, he wonders, that Donald Regis Shoaf—"Divine Right" Shoaf, a stiff-collared Republican famed across the region for waging unrelenting war against unions during his three decades in office—how could such a man have been elected to seven straight four-year terms as the mayor of a mill town where wage workers comprise a huge majority of all voters?

Miravich decides to tap the political wisdom of Councilman McPhee, whom he's known since he drove a beer truck for Pete Bonner in the thirties. In those days they spoke a common language of political discontent, the crippled old fireman and blacklisted coal miner, and became friends. They meet in the back room of Mulckey's Tavern. McPhee throws down a shot of Bushmills and launches a monologue of stupefying length. The Party of Lincoln became the dominant political force in the Monongahela Valley in the late 1800s when the mill towns, with visions of exploding industrial growth, chose capital over labor. The steel union was practically wiped out after Andy Carnegie "and his lap dog Henry Frick" broke the 1892 strike in Homestead by calling in the state militia. The other owners eagerly aped old Andy and broke all the unions. "All of western Pennsylvania..." he spreads his arms and turns the empty shot glass upside down "...became a Republican duchy, and the workingman couldn't even mention the word 'Democrat' for fear of being fired."

"That brings us up to thirty-seven," Miravich says, impatiently. "When the union came in, all those mill towns like Duquesne and Clairton elected Democratic mayors. But not McKeesport. How does that old fool Shoaf keep getting elected?"

"'Old fool?'" McPhee replies, raising his eyes to engage Miravich with a fierce stare. "I'll be second to none in ridiculing King Shoaf. But a fool he is not. Kept the city solvent during the Depression and made sure the needy didn't starve. His Presbyterian rectitude, of course, don't extend to ensuring free speech and the rights of wage workers."

"Okay, okay," says a chastened Miravich. "But why didn't we do like Duquesne and Clairton in thirty-seven instead of electing that wonderful old Presbyterian...who hates union people?"

"History, lad. Clairton and Duquesne was only empty fields when the mills come. The company imported boatloads of immigrant workers and packed them in the river flats. When the union organized the mills in thirty-seven, the workers themselves took political control of those towns. But McKeesport, see, was a riverboat town eighty years before the mills came. For all them decades merchants ran the town and elected King Shoaf in 1913, I think it was." McPhee quaffs a third straight shot, licks his lips. "Pat McNally was the first president of the Watts local, a good man but he stuck to the mill and left politics to the spineless local Democrats. And then, a'course, Sal Grotto stuffed cash in the right pockets to make sure he could operate without interference."

"Well, it's going to be different this year," Miravich avows. "We'll put some backbone in the Democratic Party—make sure they pick a candidate we can live with."

"Well, now," McPhee says, "and who d'ya have in mind?"

"I'll tell you this much. He's got to be pro-labor and against the rackets."

■

Every time President Miravich raises a hand to calm his members, the peculiar lighting projects him as a monstrous wall shadow commanding obedience. "C'mon! C'mon!" he says, banging a gavel on the podium. Out of the corner of his eye he sees his image vent its fury on an indistinct, dark mass that could be taken for the collective head of all those gathered in the meeting hall—a shade of reality, for he has indeed been trying to bang some sense into their heads. As he waits for the noise to subside, Miravich reflects on the curious fact that your shadow always portrays you as a more violent creature than you really are, a dark, scary thing lacking even the faintest glimmer of compassion.

Only about seventy-five men are sitting out there on wooden folding chairs, but the shouting will continue two or three minutes before they settle down and actually debate the proposal. First, they react, and then they debate. Most of the best unionists—the men who think before they speak, who put union solidarity ahead of political ambition, who see the union as a brotherhood and not as a dues vault to be plundered—most of the good, ordinary, well-meaning members attend meetings only when a crucial issue, such as a new contract, is to be discussed. A few of these moderates, including Miravich's brother-in-law, Eddie Cramczak, are present tonight, but each time one rises to speak he is shouted down by fist-waving faction members. In the wake of Miravich's election, three or four political factions, each dedicated to some extremist position, sprang into existence. Tonight, Miravich counts three such groups sitting in tight clumps of frustrated ambition. There are also political hangers-on who jump from faction to faction to curry favor.

Pat McNally, attending the meeting as an observer from the district office, sadly shakes his head. What has become of his local? He makes a throat-slitting gesture to Miravich, urging him to cut off debate.

Miravich agrees the time has come to guide this chaos of democracy into proper channels. "Okay!" he says, holding up his hands. "You've had your fun. Now we're going to debate this motion like gentlemen. No more funny names, no more points of order, no more filibustering. Say what you got to say in two minutes and sit down or get thrown down by the sergeant-at-arms."

Everybody looks to the rear where two sergeants-at-arms, the formidable Johnnie and Ernie Chubb, stand in the center aisle with folded arms.

"Any questions?" Miravich shades his eyes against the back lighting and looks over the floor with the grimmest face he can put on. His shadow assumes menacing proportions: the specter of dictatorial control imprinted on a background of suspected violence. People have heard rumors about his exploits in the coalfields. The hall goes thickly silent. It can help to have a bad reputation to fall back on.

The motion on the floor is simple enough: it authorizes the local's political action committee to choose a candidate to run in the Democratic Party mayoral primary, ignoring a candidate already selected by the party. Miravich's appeal to reason, backed by Chubb force, has a calming effect. The debate sails along more or less smoothly. All points of view are heard, briefly. Leftist faction leaders demand that the union create a labor party of its own. Opponents on the right argue that the local should stay out of politics and devote itself exclusively to their personal gripes on the job.

"Look," Miravich says after one speaker makes that argument, "we already have the union in the mill. Now we need a way to deal with living conditions outside the mill."

"Like what, Joe?" a member yells from the floor.

"Like giving city workers the right to join a union and earn a decent salary. Like cleaning up this pigsty of a valley and riddin' the rivers and creeks of sewage and the air of this filthy red gunk that clogs our lungs. Like cracking down on the numbers guys."

His argument, he knows, does not really change many minds. But it disrupts the debate sufficiently so that the left and right factions temporarily lose steam, leaving the balance of voting power with his compromise.

"All in favor of the resolution as stated signify by saying 'aye,'" Miravich shouts, banging his gavel. And a moment later, before the roar of the 'ayes' fades, "All opposed, give a 'nay.'" He strikes the gavel again before the rumble of "nays" dies down. "The ayes have it, resolution adopted."

As the meeting breaks up, McNally comes to the podium. "This is a stupid move, Joe. We always go with the party's choice."

"You always *went* with the party's choice," Miravich corrects him. "We talked to the party. You know who their man is? Harley Pogue." He purses his lips and adds, "And then we talked to Harley Pogue."

"Well?" McNally scans the faces of other executive committee members who have gathered around Miravich.

"Harley Pogue," says Len Mrvos, always informative, "runs a hardware store."

"So what?"

"Pogue's got putty for brains, for Chrissake!" blurts out Red Terhune.

"Shit, Red, that's never held you back. Don't you guys know you're going to split the party?"

"How d'ya split a pool of weak piss?"

McNally says, "What dope would agree to run against the party's candidate?"

"We got our eye on somebody," Miravich says. "And now, Brother McNally, with all due respect, the motion has been made, seconded and passed, and you hereby are out of order." *Crrrack!* goes the gavel. "But you're always welcome here."

■

The April snow is pure and feathery, like wisps of ash blown from charcoal embers. Leaving the mill building, Miravich turns up his jacket collar and trudges solemnly beside Rooster Wooster, who is in a depressed mood. One of his sons, a waist gunner on a B-17, has been missing in Europe for a month. Miravich says nothing and hopes that his presence helps. They part with a nod outside the Lower Gate, Rooster turning south to his car. Miravich crosses Lysle Boulevard and walks toward the two-story brick garage that now encloses the loading dock at Bonner Beers. He slows down, hesitant about revisiting the past. But he is lured on by faintly remembered rumbling sounds of cooperage on the roll. Wooden and aluminum kegs are barrelling out of a small opening hung with leather strips, the cooler doorway, onto the dock. Two guys are standing spraddle-legged opposite one another, lifting the kegs together and heaving them into the back of a truck. A closer look reveals that one of the two is a boy of high school age. Bonner employing child labor? Kegs continue bursting out of the opening and waddling drunkenly down a short ramp, threatening to run down the youngster.

Miravich halts one keg with his foot just short of the boy. He bends over and parts the leather strips over the doorway, and shouts into the cooler. "Hold up in there!"

The lifters gape at him. He wags a finger. "Never turn your back on a moving barrel, young man."

He enters the store through the same door that the mine dicks exited to meet their fiery doom on that summer day in thirty-eight. Practically empty then, the storeroom now is loaded with beer. Duquesne must be the big seller this year, its stack twice as large as the Fort Pitt, Iron City and Tube City piles. Schlitz, Budweiser and Rolling Rock are miserable one-stackers; not much call for premium beer in a mill town. A loud noise crackles through the fetid air, followed by a sharp whistle. He looks up, expecting to see a crane load dangling overhead. Instead there comes a woman's voice, floating on static: "Attention! Drivers to the office! Drivers to the office!" There is a brief pause, then on a courteous, apologetic note: "Please?"

Miravich realizes that Bonner has installed a squawk box communication system and that the voice can belong to no one but Mae Bonner. Looking to the front of the storeroom, he sees her and Bonner in the office.

Mae sees him first. "Joe Miravich," she says, surprised, banging it out over the squawk box.

Right away she notices how he favors his right foot. It's as close to gawking as he has ever seen her. "You could get a job bossing in the mill, Mrs. Bonner." He leans on a filing cabinet.

Mae turns off the squawk box and smiles shyly. "Pete makes me use this silly thing. How is your wife?"

"Going on her third month."

"Pregnant? Joe, that's wonderful." Her eyes retreat slightly, turning inward as she contemplates a world with another male Miravich.

Bonner says, "You're putting on weight. Kielbasa and mashed potatoes, I'll bet." He arches his eyebrows, as if to ask a question.

The same old question. Miravich is convinced it will follow him through life: *Any messages from Mr. Buck?* Miravich blinks twice, their sign language for "no." "I was in the neighborhood and thought I'd drop in."

"We've been reading about you in the paper," Bonner says. He makes a final flourish in a large, ledger-style checkbook, then rips out a check and drops it into a bank deposit bag with a zipper and small padlock.

From the way he signs the check, ending with a trailing line exuding confidence, Miravich knows this is no paper game: the money is there. "Don't believe everything you read," he says. "I'd like to discuss something, if Mrs. Bonner doesn't mind. Can I buy you a beer?"

It is clear from her frown that Mrs. Bonner does mind. But she is in the middle of counting a stack of dollar bills and doesn't look up.

"Well—" Bonner turns to Mae who is sitting sideways at the other desk with her legs crossed.

His gaze halts there, and Miravich is aware that he is considering more than the consequences of going against her wishes. "Nuts!" Miravich thinks, realizing that he has blundered into something that started before he arrived. Mae doesn't look up, but the rouge on her cheeks seems rosier. Miravich has never thought of her that way before. He feels as if he's intervening in Nature; they are, after all, man and wife. He begins backing out of the office.

"Hold on," Bonner says, making up his mind. He swiftly pushes papers into piles on his desk. "Look, Mae," he adds, displaying a clipboard. "Only one more route to load and it's ready to go. I could use a bite to eat." He reaches quickly for his hat.

Mae ignores the clipboard. "We should be home by five-thirty."

"I'll be back long before then, hon."

The boy from the loading dock walks in.

"My son Albert," Bonner says to Miravich. "The last time you saw him, he was a boy. He's fourteen now."

"Yeah, I remember. Hiya, Al. A boy no longer, huh?" He extends his hand.

Young Albert replies with a moderate grip and mumbles something. His eyes drift toward a wall calendar with a drawing of scantily-clad Miss April sitting on the barrel of a destroyer's five-inch gun. He is about five-six and has strong shoulders, the result no doubt of hefting halves on Saturdays instead of playing basketball at the YMCA. Perhaps that's why he seems sullen and down-at-the-mouth: forced labor.

Day-turn drinkers still crowd the bar at Saboulovich's. Some are liquoring up, gathering momentum for the weekend, but most are loafing over the usual shot and a beer. Many of the men know Miravich by sight, and he goes down the line of stools, slapping backs and saying, "Howzit, brother?" Old John Saboulovich expresses pleasure that his friend Pete Bonner has brought this hero of the working-class to his saloon. Union officials of the past, all Irish and English, did their drinking in taverns uptown. He insists that they sit in the adjacent dining room, at a table normally reserved for his two senior boarders. Twenty pairs of eyes follow the old man on his arthritic trip to the table with a tray trembling in both hands.

Miravich raises his glass of Fort Pitt tap, selected to rekindle certain memories. "Good health!"

Bonner sips his double rye from a tall, thick shot glass with flaring lips. "I thought you didn't like beer."

"Still don't. But my pap told me, always drink with a man who drinks, especially if you need a favor."

They trade bits of personal news. Finally, Bonner says, "That was quite a bombshell, your choice for mayor." Raised eyebrows accentuate his surprise.

Miravich cocks his head. "You unhappy, too? Holy Christ, the working-man can't take too deep a breath in this town, can he? I thought McPhee was your friend. Old drinking buddy and all that."

"Sure. But—" His voice rises with annoyance. "Tommy McPhee for mayor!" Bonner might as well be marching under a McPhee banner with a bullhorn. Hearing the declaration, men at the bar collectively do an eyes-right.

The whole town knows that Miravich's local has defied the party and announced it will support Councilman Thomas McPhee in the Democratic primary. Political analysts say that union upstart Miravich is jeopardizing a golden opportunity for the Democrats finally to oust Mayor Shoaf. Harley Pogue, the party's choice, may not be a luminous candidate. But as the owner of a prosperous hardware store and a valued member of the Methodist Church, Rotary Club and the Elks Drum & Bugle Corps, he is a hell of a sight more acceptable to the business community than the maverick McPhee.

"I guess you know Harley Pogue," Miravich says.

"Sure. I see him all the time practicing in the Elks drill room. The only thing Harley really wants is to lead the Armistice Day parade. But why Tommy?"

"He wants what we want." His campaign promises include increasing the industrial use tax on the Watts Works, supporting retail business, building low-cost housing, allowing municipal employees to form unions and reduce their work week to 40 hours, and—Miravich emphasizes—cracking down on the rackets.

Bonner leans closer. "You don't really think Tommy himself can wipe out the rackets, do you? And who says workers want to stop playing the numbers?"

"At least he's not owned by Grotto. Harley Pogue is." The word is out, he says, that Pogue's primary campaign is already receiving rackets' money. The union, therefore, is seeking allies in the business community—enlightened, Roosevelt-style Democrats like Bonner. Miravich pauses, gazes earnestly at Bonner, and plunges ahead. "We want you to sign on as chairman of the Businessmen for McPhee Committee. Then people will see that this is not a union power grab but a movement of concerned citizens."

Bonner is stunned. He signals for more drinks and lights a cigarette. Finally he says, "I'm not political, Joe. Just a businessman."

"Not political! You've always been strong for Roosevelt."

"That wasn't politics. That was saving the country."

"McPhee is your friend, isn't he? You want an honest mayor, don't you?"

"It's not that simple. Tommy's a swell guy, yeah, but..." He pauses, pours a half-finger of rye into his soda chaser and tosses it off. "You shouldn't put me in this position, Joe. Yes, Tommy is my friend, but..."

"But what?"

"He hits the bottle...you know..." Bonner drinks quickly, orders a third round, tries not to face Miravich. "Look," he finally says, "you send Tommy into a burning building, he'll come out a hero. But you put him in the mayor's office—" He raises his hands in a helpless gesture.

Miravich tilts his head, still looking at him. "In other words, this old drinking buddy of yours is just a working stiff and not in your exalted class of people. That it?"

"Of course not. But think, Joe! Running Tommy for mayor on an anti-numbers platform—that could get him killed."

"Yeah, well, I talked to him about that. He says..." Miravich lowers his voice to a whisper, "...he says the whole city knows how he feels about Grotto. There'd be an uproar if he gets hurt and the cops don't clap Sal in jail. Sal knows it and won't try anything."

"Maybe, maybe not." Bonner looks at his watch. "I've got to go."

"Just one more," Miravich says, signalling to John behind the bar.

The Saboulovich women are clanging about in the kitchen, stirring things in great pots. The sun is in the west, and the tap room is sinking into a late afternoon torpor. Drinkers at the bar seem to doze with their ears open. Even the war news from London, fading in and out on the small Philco behind the bar, conveys a drowsy quality.

Miravich watches Bonner, quiet now, having said his piece, studying his refilled shot glass. He's a businessman, yes, Miravich thinks, but nothing like those pinch-vested financiers from Yale who run the steel business, sitting around in committee meetings, toying with pencils and pads, making big decisions. Bonner whirled out of the ground like a cave wind, an elemental force, buying and selling, trading, bargaining, dealing under the table if necessary. The son-of-a-bitch fought the Depression like a man wrestling a tiger.

"Joe, you're moving too fast," Bonner finally says. "You don't know politics yet."

"I know enough to know we're getting suckered—workingman, businessman, you, me...all of us. Are you willing to sit here and let them give us a drum major for mayor? The Pete Bonner I remember was independent and didn't take no man's crap."

Bonner merely shrugs. Or was that a hiccup? He stands. "Mae's waiting."

"Okay, but a toast before you go. It's nearly eight years since Charleston?" He rises unsteadily. "Here's to those eight and many more to come."

Bonner also stands. They clink glasses and Miravich impulsively pats his shoulder. The bar goes silent, caught up in the back-room drama. Businessman and union man toasting, even embracing. History in the making. But in the last few seconds before parting, Miravich sees the no-deal-today look in the salesman's eyes.

Bonner marches past the bar, scooping his hat in a jaunty wave to old John. All heads watch him go. A spittoon rattles as if someone spit out a tooth. The Saboulovich women encircle the boarders' table with armloads of plates and silverware. It is dinnertime on the second Saturday in April 1945.

CHAPTER 2: April 1945

At eight-thirty on a Monday morning, Pete Bonner leaves Mae in charge of the business and drives up town to do some banking. His old Pierce-Arrow succumbed some months ago to a burst oil line, and he now drives a second-hand '39 Buick. He finagles the car into a coupe-sized curb space on Fifth Avenue and with time to spare takes a stroll up the main street. It is a mile-long brick gulch winding between seamless rows of narrow, three- and four-story, sooty red buildings with ground-floor store fronts and upper level offices and rooms-to-let. Built during a mad commercial spree shortly after the turn of the century, the buildings stand joined at hip and shoulder, their formation broken only by occasional alleys and cross streets, and if one building leans to the east, the entire block, like a rank of drunken sailors, inclines in that direction. Windows topped with ornate wooden lintels and drip-mouldings impart a heavy-lidded, dopey appearance to each façade. Yet, two blocks away, the Watts Works rumbles and sputters, awake all night, pouring out steel that will help defeat fascism.

He continues his stroll, enjoying the shop owners' opening rituals—unlocking doors, turning on lights, raising blinds, sweeping off the sidewalk. There are hundreds of tiny shops where mostly poor merchants grub out a mostly honest living. For Bonner, this is the heart and soul of the city. He nods hello to Harry Futch the skinny optometrist who is wrestling with a man-sized cardboard cutout of eye glasses in his storefront window. Bill Hobbs the butcher, his apron already bloodied from hacking at hindquarters, stands in front of his shop, arguing baseball with Sergie the garbageman. Early-bird shoppers are swarming in and around Balsamo's Fruit Market. Old men in threadbare suit coats pick over apples and pears. Old women in babushkas waddle homeward, carrying in each hand a stout brown bag brimming with vegetables.

Next comes a second-run theater district, three moviehouses in one block. Stopping under the marquee of the Victor, he watches a workman on a wobbly ladder prying out yesterday's feature presentation, letter by letter. The Victor will open at noon in time for men to catch a movie before the three to eleven turn. A poster promotes a coming attraction, "Meet Me in St. Louis" with Judy Garland. "Clang! Clang! Clang! Went the trolley!" says the blurb. "Get happy-hearted at MGM's glorious romance."

At this time of morning, deep shadow enshrouds the entrance to Jefferson First Federal, where people stand waiting to deposit what's left of Friday's paycheck. At last the thick glass door opens. When his turn comes, Bonner deposits a thick wad of bills and checks comprising Saturday's receipts and asks the eyeshaded teller to compute the new balance in his savings account. Back on the street, he feels so good he would jump in the air and click his heels—if he could get more than two feet off the ground. Money! Money with no liens against it, money not owing, money unattached. Profits free and clear. Real money and Bonner have been reunited! Real money opens up all kinds of investment possibilities. He feels as if he's been hibernating, afraid to show his head. Now he's emerging from darkness, taking a fresh look at the world. It's time to re-enter the marketplace, gauge business activity, nose out deals. He stops at a real estate office and inquires about a property he's had his eye on. It's still up for sale, he finds, still available for some venture, retail or wholesale, or perhaps even industrial. It is like the old days: he is free to choose.

By mid-morning Fifth Avenue is jammed with automobiles and street-cars, sparks popping on trolley wires, traffic cops impatiently waving drivers through intersections. Crowds of shoppers surge this way and that, pausing in front of store windows. Men's stores, women's stores, shoe emporiums, Murphy's Five-and-Ten. People dart across the street between car bumpers. Sidewalks glitter with specks of graphite deposited during a recent volcanic "slip" in one of the Watts's blast furnaces. It seems you could scoop up that glitter by the handful, just like money. Money generates money, he exultantly tells himself, remembering how, back in the twenties, invested ten-dollar bills spawned hundred-dollar returns, from which magically blossomed stocks, bonds and notes worth thousands and then tens and hundreds of thousands—on paper anyway. Fast money and fast times in those pre-Depression days. Now he has a second chance—has made a second chance, with the help of war wages. Despite Mae's feeling that there's something tawdry about the beer business, beer has been good to them. Money is good if you use it to build to make more money and build more things, and so on and on.

Noontime in Mulckey's Tavern, the workingman's bar and grill. Men up from the mill on lunch break, down from their homes on a day off, women not welcome. Crackle of sizzling fat on the big slab stove lined with neat rows of yellow-eyed eggs and bubbling chunks of ham, bacon and sausage. One short-order cook performs spatula wizardry on the grill just inside the front window, while his co-worker at a cutting board slaps together sandwiches on hard black sourbread stacked with kielbasa, pastrami, salami, corned beef, and marbled head cheese. Bonner skirts the lunch line and stops at the bar where men are hoisting beers, chomping on sandwiches, chawing on big dill pickles plucked out of a briny barrel. He remembers Depression days, when people stood outside in groups and watched, salivating, as Connie Mulckey himself worked at the grill, basting a lonely fried egg. The hungry no longer stand watching; now they come in and partake. America as she ought to be.

Rye whiskey has never been more invigorating, but he limits himself to one warming mouthful, which he throws back with an expert toss of his head.

He has never seen the town so active, not even in 1919 during the natural gas boom. What a time that was! Someone discovered gas seeping out of a rock formation in the hills south of town. Within days drilling rigs were breaking up the pavement as they rumbled through town, and scores of wildcatters were sinking wells and borrowing money to sink more wells. In the wake of the boom—the all too brief boom—twenty-seven wildcatters declared personal bankruptcy, one committed suicide, and one emerged a millionaire: Gas Stowe.

Stowe is the man that Bonner wants to see. Their relations cooled for a time after he and Crabtree rejected Bonner's plea for seed money in thirty-eight. Bonner never again brought up the subject; never will. He believes in making money, not holding grudges over it. After Stowe's only son was killed on Guadalcanal, he became again the rakish, generous gadabout he had been before he became a millionaire, shedding the self-righteous arrogance that goes with the acquisition of great wealth through pure luck. He gave up wearing jodhpurs and riding to hounds on his country estate up the Youghiogheny. Pete and Mae Bonner occasionally dined with Gas and his wife in their baronial manor house. And he and Bonner went on a couple of weekend binges to commemorate the old days. Now, Bonner thinks, his old friend might be interested in a joint business venture.

Bonner finds him at the bar in the Elks Club, along with a half-dozen regulars, including Crabtree, Fat Charlie Pritchard, and Henry Parsimmons. There is the usual hand-shaking and back-slapping, but Bonner notices some reserve on their part. The men have been discussing unions, about which no one in this group has anything good to say. The damned things have become an overwhelming fact of life, and you can't dismiss them as something happening to somebody else. Ed Crabtree, lean and balding, is the leading denigrator. Recently he changed his company's name from Ed's Bus Co. to one more befitting the only bus operation in the lower middle quarter of the Monongahela Valley: Crabtree Surface Transport Inc. Having become a transportation tycoon, he sees his control over the distribution of profits threatened by a CIO bus-drivers' union.

"The sonsabitches want to suck me dry," Crabtree says. "The government says no pay raise for the duration, so my union guys—those greedy bastards—they're demanding another week of paid vacation. Next thing you know they'll be asking for pensions."

"Just for driving a bus eight hours a day?" Stowe says, not without irony. Secretly, he sympathizes with blue-collar workers, possibly because unions have not yet discovered a way to interpose themselves between him and the mailman who delivers his oil and gas dividend checks.

"How do you," Crabtree says, emphasizing "you" as he looks at Bonner, "keep the union out?"

"They haven't come to my place yet." He signals for a round of drinks.

"I have a pretty good idea why," Parsimmons says. He regards his handsome face in the back-bar mirror and slowly turns to Bonner.

"How's that, Henry?"

"That union friend of yours, the president of the Watts local. That hunky—whatzisname?"

Bonner laughs.

"He does you a favor, you do him a favor."

"Such as?"

"Such as financing the union's candidate for mayor, old Opposer."

"Where in hell'd you get that idea?" In the same instant he detects a general relaxation, a barely perceptible release of pent-up breath, as if Parsimmons has finally said what all have been thinking.

"I heard that, too," Crabtree says. "Hope it's not true, Pete. Opposer's a good old guy, but mayor? Jesus!"

"Maybe it's more than a rumor," Parsimmons says. "You know how those hunky bars have eyes and ears. The story is, you and Joe whatzisname met in that saloon down near your store on Saturday. People heard you talking politics, Pete. They saw you shake hands on it and drink to it."

"Come on, Henry, that's really dumb." He looks over the lunch crowd, hoping that McPhee— But no, why should he need McPhee to deny it.

"If it's not true, it oughta be true," exclaims Fat Charlie, the comedian. "With Pete and Tommy in power, stealing streetcars will be legal." He mimes a trolley motorman jerking a bell cord. "Campaign slogan—ding, ding!"

"Hold on," Stowe says, watching Bonner. "Let's not go off half-cocked on this."

A waiter tells Bonner that he has been invited to Mayor Shoaf's table.

"What for?" Bonner says gruffly. But he sets down his drink and follows the waiter to Shoaf's table. The mayor has one companion, a thin-haired scowling man whom Bonner recognizes as Martin Dinsmore, superintendent of the Watts Works.

"Sit down, Pete," Shoaf says imperiously. "What're you drinking? We're having a Canada Dry before lunch. Helps the digestion."

Since Shoaf is the only mayor Bonner has known as an adult, instinct forces him to be respectful. But they never have been friendly. Shoaf is a slim man who walks as if his stiff, sixtyish bones have been wired in an upright position, and his mouth opens about as narrowly as a mouth can open and still emit speech. He stood firm against organized labor during the great steel strike of 1919, and he stood firm against the Depression, performing a thousand paternal acts of kindness for the poor.

"No point in saying we're all busy people," the mayor says. "So, right to the point. It's all over town. You're hooking up with the union and backing Opposer in the primary. And contributing money to the campaign. Five hundred, we hear. That's plain foolish."

Martin Dinsmore shakes his head, appalled at the stupidity of retail businessmen.

Bonner laughs. "What rubbish!" He sees the fellows at the bar staring back at him. Pritchard has moved to another group of men and is doing his cord-pulling joke. A faint "ding-ding," followed by a burst of laughter.

Shoaf lowers his voice. "We can add two and two. Opposer is an old friend of yours. So is that union fellow Miravich. The two of you were seen the other night drinking for hours and talking about the primary. You drank a toast to Opposer's victory. Mill town politics is very simple, Pete. Believe what you see and hear." He sits back and turns both hands palms up. "You explain it."

"I don't explain private business."

"Then listen to this." He leans over the table, speaking precisely as befits a mayor. "Ordinarily, we do not concern ourselves with who the Democrats send to our chopping block. They're all monkeys. But with that fool McPhee in the race, certain issues will be injected into the campaign that will hurt this city." He dabs his lips with a napkin. "Tommy McPhee is a populist Irish bull artist who'll say anything to inflame the people. Our steel friends want decorum and stability. That's what we've had in this city for twenty-eight years, and by God, we're going to keep it."

"Stability most of all," Dinsmore says.

"Stability," Bonner repeats, hearing the word uttered in another voice.

"If McPhee gets into office," Dinsmore says, looking hard at Bonner, "the union will be calling all the shots. We can say goodbye to everything the Corporation has built up. Businessmen will be taxed down to their underwear! This Miravich is a radical. We have files on him. He's probably even a..." Dinsmore only mouths the word "commie." He adds: "You don't want him for a friend, Mr. Bonner."

Bonner stands and says, "There should be a sign on this table—'free advice.'"

"And you'd be wise to take it," Mayor Shoaf says.

Bonner turns and leaves without a word. Gas Stowe, he sees, is sitting with a couple of lunch partners. Bonner has lost his appetite. He goes downstairs to the coat room. As he slips into his overcoat, Opposer McPhee comes out of the men's room. A red and white "McPhee for Mayor" button is pinned to his lapel.

They leave together. "Nobody'll talk to me at the bar," McPhee says. "You'd think I was the Black Death. At least my dues buy me the use of the men's room."

Outside, the wind still howls. A storm of scrap paper blows along the street. Red-haired McPhee wears no hat. His round, solid face is a fiery blob sitting precariously on upturned coat collar.

"Listen, Pete," McPhee says as they turn into the wind, "I didn't know Joe was going to talk to you. I wouldn't put you in a spot like that."

"I know," Bonner says.

"I heard what's going around, and I told people it's a damn lie. But there's too much water to bail now." He stops. "Maybe you don't want to be seen with me."

"You're still a friend, Tommy."

They resume walking. "All my life," McPhee says, "I've been this mick fireman and politician. I had some luck. Got out of the firehouse with a disability pension, got elected to Council. Well, not all luck. I paid my dues, did my job—"

"You were a hero."

"Yeah, that too. Why shouldn't I move up? I'm not no neophyte. I put in fourteen years on council."

"Not that you could do much in the minority."

"Yeah," says rueful McPhee, "Not much to show for fourteen years." He kicks a fire hydrant. "But, see, it's those two things. In a way they owe it to me, and in a way I owe it to the people. Joe and his lads came to me. They didn't demand anything, just said 'we like your philosophy.' I didn't know I had a philosophy. But I thought about it. Here's maybe a chance to pay back. I cut out boozing, and I started thinking about things this city needs. Make sense to you?"

"Sure, Tommy."

"I never seen such fear at City Hall. Shoaf comes to me and says, 'You have gone over the cliff, you dumb mick!' Yeah, old Morals Incorporated put it that way. Even he's scared and not just of commies, which I don't think Joe is. It's the numbers guys, Peter, they got such a hold."

They keep walking, watching women's skirts blow their way.

"See, running a city you got to do shady things. Sure, I flushed shit into the river and I set fire to a city garage in the dead of night so's we could collect insurance to balance the budget. But all that's nothing compared to letting the rackets operate free and clear. It's Godalmighty wrong to let them people profit off of vice."

"Tell me about Shoaf. Is he...on the take?"

McPhee walks for a while. "I don't have proof, see, but I have questions. First off, do the numbers guys operate openly or don't they? That's an easy one. Second, do you ever see any of them go to jail? Do you ever see any of them even get raided? Do you ever see a cop at the corner of Fifth and Sinclair at five o'clock when Grotto's runner drops off his sacks of cash at Jefferson First? If that makes you suspicious of the police, answer me this: Who's the grand poobah of the police? In our commission form of government the mayor is commissioner of police, that's who. Catch my drift, Peter?"

They stop for a traffic light. McPhee resumes after they cross the street. "It's not so much about getting rich as about getting elected. Payoff comes at election time. Don't know how because I've never got one. But the beneficiaries, I guess you'd say, start spending like crazy, paying off ward workers and running radio commercials. It's like a blizzard of money comes down on the election system."

They walk in silence. A man chases a fedora flipping end over end down the sidewalk. It halts with him in mid-stride, and when his foot comes down, it crushes the hat. Rotten luck, Bonner thinks. At the corner of Sixth and Locust, he stops, takes a deep breath, and says, "Tommy, I just can't afford to get involved. It wouldn't be right."

"I know, Pete, I know."

They shake hands. "Good luck, Tommy."

■

Ernest Grubmann of the Greater Ohio Industrial Propagation Association appears at the beer store the following morning. "We met years ago, Mr. Bonner." He turns to Mae. "Is this the little lady? Let me give you my card."

"Are you the trash collector?" she asks, grimacing with distaste.

In response to Bonner's prompt refusal to join his organization, Grubmann warns that the Steelworkers union is trying to take over the city government. This must be viewed as a serious threat to business stability. "The future of free enterprise is at stake in this election," he says, swiveling his horse's head from Bonner to Bonner. "Mr. Bonner, you'd be smart not to alienate yourself from the business community."

Bonner escorts him to the front door.

"Detestable little man!" Mae says. "What was he talking about?"

"Oh, you know, Tommy McPhee's got himself in a political jam. Don't worry, I'm not involved." He attacks the mail with a letter opener.

Later, he receives a phone call from Harley Pogue, Democratic candidate for mayor. He asks Bonner to change his mind about which candidate he'll support.

"I haven't made up my mind in the first place."

Silence, on the other end of the line, then a sigh. "I've never done this before, but I am prepared to offer you a discount. What do you need, nails, tools? I can get you a good price on barrels."

"I don't need barrels, Harley. The breweries provide them."

Still later, after Mae has gone for the day, Grotto calls on the phone. "Is what I hear true? After all I did for you?"

"Not true, Sal," Bonner says wearily.

"This city has seen wonderful stability since I come on the scene," Sal says. "It's a four-way partnership. Business, industry, government, and recreation, and I'm involved in all of 'em. Now labor's trying to horn in. Our stability'll be shot to hell. Is that what you want, Pete? After everything that's passed between us?"

"Why is everybody so riled up over nothing?"

"For me it's the whatchamacallit...symbolism. Beer on the side of reform? It's a contradiction, see." He pauses, resumes with a change of emphasis. "You know, Pete, I think you screwed me that time I offered to be your partner. It better not happen twice. A deal like this, see, will come to the attention of those people I warned you about years ago. You know who I mean. I'm not rushing to judgment, see, but you better look out for your interests."

Bonner closes up shop and goes for a drink. Staring into the backbar mirror, he lines up all the opinions about his conduct vouchsafed to him in the last two days. They add up to a profound truth: keep your mouth shut. His better judgment tells him to do precisely that. His sense of fairness tells him it's unfair that he, your common ordinary businessman, should face such a dilemma. On one side are friends pursuing a dream, one that has certain merits but is also idealistic and crazy and probably will fail, and on the other side are the villains, Grotto and Mr. Buck, with all kinds of punishments at their disposal. Who decreed that he should have to make such a decision?

Two days later, a one-paragraph story buried deep inside *The Daily News* announces the formation of a "Businessmen for McPhee" committee chaired by A.P. (Pete) Bonner. Other members are John Saboulovich, two of Bonner's shopkeeper brothers-in-law, two Jewish haberdashers, and Howard Murmelstein, the criminal defense lawyer. An imposing group representing beer, groceries, butchered meat, men's clothing, and legal protection. On the same day, bus depots are flooded with campaign buttons, and a red and white banner appears in public places: "McPHEE FOR MAYOR—THE PEOPLE'S CANDIDATE." Miravich proposed "the Working-Man's Candidate." But Bonner wanted no part of a slogan suggesting class struggle.

Bonner will always remember this day, Thursday, the 12th of April 1945. A dozen angry callers. Cancellations of orders. No more business, ever, say a few customers.

When Mae sees the newspaper story in the office that afternoon, she goes into a deep pout over not being consulted. "You always told me it was stupid to get involved in politics," she says. "And Tommy McPhee yet! He's the one who always got drunk at your poker parties."

"He's a changed man, Mae. Harley Pogue can't hold a candle up to him."

"Of course not! He'd explode."

Bonner laughs. Anger brings out the best in her. He tells her about the pressures put on him by his friends at the Elks, Mayor Shoaf, Marty Dinsmore, Grubmann, Pogue... unnamed others. Only an hour ago Henry Parsimmons called to warn "my good friend Pete Bonner" that Bonner's credit may dry up if he helps union roughnecks capture the city. "The Huns," Parsimmons said dramatically, "are at the gates of Rome."

"What a foolish man!" Mae exclaims. "I don't blame you for getting angry. That's what this is all about, isn't it? You just don't want people telling you what to do. But, Pete, aren't you taking a risk with your business... our business?"

"Maybe," he acknowledges grudgingly. "Maybe I got carried away." But I can't back down on my word. Not with Tommie and Joe."

The front door bangs open, and a panting John Saboulovich lurches into the office, his white hair flying. "He's dead!" he gasps. "Gone!"

"Sit down, John. Who's dead?" Bonner guides the old man to a chair.

"Roos'felt...gone, gone! It's on radio." He points to a small radio on the desk.

A funereal voice on the radio confirms it. The president suffered a stroke while vacationing in Georgia and died in early afternoon. Mae begins to cry, joining Saboulovich, who is weeping into his apron. Bonner feels a chill creeping down his arms. That's what is at the gates of Rome, he thinks: death.

CHAPTER 3:
May 1945–June 1945

As Opposer McPhee enters the Elks banquet room, his shriveled leg forces him to walk with undulating hips in a motion vaguely suggesting high wheat rippling in a breeze. A few dozen local merchants are gathered for an informal get-together with the man who wants to be the next mayor. Most already know Councilman McPhee, and he moves easily among them, slapping backs, shaking hands, and addressing each person by name, rightly or wrongly. He remembers peoples' business or occupation and ethnic origin, but many first names have fallen by the wayside. Undaunted, McPhee assigns the name "Pat" to every second or third person. "Pat, you old cut-up," he says to Walt Hobbs, the butcher. He thrusts out a hand to Roger Theobold, the undertaker, saying, "Give me a stiff one, Pat." To Ted Borous, the watch repairman, McPhee says, "Hey, Pat, got a minute?" And so on down the line. When he comes to Nathan Weiss, men's clothing, he pauses only momentarily before asking gravely, "And how are you, Abe?"

Emerging from a gauntlet of businessmen, the candidate spots a red-jacketed bartender smiling engagingly behind a table laden with whiskey, gin, vodka, and beer. McPhee slaps the thigh of his lame leg, as if signaling a change of course, and makes a sharp right turn. "Oh no," Bonner says to himself and hurries forward. Ahead, McPhee reaches his goal, pauses with outstretched hand, but swerves to the left and undulates past the table. His torso, still bent to the right, sweeps low over the booze, and each bottle glows momentarily under a halo bestowed by his desire. He passes on, following his host to a podium at the front of the room.

Seeing this battle decisively won, Bonner stops and orders a drink himself. He greets several acquaintances, then turns to the podium where McPhee is being introduced. His wife Myrtle has appeared and stands beside him, a short, gray, uncertain woman. Across the hall Joe Miravich stands with folded arms against the wall, staying in the background. The union is not a popular institution with many of these businessmen; on the other hand, the audience is not violently anti-union, for these are retail merchants whose customers happen to be in large part mill workers. It is this fact, Bonner thinks, that accounts for the generally good turnout at this first event of the primary campaign.

"First off," McPhee says after a brief introduction, "I'm here to say you won't have to worry about this mayor driving business out. I don't care what you heard about me and the union. They support me but they don't own me. They want to keep this city strong, too, and that means proper care and feeding of retail business. If we need to raise taxes, it'll be on the mills and factories and not little guys like you. We're going to remove the ban on unions for city employees, but there'll be no forcing unions down the throat of private business."

McPhee continues: "Most of you know me as the fire commissioner. I can't fight fires no more, but I still ride to the big fires and haul hose, if I can get my leg to work. That's the kind of mayor I'll be, on the job every minute of the day and hauling hose. My platform is fight all fires, capture all burglars, plow the snow, pave the streets, build housing for the poor, raise the pay of cops and firemen, promote retail business, and keep the sewers flowing."

Scattered applause ripples through the hall. Bonner is beginning to be impressed. For all his years as a politician, McPhee never acquired the art of saying nothing in flowery language.

"And one more thing." McPhee raises a fist. "The illegal elements in this city will not be coddled and protected no longer."

Miravich gives out a shrill whistle. In the general audience, a wave of tepid applause starts in the back and moves to the front, coming to a halt as if on command as it washes up against a very large man in the front row. Louie Grotto, merchant of confections, all three hundred fifty pounds of him, turns halfway around to see who's clapping and who's not. McPhee also spots him and opens his fist with a finger pointing generally, but not too exactly, at Louie. "And I mean," he says with quavering voice, "all associates and relatives of said illegal operators."

The man who introduced McPhee steps back into the shadows, and Myrtle McPhee puts a hand to her mouth. Bonner can't see Louie Grotto's expression, but he guesses it's something like the hooded half-smile with which he scares little kids who try to filch gum drops from the jar on his candy counter. Bonner wonders how McPhee has remained healthy these many years. Perhaps because he was a hero and a cripple. But suppose he wins the primary. Grotto couldn't risk making a martyr of this gimpy old hero who wants to put numbers writers in jail, Bonner thinks, which means *they will not let him win the primary.*

When his battle of stares with Louie Grotto is over, McPhee says a few more words and ends on a brighter note. "Well, that's who I am, folks. I know this city backwards and forwards, and I want to do right, and I'm a fighter.

Everything you've heard about me is mostly true. Except—" He steps out from behind the podium, stretches out his bad leg, and raps on the thigh with his knuckles. "This limb is not hollow, like some say, and it don't contain booze."

All in all, not a bad performance, Bonner and Miravich agree after the meeting. If McPhee talked passionately about doing right, he did not come off as a foolish crusader. Louie Grotto may have been present to intimidate, but his bulky presence, perversely, was incontrovertible evidence that McPhee was tilting at something more substantial than windmills.

For the next week or two, Opposer McPhee looks like the front-runner in the Democratic mayoralty race. He bounds from event to event, putting the lie to rumors about his inexhaustible thirst, and making brief, to-the-point speeches. Urged by Bonner and Miravich to be prudent in his remarks, he avoids inflammatory phrases or names, such as "rackets kingpin Sal Grotto" or "fascist dictator Donnie Shoaf." Instead he emphasizes his knowledge of city government and his proposals for improving the services and protections it provides. Harley Pogue, meantime, is making vague speeches touting industrial progress, urging people to trust their mayor, and demanding the quick return of "our boys from the waning conflict abroad." He denounces McPhee as the candidate of a "narrow and spiteful interest group," and proclaims himself the rightful nominee of the "great Democratic Party of McKeesport."

At the beginning of the third week, money begins showing up in the campaign—all on Harley Pogue's side. Handbills with Pogue's portrait appear everywhere, reproducing themselves, it seems. Radio WMCK blares pro-Pogue commercials at station breaks throughout the day. While Miravich and his union boys stand for hours every day at plant gates, soliciting 50-cent contributions from workers, Democratic Party officials hire some of the same workers at $3 an evening to pass out leaflets door to door. McPhee is belittled, defamed, and scandalized. One leaflet carries a caricature of him with an upended whiskey bottle to his mouth, riding downriver on a huge turd. It takes only a few days for the political tide to run away from McPhee. Sensing defeat, he throws off all restraints and denounces Pogue for allowing his campaign to be financed by "racketeers."

On the night before the election, McPhee calls Bonner at home. "I'm sorry, Pete. I lost my temper. But maybe I got people to thinking what an evil, corrupt system we got here." Fumbling over a reply, Bonner can only think of this shriveled old man, standing as straight as possible and watching unflinching as a burning building topples over on him. On election day, in precincts where McPhee has always won his council seat by wide margins, voters are turned from the polls by men handing out coupons for free beers at saloons after the polls close. The turnout is extraordinarily light, with the public still mourning the death of FDR and celebrating the defeat of Nazi Germany. Pogue defeats McPhee by a nearly two-to-one vote.

■

It is a muggy day in mid-June. More than a month has passed since the election. Bonner is driving Mae to a beauty parlor on his way to work. She awoke this morning as usual with a fear of being late for an appointment. He would rather have her fear than his, that Sal Grotto will follow through on his threat to exact revenge. After the election, Bonner hired a private detective for a couple of weeks to watch the house at night—from a distance, so Mae wouldn't know. He felt great relief when school let out, and the boys went to a Boy Scout camp on Laurel Ridge for four weeks.

"You're cranky this morning," Mae says, studying him from the passenger seat. Are you still disturbed about the election?"

"You were right in the first place. I should never have gotten involved in politics."

"Of course not. But I understand. Tommy McPhee always was a sweet man, he just drank too much. I was impressed at that rally, though, when I heard him speak. Myrtle told me he really did quit drinking, mostly."

"Yeah, I was proud of Tommy." He pulls a Chesterfield out of a shirt pocket and lights it, holding the car on course with his chest pressed against the steering wheel. "It was probably a lost cause to begin with," he says, expelling smoke. "Money! It was like a cloudburst pouring down on that moron Harley Pogue."

"Money from where?" Mae asks.

"From the rackets." He turns down a street lined with overflowing trash containers. "Tommy is no Woodrow Wilson, but he's done everything in city government there is to do, except go on the take. And that's the only thing Harley *will* do."

Stopping in front of the beauty parlor, he leans over and kisses her cheek. "I could use some help at the office. Can you come down after you get your hair done?"

"Sure. I'll take a bus."

"Here." He hands her a five-dollar bill. "Take a cab. I love you."

He parks in front of his store, unlocks the outer and inner office doors, and slumps gratefully on his chair in front of a tall, whirring fan. He hears his men coming in through the back door, a half-dozen drivers and helpers, one or two at a time, but he doesn't look up. He begins arranging the route lists.

An hour later, he is alone again, all of his men out on trucks, making deliveries. His desk radio, tuned to KDKA, fills a temporary void in war news with Betty Grable softly crooning "I Can't Begin to Tell You." He has calmed down after discovering that a new helper, who checked in this morning, left the premises and never returned. The man was lazy and slow, and Bonner is better off without him. He opens his account book, erases a 20 in the payroll column and raises net profits by 20. Welcome back.

> So take the sweetest phrases
> The world has ever known
> And make believe I'm telling them to you.

His left elbow rests on the desk. His left hand, with a cigarette clamped between the first and second fingers, holds up his tilted head. With sudden inspiration, he jots down a figure, drops the pencil, holds his head with his right hand, takes a long drag on a cigarette and a sip of hot black coffee. Hearing the front door open, he finishes summing a column of figures and turns to the newcomer. Motorcycle Officer Rhino Rafferty fills the inner doorway, looking strangely agitated. He takes off his cap and tears open his shirt collar with both hands, popping a button which dribbles down his uniformed chest on a thread. His hair is matted, his shirt dark with damp, and large beads of moisture run down his florid cheeks, as if someone has doused him with water.

"My God, Rhino," Bonner says, concerned yet amused. "What's wrong?"

"The heat...I'm suffocating," Rafferty croaks in an unnaturally high voice. "Got to use your cooler."

"Well, no wonder. There must be ten pounds of leather in your jacket and those things on your legs. Take them off while I get you a cold bottle of beer." Bonner gets up.

"Nah, nah, no beer. But if I could just lie down in your cooler for a while."

Bonner holds back his laughter. Rhino Rafferty has been known to do some dumb things. "Well, sure, Rhino, if that'll make you feel better. I'll show you the way."

"Don't bother, don't bother," Rafferty blurts out. "I been there before."

"Go ahead. But don't fall asleep in there."

The big man walks bowlegged in his shiny black puttees, like chappied cowpokes in the movies. Bonner half expects to hear the jingle of spurs. He turns back to his calculations.

A few minutes later Rafferty comes back to the office carrying two large shopping bags filled with goods of some kind. When he deposits the bags on Bonner's desk, one of them makes a clinking sound.

"What's this?"

"Take a look," the officer says in an official voice.

Bonner looks in the bags. One is filled to the top with cartons of cigarettes, and the other contains bottles of whiskey. "Where'd these come from?"

"Right now they come from your cooler. Last night the cigarettes was stole from Marsh's Grocery. The name's on the bag. The booze was stole from the state liquor store next to Marsh's. And there are three more bags in the cooler." Officer Rafferty straightens his tie. "Pete Bonner, I place you under arrest on suspicion of receiving stolen goods."

To the police station for questioning. In a state of shock, Bonner denies all but can explain nothing. His lawyer, Howard Murmelstein, advises him to remain silent. The detectives shrug. They seem intent on getting him, and no one in this new generation of McKeesport cops will vouch for him. His old poker cronies retired years ago. Charges are filed, a felony. An arraignment date is set.

In the afternoon, back in his office, he receives a phone call. Sal Grotto. "Did you get our message, Pete? Any questions?"

"Sal!" he says despairingly.

"Look, I gave this due consideration, see. It wasn't just striking out in anger. One thing I've learned, people take punishment better when they know a rational mind is behind it. I like you, Pete, and maybe if it was totally in my hands…but other people got into it, see. Nasty people. I had to restrain them. But that's my role."

Grotto sneezes. "Summer cold coming on," he says. "I warned you, remember. You can't just go and elect any old somebody to run this city. There's a lot at stake here. For one thing, that person you call Mr. Buck, he's still got you and the coal miner on his shit list. He hates unions and businessmen who won't go along. He'd have finished the job long ago if it wasn't for your pal Sal."

Grotto sneezes again. "It was a joint effort for the good of the city. The plan came from me, the party of the first part. Got a pro to steal the goods, party of the second part. Mr. Buck, if you want to call him that, was party of the third part. You hired one of his industrial spies as a helper, and he stashed the goods in the cooler when no one was looking." (The no-good helper who disappeared this morning, Bonner thinks.) "And poor Rhino, we kept him in a car with the windows closed and the heater running on a hot day." Grotto continues, "Take my advice. It's an airtight case. No shyster can help you. But it's just a penny-ante felony, no more than six months to a year." He continues, "As for your pals, McPhee couldn't be elected to sweep up spit. Miravich was castrated by his own members in the primary. Anyway, another party has dibs on him."

Bonner clears his throat. "Listen, you sonofabitch, leave my wife and kids alone!"

"You mean you're angry?" Another sneeze ushers in a mood change. "You should've thought of them before you stuck your finger in the pie. I hate threats. But we honor women and children. Trust me."

■

Miravich calls and asks for a meeting. They rule out public places to avoid wagging tongues and settle on Bonner's Buick. At dusk Miravich slips into the passenger side of the car parked near the main gate of the Watts. A uniformed guard stands in a pool of light just inside the turnstile entrance. Pounding, throbbing noises resound inside the mill, causing a light to flicker above the large SAFETY FIRST sign with its scoreboard of lost-time accidents this year and last year. According to the figures, 1945 is a banner year for accidents.

"Another message from Mr. Buck?" Miravich asks.

"And others. Grotto, some bad cops, maybe Pogue. But I can't prove a thing."

"Mr. Buck! What's he want from us? All these years we never got a clue about who he is or where he is or what he is. I'm getting damn sick and tired of this!" He kicks the underside of the dashboard. A harness of electrical wiring falls out and dangles below the radio. "Sorry."

With his eyes still on Bonner, Miravich bends over and stuffs a handful of wiring back up the hole. "You know what I'm thinking? Maybe there is no Mr. Buck. Maybe they dreamed up this Mr. Buck to frighten us, keep us in line. The boogie-man."

"Who's 'they'?"

"I don't know. The company, the cops...officials...all officials everywhere. Everybody who wants to keep us in line."

"You should have left well enough alone, Joe. Tommie was contented doing what he was doing. Now look at him. Bitter, hurt, ridiculed, defeated... gave up his seat on Council... And for what?"

"For a damn good cause, that's for what." Miravich takes off his fedora, the one he began wearing after his election as local president, and slaps it on his thigh. "Leave well enough alone, huh? You mean keep your trap shut and let these politicians and robbers walk all over us. I did what was best for my members."

"'My members,'" Bonner says sarcastically. "The members don't mean anything to you, Joe. You don't love the men or the union. You love the power they give you. Order people around, call strikes, put your own mayor in office."

"Who stuck the wild hair up your ass, Mr. Beer Man? You, the patron saint of alcoholics. There's men walking around town drinking wood alcohol because of you. Getting rich is all you ever think about. If you went to church, the poorbox'd be raided every Sunday."

"I should have let those mine dicks plow you into the ground."

"Screw you, Bonner!" Miravich gets out of the car but leans back in the window. "How's Mae taking it?"

"How do you think she's taking it?"

"Tell her if she needs any help, call Mitzie or me."

CHAPTER 4:
August 1945–November 1945

Bonner's trial opens three days after Hiroshima goes up in smoke, a cloud of "boiling dust" rising to forty thousand feet over the destroyed city. Any interest on the part of judge and jury in Bonner's fate ebbs faster than an outrushing flood tide. Their minds have fled to other dimensions, other universes. It is, after all, one of the most eventful weeks in recorded history.

On the first morning of the trial, the prosecution presents its star witness, Officer Rhino Rafferty, who testifies to his discovery of the stolen goods in Bonner's possession. He appears in civilian dress, having been promoted to detective. Rhino the detective! Charlie Pritchard, sitting in the audience, is heard to quip, "Every day when he finishes work he calls his wife and says, 'Hide something, honey, I'm coming home.'"

Store owners identify the goods as having been stolen from their premises. The district attorney suggests that Bonner has been trafficking in the black market and presents evidence that he once purchased meat without the required ration stamps, indicating a pattern of criminality. This makes an impression on the jurors, patriots all and sticklers for honesty in their own use of blue stamps, red stamps, and windshield stickers.

The judge adjourns the trial until Friday. When it resumes, everybody is talking about the dropping of another atom bomb yesterday, this one on Nagasaki. Not only has a second Japanese city been obliterated, but Russia has declared war against Japan. The end of hostilities seems imminent. The judge denies a defense motion to dismiss charges and orders a rush to judgment against this presumed black market profiteer.

Attorney Murmelstein does his best against great odds. The key figure in the plot against Bonner, the man who planted the goods, cannot be found. Bonner will not allow Murmelstein to call any other of his employees to the stand and grill them as possible suspects. He has no defense on grounds of unreasonable search and seizure because he freely granted Officer Rafferty access to the cooler. Murmelstein cannot present an alternate theory of the case involving Bonner's frameup because no sane person would testify against Sal Grotto, with the exception, of course, of Opposer McPhee, who cannot testify of his own knowledge that Grotto was involved in such a plot.

In desperation, Murmelstein stages a parade of character witnesses including Stowe, Crabtree, McPhee, an ancient Episcopalian minister who baptized Bonner, and the director of the McKeesport Boys Club of which Bonner is a trustee. But the lawyer rejects Miravich's offer to put in a good word. The last thing Bonner needs, Murmelstein says, is testimony by a man whom the prosecutor would portray as a radical unionist.

A saintly portrait of Bonner emerges, though in cross-examination the D.A. elicits damaging testimony from the three close friends. Bonner, they grudgingly admit, trafficked in booze during the twenties. "In other words," says the triumphant D.A., bending close to McPhee in the witness box, "this good, kind, generous man, this outstanding citizen..." he points to the defendant, "...this Albert P. Bonner who sits there so innocently today, was nothing more than a common bootlegger a few years ago?"

"No, not like that," McPhee cries. "No gang stuff and no rough stuff. Pete Bonner was a nice bootlegger."

It being late afternoon, the judge decides to delay closing statements until Monday morning. On Saturday, Bonner's home deliveries and saloon sales set a record: everyone is laying in beer for an end-of-war celebration. On Sunday, Bonner plays ball with his sons at Shoaf Field. Still able to smack the pill, he chops downward with the bat so as not to send the ball too high or too far.

"That's a dumb way to bat," Paul observes. "Is that how they played baseball way back when?"

"C'mon, Dad," Albert says. "Paul Waner didn't bat like that."

The boys pound their gloves, kick the dirt. Dad isn't all they thought him to be.

"Okay," he says, "just once." He hitches his trousers, spits on his hands, and takes up the bat. "Give it to me high and fast," he tells Albert who can deliver occasional hard pitches over the plate. Bonner misses once, misses again, then whacks the ball a quarter-mile high. It soars into the trees, slashes through a patch of woods, flies out the other side, and disappears into Kingdom Come. Bonner trots to first base and back. The boys' heads are still swiveling, following the path of the ball, as leaves and limbs rain down.

The case goes to the jury at noon on Monday. After an hour of deliberation, the jurors file back into the courtroom. Bonner's hopes rise. They must see through the D.A.'s distortions and, besides, the war is almost over. What jury could convict on such a happy occasion? He turns to show a smile of confidence to all his friends in the courtroom. His eyes rove from Mae to McPhee to various relatives in the first row and thence, in the second row, from Stowe to Crabtree to...but wait! In the space between Stowe and Crabtree there appears the elephantine head of a man leaning forward from his third row bench. It is the face, Bonner notes with surprise, of Somebody Grubmann, the ardent representative of some trade association. Why, wonders Bonner, as the judge speaks to the foreman, why would Grubmann take an interest in this two-bit trial?

Murmelstein is tugging on his sleeve, telling him to rise and be judged for an act he did not commit. It takes only a moment: Guilty!

"Ohhhh!" gasps the courtroom. The jurors, having judged him falsely, like the faceless horde that streams through Bonner's dreams, file out a rear door. He turns, seeking Mae's shattered face, and sees Grubmann bolt from the courtroom in the company of a jubilant Rhino Rafferty.

Murmelstein asks for a suspended sentence, citing Bonner's contributions to society. The prosecutor demands that he be put away for two years. Six months in Western Penitentiary, declares the judge, with possible probation in three, and "may God cleanse your soul of the stink of profiteering and black-marketing in the midst of war."

Bonner feels a strange coldness in his chest, as if a refrigerating unit just kicked on. He sees that Mae has turned pale and is wobbly in the knees. "Mae, darling. I'm so sorry..." He holds out his hands to her. She straightens and looks at him with the biggest, softest eyes he's ever seen.

Murmelstein gets him out on bond and files an appeal.

■

He awakens one morning and rolls over to kiss his sleeping beauty. Today he must tell her. Murmelstein's appeals are still pending, but there is no hope. Her pillow is damp. She has not wept in public or at home in front of him or their sons. Instead she is a firm presence of cheer and hope—until the dark of night when, privately, quietly, Mae Bonner sobs against her pillow.

"Are you awake?" he says.

"Barely. Is it dawn?"

"Not yet. A few minutes."

She turns over and faces him, hair splashing over the pillow. "Wasn't that a movie? 'Hold Back the Dawn?' If there are no more dawns, you won't go away."

"That's just it," he says propping his head on an elbow. "I am going away, Mae."

A tremor runs across her chin. She brings it under control, sniffs, and grits her teeth. "I'd like to kill that man Grotto. If I ever see him."

"If you ever see him, turn around and walk away. But now, we've got to face up to it. Howard says he'll appeal, but it's hopeless. If I'm careful and lucky, maybe I can get out in three months." He pauses, then says, "We have to talk about running the business while I'm...away."

"We'll hire a manager."

"No, Mae. I want you to run the business."

She sits up in alarm. "Pete, that's crazy, you can't mean it. You know I can't run a business. You know I go to pieces over important decisions."

"You go to pieces, darling, over unimportant things, like being late for your permanent, like children making noise, like me going over the speed limit on an empty highway. But when the sky is falling on us, you always pull yourself together. In a crisis Mae Bonner is a strong woman."

"I don't believe it," she says, even as she begins to wonder if it is true. "What did I ever do right in a crisis?"

"You didn't fall apart when I was on the road so much in the Depression. When they wanted to repossess our furniture, you kept removing the sheriff's sign so the moving men couldn't find our house. Remember when Albert came home crying because a kid told him that babies come from men sticking their thing into women?"

"He couldn't figure out where it went."

"And it was you who drew the pictures and explained it to him."

"Only because you wouldn't."

"Well...I just couldn't. By the way, have you talked to Paul yet?"

"Three years ago." A resigned sigh. "He knew so much already! He seems to travel in a faster crowd than Albert."

"It's the war. Rumors travel faster in wartime. But you see what I mean? You already know a lot about the business. You know how to order, map out the routes, take inventory, keep the books."

"But there's so much I don't know. Like guessing how much people will drink next week, or deciding whether a truck needs new tires or a new...gear shift."

"You'll pick it up. You're a smart woman, Mae. And you'll be able to write to me and visit now and then."

"Why not hire somebody?"

"Who can I trust? You bring in an outsider, you never know who he's connected to." He doesn't mention the most important reason, that keeping busy will help her get through the ordeal. "So, is it settled?"

"I guess so," she says tentatively. "I just wish—"

"Wish what?"

"That it wasn't beer. Managing a beer business was not in my upbringing."

■

"We laughed and joked...after I stopped crying, of course," Mae says on the telephone, describing her first visit to Pete in prison. "He's in wonderful spirits. I couldn't believe it. And he looks good. He's losing weight, and there's color in his face, not that sickly pallor he had before going away."

"I'll tell people he went away for his health," says her tart-tongued sister Irene.

"He works in the library," Mae continues, "and reads five newspapers every day, which is very good because he always liked the news. He's begun teaching a course in bookkeeping. Oh, and listen to this—he even goes to chapel on Sunday!"

"A truly inspirational experience."

"Irene!" Mae scolds her for the record. Off the record, she doesn't mind Irene's biting sarcasm and, in fact, finds it a useful antidote to her own unrealistic enthusiasms. Talking to Irene also reminds Mae that her travails are nothing when compared with her sister's miserable life.

"What kind of accommodations...what is his cell like?" Irene asks.

"Small and cramped, he says. But his roommate isn't a hardened criminal like a bank robber, thank goodness. His name is Bob, Sewickley Bob..." Mae can't suppress a giggle, "...because he owns a used car lot in Sewickley. He got into trouble with the OPA because of his rubber business."

"They're sold on the black market, too?"

"No, no. Rubber products, I mean, like tires. Stolen tires. Of course, he's always trying to sell something. There's a black market in there, too, you know. But at least Bob isn't the violent type."

There is an awkward silence, then a caught sob.

"Are you still there?"

"Oh, Irene, it's all so horrible! They make you pour out your purse, and the guards with their filthy fingernails sort through it. The way they look at you—everyone is a criminal. The windows in the visitors' room are streaked with dirt, and that awful clanging noise always echoing in the background, like the mill. Everything is so dreary and...prisonlike. I can't stand him being there."

"Now, Mae, honey, you knew it would be like that."

"Like that, but not like...*that*." Through sobs and sniffles she adds, "I feel so alone. I don't think I can take it for even three months, and if they keep him longer…"

"If he can take it, you can. Stop feeling sorry for yourself. You have your family. You have your friends. Three months of hell is nothing. Ask me, I know."

Feelings of self-pity turn into feelings of guilt. She hadn't meant to imply that the Bonner and Dempsey families have deserted her. On the contrary, they have responded with an avalanche of phone calls, flowers, and gifts. Food is the leading item—chickens, sausages, meat loaves, puddings, pies, and even extra food ration stamps. The message seems to be that full stomachs will override aching hearts. Mae's mother and her mother-in-law vie for the right to come and live with her and look out for the boys. Friends are another thing. Many have stuck with her but some pretend she no longer exists.

"Do you miss it, Mae?" Irene asks.

"Do I miss what?"

"You know, doing the rhumba."

"For heaven's sake, Irene!"

Of course she misses it.

■

Mae never learned to drive and her older son, Albert, unfortunately, is too young to get a driver's license. So the Buick sits rusting in the Bonners' garage. Before he went…away, Pete arranged for Crash Tatum, his lead driver, to drive Mae to and from the office every day. Since Crash doesn't own a car, he uses the truck that he drives on his route. Crash is fortyish and paunchy. He has puffy cheeks from years of chewing tobacco, first one side then the other. On the first trip, every quarter mile or so, he opens the window and shoots a spray of chawed mash through a gap between two front teeth. Mae closes her eyes and prays. Sensing her irritation that first time, on all subsequent trips he saves it up. When she gets out of the truck, she hears him giving one huge spit on the other side. Tatum is courteous and works hard, but Mae quickly learns that they call him "Crash" because he unfailingly smashes into the loading platform when backing up. After a few of these occurrences, she asks him to pull into the warehouse garage instead of backing in.

Mae recites the Rosary daily instead of once a week, dedicating the prayers to Pete's well-being. She never has expected dramatic results from prayers, knowing that God will respond, if He has a mind to, in His Own way and in His Own time. She notices that Albert and Paul seem to pray more. The intensity of their faith, of course, is diluted by a universe of sensory experiences, undoubtedly including thoughts of girls. Both have been in a state of shock since the trial. They walk around with their lips parted, eyes staring blankly ahead. Occasionally at night Mae hears one or the other crying behind closed doors, just as they must hear her crying early in the morning.

Mitzie Miravich calls and says she would like to bring her baby and visit Mae some Sunday. "What a nice idea," Mae says and sets the date. She liked Mitzie when they first met at a campaign rally for Tommie McPhee. Such a bright-eyed and polite girl, radiating a sense of good taste about her appearance (the simple, honest, few-frills look, light on the rouge and mascara, medium emphasis on the bosom) and good judgment about things in general. All told, perhaps a level or two higher than Joe Miravich, given his peculiarities, might have expected. Looking forward to a pleasant Sunday afternoon chat, Mae considers the advice she can give the young mill wife about bringing up baby, making do on a limited budget, and not buying on credit.

Mitzie arrives with her infant daughter bundled up in a blue winter suit and blue blankets. "I let all the men relatives down by delivering a girl," she says. "Blue helps a little, I think. It's odd. They all hate the mill and say their sons will go to college. But you know what'll happen? Their sons will go into the mill. It's too easy, the money's too good. Well, not my Dolly, not like me, not even if there's another war."

"Dolly! What a cute name."

Mitzie wipes nonexistent hair out of the infant's eyes. "Thank you, Mrs. Bonner. We named her Dorothy so we could call her Dolly."

Unexpectedly Mae finds herself saying, "Please, call me 'Mae.'" Although Pete was railroaded to jail, his being there for whatever reason has made her acutely aware of the arbitrariness of social distinctions. Pete would be pleased with her display of tolerance.

"Okay, Mae. That's how I feel about you anyway."

Hearing herself addressed that way is a bit jarring. "What do you mean... Mitzie?"

"Joe always said you were sort of forbidding, sort of remote. The way you dress, the way you carry yourself. It's obvious you have standards. But I felt from the first time I met you that down inside you weren't stuck up at all. You're just Mae Bonner, a simple lady, good at heart, but very shy."

Mae is aghast. No one with Polish parentage and a Croatian husband has ever spoken to her so directly. "Is Dolly talking yet?" she asks foolishly, changing the subject.

"At the age of three months? What a compliment!" Mitzie smiles and rocks the child. "Would you like to hold her?" She carries the bundle to Mae.

"Of course." Mae holds the baby at elbow length, as if it were a carton of eggs. Tiny red face, blue eyes establishing Mae's fuzzy shape, hands grasping at air. Gradually the infant's hypnotic blank stare draws Mae closer and closer. Now the baby is in the crotch of her arm. She gently squeezes it and pretends to bore in with her nose and makes babyish sounds.

Mitzie talks a little about her life. Joe is conscientious about his job and works long hours. Mitzie has enrolled in night school at Pitt and goes to the city by streetcar twice a week. Her father watches the child if Joe is working.

"Night school?" Mae says. "I never heard of women going to night school."

"That's what Joe said. And the men in the admissions office at Pitt, too." She laughs. "It was a struggle to get in. I just want to learn more. Some day I'll get a degree and maybe teach like my mother."

Mae says, "I taught first grade in Catholic school when all you needed was a high school diploma."

"Same as my mother. But she always said I should be the first in the family to go to college. I don't like just sitting at home, reading *Redbook*." She sees Mae's eyes swerve to the coffee table where a copy of *Redbook* lay. "Oh, that was stupid. I didn't mean to be patronizing, Mae."

"No, no!" Mae says, waving her hand. "I didn't take it...patronizingly... Mitzie." She stares at the baby, and her eyes feel like the baby's look, sort of glazed over.

"*Redbook* has a lot of helpful stuff about bringing up children and so forth. But women can do other things. Like you, Mae?"

"Like me?" She looks up with alarm.

"Sure, you run a business. I can't tell you how much I admire you. Not many women would even try to walk in their husband's shoes."

"Well," Mae says, at once blushing and laughing, "right now I feel like I'm swimming in them."

■

Swimming is not quite the word for it. By the middle of December, under Mae's stewardship, Bonner Beers is barely treading water. Sales have fallen.

Some tavern customers have defected to other distributors. Men dislike doing business with her; she can tell from their voices. "I wish Pete was still around," they say, or "If Pete was there...." The employees grumble about working for a woman. Some have quit. She is indecisive and, when occasionally decisive, ineffective. Her work day is a dawn-to-dusk horror of men demanding and Mae not delivering. "Put the boss on, honey," male strangers say when she answers the phone. When she tries to explain there is no male of final resort, the men callers become outraged. "Whaddya mean no man?" Even women callers want a man. She understands. She apologizes. On occasion she even begs forgiveness. She herself wants a man. How can a woman survive without a man? If she were a man she would kill the men who took her man away.

One blisteringly cold day, a week before Christmas, she has a particularly grueling time. No sooner does she open the office than the telephone brings more aggravation. Connie Mulckey of Mulckey's Tavern orders a keg of premium Rolling Rock to be delivered by eleven o'clock for a "luncheon gathering" in his back room. Mulckey is one of Pete's oldest and best customers. Mae gets on the squawk box and sends men scurrying to the cooler. But there is no premium Rolling Rock in storage, just a keg of regular Rolling Rock, brewed from ordinary mountain spring water, not the premium mountain spring water that gives premium Rolling Rock its lilt and elegance.

Mae checks with other distributors in town. They deny having a spare keg of premium Rolling Rock to sell to her. But incidentally, they ask, which of Bonner's customers wants it? Mae knows enough not to tell them.

"Well, cripes!" Mulckey says, when she calls him back. "I've given you my business for five years, and you can't get me a lousy keg of beer?"

"Mr. Mulckey, you needn't curse at me. I'll keep trying."

"If Pete was around, he'd find a way to get it. If I don't hear from you in half an hour, I go to a guy who can get it—and maybe I stay with him, too."

Mae hangs up and leans over the desk, head in her hands. What to do? Pete would be extremely unhappy if she lost Mulckey's business. There's not enough time to send a truck to the brewery. She sees Crash staring through the glass partition, his right cheek bulging, lips pursed, sadly shaking his head, undoubtedly thinking that Pete would know what to do. What would Pete do? Her mind is a blank. "Damn you, Pete," she mutters. "Why did you have to go away?"

She pulls herself together and with a sudden burst of resolve steps to the doorway. Crash and two other men stand there. "All right," she says, "how can you tell the difference between premium Rolling Rock and regular?" As far as she knows, a keg of beer is a keg of beer.

"With Rolling Rock," says a helper, "premium has a red bung and regular don't." His eyes say, 'Everybody knows that.'

"A red bung? Red cork, right?" Mae thinks a moment, then grubs in her purse.

She marches to the cooler, trailed by a column of men. Crash leaps forward and opens the door for her. Two others pull down the keg of Rolling Rock.

"Stand it up with the cork on top." It is a regular, cork-colored bung. She unscrews the lid on a bottle of fingernail polish and paints the bung red. "Premium Rolling Rock," she declares. "As soon as it dries, take it to Mulckey's."

At night Mae prays for forgiveness and vows to send Mulckey a keg of real premium the next time he orders regular.

PART 4: 1948–1950

CHAPTER 1:
May 1948–June 1948

For the first two hours of the drive, the passengers alternately doze and take in sights going east on the Pennsylvania Turnpike. Miravich and four committeemen from the Watts local are traveling on the cheap in Rudy Semchek's 1940 Dodge, heading for Boston to attend the Steelworkers' 1948 convention. Compared with slipsliding through the narrow streets of the valley, driving across the turnpike feels like racing downhill, slowing only to crawl through tunnels burrowing under forested ridges.

Miravich nods off and awakens to a political dispute in the back seat. Red Terhune is complaining about a resolution adopted by the Watts local, commending Phil Murray's "courageous" stand on the Taft-Hartley Act. Sure, Terhune says, the new law is anti-labor, especially the ban on secondary boycotts and so forth. But there's not a damn thing wrong with the part that requires union officers to sign a non-communist affidavit. Phil Murray shouldn't be challenging the provision in court, and the Watts local sure as hell should not be supporting him.

The more he talks, the angrier he gets, which is usually the case with Terhune, who can incite himself far easier than any demagogue. "Damn you, Joe!" he says, addressing Miravich in the front seat. "The local should of kept out of that mess. But you pushed it through, and now everybody's asking, 'Are you guys commies?'"

Miravich twists to face him. "So what? I know who and what I am. Don't you, Red?"

"Bullshit, Joe! I've had it with this commie stuff."

The atmosphere in the car has changed. The other three men—Semchek, Fran Luptak, and Len Mrvos—study the passing scenery. Terhune is a red-headed barrel of a man, a good unionist, a loving father, a generous friend—but a man in whom resentments unceasingly burn. If you could open him up, Miravich thinks, you'd find liquid anger coursing through his veins, fueling the flames of perpetual devotion to hotheadedness. He's the last remaining of the old Irish bloc who defected to Miravich's Unity Team in 1944. All the others have slipped away and joined a steadily-growing faction that opposes Miravich. Recently Red has been acting standoffish, as if he wants to pull out but needs a good issue to ride away on. The communist issue, already splitting the labor movement, is as convenient as any.

"It's the principle of the thing," Miravich says. "Why should Murray have to swear what we believe or don't believe? Murray's already fired a bunch of communist organizers and he forced Lee Pressman to resign. Commie or no commie, a helluva good general counsel."

"If Murray's half the good Catholic he pretends to be, he'll sign the stupid paper and get it over with."

"So that's where this is coming from. You must have gone to Mass last Sunday?"

"The Pope says communism is Godless and a mortal sin, and I believe it. You always was a little crazy, Joe. I don't know what you might of been or done before—"

"Hey, lay off that stuff, Red." Len Mrvos thrusts his puny elbow into the big man's ribs.

"According to the Pope and the priests, to be a good Catholic you got to name names and betray your friends," Miravich says acidly. "Some religion that is. Even pro-union priests like Father Rice up in Pittsburgh are taking this line."

"Who?" says Semchek.

"Charles Owen Rice. He writes pro-labor columns in the *Pittsburgh Catholic* and shows up on picket lines. He and Murray are real close. But he's loaded a ten-ton cross on Murray's back with this Red-baiting."

Fran Luptak, the learned local grievance chairman, adds information. "Rice belongs to a national association of priests against commies in unions. Father Strunka is part of it, too."

"Well, shit," Terhune says, raising his voice, "what's Miravich holding out against his own priest for?"

"A Catholic doesn't sign away his right to have opinions," Miravich says. " He cranes his neck over the back of the seat. "So put that in your Pope and smoke it!"

Semchek stamps on the brake pedal, throwing everybody forward. He pulls onto the road shoulder. Honking cars whiz by. "Listen, you two, this car isn't a meeting hall. Save it up for the convention."

Terhune's face glows, but he lowers his quavering voice. "I was a committeeman in this local," he says to Miravich, "when you was shoveling scrap in the hole. I almost got myself thrown out of the union for helping you organize that strike in forty-three. Four times now I've backed you for president. For four years I've went along with your crazy stuff, my friends calling me 'hunky-lover,' and now the priests're climbing on my back. The ball don't bounce no further, Joe." He folds his arms and settles back in his corner.

Semchek pulls back onto the highway. A heavy silence fills the car. Everyone knows that Terhune has sung his swan song. The last Irishman.

■

The Watts delegates emerge from a subway station next to Symphony Hall in the South End section of Boston. They inhale deeply, glad to be rid of the stink of brine and rotting fish that permeates their cheap harborside hotel. Catty-corner across the street, hundreds of union members are surging up the steps of Mechanics Hall to attend the second day of proceedings at the Steelworkers convention. Already in an ugly mood about charges of communism being hurled at the union, the delegates are none too polite as they split left and right around a man in a commissar cap on the top step, holding aloft a copy of *The Worker*, with a headline: "MURRAY SELLS OUT." Red Terhune rams his shoulder into the vendor, and papers fly in all directions. Semcheck bends to pick one up. Miravich pulls him back. "You want to get killed, Rudy?"

Entering a Steelworkers' convention is like walking down the aisle at Sunday morning Mass—which is not surprising, Miravich thinks, since Phil Murray has modeled the union on the Church. The delegates take off their hats and shuffle quietly to seats in the nave, while up on the stage, or altar, Murray and his aides make preparations for the services. At his insistence, all delegates wear a suit and tie; no open-necked shirts or raffish sports jackets. The delegates sit at long tables, grouped by union district. Terhune takes a seat at the far end of Miravich's table, among five other former members of the Unity Team, who comprised a second carload of delegates from the Watts. So now it's official: Terhune has gone over to the anti-Miravich faction.

Up on the stage, on either side of the podium, a dozen or so union staff men—corresponding to the concelebrants at a High Mass—sit at tables that extend to the wings of the stage. Behind them are rows of honorable clergy, distinguished guests, and district directors of the Steelworkers—visiting cardinals and bishops, so to speak. Pope Murray now steps to the podium and raps the delegates to order. He gazes out on a spectacle that evokes an illusion of enormous power. Drawn up before him are rank upon rank of steelworkers, nearly three thousand delegates. It is said to be the largest labor convention ever held in America. Huge banners proclaiming the union's economic goals festoon the walls: "GUARANTEED ANNUAL WAGE...SHORTER WORK WEEK...A LIVING PENSION...SOCIAL INSURANCE." The visitors' gallery in the balcony is jammed with the wives of delegates, foreign unionists, government officials, clergymen, and even company negotiators.

Murray makes a few announcements, and gives the podium over to a committee chairman, who commences reading, in a sing-song voice, a long, inconsequential resolution. The president, meanwhile, paces back and forth behind the podium. Aides scurry off left and right, like altar boys who have forgotten to set out wine and water.

"Murray looks like he's worried," Semchek whispers to Miravich.

"You'd be, too, if you were caught in the middle like him," Miravich says. On one side, anti-communist unionists and priests like Father Rice are demanding that he purge the CIO of communists. On the other side, powerful communist factions in some unions are supporting the former vice-president Henry Wallace for President. Wallace is hugely popular on the left, Miravich says, and a big vote for him would split support for Truman and give the '48 election to the Republicans. "The question today is, which side will Murray come down on at this convention."

By the time Miravich finishes the lesson the convention has disposed of early business. Guest speakers now lash out at Wallace and his supporters, whipping the delegates into an anti-communist frenzy—well-timed for the introduction of a resolution repudiating Wallace's Third Party. Returning to the podium, Murray calls for a floor debate. Dozens of members scramble into aisles and line up behind microphones, hoping to get their voice and name on record. Murray moves from mike to mike, recognizing speakers, patiently listening to their attacks on antiunion tormenters at the forefront of the communist hysteria, cutting short speakers who exceed the five-minute time limit.

By the time Miravich gets his turn at a mike, he feels, like his pap always used to call him, contrary. He pulls the mike to his face. "Joe Miravich, Watts Works, McKeesport," he growls with a booming hiss, standing too close to the mouthpiece. "If you people think we are doing ourselves proud here this day with all this intimidation, well, you better think again. Maybe it feels good to ram one up Stalin's ass, but who's ramming one up our own? The business interests and right-wing politicians, they got us hanging upside down with a enema hose between our legs."

Murray interrupts him. "The delegate is off the resolution."

Shouts of "Sit down!"

Miravich feels he is sliding back into his old self: radical, wise-cracking, hunky Joe-miner. He tries to stop the slide, but cries of "commie lover" have put him on a greased chute to perdition. He shoots back at Murray, "Maybe off the resolution, brother chairman, but not off the topic. There's more'n one way to diddle a pig. I'm no big fan of the Third Party, but we should condemn all the politicians, including Truman. John L. Lewis is right. The sooner we get ourselves out of the politicians' pockets, the better off we'll be."

Murray raps once with his gavel. "The delegate seems to have wandered into the wrong convention. This is the United Steelworkers of America." A deep rumble of applause lets Murray know that he's the boss now instead of old curmudgeon Lewis.

A shrill voice yells, "Send this jerk back to the pits, Phil!"

The chairman gazes down at Miravich. "If you're testing my patience, brother, believe me, it has limits."

"No, no, brother chairman. I rise to applaud you for not signing the damned affidavit. But I say the international ought to let some of its power seep out of Pittsburgh and out into the locals where we have to deal with these dictatorial plant managers..."

BAM! BAM! goes the gavel. "The delegate from McKeesport is out of order. Sit down, brother!" Twenty-five hundred Red Terhunes roar assent.

The mike goes dead in Miravich's hands. He returns to his seat to incredulous stares from Semchek and Mrvos. Luptak says with a grin, "What're all these ways of diddling a pig?"

A few minutes later, Murray calls for a voice vote on the resolution, first those in favor. "Ayes" resound in a roar that reverberates from wall to wall. Some dozens of spirited "no's" respond on the negative side, and Murray declares the resolution adopted.

Semchek whispers in Miravich's ear, "If there are so many Reds here, where were they on the vote?"

"Being a radical is dangerous to your health in this gathering," Miravich says.

The convention moves on to other matters. At lunchtime, Miravich and his pals push through a crush of people at the rear of the hall and emerge into bright sunlight. Most delegates have left the area to eat at restaurants and bars, but a few dozen lounge about in front of the hall. On the steps stands Father Miroslav Strunka, holding a hot dog with mustard drooling around the edges and talking animatedly with a sharp-faced man overdressed in a belted camels-hair overcoat. As Miravich approaches, the stranger gives him a cold, appraising stare before moving away.

"That was some speech, Joe," Strunka says, finally taking a bite of his hot dog. "But," he adds, chewing and studying his parishioner, "I didn't fully understand its import."

"Thanks, Father," Miravich says, watching the stranger disappear into the hall.

Strunka licks mustard off the bun, keeping his hard brown eyes glued on Miravich's face. "So what did that mean, Joe? Intimidation? Who's intimidating who?"

"Ah, well, you know, Father...you rile up three thousand delegates and someone might get hurt." Miravich suddenly points to the crowd milling below. "Look, roasted peanuts. C'mon, guys. See you in church, Father."

Next morning, Boston newspapers report that police last evening found a delegate named David Migas, an admitted Communist Party member, lying beaten and bloody in a gutter outside Mechanics Hall.

■

In the six days Miravich has been away, everyone seems to have changed, either grown or shriveled or aged or taken a new name or gotten a new job. As he and the boys drove into the valley, bodies stiff from twelve hours on the road, an odor of coal smoke rose to greet them, carrying with it a faint smell of fish—impossible, of course, because fish had vanished from the lower Monongahela fifty years ago. All said they smelled it, even Red Terhune who hadn't spoken a word the entire trip except to demand a relief stop at Breezewood. Fran Luptak stated his theory: "A mild form of group hysteria. We carry powerful sensations back from Boston which, as they collide with the home atmosphere..."

Still later, at home, he and Mitzie have a rollicking good ride. "You didn't forget how," she says, regarding him from above.

"I've only been gone six days, Mitz. Are you saying we don't get enough practice?"

"You've been away a lot."

It is true. Union business takes a lot of time. "Can we talk later?" he says. "I should concentrate on what I'm doing." It is then that he notices her black hair no longer brushes her shoulders but hangs an inch or two shorter. Strange, he thinks. But his attention is diverted to a single bead of sweat glistening on the tip of her nose. Its sweet taste and the faint scent of a refined soap drive him to exquisite exertions.

First up in the morning, he goes downstairs to put the coffee on. Stosh already sits at the kitchen table, his ancient pot rattling over a high flame. He greets his son-in-law with a growl and nod that are akin to friendliness compared with his attitude when Miravich started courting his daughter. The old grouch began softening up when the Miraviches moved into his home at his invitation. When Mitzie got a job in Pittsburgh, her father, although he disapproved of Mitzie's working, urged them to move in with him, paying the same rent they paid for their two-room apartment. He would watch over Dolly during the day. He was still fit and able, and he remembered from his youth in Poland how to care for calves and kittens.

Miravich said, "Listen, old man, we didn't bring her into the world to be your liquor-drinking companion."

"Whiskey I quit long time'go," he said. And this is true. Now he drinks peach brandy, and only after dinner.

It would have been impossible to find a more devoted and patient baby-sitter. After a few weeks, he announced another change of some magnitude. He was tired of being called "Stosh," a nickname that he despised. He never complained about it before, thinking it was some kind of rule in America, all Polish immigrants named "Stanley" automatically became "Stosh." Now he wants to be called "Dad," his first step on the road to becoming not merely a Pole in America but a Polish-American.

When Dolly appears this morning, wrapped in a pink robe and still rubbing dreams from her eyes, Miravich gathers her up and covers her with kisses. She is strangely unreceptive and reaches out for "Pap-Pap." She is only six days older, and still only two-and-a-half, but in her father's absence she has begun sitting at the kitchen table without a dictionary under her bottom. Her little wrist curves around a spoon half-submerged in a bowl of Cream of Wheat, and she stirs. Stir, stir, stir. With her eyes barely above the rim of the bowl, she watches circles form and disappear on the surface of the cereal.

"Dolly," her father says, gently, reprovingly. "Eat your cereal, Dolly."

She goes on stirring, ignoring him.

"Dolly!"

She grips the spoon in both hands and grinds it round and round, staring fixedly into the cereal, working as if possessed. Mush sloshes over the bowl.

"Dolly, I'm talking to you." Ordinarily he is amused when she shows her female ornery streak. Today she is carrying it too far. He looks at Stanley to see if the old man is egging her on.

"She don't remember you, you been gone so long," Stanley says. He gnaws on a heel of black bread and sips black coffee. White hair sticks out at all angles from his head. "Where you been?"

"You know where I've been. The union convention."

"Union, sh—!" Stanley exclaims, silently mouthing the second word in deference to the child.

Mitzie enters the kitchen, high-heeled pumps attacking the linoleum floor. "What's all the commotion down here? "She wears a blue suit with a white blouse clasped at the neck, primly secretarial.

"You got your days mixed up," Miravich says. "It's Saturday."

"I'm working today. If you'll give me a ride, I'll explain in the car." Snatching a dish rag from the sink top, Mitzie wipes off her daughter's hands and lifts her off the chair. "You'd think two grown men could control one child."

"She's as stubborn as her mom," Miravich says. "You can't do nothing with stubborn women." Dolly finally looks directly at him from over her mother's shoulder. Withering. "Okay," he says, "I'm sorry for going away. I'll make it up to you, honey."

Mitzie kisses her and puts her down. "Be good today for Pap-Pap. Take a nap when he tells you."

Dolly derisively jerks one tiny pigtail and runs out of the room.

Stanley goes into a Polish tirade, ending with, "Union, shit!"

"As eloquent as the day I first met him," Miravich says, as he and Mitzie go out to the car. "What'd he say in foreign?"

"His daughter should stay home and take care of her family, and her husband is a jerk for not making her." She gives him a lewd smile.

Their first car is a red 1947 Ford coupe, $200 down and twelve months left to pay. Miravich edges out the choke and starts the engine.

Mitzie says, "I'm not going to the train depot. While you were gone, I got a new job, here in the city."

"What?" He almost drives into a parked car. They are gliding down the hill between rows of frame houses with awning-shaded porches and shallow strips of grass called "front yards." A half-mile ahead at the bottom of the hill lies the Watts Works, already swimming in waves of heat. "Why didn't you tell me? We should of talked about it."

"The night you called, it sounded like you had enough trouble at the convention. Anyway, it was an easy decision." Mitzie turns the car mirror and inspects her face. She dislikes lipstick but wears a pale shade because only old women in babushkas go downtown without wearing makeup. Some say there's an ordinance to that effect.

"The best thing is," she continues, "no more train rides to and from Pittsburgh."

"Grass doesn't grow under your feet, does it, Mitz?"

Miravich has found it hard keep up with his wife. After Dolly's birth, she attended night school at Pitt for a year, then took a clerical job in a corporate office. When her boss began making advances, she abruptly quit. Miravich found out about this after the fact. Mitzie hadn't wanted him to know, guessing that he would beat up the boss and land in jail. She next went to the phone company and worked for a couple of months as a switchboard operator. Hating the regimentation, she argued with the matron over a stupid procedure and was fired a week before her probationary period ended; the union could not protect her. In recent months, she worked in a law office in Pittsburgh. But there, too, the men addressed her as "Honey" and expected her to keep their coffee cups full.

She wants more responsibility. She is a loner, not an automaton in a clerical pool. But the business world is not ready for such women. What is she to do? At home she has worked at her woodcarving, teaching herself, steadily improving. She has sold a few figurines, but she is not yet skilled enough to earn decent money at the craft.

Her new job, she says, is with a small law firm, Graham & Graham. The junior partner, Kirby Graham, remembered her from high school and hired her on the spot.

"Kirby Graham? I've heard of him," Miravich says. "High school football star. He and his dad represent all these estates and trusts."

"I'll save a lot of money on train fare and get home an hour earlier every day."

"Why not just stay home, period?"

"Old stuff, Joe. We settled that long ago." She strokes his arm. "Oh, and another thing. There are lots going up for sale in White Oak. I think we ought to drive out to take a look next weekend. Dad could sell his house and move in with us."

He says nothing. He feels like he must sprint to keep up with her. He stops the car where she says, in front of a shoe store with doctors' and lawyers' offices on the second and third floors. A tall, blond man in a dark suit comes over to the car and opens the door.

"There's a coincidence," he says, bending to look at Mitzie. "We even get to work at the same time."

Mitzie gets out of the car and introduces Miravich to her new boss, Kirby Graham. "Hello, there, Joe," the lawyer says. "On your way to the old hall?" He affects a tone of close familiarity with unions and their halls.

"Me hunky mill man," Miravich answers. "Me go mill." He drives off, ignoring Mitzie's annoyance.

■

As summer glides into fall, he senses something in the wind, an unidentified something that means him harm. It has been gathering force, he thinks, since he spoke his mind at the convention. His words, duly repeated in *The Daily News*, followed him home and provided fuel to anti-Miravich factions in the local which are plotting to unseat him in 1949. Meanwhile, tension is growing between him and Mitzie. She refuses to stay home, take care of Dolly and do as he says. She argues that he's possessive, too traditional in his attitudes—which is pretty odd, come to think of it, for a man who wants to upend society.

In October, without much enthusiasm, Miravich campaigns for President Harry Truman, despite his attempt to break strikes by coal mine and railroad unions in '46. His Republican opponent, Tom Dewey, would do far worse damage by eviscerating FDR's New Deal social programs. Politicking is slowed by a four-day fog that lies winding along a sixty-mile stretch of the Monongahela like a vaporous serpent, trapped at ground level by a temperature inversion. People begin calling it "smog," a term coined in Los Angeles to describe fog containing carbon dioxide from car exhaust. In Pennsylvania, mill exhausts join with car fumes to produce a more sinister sub-species of smog, so thick and soupy that one morning Rudy Semchek handed a leaflet to a telephone pole.

On Tuesday, November 3, Truman defeats Dewey by a surprisingly large margin of two-million votes. Henry Wallace ends a distant third. Next morning, Miravich turns his attention to a horrible disaster that occurred up the river in Donora the previous weekend. The smog had piled up like a snow drift in the hollow formed by river bluffs on three sides of town, immersing its citizens for three days. Hundreds of people became ill, and more than twenty ultimately died. Lacking a newspaper and radio station, Donora endured its catastrophe alone for two days.

Miravich guessed what happened. How could anyone who breathed milltown air not know? In Donora, U.S. Steel has a zinc works as well as a steel mill, and both were emitting smoke and dust into clammy, unmoving air without the normal aerating effect of winds and sunlight. As a result, Donorans were breathing a toxic mixture of chemical compounds, including heavy metal dusts, nitrogen oxide, sulfur dioxide, and zinc sulfate. U.S. Steel, however, has blamed the tragedy on "unprecedentedly heavy fog."

The company's position is so ridiculous that Miravich wonders why he has not heard of a protest march, or even a strike, taking shape in Donora. Why is the union quiescent? He phones Bill, an officer of the Donora local whom Miravich has met at Steelworker conventions. People are not marching in the streets, Bill says, because they fear that U.S. Steel would close the plants and throw everybody out of work. On the other hand, there was some talk of organizing a protest on Sunday after lists of the dead were posted in the community center. People were confused; the authorities had not given a credible explanation of the incident. Was there a continuing health threat? Should the mill and zinc smelter be allowed to operate? People wanted answers, but nobody was stepping forward to provide them. Just as a protest movement began to coalesce, a man identifying himself as a scientist arrived from Pittsburgh and began speaking knowledgeably as people gathered round. He was a strange-looking fellow wearing a hairy yellow great coat, but he seemed to know a lot about industrial processes, chemistry, meteorology, and atmospheric pollution. He gave factual answers to every question, rejected the notion that Donorans breathed harmful amounts of mill dust, and in the end concluded that the tragedy could only be explained as "an act of God." He sounded so sure of himself that people, hungering for reassurances, listened and believed, spurning the idea of protest. He disappeared before Bill could learn more.

"Do you accept that stuff?" Miravich says.

"Wherever God is," Bill says, "he ain't in that zinc smelter. But how do we prove that? We don't know a damn thing about smoke. Do you, Joe? Does Phil Murray?"

As for the scientist's identity, Bill remembers only the last name, which he speaks hurriedly before rushing to a meeting. Miravich scribbles what he hears, then hangs up and examines the name. "Dr. Doobay." It looks phony.

CHAPTER 2:
April 1949–November 1949

By the end of April 1949, crocuses are pushing through in a planter next to the Watts's main guard shanty, and fat robins are tracing erratic grub-search patterns on strips of lawn recently caked with grimy snow. The Sunday after Easter comes up warm and lovely. Only a faint glow hovers, halo-like, over the mill, and glittering sunlight fills an opening between flocks of low gray cloudlets in the east. Celebrating this delightful weather, church-goers stream into and out of church parking lots all over town.

At St. Stanislaus, Father Strunka himself sings the noon High Mass. Joe, Mitzie, Dolly, and Stanley, got up in their Sunday best, sit halfway back in the center of the nave, a proud foursome lined up across the pew. With the local union election only two months away, Miravich does not mind being seen as a church-going family man by the wives and mothers who attend High Mass and who will strongly influence the way their men vote. Today he notices that many women are decked out in saffron, peach, and rose-colored spring dresses with puffed sleeves, pinched waists, and voluminous, swirling skirts. Why, he asks Mitzie, do they all look like they've just stepped out of a fitting room? Because, she replies, Christian Dior's wasp-waisted "New Look," unveiled in the fall of '47, has just arrived in town. Women's clothing has finally escaped wartime dreary. Mitzie, disdaining fads, wears a simple beige suit.

Everybody stands as Father Strunka reads the Gospel for the first Sunday after Easter, a fishing tale related in John 21:1-19. Finishing, he kisses the page and turns a purple ribbon across it with an ostentatious flip of his hand. People commence coughing and clearing their throats. "My children," Strunka begins his homily, "today's Gospel contains an especially instructive story for us here in McKeesport. We find Simon Peter and his friends fishing in the Sea of Tiberias. When they haul up their nets, they contain no fish. Jesus, who sees this from shore, calls out to the fishermen." Strunka cups a hand at the corner of his mouth as if shielding his words from the wind. "'Cast the net on the right side of the ship and ye shall find.'" He continues reading. "'They cast therefore, and now they were not able to draw it for the multitude of fishes.'"

Strunka closes the Good Book. "My children, this story of simple fisher-men has special meaning for working-men as you vote in the coming union election. When you mark your ballot, will you cast your net on the right side of the boat for good, honest, American, God-fearing moralistic unionism, or will you slink to the left side of the vessel and drop your net into the slime of Godless, atheistic communism?"

"Oh, Jesus!" Miravich whispers, his premonition finally fulfilled. The unidentified thing is identified.

"You must ask yourselves," the priest continues, "whether foreign ideologies have subverted your union these years past. You must decide whether your current officers—out of ignorance or fear or just plain communistic subversion—I judge not their motivations, for they themselves must answer to God...whether these current officers of the Watts Works local have succumbed to atheistic communism. You must ask yourselves whether unprincipled men are intent on creating an economic, egalitarian Godless Utopia here on earth, here under our very noses, here in this city...even in this parish."

People direct furtive glances at Miravich, not wanting to—he can see that—decent people not wanting to accuse him without evidence, but glancing nonetheless, reacting to the priest's words. Mitzie squeezes his hand on the bench between them. They sit stonelike through the remainder of the Mass. As soon as they step outside, the sun burns into Miravich's forehead as if someone were pressing to it a Crucifix directly out of the soaking pits. A few men express their indignation over Father Strunka's accusation as the Miraviches walk to their car. Most people clear a wide path for them on the crowded sidewalk.

When they get home, he wants to be left alone to boil in his own water. But Mitzie makes him sit down and talk to her over coffee. First off, she regards Strunka's accusation as outrageous and doesn't believe a word of it. Second, she wants to know whether that falsehood will hurt Miravich's chances of reelection.

"You figure it out," he says. "Half the members are Catholic, and the other ninety percent hate the commies."

"What does he have against you?" She takes one of his hands and turns it over and over like a flapjack. "Does he know something?"

Miravich shakes his head. "I guess he's been suspicious of me ever since we got married. Asked me a lot of questions about where I came from and what I did before. So I told him some stuff in confession, never thinking it would come back to haunt me. It was either that or not get married. But there was nothing political about it. I just...well, I hurt some people."

"Whatever you said in confession, a priest can't use that against you."

"What should I do, report him to the Pope?"

"Father Strunka? I've known him forever." She rotates her cup, round and round, watching with profound interest as coffee slops into the saucer. "Are there...were there communists around here, Joe?" she says in a thin voice.

"Depends on what you mean by 'here.'" He guesses she means here, in this house, but can't bring herself to say it. It is one of the few times she has ever blunted her words. "I knew some commies, yeah, especially in the real hard times. You know what I remember? I remember them bringing food to the coal patch. There was times when the commies were the only ones who seemed to care."

In the evening, he and Mitzie go to the St. Stanislaus rectory and wait in the parlor for the priest to return from sick calls. The room is heavily draped and dark, the furniture dolefully overdone with hard little throw-cushions and doilies crocheted by the women of the parish. Dozens of small ceramic statues of angels, saints, and disciples march across a mantelpiece. An etching under glass of the Immaculate Virgin Mary holding the Christ Child to her bosom hangs on one wall, and a heavy Crucifix, resembling an iron forging, hangs on another. Miravich becomes aware of the quiet. Even a grandfather clock, shorn of its pendulum, tells silent, celibate time. A housekeeper let them in and padded noiselessly away.

At last Father Strunka appears from the direction of the kitchen. Attired in dickey and collar under his black "sick suit," the priest sits in a chair opposite the windows and lights a cigarette. He has only a few minutes to talk, he says, glancing at his watch, for he must eat dinner before making hospital rounds.

"I can guess why you're here." He holds the cigarette up to his lips. Late afternoon light bounces off his horn-rimmed spectacles.

Miravich begins to talk, but Mitzie shuts him out. "Father," she says, bending her head to show respect, "your sermon was terribly unfair to Joe. To accuse him of being a communist—"

Strunka raises a hand to stop her. "We did not accuse anyone of being a communist. We merely urged the men to look carefully before they vote. That is our duty." He softens his voice and gives her a look of clerical compassion. "Of course you are angry. We understand. You feel betrayed, and rightly so. We also feel betrayed. It is we who married you and put the Church's stamp of approval on Joseph Miravich."

"Who's this 'we'?" Miravich says. "I saw only one priest in the pulpit."

Strunka crushes out the cigarette. "You forget, Joe, we were at your convention." He makes it sound as if he had spied upon a secret cult meeting. He tells of listening "with horror" as Miravich urged his union brothers to defy the laws of the United States by supporting Murray in not signing the non-communist affidavit.

"I don't get it. Murray himself refuses to sign. Are you saying he's a communist?"

"Mr. Murray is well known for his anti-communist views," Strunka says. "We understand what he's doing, merely testing a legal principle."

"Yeah, for Murray up there in Pittsburgh, it's a legal principle. For Miravich down here in McKeesport, it's a mortal sin."

"There is more to it than that." He gets up, leaves the parlor, and returns in a few moments with a file folder. "It's all here, Joe. Things you did back in the thirties. Violence, strikes, sabotage, agitation."

"You mean someone's keeping book on me? Who is it? I got a right to know." He feels Mitzie squirming beside him. Is he losing the battle?

Strunka shakes off this demand, loose skin flapping in the crook of his throat. "The source is not important. The information speaks for itself. When the record shows so many acts of violence, one must assume they are part of a plot to overthrow existing institutions."

"So I was young and angry and maybe dumb. You don't have nothing there that shows I ever knew a commie or even talked to one."

"Oh?" The priest smiles grimly. He pulls out two sheets of paper stapled together and reads to himself, shaking his head.

What a faker! Miravich thinks. But a chill shoots through his body and settles in his lower parts. Mitzie clutches his hand.

"Did you ever hear," Strunka finally says, "of the National Loyalty Review Board set up by President Truman?"

"I heard of it. They're firing government employees on the basis of accusations, without a trial. It's a witch hunt."

Strunka ignores the comment. One recent case, he says, involved a woman who had worked in Washington for the Department of Labor since 1940. Accused of belonging to a communist-front organization, she testified in secret before the local board in Washington. A portion of her testimony, not yet made public, has found its way to St. Stanislaus. The priest holds up the two pages.

"Couldn't be. I don't know any woman like that."

"Oh, but there is such a woman. I've checked her out. A friend of yours, Joe, named..." He pauses dramatically, then continues on a note of triumph, "Dorothy Klangensmith." Now he holds out the pages. "Here, read it."

Miravich's heart practically stops beating. With Mitzie leaning across his shoulder, he reads what apparently is an excerpt from testimony given at a hearing.

Chairman: Miss Klangensmith, did you attend meetings of an organization known as End Racial Intolerance?

Miss Klangensmith [Witness]: I believe so. We discussed the horrible effects of segregation in a country that...where the Constitution guarantees equal rights to all.

Chairman: And you discussed various actions that might be undertaken in defiance of certain laws and practices?

Witness: Well, yes. But what's wrong with that?

Chairman: Our experience is that there is a strong correlation between organizations preaching racial integration and the Communist Party, USA. A similarity of thinking, you might say.

Witness: Oh, for God's sake!

Chairman: As well as a link with irreligious atheism. Miss Klangensmith, your associations are strong evidence of subversive activity, and I for one am prepared to recommend your severance from government service.

Miravich begins to crumple the page. "What is this crap?" he says.

"You'd better read further," the priest says.

Mitzie smooths out the transcript, and the two read on. The chairman says he might reconsider if Dottie would testify as to her knowledge of "one Joseph Miravich, an agitator and union organizer" with whom she had a "relationship" in 1937 while she worked as a teacher in McKeesport. Dottie, obviously startled, hems and haws and finally says no, she did not know such a person.

Chairman: You are under oath here, Miss. Do you want to make it worse on yourself. Isn't it a fact, Miss Klangensmith, that you in fact conducted a liaison with Joseph Miravich who was known by you to be a member of the Communist Party?

Witness: My God, no, no! I mean, who says— That is merely an allegation. What evidence do you have?

Chairman: We have the testimony of a reliable witness.

Witness: Who is this witness? I have a right to know.

Board Member: We are unable to disclose that information. But it is a person of known responsibility.

Witness: But it's a lie. As far as I know, Joe Miravich—

Board Member: Aha!

Chairman: Then you did know Joseph Miravich.

Witness: Not that way, no...no—

Chairman: But you knew Joseph Miravich. In other words, you confirm the information contained in this file. The witness is dismissed subject to recall.

Witness: Oh, Joe!

Miravich finishes and looks up. The priest shrugs, as if no more need be said. "Do you know this woman, Joe?"

"Yeah, I knew her." A flash of anger at the thought of the smug men who would reduce her in such a manner. "She was harmless, for Chrissake!"

Mitzie touches his arm.

"We don't know that, do we?" Strunka says.

"She taught Latin...and English, too, and she had ideas about educating mill kids—"

"Indoctrination."

"Where'd you get this information?"

"Sufficient to say I received it from a reputable organization."

"Father," Mitzie throws in, "this is not fair..." Her voice rises. "This is—" She breaks off with a sob.

"Calm yourself, my child. We must not become hysterical. I don't know all the facts yet, but I can put two and two together. In deference to Mitzie, I'm willing to keep this confidential on condition—"

"Who are you to lay down conditions?"

"...that you resign from the local leadership and not run for reelection. I believe the board will want you to name other communists."

"Bullshit!" He stands. "I don't resign, and I don't name nobody."

Mitzie stands beside him. "Not on your life, Father. I'm ashamed and disgusted by what you've done today."

They walk out. In the car, neither speaks until their home comes in sight up the hill. She says, "I have just one question."

"What? Was I a Party member? Did I belong?"

"No."

"Did I love her?"

"No."

"What?"

"Can I still vote in union elections?"

A brave front she is putting on, but he can imagine her distress. Her husband may be a Red or, at the very least, have had a love affair with a Red or a sister traveler. And more: The church she loves has immense power to do wrong as well as right.

■

The news is all over the mill on Monday. Enemies stare at him boldly, challengingly, elated that their worst suspicions have been confirmed. Friends avoid his eyes and pretend not to see him when he passes within a few feet.

When he goes to the wash-up room, men scatter like roaches. Since he works only one day a week in the mill (and four in the union office at the local's expense), he usually is assigned as a spellhand on whatever crew happens to be working the day turn. Today, by chance, it is Rooster Wooster's crew, the old gang that he started with ten years ago, minus Mickey Totten, killed in the Philippine invasion. Even these men, his old buddies, brush by with eyes averted or give him no more than a mumbled, "Hiya, Joe," as he relieves them for breaks. He feels hurt and irritated, but seeing the embarrassment his presence causes, he keeps to himself.

After work, Miravich holds his regular Monday afternoon meeting with the Unity Team, which includes most of the local officers and committeemen. Red Terhune is conspicuously absent, and the word is that he's running for vice president on a hastily drawn-up rival ticket headed by a pipe-mill committeeman named Hostetter. During the day the rival faction has flooded the town with flyers urging defeat of the local's "Red Regime" and "Comrade Miravich." It includes quotes from the Klangensmith transcript, obained from an unknown source.

Miravich and ten of his closest union associates gather in the local's small committee room. A photograph of John L. Lewis on one wall stares ferociously across at Roosevelt, Murray, and Truman on the opposite wall. It amused Miravich to set it up this way. All ten were strong Miravich backers before Sunday, but who knows what they are now. There is much nervous shifting and cussing.

Miravich passes around a handwritten copy of the Klangensmith transcript. He outlines the background of Strunka's accusations, including a general description of his activities as a coalfields radical in the thirties. As for Dorothy Klangensmith, "Yeah, I knew her, but none of the rest of it is true. It's all buried ten years deep, and I'm not going to dig down and bring up every little detail. I'll tell you this. The accusations are lies, every one of them. Period."

"Maybe so," says a voice in the rear, "but when the *Daily News* gets hold of this transcript, we're goners."

Assenting sighs sweep the room.

"Every last one of us."

"It won't be an election, it'll be a massacre."

"We can't let this happen."

"How can we stop it?"

Indignation, resentment, outrage. No one is more indignant than Rudy Semchek, who has poured his soul into the local's financial books and who has no intention of leaving office under a cloud. "The Church got no right to butt into union business. I say we throw up a picket line around St. Stanislaus. Unfair to union labor."

His proposal is greeted by a stupefied silence. This came from Rudy Semchek? Evenhanded Rudy? Naïve, honest Rudy? Everybody is stunned except Miravich, who happens to know that Semchek has no religion. There may not be many Slovak agnostics in McKeesport, but Semchek is one of them, and he does not fear being struck by lightning if he speaks ill of any church.

"You got it wrong, Rudy," Miravich says. "I remember Strunka himself on the picket lines when we were organizing. Him and Father Rice in Pittsburgh. The Church is the best friend union labor ever had. Even the Popes are on our side. But they hate communism, and this hate, see, makes the priests do things they wouldn't ordinarily do. They got to find some commies to run out. It's like incentive pay in the mill. Sometimes you get so hungry for the extra bucks, you push out a lot of bad tonnage with the good."

"I wouldn't advance that theory in public," Fran Luptak says. "But how are you going to deal with Strunka?"

Miravich deliberates. He already has decided to stop attending Mass. "I'll tell you this much, I won't confess to him no more."

"That's smart," Luptak observes. "A little late maybe."

"What I'd like to know is, where'd he get this secret testimony?" says a committee member.

"And where'd Hostetter get money to print up all them leaflets?"

Miravich nods sagely. "I've been wondering that myself. Some government agency, or a secret priests' group, or Watts management—"

He gets the meeting back on track and appoints a committee to investigate two matters, the source of Hostetter's money and the source of the Klangensmith testimony, with little hope of finding either. The discussion turns from conspiracy to politics, a natural progression. "We can still win," he says strongly, and against his better judgment.

"Terhune'll take all the Irish with him," someone says. "The English and Germans was gone long ago."

"Swedes, too."

"And now all the Red-baiters and most of the Catholics."

"Who's left?"

"The coloreds."

A dry observation: "All four hundred of 'em, out of seven thousand votes."

"At least they're safe for us. Terhune hates 'em, calls 'em 'jigaboos,' right to their face."

"Red's gonna get himself decked one of these days."

"Hostetter hates hunkies."

"And Poles."

"Their leaflet says, 'Vote for the real Americans.'"

"A pretty good line. Everybody wants to be a non-commie, real American."

Morose faces focus on President Miravich. He says slowly, commandingly, "They're playing right into our hands."

"C'mon, Joe! This is no time for joking."

"The question is," he says thoughtfully, "do the members really want to go back to the old days? You know, Slavs against Irish, Poles against Germans, Croats against Serbs, whites against coloreds? All that old bullshit. You think about it, that's what their campaign comes down to. Hell, we just went through a war, all Americans on the same side. Took us fifty years to get there, and what do these guys want to do? Split us all up into clans and nationalities and races so we can start fighting between ourselves all over again. That isn't what the union's about. The real issue is, is management going to control our lives and tell us what we need and how to think? If they can divide us on this commie shit, we'll be pushovers on the real issues."

Luptak, Mrvos, Semchek, and the two Chubbs give passionate, if rambling, supporting statements. There are more questions, more indeterminate answers. The men want to be defiant, stubborn, strong, but in fact they are frightened. Miravich himself is frightened. As an accused communist, he could lose his job, even land in jail.

Finally the room falls into a bewildered silence. "We all together then?" Miravich says. A few men hang their heads or look at the wall. The Unity Team, he realizes, is not as unified as it was when the meeting started. He says, "Okay, you boys decide whether you're in or out."

Tactfully removing himself, he goes down the corridor to the outer office. Peg Breen, the office manager, is flopping dust covers over typewriters, closing up for the day. From her desk radio comes a mournful dirge.

There was a boy,

A very strange enchanted boy.

Miravich listens for a moment. Nat King Cole. Good singer, gooey song. He reads a notice from the international. "Dear Sir and Brother: It has come to our attention that..." Muffled shouting emanates from the committee room, followed by a long silence.

Finally Semchek comes to him and reports that it was close, but they voted six to three, with one abstention, to stay in his corner.

■

Neighbors begin shunning the Miraviches. Anonymous phone calls warn that Reds are not wanted in this town. Even Mitzie, defiant as she is, stops walking to the corner grocery in the evening to avoid unfriendly glances.

On Friday, five days after the accusatory sermon, they receive a call from Miravich's sister, Anna Cramczak, inviting them over for coffee and dessert after supper. No reason given. They make the short trip to Duquesne, neither speaking for fear of carrying a quarrel into the Cramczak home. He drives north alongside the Duquesne Works, red and smoky, and turns up a steep cobblestone street. Dolly, sitting between them, enjoys the sensation of pointing almost straight up. "Bumpity bump bump," she says, echoing Mitzie.

They sit at the dining room table, the three Miraviches, two young Cramczaks, and Eddie Cramczak, presiding. Anna, carrying cups and plates from the kitchen, probably assumes her husband will tell them why they have been invited. She ought to know better, having been married to him for twenty years. Eddie does not talk much. His thoughts on a variety of subjects have never been ascertained, not even by his pals in the mill. Nature has endowed him with the means to conceal his emotions: cloudy blue eyes and the bushiest of mustaches. He has a high forehead and puffy cheeks, and Miravich has never seen the triangle of face enclosing the mouth, upper lip, and chin without a mess of hairs upon it.

In the first five minutes of this social gathering, Cramczak says only two words, and these to his eleven-year-old son, Tommie, who is squirming in his chair. "Settle down."

Miravich cannot restrain his curiosity. "It was nice of you to invite us over..." leaving unsaid his question, Why?

Anna stands in the doorway with fists on her hips, gazing at him like a big sister.

"Okay," he says, throwing up his hands, "I peed in the woodpile. But don't tell Pap or he'll whack me."

"Huh! You got whacked on your own doing, not from anything I said. Pap didn't like us ratting on one another, don't you remember?"

With her hips spreading sideways and her graying hair bunned in the back, Anna is getting to look more and more like Mama, who passed on two years ago. But Anna's angular face still has a pinkish glow that seems inappropriate to a mine patch daughter. You would think the flesh would be stretched here, knotted there, leathery, bitter and resentful. Anger rises in him, an irrational resentment. Anna must be faking it. How could she escape the effects of that miserable life? He remembers the day she left, not long after Pap was killed. Their mother had a sister here in Duquesne who found a job for Anna as a live-in maid. She met Eddie, a blast-furnace worker at the Watts Works, and got married just before the Depression hit.

Cramczak serves up large wedges of homemade apple strudel and passes the plates down the table. Anna goes around pouring coffee. "There's more of everything. Eat up. Dolly, you darling, you like my strudel?"

Dolly sits on her mother's lap, chewing wide-eyed, crumbs cascading down her front. She nods bashfully at Aunt Anna.

Two of the Cramczaks' children are here, Tommie and a teenaged girl named Jenny. The Cramczaks did pretty well in spacing out their children, one every three years or so, probably—as the family rumor has it—by means that the Catholic Church condemned. According to Anna, the idea was to save wear and tear on the bearer of life, which was the one condition imposed by Eddie in return for allowing the kids to be brought up Catholic. Planned parenthood in their case owed much to Eddie's belief that all good things are scarce and must be conserved. The wisdom of their spacing plan became apparent when the Steelworkers' postwar bargaining power made college a possible goal for a thrifty millworker family. Now they intend to send all their children—well, the boys anyway—to college. Their oldest child, Daniel, is a freshman at Duquesne University. A framed photograph of him in his high school graduation gown sits on the shelf of the highboy at one end of the dining room, occupying a position only slightly less prominent than a shrine to the Blessed Virgin and the Sacred Heart of Jesus.

Mitzie has been unusually quiet, struggling with some inner conflict. Out of a sense of social obligation, she exclaims to Anna, "Wonderful strudel! How did you get it so...strudely?"

Forced laughter. Everyone falls to eating in silence and very soon the plates are empty. The Cramczak children ask whether they may leave the table and play with Dolly. She slips out of Mitzie's lap and runs tottering with them into the living room.

The adults are alone. Anna pours more coffee. Cramczak turns aside and blows his nose. "We heard what happened," he says.

"Who hasn't?" Miravich says.

"You know how the mill is." Cramczak lights a cigarette.

Anna says, "I heard about it at the grocery store."

Miravich takes a sip of coffee and stares at a spot on the wall behind Anna. He can guess what's coming.

"Sounds like you got real trouble this time," Cramczak says.

"Just the Church. What the hell."

"They say you tried to subvert us with communism?"

"Subvert...convert, something like that."

Mitzie sits absolutely still.

A long pause. No one moves. Finally Miravich averts his head ever so slightly and finds his brother-in-law staring at him.

"So, all that time you lived in my fruit cellar—nineteen thirty-seven, thirty-eight—that's what you were doing. Boring from within." His eyes slowly enlarge.

Miravich now looks fully at him. Cramczak has that poker-faced look of a man delighted with his own wit. Understanding creeps tingling up Miravich's arms. He composes his face in the same way and says, "Yeah, boring. And spying, too. Did you find the maps showing gun emplacements at the Watts?"

"Yep, and the code books, too."

"Stop it, you two," Anna says. "You act like it's a big joke. Mitzie doesn't feel like laughing, do you, hon?"

"No, not laughing," she replies, even as her stony expression breaks up in a flood of relief. "Maybe smiling, though." Her voice quavers in a way that Miravich has never heard. "I've felt so cold since Sunday, like everywhere we moved was in shadow. It's good...good to know we have friends like you."

"What else could we be? Dear God, Joe's no angel, but he's my brother. All he ever did was organize unions...as far as I know. I mean, whatever else he's done—"

"You better quit while you're ahead," her husband says.

"I won't say I never done some mean things," Miravich says.

Anna continues, "Anybody can be mean. Pap was mean a lot of the time, which is where I guess you got it. But Pap wasn't unAmerican. He wasn't a..." She glances toward the living room and lowers her voice, "...a Red."

Miravich laughs. "Pap? He never knew what Red was till he was too old to care. Different generation. Anyway, I meant 'mean' in another way."

"I knew what you meant," she says tersely. "Violent mean."

Mitzie leans forward, thrusting herself in. "That isn't the Joe Miravich I married, and I wouldn't have married him if he was."

Miravich solemnly shakes his head. The conversation goes on without him, a fruitless discussion about the source of Father Strunka's lies and half-truths.

"But nobody will believe what he says, will they?" Anna says.

"How could they?" Mitzie says.

"Sure they will," Cramczak says.

Everyone turns to Miravich for the conclusive answer, and he says, resignedly, "Eddie's right. There's a hysteria building up. I saw it at the last convention. Phil Murray is being pushed to have a purge in the CIO. But it's going on all over. Look at this Alger Hiss in Washington. They won't let him off the hook even with big-shot politicians on his side. When it gets down to people like me, we just get swept away in the storm."

"Maybe you bring it on yourself, Joe," Cramczak says. "The way you talk and act, no wonder people think you're radical. The politics, the wildcat strikes...every time management makes a move, the local throws a grievance in their face."

Miravich addresses the women. "Eddie and me, we always had different philosophies about running a union."

"Your philosophy ought to be keeping management's nose to the grindstone. Every night I go to work I see the blast furnaces and stoves falling apart, almost brick by brick. They're letting the equipment wear out, Joe. People are going to get killed sooner or later. You look up and down the valley, probably see the same thing. The company's selling more steel, but producing it somewhere else. The union's got to make them want to invest in this place."

Miravich waves his hand. "Even if we knew they're going to walk away from these mills, which we don't, what do we do? They're always making dumb decisions, and we got no say." Miravich leans forward, ticking off points one by one on his fingers. "We're under a companywide contract, and I can't strike them. I can't make them report to me, I can't meet with them, I can't talk with them, I can't get them on the phone. When I go to the superintendent's office, guards come and march me out. I'm not even allowed in their men's room. I may as well be a Red."

Cramczak shakes his head as if he knows better. "One thing you can do is come down to the furnace shop and see for yourself."

Mitzie always wearies of these discussions about union politics. "Maybe you just ought to get out of it," she says bluntly to her husband. She calls Dolly. "Time to go." She kisses Anna and then Eddie. "We will never forget what you did tonight."

■

He tries to keep watch out of all corners of his eyes, but even so the next blast of trouble comes up on a blind side. On Monday afternoon, Miravich and a few of the guys are sitting around the committee room, sinking deeper into despair. Cigarette smoke curls above the table littered with ash trays, empty Coke bottles, blank pads of paper. Ideas have dried up. Peg Breen sticks her head in and announces that four colored workers led by Walt Tyrell are asking—no, demanding—to talk to Miravich.

The officers look at one another. "Bring them in, Peg," Miravich says.

As the Negroes file into the room, looking solemn and justified in whatever it is they will demand, Luptak leans over and whispers to Miravich, "I thought you said things couldn't get any blacker."

"Hiya fellows," Miravich welcomes them. "Walt, how's your wife?"

"Better, thank you." The Negroes warily array themselves on one side of the table and sit stiffly with eyes focused on spaces between the men on the other side. Miravich noticed this about Tyrell years ago. Although he stares directly at people from a distance, when up close he rarely looks anyone straight in the face. This is not submissiveness or fear, but something else which Miravich thinks he understands because he himself has felt it. When you are deeply angry, you come to think of your eyes as weapons which obey your thoughts; you don't bring those weapons to bear in ordinary exchanges but only when necessary and then in dead earnest.

When Miravich gestures and says, "The floor's yours," he knows that Tyrell, though glancing to one side, sees him perfectly well.

Tyrell introduces the three other men, all laborers attached to various mill departments. Under a Jim Crow hiring policy, Negroes routinely are assigned to labor gangs and remain for years in these dead-end jobs instead of being transferred to production crews. Tyrell himself had to work some fifteen years before getting out of a labor gang and into the blacksmith shop on a low-paying job. Now in his forties, he has white fuzz on a balding head and brown eyes swelling with suppressed fury.

He gets quickly to the point. "Remember, Joe, a couple years ago you said the time would come when everybody had to be treated equal. We figure the time has come."

"Sure, Walt, I remember that. And I stand by that. The time will come."

"We're thinking more in terms of right now." Tyrell folds his arms. His delegation unconsciously does the same, black forearms lined up muscle to muscle down the table.

Miravich dissembles. "I don't follow you, Walt. Right now for what?"

"The time to merge all the seniority lists in the plant. We want everybody to have an equal chance to bid up the ladder."

Miravich tips his chair back so he can see the faces of the people who sit on his side of the table. Fortunately, Semchek, Mrvos, and Luptak happened to be in the room with him when the colored men showed up. These three, unlike some members of the Unity Team, want to end segregation in the plant, just as he does. The desire is there, but the question, of course, is when. When do you risk your political neck to help less than a tenth of your members, the four hundred Negroes in the Watts, gain rights that a majority of members want to withhold? When do you shoot yourself in the head?

"Merge seniority lines," Miravich repeats, nodding at the soundness of the idea. He allows himself to think it over. Most departments have two different "lines of progression," one for whites and one for coloreds. The white line leads to the best jobs in the department. Even if Negroes manage to get out of labor and into a production crew, their line of progression halts at a low wage level. Merging seniority lines would boost long-service Negroes above younger whites for promotion and layoff purposes.

Still nodding, Miravich says, "Merging seniority lines is one of our goals."

"Meaning what, Joe?"

"Meaning we're aiming for that goal every day."

Tyrell laughs. "Listen, man, we've heard a lot of that shit!" Now he and his friends look straight at Miravich. "See, man..." Tyrell's soft voice edges into hard Southern drawl. "...this goal you talk about—I don't think we ever reach that goal. That goal movin'. We gain five yards, the referee put that goal back five. To hell with that. We goin' for a touchdown. Now!"

"Walt..." Miravich hates this feeling of helplessness.

"Five years ago you came to us and said you'd negotiate a new seniority agreement. Eliminate all these dead-end lines of progression. People told me, 'You a fool to take a white man's word.' I said Miravich can make the union move. Year after year, we voted for Miravich and nothing's happened. So this year—"

"So this year you figure you got a bargaining chip, right? This year the colored vote might make the difference, right?" He lowers his voice. "Walt... you sort of catch us at a bad time. There's this commie stuff being tossed around—"

Southern drawl to heavy Northern sarcasm: "No shit?" Tyrell glances sideways at his companions. "Why none of you tell me that, man?"

Luptak takes over. "Walt, you know this union stands against segregation. We put it in the constitution. Phil Murray appointed a civil rights committee—"

"Yeah," says Tyrell, "headed by a white man."

"A liberal white man."

"That may be the worst kind." Tyrell rises. "We goin' no place fast here."

They scrape back their chairs and walk out. Miravich calls after them, "We'll get there, Walt. We'll get there—"

The committee room is silent. Then Len Mrvos says, "He's a pushy one. I'm not saying he's wrong, but who elected him to represent the coloreds?"

"Walt always stands up," Miravich says. "He's an alderman in the First Ward and heads the local NAACP."

"Yeah? Where does he get off being so self-righteous?"

Miravich wads a piece of paper and throws it at Murray's picture on the wall. "I got half a mind to say to hell with politics and do the right thing."

"But," says Luptak, "the other half says if you do the right thing, you won't be elected, and you have to be elected to do the right thing. Maybe you'll gain four hundred colored votes, but you'll lose five thousand whites."

"So where do we stand?" Semchek asks.

"We stand—" Miravich starts strongly, but all the courage puffs out of him. He can almost hear it escape, farting and whistling. "...our position is, we're for racial equality. It's in the international constitution. Any questions, refer them to Phil Murray."

He goes to a saloon and sits alone, scraping the label off a bottle of Tube City.

■

For many weeks there have been no developments on the communist issue. The flow of information out of Washington has ceased. The press batters at the door of the National Loyalty Review Board without success. Miravich hears nothing from Phil Murray's office, nothing from the company. Even Father Strunka has shut up. And then word slips out of Washington that Dorothy Klangensmith, who has been recalled by the board for further questioning, cannot be found.

Two investigators from the House UnAmerican Activities Committee appear one evening at Miravich's front door. Belligerent and ill-mannered, they remind him of the mine dicks of '37, acting as if divinely-appointed to assess guilt and mete out punishment.

"Let's go inside," says one, moving confidently in that direction.

Miravich takes a step toward him, and the agent backs away. "Speak your piece and move on," Miravich says.

This man, obviously the lead agent, announces that Miravich will be invited or subpoened to testify before the Committee, and they have come to offer him a deal. First he must recant in public and give the names of Communist Party members and sympathizers that he has known.

Mitzie, hearing the commotion, comes up behind him. "Who is it, Joe?"

He ignores her. "I ain't givin' no names," he says, slipping into a way of talking appropriate to a conversation with rats.

"You'll be sorry, pal. We're offering you a way out." He wears an offensive blue and yellow tie.

"Get off of my property!"

"We represent the Congress of the United States."

"You represent shit far as I'm concerned." Miravich advances on him.

The man backs up into his companion. "You'll sing a different tune in Washington, you and all you hunky Reds."

Miravich throws a sweeping kick with his right leg, catching the agent's ankle. When he goes down, Miravich reaches in to throw a punch. But Mitzie grabs his arm on the back swing and pulls him away.

"Leave me alone, goddamn you!" he says, pushing her. He never will forget how her face seems to freeze in a mask of disbelief. He turns again to the fallen man who is scrambling backward on his buttocks, his face pale.

"Don't be stupid, Joe. Stop it!" Mitzie again is tugging at him.

The man raises a forearm to shield himself as the second agent tries to drag him onto the sidewalk, shouting, "Police! Police!"

Miravich clutches the downed man's tie, yanks him upright, and aims a blow with his left fist. The man turns his head aside in open-mouthed, agonized fear. The rage drains out of Miravich, replaced by a thumping headache. He releases the man and steps back, feeling Mitzie's arms encircling him, the first time she has gripped him in anger.

As the men run to the street, a bald-headed demon with pitchfork comes hurtling around the side of the house and down the front walk. Moving with a hop and a limp, shouting Polish curses, Stanley brushes past the startled Miraviches. The panicked investigators stumble over one another and pile into their car. He thrusts the pitchfork at the retreating car, leaving tine marks in the trunk lid. "H'America, shit!"

"Papa, shut up." Mitzie takes the pitchfork from him and walks into the house.

CHAPTER 3: April 1949

Bonner's son, the reluctant budding architect, walks backward down the grassy slope, unreeling a chalked cord from a wooden spindle. "There! There!" Bonner shouts, and Albert stops uncertainly. He looks over his shoulder. His brother Paul, a chunky fifteen-year-old, stands below, on a precipice over the Monongahela, playfully swinging a long-handled sledge. Running down from a densely wooded strip at the top of the bluff, the slope is a queer topographical feature, roughly rectangular, ending abruptly about a hundred feet above the river bank.

Up near the summit Bonner peers through the scope of a surveyor's transit. "To your right. More-rrr...more-rrr..." Bored Albert appears in the crosshairs, reel in hand. "Stop! Paul, put the peg in there." Paul's blank stare comes back through the eyepiece. "The peg, Paul, hammer in the peg!"

Bonner has taken an option to buy this land and is making plans to build a factory. He borrowed the transit from a friend in the city engineering department, read a few pages in an operating manual, and taught himself how to use the device. But his sons seem not to have inherited his capacity for hard work. Feeling peevish, he glances at Mae, who bore and mothered them. She stands slightly up-slope, skirt fluttering around her knees and babushka knotted under the chin to hold her hair against the breeze.

Her sons, despite their playful shoving and pretended leaps over the edge (halted by Mae's frantic, "Stop that!"), have finally pounded in the peg and wrapped the cord around it. Bonner walks halfway down the slope and snaps the taut cord against the ground. Puffs of chalk dust spout up, leaving a sharp, straight line closing a huge rectangle laid out in the grass. He returns to the transit and says to Mae, "Have a look."

Reluctantly she comes down, sliding one foot after another across ground still wet from runoff after a recent rain. The damp grass bows low with her passage. Reaching the transit, she shuts one eye and takes a peep. The bottom of the slope leaps at her, expanding, exploding into a dizzying view of the edge of the world suspended over an ocean. The strip of land slopes precipitously, dangling from the top of the bluff like a pharaoh's beard that she saw on a mummy's mask in the Egyptian Room of the Carnegie Museum in Pittsburgh. A good hard wind, she thinks, could bend the entire bluff back under itself, sending the Bonner family tumbling down the slope and into the abyss.

She is gazing across the valley. As a cooler breeze sweeps down, a large lump of leaden smoke separates from an even larger mass, leaving connecting wisps, as if one were pulling apart a ball of cotton. In the gaps between torn wadding there appears a view across the top of the world. When the sun momentarily shines through, the entire misty horizon seems to quiver with pleasure, ridge beyond ridge beyond ridge, green turning to turquoise then to grayish blue, a soft, rumpled comforter where angels sleep.

Shifting again, the smoke closes in, isolating them on the slab of earth above the fire below, creating again the feeling of being on a sliding board into hell. She grips her husband's arm. "How high are we?"

"A hundred or so feet above the river, I guess. You don't have to look down."

"If I'm watching the boys I do. Paul! Albert! Get away from that cliff!" She turns to her husband. "So you have an option to buy this whole...thing?"

"The way business is going, we could pay it off in no time," he says. "It's the best buy in the valley, Mae. Never-developed land. Too far off the water and too small for a mill, too steep for farming in the early days. We'll do some flattening down below and put the factory on a sort of plateau. We'll get the state to put in a four-lane highway for trucks from Route Thirty—"

"Level it off? This lovely cliff?"

He laughs. "Mae, you're afraid of heights. You hate cliffs."

"Yes. I can't imagine why I'm even standing here." She laughs. "But you can't chop down everything I'm afraid of."

"This will be for you and the boys...an investment in the future."

A shout from above. Gas Stowe waves hello and starts toward them. Mae waves back. Of her husband's oldtime friends, she likes him the best, a generally kind and good man, though a notorious womanizer. This spring Sunday finds the handsome devil in a purple turtleneck sweater and a dark brown sports jacket. Coming down the hill, he picks his way almost daintily in the spongy turf, holding up his trousers so as not to get the cuffs wet. He earned his fortune years ago as a roughneck wildcatter, tramping all sorts of rough ground in woolen pants and shin-high boots. Now his old hightops must be rotting in the attic while he prances around in expensive loafers. As Charlie Pritchard says, success didn't go to Gas's head, it went to his feet.

"Sorry I'm late," he says. "Thought I knew all these hills, but I couldn't find this one. Hey, fellows!" He shouts a greeting to the Bonner boys who are engaged in mock combat half-way down the slope. As Mae walks to the car,

Gas watches her sashaying fanny. "Okay," he says, turning to Bonner, "what's this new idea?"

Bonner outlines his plan, prefacing it with a brief history of this forgotten strip of land. Bonner's option to buy includes a large part of the bluff. He will shave off the lower part of the north face, creating just enough space for an aircraft parts factory with a rail spur leading right into an existing railroad track.

Stowe knows better than to laugh outright at a plan hatched by Bonner. But extreme dubiety shows in his smile. "Aircraft parts? Pete Bonner in manufacturing?"

"It depends on what you mean by 'in,'" Bonner says. He is forming a consortium of businessmen who would invest in and own the plant, but they would give operating control to an experienced group of manufacturing managers. Bonner already owns controlling interest in a small foundry run by a professional foundry manager. "Same principle here," he says. This valley would be an ideal place. Nearby mills could furnish steel at practically no freight cost by barge or rail car. The milltowns have a large pool of experienced labor. Bonner has leads on several potential investors, and now he needs a principal investor, a partner. He needs Gas Stowe.

"Christ, Pete, where'd you come up with this one?"

Bonner smiles. "In the prison library, I read a lot of articles in business journals that never made the daily paper." Even in 1946, analysts and steel executives were predicting there'd be a huge postwar growth in steel demand in the midwest and far west. To meet that demand, the experts forecast that producers like U.S. Steel and Jones & Laughlin would build new mills in the chicago area or farther west. Anyplace but in this valley. "So," Bonner continues, "if we want to keep steel, we've got to bring in a new industry that'll consume a lot of steel and help us diversify. If we start with a small aircraft-parts factory, we might persuade a big manufacturer, like Boeing or Grumman, to build a major plant in the valley. That'd give U.S. Steel a good reason to modernize these mills."

By chance, Bonner says, he met an aircraft manufacturing consultant named Max Trippitt who helped develop this idea. "It's hard," he admits, "to sell the idea to people around here. You know the feeling, the mills will be here forever."

Stowe nods. "After three generations, it's hard to think of them not being here."

They have been walking back and forth across the property, Stowe listening intently. Now they stop where the transit sits on its tripod. Stowe moves a few steps to his left, as if to take a neutral stand, and gazes out over the valley for some minutes. The clouds and smoke keep moving around, coming together, pulling apart. Stowe takes a look through the transit scope, handling it like the old surveying hand he is. He sees plumes of smoke spurting from smokestack after smokestack planted in factory after factory—steel mills, tin mills, glass works, metal shops, foundries, pipe mills, furnaces, power houses.

"Where's that coming from?" He indicates a white blob hovering over the farthest ridge up the valley.

Bonner shields his eyes and looks up range. "I'd say that's from the Clairton coke ovens. We can't see Donora from here. Too far upriver."

"The citizens of Donora can't see Donora," Stowe says, slowly swinging the scope. "What a sight! I've got five whole steel plants in my sights and I can't even see Donora and Monessen." He rotates in a half circle. "And going down river, there's Braddock, Rankin, Homestead, and I can't see the two mills in Pittsburgh." He removes his eye from the scope and says, musing, "The largest concentration of heavy industry in the world. Those old steel guys and financiers really laid it down, didn't they—all that money, that investment, I mean. They ripped out the old valley floor and laid down capital like linoleum."

"They took out plenty, too."

"Yep. They took it out in bundles." He walks downhill, craning his neck for a view of the river.

Bonner stands beside him, a picture of patience, veins pulsing in his forehead. "Boys," he says to his sons, "go up to the car and make sure Mother's okay. Tell her we'll be up in a few minutes. Don't forget the tools."

As he reaches the brink, Stowe turns and puts a hand on his shoulder. "Pete, listen. A steel-consuming industry is a good idea. But nobody in his right mind would invest in this valley. Look at that stinking river. You stick your big toe in, the acid'll burn it right off. Look at the sky...nothing but smoke and haze. Look down there at all those narrow, crammed streets. Look at the riverbanks. There's not a pretty sight in the whole damn valley. This is the asshole of the world, Pete."

Stowe kicks at the turf. "Anybody who's ever made money in this valley, he didn't put it back in, not after the first ten years. Carnegie sold his steel company, built a few more libraries, and got the hell out. I've studied it, see. The dozen or so guys who invested in the original Carnegie Steel, all of them became millionaires. Not a one of them reinvested in western Pennsylvania. Now, Dick Mellon, he's leading this campaign to clean up Pittsburgh. Is he building any plants in the valley or cleaning up these mill towns? Ha! He knows better."

Bonner stands stock still, gazing out over the valley.

"My theory is," Stowe continues, "you develop industry in a town, or a valley, you put money in, and then you start taking money out. Once you do that the place has become a mess. It's a taking-from place, not a putting-into place. When I look ahead, I see this valley, fifty years from now, a sinkhole. You don't invest money in a sinkhole."

Bonner nods and takes his friend's arm and gently pulls him away from the cliff. "What time did you tell Olympia you'd be home?"

Stowe carefully steps over a chalked line as they walk up the hill. "Who said I was going home?" With a nudge of his elbow, Stowe indicates he's going to cash in on another kind of investment. He opens the door of his lime-colored Cadillac convertible and waves goodbye to Mae and the boys.

■

Every day, Miravich opens *The Daily News* expecting to find more lies about him. Every day, he expects the Corporation to fire him. When the day slides by without something bad happening, he is not relieved; there is always tomorrow.

The tension makes Miravich irritable at home; he loses his temper over small things, quarrels with Mitzie. She tries to ignore his sarcastic comments and flashes of anger. But she is high-strung, too, and sometimes just can't avoid shouting back. In the morning, they pledge to one another that they will hold their tempers, but in the evening they get into a heated argument. Both realize that the cause of their immediate problem lies outside their home, in that damnable Red business, but knowing the source doesn't help them avoid the friction. They begin slamming doors on one another.

CHAPTER 4: June 1949

Another door-slamming episode: He slams, she slams, baby wails, he slams again—this time the front door—and heads downtown. He walks quickly, locking knees and hip joints to brake his headlong rush down the steep street. A deep and penetrating ache where the toes used to be. It is a half-hour after sundown, but the sky has a weird brightness. An orange remnant of the last Bessemer blow hovers overhead licked upon by a strange flickering that eats away its vitals. People sit on their tiny front porches under dark awnings, like crickets imprisoned in boxes, the radio murmurs and laughter sounds. It occurs in cycles, a minute or so of talk, then a gush of laughter, a comedy program—probably the Fred Allen show, judging from the unmistakable bass voice of Senator Claghorn. It is not yet bedtime and front doors are open to the night, and through each streams a shaft of light. Walking faster, propelled by fury, he goes from light to shadow to light, like a stick dragged racketing along a picket fence.

Everything seems to be going wrong between him and Mitzie. She is too pushy, always doing what she wants instead of listening to him. He thought she would settle down as Dolly grew up, but no, she has become even more impatient and independent. Layered on top of this are new tensions growing out of the communist business. Mitzie is a hundred percent behind him in a political sense, but she is constantly chastising him over the way he is handling himself. He is angry all the time these days, his temper flaring and burning everyone around him. She doesn't like his tendency to violence. He thinks she should be more understanding. His job and union career are in jeopardy. How does she expect him to act?

The pitch of the hill begins to level out, and the Watts disappears from view when the street doglegs behind an apartment building. It takes him a minute or so to get around, but in that time jagged blue flames tinged with orange have begun spurting out of blow-off stacks atop the boiler house and blast furnaces, creating a large pool of flaring light that spreads across the river gorge. The opposing bluff, sun-burned to a brownish-green, appears to have been caught nude in a spotlight as it tiptoed across a dark stage. Miravich has never seen such a display. This is not the joyful incandescence of a blowing Bessemer but the harsh luminescence of runaway gases combusting and searing the sky. Great volumes of superheated gases, generated by God knows what uncontrollable chemical reactions, must be flooding the maze of piping that connects ovens, furnaces, and boilers—glutting the entire system, overwhelming internal regulators, flowing wildly through valves stuck in the open position, seeking an escape route.

Changing his mind about going to the union hall, Miravich hurries across Fifth Avenue at the bottom of the hill, then Lysle Boulevard, and heads for the Lower Gate. Suddenly, the blowoff flames disappear as if sucked back into the stacks. Above the street traffic, the valley goes dark, an unseen hand at the blinds. Now he knows what his mother felt the day his father died in the mine. A siren sounds at the hot end of the mill, piercing, over and over, proclaiming death.

As he passes through the gate, a friendly lieutenant guides him through the crowd. "Accident in the blast furnace department, Joe," he says, giving him a push in that direction. Sirens are still shrieking, and now the plant steam whistle, normally used only to announce a shift change, puffs out three short mournful bursts.

Blast Furnace Betty looms ahead, exhaling icy blue jets at the top, squatting in a puddle of floodlit clamor. Outside are ambulances, cars, trucks, workers. Miravich goes through a thin line of men and into Betty's cast house, an octagonal structure encircling the bottom quarter of the furnace. This lower part of the furnace consists of the bosh and the hearth, where superheated air blasts through a "burden" of iron ore, coke, and limestone to produce molten iron and slag. The cast-house floor, made of whitish-gray fire-resistant brick, slopes gently upward, cinching corset-like around Betty's buttocks. A plant guard recognizes Miravich and leads him around the furnace. Just outside the cast house, between Betty and Myrtle, the next furnace to the east, are three, fifty-foot high stoves that heat blasts of wind fed to the furnaces. The stoves stand stiffly like cloned attendants to a queen.

Miravich sees men standing in small groups near the edge of what appears to be a square black pit in the milky brick floor. Drooping heads, hands in pockets, a sense of helplessness. He has seen it before, the look of men at a death scene. The black square turns out to be a tarp spread over three cigar-shaped lumps lying in a row.

Rudy Semchek emerges from the group and hurries over. In the weird flickering light, his high cheekbones protrude cliff-like over an avalanche of dark whiskers. His presence makes Miravich feel a little better.

Semchek reads the question in Miravich's glance. "It's real bad, Joe." He sidesteps to stay in front of Miravich. "It was gas—carbon monoxide. They didn't know what hit them." Now he inserts himself squarely between Miravich and the bodies. "You don't have to look."

Oddly aggressive behavior for Semchek. Miravich pulls away from his restraining hand, moving slowly and deliberately so as not to lose control of himself. "Who are they?"

"Bonczek, Oleska and..." Semchek averts his eyes, "...Eddie Cramczak. Sorry, Joe."

Miravich slowly approaches and gazes down. Three motionless mounds under the black tarpaulin. He gestures with his head, and Semchek and another man turn back a corner of the tarp. All three lie on their backs, eyes closed. Eddie's mustache conceals whatever message may be on his lips.

Another gesture, the faces disappear under the tarp. Miravich recognizes a hat lying nearby with Eddie's badge pinned to one side. Dazed and shaky, he picks it up and looks inside, he doesn't know why. He feels men staring at him. He rolls the brim on his fingers, then places the hat carefully on the mound of Eddie's body.

It is a bad day for Slovaks. Years ago, when furnace jobs were even more hazardous and physically punishing than today, work that no self-respecting Anglo-Saxon would stoop to, Slovak immigrants came to dominate the blast furnace department, handing jobs down from father to son, uncle to nephew, old immigrant to new arrival. In the pre-union days it became the only department in the Watts where Slovaks could climb the ladder to well-paying jobs, or die of carbon monoxide asphyxiation.

Ambulance men come with stretchers and carry the bodies away.

Miravich draws Semchek and a crew man named Marbak, who saw the accident, to one side. "Leaking gas?" he says at a guess.

Right, Semchek says, and it happened during a "stove-changing" episode. The stoves provide hot blast to the blast furnace in sequence. At any given time, only one stove is "on blast," while the other two are being reheated with carbon monoxide gas recirculated from the furnace. Every few hours the stove-tending crew must switch stoves, diverting the wind blast from the cooled stove to a reheated stove. Moving between the two stoves, a tender opens and closes several valves by hauling on chains that turn large wheel-handles on the valves. This operation takes fifteen minutes or more. Changing stoves presents one overwhelming hazard: Carbon monoxide often leaks undetected from valves. It is odorless and invisible, and lethal if it constitutes even a fraction more than one-fifth of one percent of the air breathed by a man. Death occurs within a minute or two.

"Bonczek was changing stoves," Semchek says, his dark eyes blazing. "The valves was leaking, Joe. We've reported this a dozen times in the last month. Nothing happened, fucking nothing!" The exclamation sounds strange out of Semchek; Miravich has never heard him curse. "Bobby should of had a mask on, but he didn't, and he collapsed on the platform at Number One Stove. Oleska happens to pass by, sees him lying on the platform, runs to help him. But he forgets to bring oxygen. Too excited. He tries to drag Bobby away, but he falls, too. It don't take long, Joe. If there's enough of it, you take a couple deep breaths, you're gone."

Marbak takes over. "Eddie must of seen Oleska run out and follows him. But Eddie is smart. He grabs an oxygen tank and a mask and runs to the platform. He tries the tank first, to revive Bobby and Steve, even before he puts on the mask. But the tank don't work. Fucking thing is dead! He drops it and reaches for the mask. This much I seen from right here, just coming off break. I see Bobby and Steve lying there and Eddie with the mask. I give a big holler and run toward the oxygen rack. Last thing I seen, Eddie was trying to pull Oleska off of Bobby. By the time I turn around, they're all three piled one atop the other."

Miravich walks a few steps toward the roped-off stove area. Repair crews are at work.

Semchek is with him. "It was company negligence, Joe. Over and over we complained about loose connections and old equipment. Eddie more than anyone. We filed grievances and demanded meetings, but—"

"I remember, Rudy," he says calmly. "You told me, and Eddie told me. I should of listened more." He sees shadows scurrying around the stoves. A floodlight plays on a scaffold dangling about fifteen feet above the platform on Number One stove. Men wearing face masks and oxygen tanks strapped on their backs are up there, working on the valve fittings. "But the company screwed up here, and we're going to go after them. Who's the foreman?"

"Jack Kiefer. He was in the foremen's shanty when it happened. But he's okay, Joe. On safety, he's on our side."

"We'll see. Meantime, you and Marbak talk to every man in the crew before they go home. What did they hear and see? Who did what or didn't do? Get a list of all the grievances and when they were filed. Inspection records for valves, oxygen tanks, masks...safety meetings."

"Right, Joe. First we have to notify the families."

"I'll take care of Eddie—" He stops with a grunt. Too late to take care of him.

Miravich stands by the rope, staring down Stove Alley. The repair crew is rattling chains and banging on a hard metal surface, the noise resounding throughout the area. Immediately the other side of the rope barrier is a pool of blackness into which he coughs and spits accumulated ore dust and the taste of death. With a jerk of his wobbly head he brings into focus Eddie's face: Eddie the big brother, sticking his head in the fruit cellar to wake him up for work; Eddie the skeptic, sitting in the front row at the monthly meeting and shaking his head. Eddie was not a political animal. "You don't know where you're going," he once told Miravich, "you just follow your instincts." Miravich replied, "I'd rather follow my nose than sit on my ass." The fact is, he ignored Eddie's warning about poor maintenance; well, not completely, but certainly he allowed his own predicament, the danger posed by Father Strunka and the commie-hunters, to occupy the space where his sense of duty should have been.

"Kiefer!" he yells down the alley. "Jack Kiefer, where are you?"

A throbbing off to the right, in the blow room, sets the ground to rumbling: the shuddering, muffled roar of a turboblower starting up. It must have been turned off shortly after the accident, and now someone has turned it on to generate and blow wind into one of the stoves. A man bursts through the blow room door. He is tall and bow-legged, dressed in wartime khaki, and he comes forward in a fast, driving gait. Here finally is Kiefer, the blower foreman. They have never met, but Miravich has heard about him. He is no ordinary turncoat foreman but a former G.I. and graduate engineer who refused a shirt-and-tie job when he came to the Watts and volunteered to work as a foreman so he could learn steelmaking from the ground up.

Kiefer does not merely take off his mask; he rips it off. "You're Miravich, right?"

"What the hell you doing?" Miravich says. "Three men dead and you're going to tap the furnace?" Already they are jaw to jaw, but Kiefer's V-shaped face appears to confront him from an oblique angle. He clenches his fists. "I ought to pull this crew off the job right now."

Kiefer makes a half-turn and walks toward the rope barrier. "You do that, we'll all be ass deep in hot metal. Don't you know anything about blast furnaces?"

Betty's heat rises in Miravich's face. He thinks about it. Betty hasn't been tapped since before the accident and must be bottom-heavy with molten stuff, like an overdue cow. Except she is not a cow but a cauldron, and if she is not opened up and drained, the seething, superheated burden could blow out a side, flooding the entire area in a scalding white sea. This would surely destroy the furnace and possibly kill more people.

"A criminal act was done here, Kiefer, and the company isn't getting away with it. You make this place safe for my members. Then we're going to talk."

Kiefer unstraps his oxygen tank with quick sure hands. "Don't think you're the only one who's angry here. Yeah, we'll talk, after my relief comes on. You want to wait that long, I'll meet you in the motor shed. Alone." He sets off around Betty's perimeter, pumping an arm as a signal to his crew.

Miravich follows him around and is joined by a solemn-looking Semchek. There is nothing more to say. They can only stand, sweating, and watch. Men have died, but this brutish apparatus must be served. It controls the workplace, it controls their lives, and the Corporation owns everything. He tries to hold himself immobile so as not to give in to an overwhelming desire to dash his head against something. Seeing his bulging eyes, Semchek takes him by the arm as if to shake his eyeballs back into their sockets.

Kiefer's men are preparing to cast. A trough made of sand and refractory brick leads from Betty's "iron notch," splaying out into various runners in which the molten iron will flow down the sloping floor and spill into a ladle car positioned on tracks below the cast house. Three men dressed in yellow asbestos suits gather near the notch as the cast siren begins to wail. At Kiefer's signal, one presses a button on a hand-held controller. Out of repose comes a mechanical arm, swinging over the notch and driving its pneumatic drill in against a clay plug. When the arm moves away, another man thrusts an oxygen lance into the notch to burn through the iron "skull." A cloud of sickly-looking greenish vapor puffs out, followed by flame and red smoke. Molten iron and slag gush into the trough. The men skim slag off the top and divert it to another runner leading to the slag pit. Star flashes dance wildly, and a heat cloud spreads through the cast house.

Miravich thinks of his sister Anna, probably asleep in the bed where she will sleep alone for the rest of her life.

■

He waits outside the motor shed, refusing to dwell on the last time he was called to a meeting in this place. It is well after midnight when Kiefer appears and leads the way to a side door. Inside, he closes the door and stands under a dim light.

"What's all this for?"

"Just listen." Kiefer stands right up to Miravich, glowering in his face. He is slightly taller but has the same lean, tough build as Miravich. "I don't like your politics, Miravich, but I've heard you can be trusted. Is that right?"

"All depends. A snake in the grass better not trust me. We're not playing a game here, Kiefer."

For the first time, the foreman sounds regretful. "I just heard Cramczak is your brother-in-law. I'm sorry. He was a good man."

"They were all good men, and I'm going to find out who killed them."

Kiefer sinks back against the door, his face out of the light. "It shouldn't have happened." His voice breaks, then firms up. "We've probably had gas leakage for months because of bad valves and fittings. They wouldn't allow us foremen to order new parts."

"Are you saying this on the record?"

"If I could, I wouldn't be meeting with you here. Trouble is, I can't prove anything. All I can do is suspect."

"Suspicion's cheap. I got suspicion." Miravich reaches for the door knob, sensing that somehow he has gained leverage.

"I know where you might get proof."

Miravich glances at his watch, though he knows it's too dark to tell time. "Yeah?"

Several months ago, Kiefer says, speaking low and fast, an outfit came in and took carbon monoxide readings around the stoves and furnaces. The results were transmitted, as usual, in a report to Frank Mudge, blast furnace superintendent, who told Kiefer and other foremen that the readings were "pretty much normal." The superintendent rejected a flood of requests for new equipment, saying the report indicated that the stoves needed only routine maintenance. Kiefer was stunned; even the untrained eye could see that many moving parts were worn out. His surprise escalated to suspicion when Mudge refused to let him see the report. Kiefer says bitterly, "A turn foreman can't get anything done in this plant."

Miravich almost laughs. "Join the crowd, pal." He thinks for a moment. "What it comes down to is, they let our people work these stoves knowing the equipment is old and worthless, knowing someone was going to be killed?"

"They don't look at it that way. The way they think, as long as there's a chance nothing bad'll happen, nothing bad will happen. Wishful thinking. But they're scared shitless of what Marty Dinsmore will say if they go over budget." Kiefer pauses. "I'm guessing, but I think they've already decided the Watts is on a downhill slide. Our furnaces represent overcapacity for the Corporation. So why spend money on them? Let them wear out."

"All this don't help the people they just carted off."

"I warned Bonczek over and over, 'When you go out to change the stoves, wear a mask and take a guy with you.' But Bobby is an oldtimer. It injures his pride to have someone watch over him."

"So you're putting it all back on Bobby?"

"No, no. It's ultimately our fault, management's fault. But if you know management is screwing up and you don't protect yourself—"

"Why are you telling me this?"

"I'll fight the union ass over tincups on most things, but not safety. Someone's got to shake up top management on safety. But you've got to get that report from Mudge."

"Sure, I'll go in and ask old Mudgy for it," Miravich says dryly.

"Good idea. You'll see he keeps it under lock in a filing cabinet."

"Uh-huh!" Miravich stares into the walnut-shaped eye cavities where Kiefer conceals his soul. "You hate the union except when it comes in handy. You can't force management to do right, but you expect us to."

"The union's got to have some use." By the way, he says, turning after he opens the door, it might help Miravich to know the name of the testing outfit. "It's one of those business organizations with a mile-long name. The Greater Ohio Something-Or-Other Association."

■

The next week is the saddest and busiest of Miravich's presidency. He sees three of his members into their graves. He and Mitzie attend each funeral and spend several nights with Anna Cramczak and her three children, trying to help them "accept God's will," as the priest urged the family to do. So what would become of them? The only money coming from the company is Cramczak's last paycheck. Years ago, U.S. Steel instituted a pension plan, but few employees below upper managerial ranks can afford to enter the plan, which requires workers to pay ninety percent of monthly contributions. How could an hourly worker, living hand-to-mouth during the Depression, set aside anything?

The union now is talking about negotiating a company-paid pension plan, but it will come too late for the Cramczaks. Anna is entitled to a small Social Security stipend based on the ten years or so that Eddie worked after the law was enacted. There are five years left to pay on their home mortgage. "I'll go to work," Anna says. Unskilled women without high school diplomas are not in demand, and she will have to return to housework, if anything. There is no way around it: Patrick, the eldest son, will have to leave college and go into the mill. Anna is resolute, comparing her plight with that of her mother, widowed with six kids by a flash mine fire and turned out of a company house. "It's better than what Mama had to face," she says. Some better that is! Miravich thinks. Anna doesn't look so fresh now. She stares with uncomprehending eyes at Eddie's medal for heroism presented by the union.

Miravich and Mitzie have declared peace for the time being. They join together in grief. Beneath the surface, though, a rift has opened, and they both know it without understanding it. They are in a bad fix, as Miravich sees it, still loving each other but unable to cut through all the slights, grievances and unexplained shouting matches of recent weeks. He suspects the fault is mainly his, and he keeps trying to make it right by explaining or apologizing. Each attempt makes it worse because the two of them get confused over which incident they are discussing.

Working day and night, Miravich and his committeemen interview dozens of blast furnace crewmen from all shifts. Many recall the day four months ago when technicians from an outside agency conducted emission tests in the blast furnace area. Some say the same outfit has been carrying out these tests at regular intervals for several years. The leader of the testing unit is a tall, thin, sallow man. Armed with signed statements from these workers, Miravich and Semchek demand a meeting with Frank Mudge.

His office is in a detached building that sits atop the river embankment behind the blast furnaces. Constructed of prefabricated corrugated metal, it has a semicircular arched roof resting on end panels and looks something like the Quonset hut of World War II fame. Mudge had this curious structure erected to demonstrate his prudence in spending the company's money. A fortyish, pudgy man, Mudge is frontally bald but for a carefully-arranged spray of black hairs that tempt passersby to grab and run. No one could reasonably argue that he is a "bad" man or inexperienced. On the contrary, Frank Mudge knows first hand the hazards of steelmaking: He always wears a high-necked shirt to conceal a white spot where a thimble full of hot iron splashed him. He began working at the Watts before the union came and, like most managers of his generation, considers it an intruder on his property.

The meeting is brief and unpleasant, as Miravich expected. Mudge, seconded by Bert Twinkle, the labor relations man, notes that the union has filed a grievance. The company will say nothing outside the grievance procedure. "I knew every one of those men," Mudge says, "and I'm sorry, and I grieve for their wives and kids, but accidents happen. We'll wait for the evidence, but I wouldn't be surprised if it shows human error."

"The human error occurred right here in this office," Miravich says.

"Come on, Joe," says Bert Twinkle. "Let's not get personal about this."

Miravich brings up the emission tests. When Mudge responds with a perplexed look, Semchek hands over a folder filled with signed statements by men who witnessed the testing. The union men ask for a copy of the report.

"If there is such a report," Mudge says, "it's confidential."

Miravich shifts tactics. "Let's cut the crap. We know there's a report. I can name people who've seen it. It's in that second drawer behind you, unless someone stole it."

The maneuver doesn't fool Mudge. He doesn't turn to look and merely says, "We're not going to open up any files to the union."

When they leave the office, Miravich tells Semchek to watch the door and whistle if anyone comes out. He hurries around the side of the building and peers into a side window. Mudge is leafing through folders in his filing cabinet. He pulls out a red binder, closely inspects it, puts it back in the top drawer of the cabinet, and twists a key in the lock.

Over the next two days, Miravich tries everything he can think of to pry the emissions report from the company, with no success. Generally, mill accidents take one or two lives a year at the Watts, and generally management and the union cooperate in tracing the cause and taking corrective action if any is needed. The bosses, after all, are not heartless. But management has the right to run its mills as it sees fit, which includes the right to withhold "operational" information. Miravich appeals to district union officials who fare no better in talks with regional company managers. Phil Murray's office sends condolences down to the local, but Murray himself is out of the country.

It appears that the company will escape responsibility, and it is not hard to guess why: a conspiracy at top levels to avoid spending money. On the third day, Miravich and his braintrust gather in the union office to discuss what can be done.

Luptak, who is in charge of pushing through the grievance, sums up the problem. "All these statements by eyewitnesses don't mean a thing without proof that the company knew the valves were defective."

"They knew," Miravich says with certainty.

"How do you know they knew?"

"I got my sources."

"Do you think maybe you should let us in on these secret sources?" Luptak says. "Or do you stand on management rights, too?"

"Save the sarcasm, brother. I gave my word."

Mrvos says, "We could threaten to walk out."

"Go on strike?" Semchek says. "With this Cold War in Europe heating up?" He definitively shakes his head. "Then the 'commie' tag would really stick."

Miravich regards him with mock surprise. "What's next for you, Rudy? Secretary of State?" His smile fades. "Rudy's right. We've got only one move left." He pauses to gather strength from the suspense. "We've got to steal the report from Mudgy's office." Before the men finish whistling under their breaths, he adds, "It's a risk we've got to take—I've got to take. But I'll need help, and there's only one guy in this local crazy enough to make it work."

They all know instantly. The best man for industrial sabotage this side of Chicago happens to be sitting in the next office, plotting his campaign against Miravich. Miravich pounds a fist on the wall. "Hey, Red, come on in here!"

Red Terhune grudgingly enters and stands stiffly with his back to the door. His fury is always at the ready. But the truth is, he is ashamed of the lengths to which his new allies have taken the Red-baiting accusations and has admitted as much to Semchek. Slowly, as Miravich outlines the situation and the one remaining option, Terhune's resentment finds a new target.

"So that's what we're asking," Miravich concludes. "For the good of the local, and in memory of Eddie, Bobby and Steve. We can't let them die like this."

"This have anything to do with the election coming up?"

"Maybe so, Red." Miravich nods thoughtfully. "Maybe in addition to the fact that three good men are dead, maybe in addition to my sister being widowed and her kids going fatherless—maybe none of that means a thing and all I really want is to be reelected. You'll have to figure it."

■

By two o'clock in the morning, after several minutes of wallowing in breeze-whipped water just off the Monongahela's northern shore, they finally get the canoe headed in the approximate direction of the opposite bank. Miravich, in the bow position, digs and pulls, digs and pulls, already cold, damp, and nearly lost in this vast expanse of black water on a moonless, starless night. Being in the river is a lot different than he had imagined while gazing at the river from bridges and bluff tops. How very small he feels, and how very frail this craft seems. Nasty wavelets dash against the prow, stinging his face and bare arms with cold sprays.

"On the left!" Terhune hisses from the stern seat.

Miravich obediently draws twice on the left, deep and hard, and the bow swings left, pointing toward Pittsburgh.

"On the right, for Chrissakes!"

He draws equally on the right, and the canoe swings back on a line bearing for distant bobbing lights that mark a dredging barge anchored some thirty yards off the Watts's river wall. Once they round the barge, they should be able to spot a green light that is to be suspended over the wall, just below

Frank Mudge's metallic hut, by one of several union members involved in the caper. Pulling off a simple theft from a mill office has proven to be an event requiring a conspiracy whose many variables only a mind like Red Terhune's could weave into a whole.

Miravich shifts his weight to ease an aching knee, and the canoe rocks threateningly. "Sit still, Joe, or you'll be swimming." A command brimming with contempt, experienced canoeist to landlubber. But the joke is on Terhune, who doesn't know that his bow man came aboard unable to swim a stroke let alone stroke a paddle. The latter became apparent shortly after shove-off, when Miravich, using a pickaxe grip, drove his paddle into the rocky bottom. If not an accomplished canoeist, Terhune at least has been in one, having accompanied an outdoors friend (the owner of the canoe) on an outing on the upper Youghiogheny. As the canoe spun around, and with their buddies on shore—Mrvos and Semchek, who had driven them and the canoe in a borrowed pickup—shining flashlights and stabbing directional fingers at the far shore, as if to say, "The mill's over there!", Terhune remonstrated with his partner and demonstrated how to fucking hold a paddle, cross-over hand at the top with fucking knuckles up.

Miravich is beginning to get the hang of it, twice on the left and twice on the right. He pulls hard through the greasy, black water, and the odor of engine oil wafting up indicates that they are approaching the mid-river boat channel. There is also a pungent hint that flushing valves in the city sewage plant are open, probably have been stuck in the open position since Opposer McPhee bowed out as Sewer Commissioner. Except for the swish of the canoe breaking through small waves, it is quiet out here on the river. The Watts fills the skyline from west to east, a craggy dreadnaught with dark towering structures and satanic licks of flame erupting and receding from a dozen unidentifiable spouts. From her bowels comes a clamor of men trapped below the water line in airtight compartments. Miravich digs deeper and pulls harder, and black water splashes back.

A loud hissing from the captain in the stern. "Sheee-it! Back, Joe! Back paddle!"

Miravich throws himself into reverse, stabbing at the river in what he conceives to be a backward movement. Hearing a smooth, gliding *whooosh* on his right, he glances up and sees a great dark form bearing down on them with the inevitability of a speeding locomotive. He back-paddles furiously, knowing from his grunting and farting that Terhune is doing the same. The great dark form rushes by, missing them by a few yards at most, and only then does he realize it is a barge carrying pyramidal mounds of dark something that must be coal or coke. After the first barge comes a second and then a third. Only then do the running lights on the tow boat, far to the rear, come into view. She is pushing a seven-barge tow whose lumpy cargo would hide the boat itself from anyone stupid enough to be down low, right in the mid-river boat channel.

Puffing from the exertion, both men let up for a few moments to watch the tow slide by. Then comes another unfamiliar sound, a simultaneous rumbling and threshing that seems absurdly out of place on the river. Louder and louder sounds this underwater rumbling, making the river itself tremble in the shock waves. And now the canoeists see that the tow boat is not one of the new diesel-powered vessels but an old steam-powered sternwheeler plowing majestically toward them. At the rear a massive shape goes round and round, scooping up Mother River and flinging her off with cruel abandon, bruised sprays glinting silvery against the mill's dark mass. The canoeists sit in their craft, idly treading water, while the big boat glides past. Miravich sees no sign of life, not even inside the lighted wheelhouse. At the same moment he sees the boat's name on the front of the wheelhouse. For a moment, he can't believe what he sees. He again reads the name, then cries out and lunges as if to snare the boat. But the *J.T. Buck* rushes past, pistons throbbing in the belly, oblivious of the canoe and its puny occupants.

Terhune's bulk in the stern has turned the canoe rearward as it floats downstream parallel to the towboat. Waves from the paddle wheel will hit the canoe broadside. As the great wheel comes abreast, he shouts, "Hard ahead right!"

Miravich thrusts and draws, thrusts and draws. Slowly the prow comes around to face the waves head on. He feels a surge under the canoe, and he rises swiftly, still paddling but catching only air, and then down into the trough, and the next wave smashes him like a giant fist. He fights back, screaming at the top of his voice, "Buck! Buck! Buck!" and paddling for his life. The canoe, rocks, tips, wobbles, yaws, does everything except capsize. Within seconds they are merely bouncing through a rough wake. Miravich shakes his fist downstream, but the *J.T. Buck* has been swallowed in darkness.

"We're out of the channel," Red whispers, as they rock on lessening swells. His voice is hoarse but exultant. "I told you we could do it."

"It's not over yet. Let's go." Once more he plows ahead, putting the *J.T. Buck* out of mind to make room for what has to be done.

Terhune was right about one thing: This was the only way to enter mill property without being seen. The Watts's three gates are always manned by guards, who also patrol the fence line along the railroad tracks. But no patrols come anywhere near the river side of the plant, which is the backside, so to speak, of most mill buildings. The only activity back here occurs during the day turn when coal and coke are unloaded from barges. Otherwise, the riverbank is a lonely place.

For a hot-headed Irishman, Terhune has calculated the current with surprising accuracy. They pass by the southern end of the dredging barge with only a minor amount of pulling upstream, and there it is, the green light dangling over the river wall. Two minutes later, they thud against slimy stones, and Miravich, line in hand, scampers up a ladder bolted to the wall for use by Watts chemists who come down here to pick up water samples whose content will never be disclosed to the outside world. He ties off the canoe on a heavy iron cleat, and Terhune comes up with his bag of tools. Luptak emerges from the shadows. He has timed his break in the pipe mill to be here when they arrived. It is very dark. A complicit electrician has shorted out the lights on the roadway in front of Mudge's office building.

The three edge around to the front door—and here is where they come up against the unknown: not just an ordinary lock, but a very large padlock that was not there only two days ago. Miravich's visit to Mudge's office must have made the superintendent even more cautious.

Terhune roots in his bag of borrowed burglar tools but finds nothing that will dismantle this thing. "Gimme a crowbar," he whispers.

Give him a crowbar! As if Miravich has a dozen gleaming tools laid out on a surgical towel, just waiting for instructions: "scalpel...scissors...crowbar." He growls back, "Now where am I going to find a crowbar?"

Terhune tests the door with his considerable shoulder. "Uggh! No give."

"Steel don't give, Red."

"You should of told me about this lock. Give me a rock."

Unpaved ground in a steel plant is composed of decades of compacted dust. The very last stone to be found on this site was skipped into the river by a puddler's helper in 1881. "This isn't a coal mine," Miravich says.

"We'll have to smash a window," Terhune says.

"No can do. Covered with outside metal shutters. "

Miravich turns to Luptak who shrugs. He is an intellectual, not a mechanic. They hear movement and, wheeling about, see Terhune sprinting toward the slag pit some thirty yards up the roadway. They have no idea what he's up to until he jumps on the runningboard of an idling slag truck and looks in the cab. Apparently no one there, the driver presumably having gone to take a leak, and Terhune slides in behind the wheel. He softly puts her in gear and edges toward them, careful not to throttle up and disturb the peace.

"Stop him, Joe," Luptak says. "He's going to do something stupid."

Miravich jumps in front of the truck, waving his arms, but quickly jumps aside.

"I'll just give her a budge," Terhune says from the cab, passing Miravich and Luptak. He shakes his head: not to worry.

With utmost caution, he pulls right up to the door of the hut. Miravich and Luptak run up to observe. The truck edges ahead ever so little, and the bumper presses against the door. Nothing happens. A little more. Nothing. In the cab, Terhune's entire upper body is rocking forward and backward, as if he himself is butting the door with his head.

Luptak's low voice: "Joe."

"What? What?"

Terhune puts it in reverse, backs up a few yards, grinds down into low-low.

A more urgent "Joe!"

Miravich leaps onto the running board. "What're you doing, Red? Stop!"

"Fuck 'em!" The truck jerks ahead, bashing into the door. Once, twice.

The entire front of the hut seems to bend backward, then spring forward as if gasping for breath, then fall backward in a final paroxysm that rips it out from under the roof. There is a loud rending of metal, and a victorious toot of the air horn. Miravich jumps to the ground while Terhune backs up the roadway.

Miravich has an overpowering urge to run or dive into the river, but there seems to be no immediate danger. The continuous roar of the furnaces concealed the noise of the falling wall. He grabs Luptak who is backpedalling, nearly in panic, and tells him to shine his flashlight into the wreckage. The front side of the hut lies flat across the outer reception area of the building. Everything is crunched toward the rear, and as the light rapidly crosses the ripped metal, he instantly sees the filing cabinet in what is left of Mudge's inner office. They pick their way across the debris and find the cabinet lying on its side. What luck! Miravich grabs a hammer from Terhune's kit and with a few hard bangs springs the drawer lock. He snatches the red binder and gives it to Luptak who, by prearrangement, will pass it on to a night-turn clerk in the test lab who has the run of the plant on his bicycle. He will take it to the blueprint office where another night-turn clerk will make a copy. Tomorrow, a receptionist in the headquarters building will find the original on her desk, deposited by unknown persons.

As Terhune trots back down the road, the slag truck with the regular driver behind the wheel does a quick turnaround and speeds toward the nearest gate. Obviously, Terhune later said, the driver had been taking a catnap, and it was not hard to convince him to forget whatever he saw and to get out of the plant while the getting was good.

Luptak takes off at a run to find his test clerk. Terhune grabs his bag and disappears over the river wall. A pair of headlights swing into the roadway at the slag pit and approach slowly, then faster and faster as they pick out the demolished building. Miravich slips the line off the cleat and clambers over the wall. Halfway down the ladder his foot misses a rung, and he slides the rest of the way, his forehead hitting every other rung. He falls dizzily into the canoe.

"Cast off," Terhune says.

Miravich lies on his back with legs dangling over the side.

"Joe, cast the fuck off!"

He raises one foot and weakly pushes off the wall. He is vaguely aware of Terhune cursing and twisting violently side to side, ladling water into the canoe as he backs out and swings around. Slowly, slowly, and with great effort, Miravich pulls his legs into the canoe and sits up. Something is not right with his head, for he sees not just double but triple versions of a weak yellow light gyrating at the top of the wall. He finds his paddle and dips it in, then flips it to get right side down, and draws.

"'Attaboy, Joe."

The night is composed of sludgy ink, and the men atop the wall have only pocket flashlights whose beams go nowhere. They shout incomprehensibly. The voices float out over the dark river and, wings gone, abruptly plummet into silence.

CHAPTER 5: June 1949

Miravich's aching head makes him shout at inanimate objects and walk sideways every fourth step or so. He remembers last night's adventure only in patches. Late rising, he arrives at the local at ten o'clock, and there, sitting on his desk, is the painfully-acquired object of the enterprise. It is a multi-page report entitled "Confidential: Emission & Leakage of Gaseous Compounds, Blast Furnace Dept., Watts Works, Selected Dates." And at the bottom of the page: "Prepared by Greater Ohio Industrial Propagation Assn."

Luptak directs his attention to the first page, dated February 16, 1949. On that day, just as Kiefer said, stove tenders were exposed to deadly doses of carbon monoxide, at least some of the time. The binder contains several dozen pages. Each set of four or five has columns of air sampling data gathered on a specified day, and the sets are arranged in reverse chronological order. Miravich flips through the first few sets. Emission levels also were high six months earlier, and, yet again in 1947 and 1946. Miravich and Luptak look at each other. It is clear that the company has operated Betty with defective stoves at least since 1946, which is evidence of gross and willful, even criminal, neglect.

"We got the bastards," Miravich says. "They've been killing us for years."

Luptak rushes out to re-draft a grievance filed by the local, and Miravich continues studying the report. The stiff, blueprinted sheets whisper in his hands. He passes back through 1945, 1944...and on back to the first set of data collected in 1939. Readings were normal in the first several years but began turning bad in 1945. Miravich guesses what happened. In that year, someone in management disregarded evidence of rising carbon monoxide levels in order to avoid spending money on repairs. To halt the sampling would have raised suspicions, and so, in true bureaucratic fashion, the company continued collecting data—and ignoring it.

He leafs through the report a second time and comes upon two sections stuck together. When he pulls them apart, a date at the top of one page leaps out at him, and a chill spreads up from his waist. *May 21, 1944.* He will never forget that day, a Sunday, the day that someone tried to kill him in the motor shed and got Billy Pyle instead. He rubs his eyes and looks again. The date is still there. His hands begin shaking.

He calms himself and dispassionately considers what he has found, if anything. On that day a crew from this Greater Ohio...he checks the name... Industrial Propagation Association collected air samples in the blast furnace area—only a stone's throw from the motor shed where he and Billy went down in an avalanche of heavy crates. Coincidence? Maybe. But he always has figured that the perpetrator was an outsider who somehow entered the mill, perhaps with a construction crew. Why not an air sampling outfit?

This thought dredges up another recollection from his night on the river: the paddle-wheeler that nearly capsized their canoe, threshing remorselessly downriver with not a soul visible in the wheelhouse, a ghost ship bearing the name *J.T. Buck*. He has no idea how to translate a towboat name into a real person. But it is a possible lead, and Miravich calls Bonner to give him the news. A new office manager at the distributorship reports that the Bonners are vacationing for two weeks in Atlantic City.

Miravich sits for a long while, trying to draw meaning from this changed situation. Two possibly crucial clues to the identity of his and Bonner's assailants have suddenly fallen from the skies as the result—wouldn't you know?—of a burglary mission. But there isn't much he can do until Bonner returns. Meanwhile, he must attend to more urgent things.

Two days later there appears Vol. I, No. 1 of a four-page tabloid edited by Len Mrvos, who worked on a high school paper. A photographic copy of the most incriminating portions of the emissions report appears on the front page. Mrvos's lead story starts off, short and captivating, "Management killed and lied about it." Continuing the tabloid spirit, Mrvos would have named his paper *Watts Up?* if Miravich hadn't objected to the light-hearted tone and insisted on *The Watts Worker*.

Distributed in every mill department, handed out at the plant gates, passed out on busy corners, at bus depots and in the train station and saloons, the local's paper creates a sensation. Even *The Daily News* picks up the story. Watts management stands accused in the press of planned neglect, working Betty and her stoves until they all but fall apart. No one would charge Marty Dinsmore, Frank Mudge, et. al. with outright murder, but common sense tells most readers that manslaughter has occurred.

"Burglary," Luptak declares, "will now take its place beside negotiation as an approved tool of collective bargaining." He makes the comment at a committee meeting after three days of uproar in the press and at the Watts Works. "But it looks like the company is going to slip out of this mess with just bad publicity."

"After committing murder?" Semchek exclaims.

"The way the district attorney sees it, the Corporation is guilty only of 'miscalculating the useful life of complex technological equipment.' There's no criminal liability in that. We may win on the grievance, but the families won't get any compensation."

Miravich reports that the Corporation has offered lump sum payments to the victims' next of kin amounting perhaps to $500—but only if they promise not to sue. Meanwhile, it appears that no Watts manager will be punished in any way for the deaths. Dinsmore and Mudge were called to Pittsburgh for talks with corporate people, Miravich adds, quoting his mysterious source in Watts management. "But the only thing they did wrong, from the Corporation's point of view, is let the cat out of the bag. Corporate policy is to allow our mill to wear out so they can replace it somewhere else. Probably all the mills in the valley. They deny it, and we can't do a damned thing about it."

The local's swift response to the blast furnace accident at least reversed the Unity Team's political slide. Miravich also helped his own cause by publishing a column in *The Watts Worker*, pointing out that back in 1943 the Communist newspaper *The Worker* attacked him for leading the Green Steel strike. It was "against Soviet interests," the party's mouthpiece said, to halt production of steel vitally needed by the USSR with the Germans camped in front of Leningrad. "If I was a commie," Miravich wrote in his column, "how could I have led that strike?"

With the Red Scare issue partially defused, Miravich has a good chance of being reelected. "Being an effective leader still counts for something," Luptak concludes. Leaning over to Miravich, he whispers, "Being a good thief counts, too."

■

The odds in favor of Miravich's reelection improve dramatically a week before the election. His scheduled appearance before a panel of the House UnAmerican Activities Committee is abruptly canceled. HUAC gives no reason, but a day later news stories out of Washington report that Dorothy Klangensmith, the missing witness, is no longer missing. Her body has washed up on a Potomac shore. The speculation is that she flung herself off a bridge rather than testify again. Miravich sits staring at the wire story in *The Daily News*. Dottie left no survivors—except Joe Miravich, he thinks. He knows without a doubt that she disposed of herself to save him. What a lonely and miserable life she must have led, believing that mere men can create classless utopias. He never really gave her anything, and she gave him…everything. He asks Mitzie to set aside their marital problems for the moment and light a candle in memory of Dorothy at St. Stanislaus Kostka. Only later does it occur to him that Dorothy was an atheist who would have regarded the lighting of altar flames as a heathen practice.

As men begin pouring into the hall to vote on election day, Miravich senses that the tide has turned in his favor. Around noon, he walks outside for a breath of air. He stretches, rubs his back against the door jamb. Across the street, Walt Tyrell leans against a phone pole, arms crossed, staring at him. No greeting nod, just the long, slow dark look. He interrupts his scrutiny to step in front of a group of Negroes approaching the union hall. They listen to what he says, then turn and walk away. Miravich gapes, realization setting in. The sonofabitch has organized a colored boycott of the election.

The taste of this victory must be what cow dung tastes like.

■

Stern orders come down from Corporation and union officials in Pittsburgh: Watts management and local union leaders must meet and find a way to resolve their differences. When Dinsmore proposes a meeting, Miravich surprises everybody by accepting. His troubles of recent months have forced him to look inward, to assess his accomplishments and find out where he stands. His first question is, What accomplishments? Mitzie is retreating from him, his church disowns him, the coloreds are boycotting him, and management has rebuffed his efforts on behalf of workers. He remembers his pap telling him that when the coal thins to a sliver in one room you should double back the way you came and start digging a new room at an oblique angle to the first. As always, Pap had more than mining in mind when he spake this parable.

The meeting takes place in the same conference room where Miravich years before slammed a piece of pig iron on the table, initiating what in Marty Dinsmore's view has become six years of unremitting agony for management.

"But that period is over," Dinsmore declares at the outset. "We will make every effort to improve labor relations in this plant." As a symbolic gesture, he gives up his seat at the head of the table and sits across from the union group. "Now we're equal," he declares. "We welcome this new relationship. Does the union wish to make a statement?"

The committeemen glance at one another. Dinsmore had sounded almost contrite. Could he have changed? It is said around the mill that he takes care of his long-suffering wife, crippled by polio, and that he heads the local March of Dimes campaign. Everyone turns to Miravich, whose head is sunk in conjecture. One thing he knows is that being morally upright in private life does not prevent a man from acting out of the most foolish social theories and beliefs in public life. He looks at the other superintendents, one by one. Apart from Phil Shumly, they're all probably decent guys, he thinks. Good to their wives and children, contribute to charity. When they report for work, they check their good qualities at the gate and line up for an injection of managerial control. It's poisonous, evil medicine.

Miravich folds his hands on the table and pushes ahead. "I never learned the Bible because Pap wouldn't have it in the house. But I believe the Lord says somewhere, 'Children, it's never too late to do right.'"

Dinsmore begins a grave, assenting nod.

Miravich continues, "And so I say to management, 'Children, we are ready to do right if you are.'"

Dinsmore halts his bobbing head and says, warily, "A fresh start?"

"Yessir. A fresh start. And for starters, we want to know what is the future of the Watts Works. Will the Corporation put money into this plant? Do we get modern equipment?"

"Well, Joe..." Dinsmore replies with a smile. He obviously has been coached by Bert Twinkle, whose new first principle of labor relations calls for informality and a liberal use of given names. "...that's an operational matter, you know."

"Yeah, and that's why I asked. Is the Corporation going to fix up this plant and make good steel with safe equipment? Or let everything slide?"

Dinsmore's eyes narrow. "I've just stated how we will meet our obligation. The union's obligation, Joe, is to work this plant under the direction of management. As for the future, the market will dictate that. We don't foretell the future here, we make steel."

"And when the furnaces are all worn out, you'll make steel someplace else, right?"

"Whatever is in store for the Watts Works may be a concern of yours, Joe, I will allow that much. But..." he leans across the table, "...it is none...of...your...business."

Shumly gets into the argument. "People who engage in the violent destruction of mill property have no right to demand anything."

"What?" Miravich says, turning to him. "Mudge's tin hut? Killing the three stove tenders was a lot more violent than anything we done, if we done it." He takes a deep breath and strikes out on his own. "Tell you what," he says in a friendlier tone. "These are good jobs, and we want to keep them. But management is screwing up, forcing us to work with worn-out equipment, a lousy layout, stupid operating rules, seniority lists that discriminate against coloreds...And more, too. But we got experts of every kind, in every department—the guys who do the work. We're willing to meet with management to make things work better. You say the Watts is threatened by competition. Okay, we'll show you how to beat the competition."

The committee looks aghast. Luptak shakes his head at Miravich.

Miravich rushes ahead. "With one condition. The company guarantees no jobs will be eliminated as the result of our suggestions. It's been done before. We form a committee to advise management, see, and if production goes up because of their ideas, the men get a bonus. Something like that."

Silence around the table until Luptak says in a shaking voice, "Joe..."

Dinsmore turns to Bert Twinkle. "What's he talking about?"

"A dumb scheme that's been tried at a few small companies, I hear. Dreamed up by a couple of union staff guys. Even Phil Murray couldn't swallow it, and they both resigned a few years ago."

Dinsmore has heard enough. "The Watts Works will freeze in hell before this management will be party to such a harebrained thing." He stands with arms stiffly at his sides. "This meeting is over. We will not meet with commies, or whatever kind of radical you are, Miravich." He says to Shumly. "I want these people out of here. Call plant security."

Back at the hall, Luptak berates him. "Stupid move, Joe. You give them a fire hose to put out the fire, they'll turn it on us. Worst thing is, you sprung it on your own people. We never discussed anything like that."

"So I lost my head." Miravich picks up a book on his desk and throws it at the wall. "No matter what we propose, they say no. Well, fuck 'em! We always say no, too. They want to combine jobs, we say no. They want to eliminate classifications, we say no. They want to meet to discuss efficiency, we say no. We say no till they say yes."

"That's more like it," Luptak says. "We got them by the throat."

"Yeah. And they got us by the balls."

■

A Sunday afternoon, Miravich comes home from the union hall and finds Mitzie at her work bench in the studio, an addition to the home built by Stanley with Joe's help. Knowing how much she enjoys her woodcarving, they tore a hole in one side of the house, built an alcove to the dining room, and faced it with a large bay window. Its three sides face east, south and west to catch the fugitive rays of the sun which now and then tease McKeesport.

Miravich sticks his head in the doorway and sees her hunched over the bench, absorbed in her work. She wears bib overalls over a white turtleneck sweater. His eyes trace the line of her strong back rising from where the baggy pants collapse inward around her narrow waist. Thick black hair flows down over her shoulders and ears, closing her in, like curtains concealing a sanctuary. Dolly sits on her own stool next to Mitzie, rubbing two sticks together in pretend-carving. Not quite four years old, she invests each task or bit of play with fierce concentration. Like mother like daughter.

He watches as Mitzie gouges a block of cedar with brisk twisting movements of her forearm. She quit the Graham law firm when it became clear that young Kirby was nervous about the communist business. Now she is searching for another job with an opportunity for a woman to do more than look good in high heels.

"If you're hungry, there are cold cuts in the ice box," Mitzie says.

"Dolly, honey, go see Pap-Pap, he wants you."

At a nod from her mother, Dolly slides down from the stool and runs out.

"Cold cuts?" he says to Mitzie. "Is that all we have?" He came in to make up with her, but the dismissive tone in her voice annoyed him.

She says nothing, her attention riveted on the cedar block.

"Mitzie! Say something, dammit!"

"Why should I say anything? You don't listen."

"Now you're playing with me. Why isn't there something good to eat?"

"If you'd stopped at the grocery store like I asked, there might be something."

"I had to see a guy and forgot."

"Why didn't you ask this guy to get you something to eat?"

"C'mon, Mitz!" Miravich paces back and forth behind her in the studio. He didn't come in to fight with her. Just an innocent remark on his part—Christ, he doesn't even care what's in the icebox!—and they're chasing one another in a vicious circle. And when Mitzie gets a grip on your tail, he thinks, she doesn't let go. This is how it has been for weeks, ever since Strunka's accusatory homily. They can't seem to settle even minor issues. Layer piled upon layer of misunderstandings; it's so complicated that he has no idea how to begin untangling the mess.

He goes to her side. "It's time to get this ironed out, Mitz. We haven't talked for a week."

She is wiping off her tools, one by one, and placing them in a drawer. With her head bowed, hair obscures her face. In a low voice she says, "I don't like the way you've been acting, Joe. I don't know what's happened to you." She looks at him for the first time, not with weepy eyes but with a hard, almost belligerent stare. "The man I married was confident and strong and had wonderful ideas. He was going to change society."

"The man you married," he says, "wasn't accused of being a Red. The man you married didn't realize how inflexible management is. He didn't figure on the International union stripping all the power out of the locals."

"The Red thing was awful, I know. The other stuff—" She makes a gesture of impatience. "That's not where the real problem is."

"Where is this real problem?"

She has turned back to her instruments and is holding up a penknife blade to the light. "In your attitudes, Joe." She drops the knife in the drawer. "Before we were married, I knew you had these stupid ideas about men being the boss, all that nonsense. But I could accept a certain amount of that because I loved you for other reasons, and because I thought, 'He's a smart guy, he'll figure it out.' But..." She picks up the block of cedar wood and, stretching across the table, places it on a window sill. "...you haven't, have you? I think the idea almost frightens you. It's like you're jealous of me."

"How can I be jealous of my wife?"

"You explain it, then." She sits squarely on the stool and folds her arms, looking at him. "All this resentment. If it was up to you, I couldn't make a move without asking you first. I told you at the beginning I wasn't going to stay home and sweep the porch and dust the furniture. You're closing me in, Joe, and I don't want to be closed in."

A moment of silence. Anger is welling inside him. He leans against the wall, waiting for her to say something really outrageous.

"And recently these outbursts of anger, even violence." She slams the drawer closed and snaps a padlock in the hasp. "What Father Strunka said about you was bad. But nothing justifies hurting people."

"Okay, so I went off my head a few times. So I yelled once or twice. Maybe I was wrong. People got to be wrong sometimes. Most people got flaws." He puts his face close to hers. "Except for Miss Perfect here. You don't allow for people to make mistakes, do you, Mitz?" Seeing that she won't respond, he pulls away and backs into the edge of the table. The jolt irritates him. "This stuff about what you thought at the beginning," he says sharply. "I'll tell you what you thought at the beginning. You thought, 'Boy, this guy Miravich is a tough guy who come up the hard way, which means there's not a weak piece of gristle in his whole body. You looked too much at the physical specimen, Mitz. Yeah, I was that, but maybe my upbringing left some loose ends up here." He points to his head.

"Oh, Joe, please!"

"Please what?" He takes a step toward her, feeling a surge of anger. "Are you ridiculing me?" For a moment he remains there, sort of hanging in the balance, feeling fuzzy-minded. How could he be so clearheaded in the meeting with Dinsmore and so muddled with his own wife? He steps back and begins pacing in front of her. "I could use some support, you know. You didn't desert me when that goddamned priest—"

"Lower your voice, please, and don't use language like that."

"And I thank you for sticking with me on that. But I got other pressures, you know. Every day at the mill, at the local....These management people are real assholes."

"I can think of some union people who qualify for that, too. Union leaders who don't stand up for the rights of members."

"What's that supposed— Oh, you're bringing that up again." He remembers that episode all too well, the summer of forty-five when men began coming home from the service. The veterans immediately displaced all the women who had worked throughout the war, even those with more seniority. The union rejected the women's appeal. "Okay, some women got a raw deal," he says. "I don't see that you were hurt much, being pregnant already. You would of left the mill in a couple of months anyway."

"Pretty convenient for the union, huh? What happened to the principle of equal rights for all members?"

"Oh God!" Miravich slumps over the table, holding his head in both hands. "How'd we get onto this 'equal rights' stuff?" He feels confused enough, and now her talk of 'equal rights' brings Walt Tyrell to mind. Angry at himself, he slaps the table with an open hand.

With a dust cloth she begins scraping wood flakes and other debris from her work table, using long vertical strokes, catching the debris at the bottom of the table with the other hand. "Well, Joe," she says, being infuriatingly rational and all-knowing, "maybe there's too much stacked against you in that mill. Even your members don't give a damn. It's that whole way of life. I'm not sure Dolly and I want to spend a lifetime watching you try to defeat these people. Maybe you ought to come out of the mill, Joe. There are plenty of other things to do."

"Whose life're we talking about, yours or mine? You go to the office and dick around with them high-falutin' lawyers—"

She throws down the rag and pivots towards him, her right fist pressed into her hip. "It was supposed to be both our lives, not one or the other. And if you think I...dick around, you're a fool. Grow up, Joe."

"Okay, so I'm suspicious. What'd you expect, where I come from."

"There it is again! Where you 'come from.' Whatever goes wrong you blame on what happened in the coal patch thirty years ago. It's like you buried your soul in the pits. I thought when we got married you'd begun digging it out. I guess not."

While he fumbles for a rejoinder, she unties her brown apron and hangs it on a peg. "I'm going to put Dolly to bed. Come in and kiss her goodnight, if you want to." She leaves without looking at him.

He calls after her, "Who says I wouldn't want to?" He sits on her stool, shoulders slumping.

CHAPTER 6: July 1949

At 6:30, a half-hour before morning shift change, Miravich and three committeemen are driven through the mill grounds by a lieutenant of the plant guard. Dawn came officially an hour ago, but it's a misty morning, still half-dark. Fiery reflections leap and dance in the windows of mill buildings. The lieutenant drives to the rear of the open hearth shop. Most of the day-turn furnace crew, a few dozen men, are idling around the large open doorway, standing, sitting, squatting. Obviously these men intend to continue a wildcat strike they started yesterday. They walked off the job in mid-morning and later persuaded the afternoon and night crews to continue the strike.

Across the narrow roadway, a smaller group of workers, all Negroes, stand with folded arms at the entrance of the ingot-stripping area. Over their shoulders, behind Blast Furnace Betty, the sun appears suppurating in the low margins of a turbulent sky.

Miravich gets out of the jeep, hitches his pants and slowly and deliberately crosses in front of the strikers to get to the colored men. Walt Tyrell is in the front rank.

"Hello, Walt." A friendly nod to the others. "We're going to get this straightened out."

"Depends on who gets straightened out, Joe." That slow, measured voice. "Up to now, it's been us. We been straightened out, laid out, left out, and shut out... Wherever out is, we there." His eyes, which have been traversing from left to right, jumping over Miravich, now return to center and bear directly on his face.

The union official in Miravich wants to make an officious reply, but he merely nods again. "Well, give me a chance to see what's up."

"You know damn well what's up, man. These white boys striking to keep us out. Black men can strike too, Joe."

Other colored men have crowded in close to listen, and they mutter in agreement. "Right, man"..."Yessir"..."Damn right!"

Miravich swiftly calculates: less than five hundred coloreds work at the Watts, the majority in laboring jobs, not critical to turning out steel, even if Tyrell could induce all to strike. "Look fellas, we'll all be out pretty soon anyway. Black, white and in between. Phil Murray is demanding pensions for us all, and we may have to strike."

"But it hasn't come to that," Tyrell says sharply. "It's come to this!"

Miravich walks back to the striking open hearth crew, every one of whom is described on his employment record as "male, Caucasian." Men in the front rank seem to be straining toward the Negro workers, hate flowing across ten yards of dirt road. He hears the lieutenant on his walkie-talkie, calling for reinforcements.

Mooohh! goes the seven o'clock whistle. As if produced by a harmonica player with puffed up cheeks, it starts at full blast and holds that single mournful note long enough for one-half person, on average, to die in McKeesport, then expires itself, falling down the scale and ending with a *pffft!* of used-up steam. Men look up as if they've never heard it before. An echo back in the hills plays it again. Slowly, reluctantly, the Negro workers begin dispersing, going to their jobs elsewhere in the plant. The open hearth men remain where they are. A few mockingly wave bye-bye to the blacks.

Paul Whipple, the open hearth superintendent, is striding toward Miravich, white shirt and tie demanding obedience. "Get these men back to work. This is an illegal strike."

Miravich and his committeemen, Fran Luptak, Rudy Semchek, and Thomassini of the open hearth, confer with a couple of strike leaders, giving them hell. What are they trying to do, start a race war? Miravich spreads his arms and begins herding people through the doorway. Most go willingly; they can see the situation was getting out of hand. Across the road, Walt Tyrell stands staring.

Union and company officials split off in a small group. Miravich asks for a recounting of yesterday's events leading up to the strike, and Whipple summons the melter foreman who was in charge when it started. Out of the shadows comes—by God!—Jack Kiefer. Transferred from the blast furnace department in the middle of one controversy, he has landed in another one, here in the open hearth shop.

At the start of yesterday's day shift, Kiefer found himself short of men in the production crew because of vacations and illness. He had to find a replacement quickly. One furnace had been tapped just before shift change; its two hundred tons of molten steel, dangling over the pit in a teeming ladle, had to be poured into ingot molds before it began to solidify. Most foremen would have gone looking for a white man, any white man, and wasted a half hour doing so. Kiefer spotted a Negro laborer right at hand, shoveling slag behind No. 5 furnace. Earl Busby, Badge No. 333810, eight years' seniority, a man who knew the operation and was as smart as any other guy of whatever color. The custom for sixty years has been that Negroes can work as laborers in the shop but cannot work in higher-paid production jobs. Kiefer ignored the unwritten rule and promoted Busby to the pouring platform as "slagger," a low-level but essential job. The rest of the pouring crew grumblingly worked through one pouring cycle so the heat would not be lost. When all ingot molds were filled, they walked off the job and vowed to stay away until Busby was removed. Kiefer refused to countermand his order.

Whipple has authority to assert, that's his job, and he talks a blue streak, goddamning them all to hell several times over, not excluding Kiefer. If the open hearths don't resume production by early afternoon, he says, the Watts's rolling and pipe mills will run out of stockpiled steel. The entire plant will go down, and seven thousand men will be out of work.

"You can't shut down an entire steel works because of one man," Whipple says.

Kiefer says, "Some see it as more than one man."

"We don't see it that way, and we run the plant."

Miravich and the committeemen go to the locker room where the men of the day crew are lounging around, awaiting a decision. A man named Ramsey, a first helper—the highest rated hourly worker—steps forward. A heavy man with bowed legs and stooped shoulders, he once served as a union grievance-man himself and obviously commands respect. "I'll tell you right off," he says to Miravich, "we never had colored in the open hearth crews, and we never will. We're keeping this place shut down till that nigger's gone."

He seems to speak for the whole group. A few men turn their heads aside, but most yell and whistle in agreement.

The union officials retreat and caucus. The easiest way to deal with the situation is to demand that the company stick with the local seniority rules and take Earl Busby off the open hearth crew. Whipple obviously would welcome this decision. An uninterrupted flow of steel is more important than any theoretical commitment to civil rights.

"We got seniority rules, we got to stick by them," says Thomassini, the open hearth committeeman.

"Balls!" Semchek declares with unexpected conviction. "These guys are wrong. The coloreds ought to have rights like any other."

"Rudy's right," Luptak says. "It's a matter of principle." He stops short and looks down at his feet moving in the dust.

"You're pawing dirt," Miravich says. "Say what's on your mind."

Luptak speaks in a low, even voice. "If we go against these guys and stick up for the coloreds, you'll never be elected again. You were lucky to survive the Red-baiting. Add this and you're dead. Maybe we all are."

"So what's your solution?"

"The only way to eliminate racial hatred is through education. It's a long-term process."

"Francis! For Chrissake!"

Word arrives by messenger that John Marple, the district director, will come to the Watts and take charge of this delicate situation. "Let Marple handle it. That's what he gets paid for," Luptak says.

"What do we get paid for then?" Miravich says. "To sit back and have everybody tell us what to do? Management, the district office, Phil Murray—"

Luptak walks away. After more palaver, Miravich tells Semchek to go back to the local and organize phone calls to all open hearth crew members on all turns, urging them to come down to the shop for a mass meeting at 10 o'clock. Marple should be here by then.

Miravich strolls alone into the open hearth shop, reacquainting himself with the terrain. He worked here during his first months in the mill. He remembers roaring furnaces and whirring overhead cranes, carrying enormous ladles dripping molten steel. Today, unnatural dusk has fallen in the open hearth "pit," a place normally aglow with pulsating light. The pit area extends along the rear side of a row of twelve open hearths. On the front side, molten pig iron, scrap, limestone, and other elements are fed into the 20-foot high, rectangular brick furnaces. Cooked steel is tapped on the "pit side" into teeming ladles and transported by crane across the pit to a "pouring platform" where it is poured into ingot molds. Crossing the pit, he wades through three or four inches of soot and cinders, residue of thousands of steel heats that have passed overhead. A history of the steel-framed twentieth century is buried here. If only dirt could talk. A litter of slag piles, grimy slag pots, thrown-down tools, and two huge teeming ladles lying drunkenly in the dust. He remembers a never-ending shoveling and shifting of slag starting with his first day in the Watts. A foreman gave him a shovel, and said, "Do what the nigger's doing." Which is how he came to meet Walt Tyrell, already a ten-year man at the Watts but still a laborer. He taught Miravich the ropes. Every day, for several months in the summer and fall of 1939, they shoveled, raked, banged caked slag off of slag pots, coughing and spitting black guck, and all the while they told one another stories and jokes, and laughed till their sides split.

One day a slagger's job became vacant, and Miravich's name was next on the bid list—the whites-only bid list. He moved out of the pit and up to the pouring platform. Tyrell stayed in the pit and got a new young white boy to teach the ropes to. After a while, he stopped waving to Miravich and started staring from afar. It could not have been with malice. What did Miravich do wrong? Was he supposed to turn down a 20-cent an hour pay raise and stay in the pit? Tyrell understood this, but he kept staring.

Miravich climbs to the pouring platform, a six-foot high dock extending along the east wall of the building, with railroad tracks running in front. He gazes out across the pit, imagining the crane carrying a teeming ladle with two hundred tons of molten steel hovering above ingot molds sitting on rail flat cars next to the pouring platform. When a ladle plug is extracted, molten metal streams down into the molds, with the crane operator moving the ladle down the line, filling them one at a time. Wind is moaning in the roof trusses. Somewhere the loose end of a tarp is flapping, a winged dinosaur circling the dark shop. Miravich closes his eyes and remembers his days as a slagger. When a mold is full, a slagger moves in with his tool, a technological marvel otherwise known as a board slightly larger than a two-by-four. He leans out over the track and skims slag off the top of the boiling steel, risking what is called "catching a flyer," which occurs when hot metal explodes up out of the mold, spraying everyone in the vicinity.

A slagger's job is the starting slot in a line of progression leading to a variety of higher-paid jobs. Good money may make the health risk acceptable. But how would Earl Busby put a price on the hostility of white crew members? Is he willing to take all that shit and a crappy job to boot? Maybe a union leader's duty is to follow the majority's wishes, keep the peace and, not so incidentally, protect Earl Busby from the consequences of a fired up ambition to go places where he's not wanted.

An hour has passed. Miravich makes his way to the southside entrance. A lot of people are milling around. Two jeeps filled with plant policemen are parked at the fork in the road. Jack Kiefer catches his eye and approaches.

"Management wants to get this over with." He has that caught-in-the-middle look that first-line foremen often wear to mask their feelings. "Production comes first. We'll move Busby back to the pit laboring job if the men go to work." He gives a slight shrug: What can I say?

"That's what they want to hear," Miravich says, keeping his eyes fixed on a far point. Kiefer, he knows, wants to say what he really thinks, but walks away.

Walt Tyrell approaches with a young colored man. "Joe, this is Earl Busby."

He is darker than Tyrell, darker than most coloreds, and he has a pendulous lip. Wary but eager, the kid sticks out his hand, flashing an off-white palm as if displaying a card.

Miravich shakes briefly. "The Jackie Robinson of the open hearth, huh." He turns to Tyrell. "Your foreman give you the day off? What do you want us to do if you get suspended?"

"Fuck you, Joe!" That mellow-edged Negro voice, half Deep South and half First Ward McKeesport. "You take care of union business, and I'll take care of myself."

Busby's soft brown eyes take on a glitter imitating Tyrell's. They must take staring lessons in the First Ward. Fury tinged with a feeling of powerlessness. He pulls up the pendulous lip and closes his mouth, and Miravich senses a certain stiffness of body that indicates the kid is doing something inside to hold himself together. Miravich knows what it is like to be scared shitless. It squeezes out all the good, leaving a hollow tube of a man. That's the object of Jim Crow customs and the Red Scare, to scoop out your insides and fill you with other people's ideas of what is right.

He watches them walk away, passing through a narrow lane between hostile whites.

By 10 o'clock, about a hundred crewmen from all shifts have gathered at the open hearth shop. Marple has not yet appeared, but Pat McNally of his staff, the former Watts local president, comes in his stead, saying that the district director has been delayed. He urges Miravich to delay the meeting.

Miravich says no, it's time to make a decision. He assembles the men on the railroad track just below the pouring platform. He and the committeemen climb the steps. Paul Whipple follows, probably expecting to lead off the meeting with a lecture on the illegality of wildcat strikes. No, Miravich says, this is a union meeting. Semchek and Thomassini escort him, protesting, off the stage. Jeers for the boss rise from the assembled crewmen. Over near the doorway, Kiefer is holding back the plant guards.

Miravich stands on the lip of the platform. "I'm going to make this short and not so sweet," he says to the crews. "Everything that's happened over the last twelve years makes me believe we are a union. Management doesn't want us to be a union, but we are a union." He takes a breath and calls out, "Am I right?"

"Right!" What else could they say?

"We are a union and the majority rules. Right?"

"Right!"

"Now a lot of you people were around in thirty-six and thirty-seven when we organized U.S. Steel. We needed every shade of human being we could get, and the coloreds were with us, as I recall. When the Steelworkers finally won over Little Steel, the coloreds were with us. When we struck in forty-six, I didn't see any coloreds crossing the picket line." He crouches and looks directly at Ramsey standing in the track bed. "How about it, Ramsey? Did you?"

Before Ramsey can reply, Miravich moves to the next man. "Did you, Burns?" And the next. "Did you, Matty?" He straightens and, seeing that Ramsey is turning to address the men, he roars out, "No one saw anything like that because the majority ruled. The majority said, 'Strike,' and everybody struck. That's what happened. And the majority, speaking through convention delegates, put these no-discrimination clauses in the constitutions of the CIO and the United Steelworkers of America."

Someone shouts, "We don't work with niggers!"

Miravich stands on tiptoes, gazing over the men. "Can't see who said that. Raise your hand." No one does. "That's what I thought. Ignorance always hides. Now, look, I worked with a lot of you men right here on this platform, and I saw a lot of things happen here. I saw a flyer burn off Bob Johnson's face, and I remember the furnace breakout that killed two men in forty-two. I ask myself, if the coloreds get the wage increases we've won as a united union, why don't they share in the hazards? Why are we keeping them in reserve? Maybe you think only white boys are expendable."

Someone shouts, "They can't stand the heat."

"You ever see a colored man with a sunburn? Maybe God gave them black skins to work on the pouring platform." He walks a few feet along the edge of the platform, thrusting his chin toward the men. "Yeah, I see a few of you waving me down, but I see a lot more listening to logic. Just before I came up here to talk, management comes to me and says, 'We don't like this business of a strong, united union, and so we're going to rescind that assignment of a colored man to the pouring crew. We are not going to knuckle under to the union policy on equal rights,' they said, 'because that'll make the union stronger.'" He pauses again, inflating his chest. "I'm here to tell you we're not going to let management go back on our rights. We are going to enforce the policy of the CIO and the United Steelworkers of America. We don't need any coddling by the district office or even Phil Murray. We make our own decisions here, for our own reasons. Right?"

As he talks, he picks up the handles of a wheelbarrow abandoned on the platform and quickly wheels it to the edge. He reaches in and takes out a slagger's board. "So here's the deal. We are going to renegotiate the seniority arrangement in every department in the Watts and open it up to every member in good standing whether he's black, white, red, or brown. But we have to start here in the open hearth. And we are going to do this by majority vote. All in favor of a strong union, shout it out!" Immediately upon saying it, like he's seen Murray do when calling for a vote on a sensitive issue, he slams the board down on the edge of the wheelbarrow. The metallic *bonggg!* almost drowns out the vote, which isn't so weak after all. "Passed," he says. "The majority having voted in favor, I declare this strike to be over. Go back to your jobs, and thanks for being strong."

The men turn and move slowly off. A few stand protesting, but the surge eventually carries them away also. Semchek is the first to shake his hand. "You done it, Joe." Shining eyes. Luptak looks touched and contrite. McNally pats him on the back and says, "That's just about how Marple would've put it."

CHAPTER 7:
August 1949–September 1949

Miravich climbs the Bonners' front steps at their home in White Oak, marveling at the seeming ease with which his former boss recovers from adversity. Only four years out of jail and he's wallowing in success, now directing a small empire of businesses including beer. He appears at the door, smiling broadly, wearing a short-sleeved casual shirt that reveals still well-muscled forearms. "It's been a while, Joe. Hot night, eh? We'll sit out here on the porch."

Mae appears shortly and inquires after Mitzie and Dolly. She is still a taut little figure, but she seems to have climbed down a bit from that old aloofness. Would he like beer or club soda with a lemon twist? she asks. Soda, he replies.

She serves a soda to Miravich and, to her husband, a highball, so deliberately watery that the whiskey sinks dejectedly to the bottom. Bonner draws up a wicker chair for Miravich next to his own favorite lounge. He stretches out, prepared to talk man's talk. "You've been through some tough times, Joe. Congratulations on your election."

"It was my smallest margin ever. Standing for election every year is like being smothered slowly by a pillow. Pretty soon they'll snuff me out." He takes a sip of the tart soda and feels his tongue curling up in distaste. "Anyway," he says, "I come to tell you... came to tell you about this thing that happened to me."

Bonner interrupts. "Why not quit the union and work for me?" Bonner outlines his plan. He owns majority interest in a small foundry, a supplier of mill equipment to the steel industry, and he would like to hire Miravich as general foreman. "Pretty near double your mill wages, all daylight work, and you'll be in a management pension plan."

Surprised, Miravich sits back. "You own a steel foundry? From peddling beer to making steel? I didn't know water flowed in that direction."

"A business is a business, Joe. I own it, but I don't manage it day to day." It was a good investment, he explains, a tiny firm in which he bought controlling interest from the now-deceased founder who had nobody to pass it on to. Mercury Steel Castings employs only ten workers, and he has kept the plant manager and sales manager. He needs a general foreman to replace one who is retiring. "You'd supervise the men, working under the plant manager."

"Whoa! Hold on! Thanks for the offer, but I got to look this horse in the mouth. Double my mill wages? A management pension?" Miravich feels lighter than air. "That's some offer! Can't help wondering if there's...if there's something behind it."

"Like what?"

"Something related to the union." It's getting too dark to identify the glint in the businessman's eyes, and so he stares hard at a big drop of sweat trickling down his throat. "I don't know...maybe you think I'll help you bust the union at this foundry."

"Joe, c'mon!" Bonner gets up, does a turn around the porch and comes back to stand over Miravich. "Let's not get tied up in that labor-management stuff." He sits again. "I'm not trying to run the union out. I'm not crazy. You can't operate a nonunion manufacturing plant in this valley. If I don't pay union scale, I'll lose my men to the mills. So I may as well pay up and avoid the fight."

Sitting down, he takes a long sip of his drink. "I came to you because I can trust you. The fact you're a respected union man...sure, that counts for something. I have plans down the road." He briefly outlines his parts-plant idea. "I know you don't like the mill bosses, but my foundry manager listens to the men."

"I've heard that before—listens to the men. Balls! I need more than words."

Bonner says irritably, "You want to run a business, you have to own it, Joe."

And gets an irritable reply. "Who wants to be a lousy owner? You don't hear right, Bonner. You're too damned impatient with people who don't think like you."

Bonner frowns at his glass. Miravich tells himself he ought to loosen up. Bonner is no lumphead like the steel bosses. From the side door comes Mae's voice calling, "Paul-all!" Curfew for young Paul Bonner. Only the cicadas respond. The kid must be a bit of a rebel. Again: "Paul-all!" The cicadas' choir grows shriller. The side screen door bangs shut. Mae is not happy.

Bonner changes the subject. He must soon make a business decision that depends on whether there will be a national steel strike in September. With the union weakened by a current round of mill layoffs, it probably won't go on strike, will it?

"For pensions? You bet we will, layoffs or no layoffs! So far it's only a few hundred men. The economists call it a recession. Personally..." Miravich sips his tart drink, "...I think it's another message from Mr. Buck."

"Mr. Buck even causes layoffs?" Bonner laughs, then reconsiders. "Well, why not? Somebody could be pulling strings like that. Somebody's trying to prevent me from building my factory. That's a Mr. Buck kind of...evil."

"You want to hear about evil?" Miravich says. "The Mr. Buck I know is running the mills into the ground so the owners can grab up the profits and leave us in misery. My Mr. Buck—" He stops, then leans forward, intent, excited. "Maybe it's no joke. Maybe there's a pattern here. Suppose some organization is trying to put us both out of business. *Suppose Mr. Buck is real.* And I have some evidence. That's what I came to tell you."

Bonner swings his legs around and sits on the edge of the lounge. "Go on."

Miravich tells why he thinks the attempt to kill him back in 1944 might be traced to an employee of a company that was collecting air samples in the Watts.

"An outfit called the Greater Ohio Industrial...something or other," he says, pausing when he notices Bonner straighten up at the reference. He continues, "And then I saw that towboat with the name *J.T. Buck.* Don't know how that fits in, but it's sure a weird coincidence."

"Wait a minute!" Bonner pushes himself out of the lounge and rushes into the house. He returns with a business card, saying it was given to him a few weeks ago when he visited a small company in Monessen. In preparing a prospectus for potential investors in the aircraft parts plant, Bonner had to compile a list of companies that would supply equipment for the plant. He hoped to get a written commitment from the owner of the Monessen firm, a producer of high quality pumps and valves. "His name is Joe Doan," Bonner says. "He thought I had a wonderful idea...but—" Bonner shakes his head and again glances at the card.

It is unlike Bonner to be so flummoxed, Miravich thinks. To conceal his impatience, he recrosses his legs and stares hard at the hand palming the card.

"First time I ever heard anything like this," Bonner says. "Doan said he's sorry but he can't do business with me. *Can't!* A couple weeks earlier, a man from Pittsburgh came and warned Doan that if he sold equipment to me, all the mills in the valley would cancel their contracts with him. He can't afford to lose that business." The man who delivered the warning said he spoke for the big steel companies, who were merely protecting their monopoly on labor in the valley. There are only so many men of working age, and the steel producers all pay the same union wages. A new industry might offer higher wages and suck the labor right out of the mills.

"When I asked who this man was," Bonner continues, "Doan became nervous, maybe even afraid, wouldn't mention the man's name." But he handed Bonner a business card left by his visitor, wished him good luck and ushered him out of the office.

Bonner holds the card in the light of a citronella candle and reads aloud: "Dr. Robert DuBray, executive director, Greater Ohio Industrial Propagation Association." He gives the card to Miravich.

"So that's how you spell it," Miravich says, explaining that he heard of a "doctor" with a similar name who visited Donora during the killer-smog episode.

"That's our man!" Bonner nods slowly.

Sitting knee to knee across two feet of muggy evening, candlelight flickering on their faces, they both see, or at least sense, a flush of comprehension rising in the other's face. Is that dark abyss, on the edge of which they've been teetering all these years, not bottomless after all? For a moment they remain silent, each reviewing his own memories of the violent incidents and reversals of fortune that have cascaded through their lives since the day they overheard a conversation at the jailhouse window in Charleston.

Still remaining is the question of whether and how Dr. DuBray and Mr. Buck are connected. Bonner says the name of the towboat, the *J.T. Buck*, might be a clue. "I've heard they name them after prominent industrialists," Bonner says, immediately hurrying back inside to fetch a Pittsburgh metropolitan phone directory. There is no company or private residence listed under J.T. Buck, but DuBray's association has a Pittsburgh address as well as several branch offices, including one on 11th Avenue in McKeesport.

"Grubmann!" Bonner exclaims, looking up from the directory. He tells Miravich about the pest who represents DuBray's association and probably can be found at the McKeesport office. He proposes confronting Grubmann and trying to pry information from him before approaching the head man. They agree to meet at the 11th Avenue address at ten the next morning.

As Miravich starts down the steps, Bonner says, "What about the foreman's job?"

"You can't make a manager out of me. But there's a good man at the Watts. Jack Kiefer. Try him."

■

Miravich finds the 11th Avenue address in a quiet neighborhood of churches, abandoned shops, and second-story apartments. It is a two-story building sheathed in simulated yellow brick shingles with Fred's Barber Shop on the first floor. Bonner is sitting in Fred's barber's chair, getting a trim and a shoe shine and having a fine old time, laughing and talking with Fred. Miravich soon perceives that there's method in Bonner's grooming. With his hearty good nature, he has drawn out Fred, who is describing the peculiar activities of "that jerk upstairs." Fred takes care of the building for the owner and has put up with Walter Grubmann for fifteen years. Grubmann works alone, Fred says, though now and then some "rough" characters pay him a visit. "Sal Grotto, for one," he adds in a whisper, responding to Bonner's raised eyebrows.

Five minutes later, the barber whips the apron off his patron, flamboyantly disposing of the few hairs he has nicked from Bonner's balding head. Miravich and Bonner go outside and enter a door leading to a narrow staircase. At the top is a small landing and a single door with marbled glass in the upper half and in black paint the association's name and "Walter Grubmann, Branch Mgr."

Bonner opens the door without knocking and walks toward a large desk on which are stacked newspapers, magazines and piles of clippings. Behind the desk, a stout man in shirt sleeves, tie and suspenders rises in surprise. The rest of the office is bare, except for filing cabinets, piles of newspapers, and one frail ladderback chair sitting in front of the desk. Visitors obviously are not welcome. Dustballs blow about the floor. Through an open door they see trash and beer cases heaped in the rear room.

"Walter Grubmann?" Bonner says, as if he's come to make an arrest.

"May I help you?" Grubmann does not look remotely helpful. He removes his glasses and studies each visitor in turn. His sharp glance clings to Miravich who, in his well-worn black and white, union-local softball jacket, presents a strange contrast with business-suited Bonner.

"Remember me?" Bonner says, walking around the corner of the desk. "You came to my place trying to sign me up." He picks up a brochure touting the benefits of GOIPA membership. "I saw you at my trial. Day after day, all day long, you sat there taking notes. Why'd that interest you? What the hell is this outfit?"

"We are a business organization providing services for businessmen."

Bonner is riffling through a pile of clippings and photographs on the desk.

"That's private property," Grubmann says, reaching for the phone. "I could have the police here in two minutes."

"I could crack your skull in one," Miravich says, hefting a paperweight.

"Now, now, none of that," Bonner says. He winks at Miravich and lowers his voice. "You know what I think, Grubmann?" He waves a handful of picket-line photos in the man's face. "I think you're just a lousy snoop. Look, Joe, here's a scary one for your scrapbook." The black and white glossy shows Miravich with a raised fist on a picket line during the '46 steel strike. The word "Commie" is scrawled across the print in white ink.

Miravich takes the picture. "I remember that day. They just announced the settlement and we were joking with the cops."

"This outfit you work for," Bonner says, "it's a front of some kind, isn't it?" He picks up another handful of pictures and clippings. "Industrial spies, that's what you are. I've heard of it."

"Industrial rats!" Miravich says. He moves the phone out of Grubmann's reach and, clutching his tie, begins cinching it up.

Bonner really does have to restrain him now. "Just tell us who your boss is and where we can find him."

Miravich sticks his face in. "Who's Mr. Buck?"

Is it their imagination, or does Grubmann really tremble and go pale? He quickly recovers. "I don't know such a person. Leave me alone." He slumps in his chair.

The next step would be to ransack the office, but even Miravich, furious though he is, knows this would be a mistake, in broad daylight.

Out on the street, Miravich feels a little foolish. "You know I wasn't going to hit him. He's just an old man pasting clippings."

"I know. Let's talk in my car."

"What a boat! Lincoln Continental. You're really flaunting it now, Bonner."

They sit in the car and discuss their next move. Grubmann may know more, but probably not much more. In his strong-arming days, Miravich picked only on tough scabs and finks, which gave some moral authority to the task. There's nothing moral about beating up a pathetic old man. The only thing left, Miravich says, is to visit GOIPA's main office. But Bonner can't go anywhere for a couple of weeks. He is in the middle of sensitive negotiations with potential investors and must leave tomorrow for a meeting in Cleveland.

"Do you want to get to the bottom of this or not?"

Bonner starts the car but sits there with one hand on the wheel, musing. "I went hunting once for bear in the Adirondacks. Tommie McPhee, Gas Stowe, and me. We had to crash through thick underbrush where you couldn't have seen an elephant. I wasn't at all sure I wanted to find a bear in there." He laughs at the memory. "We saw bear tracks but no bear."

■

Miravich wants to meet this DuBray, look him in the eye and intimidate him. But he can't just pick up and drive to Pittsburgh any old time; it's a half-day round trip. He intends to go on his next free day, but free days are hard to come by. Urgent business at the local commands his attention. At home, Mitzie's father falls ill and is hospitalized. Tests reveal deterioration of liver, gall bladder, heart, and other organs. Stanley is seventy years old and suffers from "the aging process," a doctor declares. When Dolly comes to his room, he touches her cheek with the knuckles of a clenched, arthritic hand. The doctor orders warm milk and bed rest. The Miraviches take him home. Outside of Dolly's presence, he rarely speaks except to breathe an occasional, undiscriminating "Shit!" and his dark eyes disclose only bitterness and anger. He seems to be regressing from his two or three years of accepting America.

Miravich becomes impatient with him. "Why did you stay here if you hate America so much?"

Stanley says one word, "Her," and nods at a framed photograph of his dead wife.

Miravich bends and studies at the picture. "You had a real beauty there, Stanley, and she gave you a beautiful daughter who gave you a beautiful granddaughter." Still bending, he looks at the old man lying on his side, his unshaven chin only inches away. "If you're determined to die," Miravich says, tears unaccountably welling in his eyes, "you ought to die happy."

Stanley reaches over and fiercely squeezes his hand. "Dumb Croat!" he says.

He dies within two days, in the end calm and sedate. Father Strunka says a funeral Mass, well-attended by the Polish community and a few men who worked with Stanley in the mill. He was not trusting enough to contribute his hard-earned wages to U.S. Steel's contributory pension plan, but he saved a large amount of cash after Sonya died. He never went anyplace or did anything. In a drawer with treasured mementos from his Polish boyhood, Mitzie finds $3,013 in cash, much of it still in pay envelopes, as well as a $10,000 life insurance policy, a deed for the house free and clear of encumbrances, and a one-sentence will taken down by the Reverend Strunka in Stanley's last hours, leaving everything to "my beautiful daughter." Stanley's bitter slice of life was larger, at least in material terms, than anyone knew.

The day after the funeral, Miravich finds his wife and Dolly in the studio. The child is playing with a block of wood, talking child talk. She has been abnormally moody since her grandfather died. Mitzie sits on her stool, gazing in bewilderment at Stanley's legacy piled on the table in neat stacks of $1,

$5, and $10 bills. A mason jar is filled with coins found in the pay envelopes. Miravich leans against the door frame, watching the two. He and Mitzie put aside their differences in order to help Stanley during his illness and give him a respectful sendoff. He is not sure what will happen next, but he knows the problems have only been deferred.

Mitzie has been sitting there a long time staring at the money. Miravich clears his throat. "Do you mind telling me what you're thinking about?"

She gives a little start, as if waking up, and half-turns to him. "I'm thinking this is blood money," she says in a low voice. "Papa earned it in a job he hated." She puts a hand over her eyes. "And then he came home and took it out on Mama and me."

"It was honestly earned, Mitz. At the end, maybe he was ashamed of how he treated you but proud that he could leave something to make up for the bad times. That's how you should think about it."

"I'll open a bank account for Dolly," Mitzie says. "This girl is going to college, that's for sure."

"Let's see," Miravich says, counting on his fingers. "She'll finish high school around nineteen sixty-three. What are we...what are you thinking of—Pitt, maybe?"

"It'll be up to Dolly, of course," Mitzie says. "But I like California. Maybe UCLA or Stanford."

■

By the third week in September Miravich is still tied down in McKeesport and Mr. Buck roams free. A fact-finding board appointed by Truman has found against the industry negotiating-coalition led by U.S. Steel, declaring that the union has the right to bargain for pensions. With a new strike deadline of September 25, Miravich works day and night at the union hall, preparing for a strike.

Bonner relays a messsage from Fred the barber, who reported that Grubmann vanished a day or two after Miravich's and Bonner's first visit. Men came in a truck and removed files from the office but left piles of trash in the back room, including four beer cases filled with empty bottles. Fred's employer, however, continued to pay the rent.

Miravich pictures the old man sitting in his underwear shirt and swigging beer as he scrawls "Commie" across newspaper photographs. Then it occurs to him: a petty cheat like Grubmann would not have left behind the empty beer cases, each worth a 75-cent deposit refund. Unless, of course, he departed under extreme...compulsion.

CHAPTER 8:
September 1949–November 1949

It is late afternoon on the last day of September. As the meeting breaks up, Miravich is swept out of a ballroom in Pittsburgh's William Penn Hotel on a tide of delegates. Excitement in the air. He and about two hundred other local union men have just authorized Phil Murray to call a nationwide strike at midnight unless U.S. Steel meets their pension demand. Twice before, the union has postponed the strike deadline at the request of President Truman, but there will be no more postponements. Murray ordered the committee to remain in Pittsburgh while he returns to the bargaining table.

Miravich goes into a lounge and sips a beer. Cigarette smoke rises lazily from a dozen men chatting at the bar, union guys from around the country, tech sergeants in labor's new army. Strong men, standing together in solidarity, collectively they appear to hold the balance of power in this latest struggle with the industry. Miravich wishes he could restore the balance of power in his own life. After the brief truce during Stanley's illness and funeral, he and Mitzie are still arguing. His thoughts drift despondently back to the union, where he's accomplished damned little during five years as the local president. Finally standing up for Negroes' job rights is about the only thing he has to be proud of, though many union members think otherwise. Walking through the mill, he hears anonymous shouts of "nigger lover," and a segregationist faction has started a movement to oust him in next spring's election.

"Joe Miravich?" The voice near at hand snaps his self-accusatory reverie.

A young man stands at his elbow. "I'm Jim McPhee, Tom McPhee's son."

"Oh, yeah, you're on the International staff." They shake hands. He must be in his late twenties, a red-headed man with a concavity of face that reminds Miravich of his dad. Miravich recalls something of his story. He worked a year at the Watts, served a couple of years in the army, and graduated from Pitt on the GI Bill. He is an economist, one of a handful of intellectuals that Murray has hired in technical positions.

"I really admire how you handled that open hearth strike," McPhee says. "That took courage and conviction."

"Let me buy you a beer," Miravich says, feeling better. Returning to the strike, he says, "Being truthful, Walt Tyrell's protest is what really made it happen."

"But you supported him, put your future on the line. It's a big problem in all the locals." He looks thoughtfully at Miravich, decides to continue. "The locals have got to revise these Jim Crow seniority setups. And that won't happen unless the International forces their hand."

"Your dad taught you right. But you better be careful what you say and who to."

"I trust Joe Miravich. My dad wrote about you when I was in the army." He tips up his bottle of Duquesne and takes a healthy sip. "I didn't come on this staff with the idea of preserving inequality."

"Boy oh boy! Now we got an Opposer McPhee on the International staff. So what kind of research do you do?"

"Mostly research on employers. Financial records, labor costs, profits, investments, corporate history. Whatever we need to know."

Miravich's beer halts on another trip to his mouth. "You know how to dig up the past, find the backgrounds of industry bosses and so forth?"

McPhee smiles. "I do it all the time."

"Do you work for the locals, too?"

"Sure. My assigned work comes first, but I can do research for the locals, especially for Joe Miravich."

Miravich practically leaps off the bar stool. "Jim McPhee, you got a customer." He leads McPhee to a quiet table and tells his story, starting at the beginning in the Charleston jail, leading up through the attempted assassination of Phil Murray, the various efforts to silence Miravich and Bonner, the killing of Eddie Cramczak and his buddies. The mysterious involvement of Robert DuBray and his hokey association, and Miravich's chance meeting on the river with the *J.T. Buck*. And the questions: What is GOIPA and who is Mr. Buck?

McPhee agrees to look into the Mr. Buck mystery as soon as the steel strike and negotiations are over. As he jots final notes in a small pad, the call comes for the committee to reconvene in the ballroom. It is a brief meeting. Murray reports that further negotiation would be futile. There is no need for debate. He will order that telegrams be sent to hundreds of locals, ordering them to go on strike at midnight.

Next morning, Bonner is pleased to hear that McPhee will do research on GOIPA and Mr. Buck. But Miravich detects a note of pessimism in his voice over the phone. "Get this strike over quickly, will you, Joe?" he says. "I've got to get my foundry back to work."

"What the hell, a little strike goes with the territory."

"It better be damned little. I...uh...put myself in a bad position." You can almost hear the sweat stand out on his forehead. "I thought we'd avoid a strike. What happened?"

"Simple. U.S. Steel doesn't want to pay a pension to sick, old men sitting around doing nothing."

■

Rain drives hard against the windshield, cascading over hapless wipers and across the hood of Bonner's car. October cloudburst. He can barely make out the curb bordering the traffic lane on his left. Leaning over the wheel, he swipes a jagged streak across the steamed-up windshield with the back of his hand. He lightly pumps the brake pedal and stares ahead, trying to spot the tail lights of a car in front of him. Instead there appears an apparition, a black-and-white snapshot that quickly fades into the downpour, of blurred faces leering at him, mimicking the foggy wraiths that danced on his windshield on that day in 1937, the beginning of a dream life that has run parallel with real life all this time. Now a sharp pain stabs at his chest, forcing him to fall back against the seat with a loud gasp. Real angina pain, not dream pain, a companion of recent months, but it swiftly departs, scared off by a great clap of thunder.

Bonner breathes deeply, cautiously, surprised to find that he has survived those few seconds without smashing into another car. The downpour continues. He turns into a parking lot behind a two-story brick factory building, the home of Mercury Steel Castings. When the rain lets up a little, he gets out of the car under a flimsy umbrella and half-walks, half-trots around to the front entrance. Four Steelworker pickets, holding newspapers over their heads, stand flattened against the building. But the narrow roof overhang is no protection from cold rain blowing from the southeast.

"Come in out of the rain!" Bonner shouts, as he pulls up puffing at the doorway.

Three of the men follow him into the vestibule, pouring water out of the clefts in their hats. The fourth man, Ben Evans, the local president, remains outside. When Bonner calls to him, he defiantly shakes his head. He takes a principled stand (albeit in a puddle) that striking labor shall not encroach upon capital's private property.

Bonner says to the others, "It's not trespassing if I invite you in." They nod, either knowingly or eagerly. "I'll have someone bring down coffee."

He slowly climbs a wide staircase to the second-floor offices, arriving at the top out of breath. He has laid off his two-woman secretarial force for the duration of the strike. Only the plant manager, Tutweiler, and an assistant maintain the small reheating furnaces in the first-floor shop. Bonner sends the assistant downstairs with coffee for the pickets, then takes off his wet clothing and hangs the suit coat and pants carefully on a rack so the wrinkles will fall out. With the office heat turned off, he is chilly sitting at his desk wearing only underwear and calf-length socks held up by garters. But he forgets his discomfort as he studies figures he has jotted on a yellow pad, assessing again his bleak situation. The first payment on a big bank loan soon will be due, but he has no cash and the strike has choked off most of the revenues normally generated by his businesses.

Bonner, the wily businessman, got himself into this jam by failing to see what should have been obvious more than a month ago: that all potential investors in his parts plant have been scared away. Banks refused to give him a startup loan; mill suppliers refused to deal with him; and opposing businessmen argued that Bonner's plan to operate as a union plant would help put the valley in perpetual thrall to grasping union labor. But he was blinded by impatience and the importunings of his partner, the engineering genius, Max Trippitt, who could be extraordinarily persuasive over a few drinks. The two of them, Trippitt argued, would inspire confidence in their project by absorbing a minimal startup cost. He produced an artfully-drawn sketch of the factory (or *some* factory) as his initial contribution. Moreover, the demand-supply logic of the plan appealed to Bonner: how could the steel companies *not* welcome an important new customer in the valley?

In early September, gambling on a peaceful settlement of the steel negotiations, he made a downpayment on the riverfront property and retained an architect to produce a preliminary design. How could the steel producers possibly ignore the recommendation of Truman's Steel Board and deny pensions to old and valued workers? They did, however, the strike is now in its fourth week, and all Bonner's businesses have lost money. To avoid a strike at Mercury Steel, he offered to sign a standard "me-too" agreement with the local union, granting the wages and benefits eventually accepted by the big steelmakers in return for continued work in the foundry. But Evans, the local president, a stickler for union solidarity, rejected the offer. Not that his piddling local of a dozen members strengthened Murray's hand in any measurable way. And now thousands of dollars worth of already-produced parts sit on the loading dock, awaiting the end of the strike. "The business world," Miravich remarked, hearing of Evans's peculiar decision, "got no monopoly on jerks."

With beer sales also declining, Bonner knew by the second week of the strike that he had lost his gamble. He halted the work and promptly received invoices totaling $10,000. Max Trippitt kicked in his "last" $100 and departed for parts unknown. Left in the lurch, Bonner paid a third of the debt by selling his interests in lumber and trucking. But no amount of fiddling with bank withdrawals and deposits could extract him from this mess. As a last resort he negotiated a six-month loan at a new bank, The Friend of the People Bank, which imposed onerous terms. His name, he was told by a loan officer, was on a "high-risk list" because of his reputation for acting on "intuition and guts." Bonner signed the note, pledging as collateral all the hard assets of Bonner Beer Distributing. If he defaults, nothing will be left of Bonner Beer, except the customers.

Sitting in the drafty office, he props his elbows on the desk and explores lines in his forehead with fingertips. Only two weeks remain before he must make the first loan payment. It is entirely possible that everything will come crashing down, and Mae and the boys will be hurt most. He suspects he does not have much longer to live. Weak heart, clogged arteries, diabetes... His physician urged him to have a thorough checkup. Not now, Bonner said.

The amazing thing is that his current situation seems to be a reprise of the twenties when he risked too much and lost all—and his father, too. How could he make two mistakes of this magnitude in one lifetime? In the Depression, at least, the heavens fell on almost everybody. This time, someone aimed the fall so that it would hit Pete Bonner exclusively. God, he wants to get his hands on Robert DuBray!

■

The national steel strike of 1949 is tame by standards of the 1930s. The steel companies make no attempt to hire scabs, and the union allows maintenance men to go into the mills to keep the furnaces "on heat." Miravich works long days, visiting the picket lines, managing a hardship program for strikers who run out of money, and distributing beans, flour and potatoes to needy families. He and other officers take no union salary during the strike, and money is getting a little tight for everybody. But every evening he stops at a few saloons. To gauge the morale of his members, he tells himself. Although alcohol has never been his particular vice, drinking five or six beers a night and staying out late is becoming customary. When goes home, Mitzie gives him the silent treatment. They sleep in the same bed only because Dolly, who is four years old, expects them to. Whatever holds them together as a family has stretched to the breaking point.

He can never tell what Mitzie might do. One morning, barely awake, he rolls over and gets a fuzzy glimpse of her standing near the bedroom door. She has taken off her pajama shirt. Her breasts, large and melony, stick out above lemon-colored pajama pants. Seeing that he is awake, she breaks into a run and lands belly down on him before he can move. As he gasps for breath, she sits up, straddling his hips, and holds his wrists tightly on the bed.

"Damn you, Joe! I'm not going to let you ruin our lives."

"You just ruined me."

"I'm serious. Do you want to lose Dolly and me?"

"You know that's a dumb question, Mitz."

"I think we're in the wrong place at the wrong time. You're not getting what you want from the union business, and I don't want to be just a mill wife."

His mouth is dry, and a hangover is taking hold. He feels spiteful. "Too good to be a mill wife? You come from the mill and married into the mill, so you'll get no pity from me. I got things to do here."

She struggles to control her temper. "Why? What things? What's going on, Joe?"

He can't help squirming under her, trying to conceal his tumescence. "Talk is cheap."

She stiffens and draws back. "It's like you're deliberately pushing me away."

An interesting suggestion: pushing her away, her and Dolly, forcing them out of his dangerous orbit, for their own good. He is a marked man, pursued by dangerous people. It would be a noble course of action, if true, and for a moment he allows it to be true. But even he can't act out this egregious lie. The fact is, he never thought of such a thing. He is no hero, just plain old self-centered Joe, and this realization adds spite to his words.

"I guess if I said the right thing now, I could get laid."

She flings herself off him.

One evening after work he and Semchek are walking up Fifth Avenue. The sky is low and mean, hinting of an approaching storm. They hear normal street noises: car doors opening and slamming, engines starting up, tires rolling over the brick paving with a hard blubbery sound, clacking of high heels approaching and receding. But something is missing. It is like an August evening without the clamor of cicadas, this mill town without the comforting background chorus of clanking, whirring, grinding, roaring, screeching, and hissing supplied round-the-clock by a working steel mill. They have spent a couple hours making the rounds of bars and downing beers while reassuring anxious steelworkers that the strike will end soon in a wonderful victory. And now they intend to ease out of the evening in a quieter place where they can talk undisturbed, the basement cocktail lounge in the city's largest hotel, the Penn McKee.

The clientele of the lounge consists largely of salesmen, engineers, and business travelers with an occasional sprinkling of steelworkers willing to spend ten cents more per bottle of beer for the privilege of mixing with a better class of drinkers. Tonight, attention in the lounge is riveted on a TV set situated high in the far corner from which issues the false note of faked melodrama in a wrestling commentator's voice as musclebound men throw themselves at one another, catapulting off the ropes and slamming to the canvas. Television arrived in McKeesport taverns only two months ago, but already "professional" wrestlers and Milton Berle are winning the battle for the minds of men. Attendance at evening church services, union meetings, civic gatherings, and what-have-you has fallen off in direct proportion.

Miravich and Semchek talk for a while, and then, despite better intentions, fall into the trance-like state of tv-watchers that they themselves disparage. After a couple bottles of beer apiece, Miravich says he has had enough for the night and goes to the men's room. Returning to the bar, he notices that four new customers have come from the dining room, jammed themselves into a booth, and are ordering after-dinner drinks. With a quick glance Miravich identifies them as management men, probably U.S. Steel executives celebrating some anniversary. He tries to ignore their loud talk and laughter until he hears the word "commie" uttered in a contemptuous way by a voice that sounds annoyingly familiar. Phil Shumly! Turning on the barstool, Miravich matches the voice with the face as Shumly expostulates about the "Reds" who control the Watts local. Against his better judgment, Miravich slides off the stool and walks toward the booth.

"What a coincidence," Shumly says, seeing Miravich approach. "I'm seeing Red right now."

"Are you talking about me, mister?" Miravich stands in front of Shumley who occupies an outside booth seat.

"If the shirt fits," Shumly says. His friends glare at Miravich.

"You shouldn't tell lies like that in public, and I'm asking you politely to take them back."

One of Shumley's companions speaks up. "Get lost, pal," he says authoritatively, as if issuing a command to a mill worker. Miravich recognizes the type if not the man.

Shumly grows bolder. "Like I said, Miravich, if the shirt fits..."

Miravich reaches down and pulls him out of the booth with a fistful of shirtfront. At the same moment, Semchek comes up behind and tugs on Miravich's jacket. "Joe, let him go."

He knows that Semchek is right. He hesitates and during that long, static moment he wonders if his whole life has set him up to do stupid things like this, and he loosens his grip on Shumly's shirt. But a sudden push by Shumly distills the hatred of a lifetime in his leering face, and Miravich feels himself sliding down a greased chute. Exploding forward, he lands an uppercut just below the rib cage. Shumly misses with a roundhouse right, then begins to collapse under a flurry of punches to the head. As he goes down with a heavy belch, Miravich smashes his face with an elbow. Blood spurts from the burst nose. Shumly's friends have been trying to pull the two apart, but now they attack Miravich. Glasses, chairs, and stools are falling all around. Other customers join in. Miravich falls under a mass of bodies as wild fists rain on his own head, and he rolls over and over in puddles of beer and glass fragments.

Sirens! Loud voices. "Clear out! Clear out!" Something whacks him on the back of the head. When he wakes up, he is being dragged, feet spragging, out the door. They throw him into the back of a paddywagon. He spends all night in jail. Shumly, badly hurt, winds up in a hospital. In the morning, a police magistrate finds Miravich guilty of misdemeanor rowdyism. Within an hour, the local radio station reports that "a U.S. Steel Corporation executive has been assaulted by a local official of the United Steelworkers of America, shattering the peaceful atmosphere of the current steel strike." Feeling too mean and angry to go home, Miravich spends all day at the local and then goes drinking by himself.

When he finally gets home near midnight, Dolly has gone to bed. Mitzie is working in the studio and doesn't hear him enter. Low music comes from a radio on her workbench. Miravich recognizes the oh, so-soft voice of Alice Faye, singing "You'll Never Know."

You went away

And my heart went with you.

He stumbles over Dolly's stool. Mitzie turns with withering eyes. "You're drunk. They should have locked you up again." She turns off the radio. "Are you losing your mind, Joe?"

"Don't worry about it." He has never seen her so furious, which irritates him because she has barely spoken for three days and is no prize package herself.

"Don't worry? You sonofabitch!"

He slaps her smartly on the cheek. "To hell with you, bitch!"

She stands still. Her cheek turns red. When she walks by him, brushing his arm, it's as if a cold wind passes.

"Mitz, Mitz, wait a minute. I didn't mean it..." But she has gone.

■

A break in the nationwide steel strike finally comes in late October when Bethlehem Steel surrenders on the pension issue, cracking the industry's united front after 31 days of strike. U.S. Steel holds out for two more weeks but finally succumbs. On the evening of Friday, November 11, local union officials assemble in the William Penn to vote on a proposed settlement. Whooping and raising fists, the delegates unanimously approve the agreement, then surge toward the podium to shake hands with Murray, or merely touch the great man. Miravich picks his way through the crowd to Jim McPhee, who stands behind Murray, sucking on an empty pipe. He has the vacant stare of a man who hasn't slept for a week, but he smiles at Miravich and says in his ear, "I have something for you, but I need two weeks to finish this business."

Miravich is grateful. Throwing his voice over the noise, he says, "Thanks, brother." At this instant, he is knocked against Murray, who turns thinking the compliment was meant for him. "Glad you approve, Joe," he says dryly.

Miravich pumps his hand. On impulse, without knowing why, he says, "You beat 'em all, except Mr. Lewis and Mr. Buck."

For a moment Murray is lost in his own blank look. But Dave McDonald shoves Miravich out of the way and ushers the president to the door.

At midnight, the Watts Works begins calling in crews. Younger men are not happy with the new contract because the union has to sacrifice wage increases for pensions. "But think of it!" Miravich tells a faction of young grumblers next day at a local meeting. "For the first time in history, a whole industry of four hundred thousand men will be covered by decent pension plans. All you got to do is stay in the mill till you're too old to piss right." A steel retiree will receive $100 a month for life, with the company paying everything except the pittance that each worker must contribute to Social Security. But for widows of men killed in the mill, like Anna Cramczak, the agreement contains nothing.

■

The settlement comes too late for Pete Bonner. The first payment on his loan is due on the Tuesday following the U.S. Steel settlement. The foundry is barely back in production, beer sales have not yet picked up, and Bonner has scraped together only $500 of a scheduled $3,400 loan payment. The bank refuses to extend the deadline. His business, his home, his family—all are on the line. In desperation, Bonner turns to the usurer of last resort.

An hour later, driving back to his beer store, an envelope containing $3,000 in cash stashed in an inside coat pocket, he experiences an exhilarating sense of freedom from default. But that feeling of relief fades into an inexplicable sodden heaviness, and, getting out of the car, he walks past his office and goes into Saboulovich's Cafe. He hasn't been there for months.

The saloon is nearly empty. Young John Saboulovich is tending bar in place of his father who, Bonner is surprised to hear, has been ill for weeks, laid up with the various ailments that can befall a seventy-two-year-old Serb transported to the dust and grime of McKeesport at the age of ten with immune systems developed by his forebears in the pristine Kopaonik mountains. His saloon, which depends entirely on mill trade, lost money during the strike. Bonner was thinking of collecting $50 owed him for the last three beer deliveries. Selling beer on credit is illegal, but he does it for a few old customers. Now he needs every $50 he is owed. Nonetheless, he writes a note absolving the debt and tells John to open the folded scrap of paper after he leaves.

He has been on the wagon for three months, doctor's orders, and the straight rye whiskey tastes like something he should stay away from. But it helps lessen the oppressive feeling. He cannot look himself full in the face because the backbar mirror has been reduced to a narrow slice by a three-bottle display of the ever-popular Four Roses. He sees only the left side of his face (or is it the right side reversed), and he thinks about right and wrong. He always has played by his own laws, some of which, he grants, are on the margins of rectitude. Up to now, he has trusted himself not to exceed the bounds of morality and good judgment, and when he's decided—or more likely when Mae has decided—that he's strayed too far, he's pulled himself back toward the center.

Bonner takes a sip of rye, deliciously harsh. He presses a hand over his breast pocket and feels the thick packet of bills that Sal Grotto handed him an hour ago. Like all loan sharks, Grotto charges triple the going rate at the banks, which means fifteen percent. "Per week," Grotto said briskly, watching Bonner's face for a reaction. Seeing none, he continued, "You can't make a payment, I get a piece of the beer business. It's up to you to figure a way around the Liquor Control Board."

Finishing his drink, Bonner smiles at young John. "Give your dad my best."

When he goes down for breakfast in the morning, Paul, a high school junior, has already left for school. Albert is away at college. Despite Bonner's wishes, he decided to study history at a small school in Ohio rather than architecture at Rensselaer Polytechnic. Bonner is surprised how little that matters now. His immediate concern is how to explain his current financial predicament to Mae. She knows only that he got into trouble by following Max Trippitt's advice, though Bonner has been vague about the extent of their indebtedness. She comes into the kitchen radiating annoyance about his fall from grace last night. But she scolds him only briefly in proportion to his one-drink retreat from sobriety while fixing a hardboiled egg and a piece of dry rye toast for him.

"Will we make the payment deadline?" she asks.

He bites into the dry toast, makes a face. "I'll deposit the money this morning." He pats his breast pocket and says, with lowered eyes, "A lot of customers owed us money."

"That's a relief. Albert called from school last night. He's heard us talking about the tight situation, and he offered to drop out of college and go to work."

Bonner throws down his spoon. "Absolutely not!" He almost sputters with indignation. "What kind of college is that? Don't they teach them anything about business? You take a chance, sometimes it doesn't work out, you land in a jam, and then you get out of the jam."

Mae is startled by his reaction. "He only asked, Pete."

"I'll take care of it, dammit!" He jams his arms into his suit jacket.

Driving downtown, Bonner pounds the steering wheel with one hand. He pulls into a gas station driveway and sits for a while, thinking. At last he walks to a phone booth, calls Gas Stowe, and says, humbly, that he needs a favor. It happens that Stowe is on the board of directors at the bank where Bonner took out his loan and agrees to meet him there. An hour later, Stowe appears in the bank lobby, wearing beach attire—duck pants and striped polo shirt under a blue coat with white, rubber-soled beach shoes. He is departing at noon for his annual marlin-fishing trip off the coast of Cuba.

Bonner can barely speak for embarrassment. He briefly describes his dilemma, leaving Grotto out of it, and asks Stowe if he, as "a personal favor," would use his influence to obtain a postponement on the first loan payment.

"Pete…" Seeing Bonner's anguish, Stowe gazes at the bank's vaulted ceiling, whistling silently. Then he says, "I can't change a loan agreement. But…" He faces his friend. "…maybe you've forgotten. I owe you one from the old days. Three thousand? Okay, you're covered. But not a penny goes into that cockeyed factory scheme."

Always comfortably liquid, Stowe withdraws three $1,000 bills from his account, hands them to a stunned Bonner, and asks him to sign a simple I.O.U. at the 1% "old pals" rate once common in McKeesport. They shake hands, and Stowe dashes out to a taxi waiting to take him to the airport. Bonner sees a pretty face in the back seat.

Stowe's $3,000 immediately goes back into the bank as a loan payment, and Bonner feels relieved of a bruising weight. But shouldering that mass was nothing, he discovers as he leaves the bank, compared with the moral tonnage of the $3,000 he borrowed from Grotto. He has refrained from opening the packet of bills, as if one glance inside would, as in a fairy tale, turn the beholder into a goat, or a pillar of graphite dust swept up from Fifth Avenue. He hurries his steps on the way to Louie's Confectionery.

When he enters the store, Louie disdainfully jerks a thumb toward the back room. His attitude reminds Bonner of continuing rumors that Louie might be conspiring with John Miomyo—known familiarly as "Johnny Mio"—to depose Sal as the rackets king. Brother against brother, a terrible thing, even for racketeers. Bonner raises a corner of the entryway curtain and steps inside. Sal is sitting at his desk, an open ledger in front of him. Pixie leans against a filing cabinet, sucking a cherry popsicle.

Gazing coldly at Bonner, Grotto takes the envelope and looks inside. "What's this? You're giving it all back?" A scowl darkens his sullen face. "Never thought I'd see you welshing on a deal, Pete."

"What deal? I'm repaying the loan before I use it."

"Money back, shit! I was looking to a relationship. This is the second time you aced me out." He counts the money. "There's only three bills here. You owe another three hundred bucks, counting cost."

"Cost? I only got the money last night."

"What time, five o'clock?" He counts on his fingers. "Fifteen hours. The rule is, four hours makes the day. You used my money for a whole goddamn day. Besides, I don't respect you no more." He sticks his hand out. "Three hundred."

"To hell with you." These are the most satisfying words he has spoken as a businessman.

"Did I hear right?" Grotto leans back in his reclining desk chair, chin tucked into his neck, eyebrows arched upward. His eyes shift to Pixie.

"You heard right." Bonner feels Pixie's hovering presence. A veil of indifference as cold as a grave shroud seems to fall into place, separating Bonner from his mortal body. He turns to the big man and says, "I probably deserve whatever you can dish out." Startled out of his sugary reverie, Pixie looks for a place to lay down the dripping remains of his half-sucked popsicle while try-ing to decide what's going on here. When nothing happens, Bonner swipes aside the curtain and walks out.

CHAPTER 9:
November 1949–December 1949

On the evening Mitzie announces that she and Dolly are leaving him, Miravich has just come home cold sober. He sees luggage piled in the living room and immediately knows this is the worst thing that will ever happen to him. Mitzie is sitting there, waiting for him. She always faces unpleasantness directly. "We have to go, Joe. I'm taking Dolly. Early tomorrow morning."

Her pile of luggage indicates this will not be an overnight trip. He drops a folder of union papers and goes rigid in front of her. "Mitzie, no! No!" He wants to seize her and crush her to his chest, but he knows this won't help. She is not bluffing. If only now and then she would bluff.

Dolly runs into the room and throws herself at him. Catching her in the armpits, he raises her shoulder-high. "Hiya, honey. My God, Dolly!" He kisses her, on the forehead, on both cheeks, on her neck, on her hands. "Dolly, Dolly, I love you."

"Well, Daddy," she says, playfully reprimanding him for over-acting, "I love you, too."

He sees Mitzie take a couple of backward steps, going weak in the knees. "Dolly," he says, putting her down, "why don't you go to the back yard and ride your tricycle? Daddy and Mommy have to talk. We'll be out real soon."

The child runs out.

Miravich is torn between love and hate—no, not hate, he thinks, never hate. He walks to Mitzie, who is barely able to stand, and puts an arm around her shoulders and gently pushes her to a sitting position on the couch. He takes off his jacket and sits beside her. She is shaking and has tears in her eyes.

"I'm sorry, Joe," she finally says. "It's the only thing I can do. We've been breaking up for months. It won't get any better, and I don't want Dolly to see us fighting. Or to hate you."

"I'd never hurt her, never, never!"

"You've been living in another world. You're not with us anymore. The drunkenness and violence…"

He feels as if blood is draining out of him. A thousand needle pricks go into his arms and chest. "For God's sakes, Mitz, can't you be a little forgiving for once in your life?"

She allows him to hold her hand. As he sits in a daze, she outlines her plans. She has one-way tickets for a train trip to California, leaving tomorrow. A cousin on her mother's side has offered to put them up on her farm in the Salinas Valley until Mitzie finds a place of her own. Her prospects, she says, are good. She will work as a secretary or a legal aide or a phone operator—God knows, she's had experience at all of these trades—while establishing herself in the arts and crafts world as a woodcarver. Or, she might work as a steel-worker for Edgar Kaiser, who owns a steel mill in Fontana and who is said to be hiring workers from eastern mills.

Since Stanley left her a tidy sum, she can afford to spend a little time look-ing around. Joe may live rent-free in Stanley's old house (he insists on paying rent). Eventually she will sell the house, but he should not feel under pressure to leave. Meanwhile, he can work out his destiny as a union politician, but this destiny will not be hers. She came to this conclusion in October.

"You mean when I smacked you?"

"That was just the final thing."

"Then it was the Red thing?"

"No, Joe, it was not the Red thing."

"The business about you working—?"

"Oh, Joe," she says with a sigh, "it was some of this and a lot of that."

Because she still believed in what the union stood for and didn't want to undermine her husband's credibility, she waited until the pension strike was over. Being a good Catholic, she does not ask for a divorce. She says he may visit her and Dolly if he wishes. She doesn't know what the future will hold. Joe could still be part of that future, but maybe not. She doesn't want Dolly to grow up without a father, but he has been acting less and less like a father and more like an indifferent stranger.

Why is she so brave, determined, so right about everything, so sure of herself even as her lower lip quivers with self-doubt? Why can't she for once in her life be weak and vacillating and take him back, or would this destroy her image of herself? If she's going to live without a man, is she ready to give up sex? Is he ready to give up sex?

Next morning, Tuesday, November 29th at eleven in the morning, he puts them on a train at Penn Station in Pittsburgh. In his last glimpse of them, as he stands on the platform, he sees Dolly's nose squashed against the coach window and behind her, Mitzie's face, already indistinct, fading into the darker background inside the train.

Miravich drives back to the union hall. A short time later, Jim McPhee calls and invites him and Bonner to his office to brief them on his research.

■

"I can tell you this much for certain," Jim McPhee says at the outset, "Robert DuBray is a truly sinister man."

Miravich and Bonner nod almost in unison: it is good, finally, to have their fears confirmed. They are sitting in McPhee's office at the Steelworkers headquarters in Pittsburgh. Makeshift shelves extending along two walls are lined with statistical abstracts, transcripts of Congressional hearings, journals, and economic texts. Scattered over McPhee's desk are newspaper clippings, incorporation records, and assorted other documents from which he assembled most of the story he now relates.

The Greater Ohio Industrial Propagation Association, or "GOIPA"— McPhee pronounces the acronym with distaste—was created in 1926 by a group of industrialists to promote the antiunion American Way movement. Its principal task was to organize opposition to labor unions and promote management-labor cooperation at large nonunion concerns which provided the initial funding. Gradually the organization expanded into a wide-ranging trade association extending across all industries and employing dozens of experts who advised member-companies on matters such as legislation, taxes, human relations programs, and community problems such as economic development, education, worker housing, alcoholism, and communicable diseases.

"What about collecting air samples in the mills?" Miravich asks impatiently.

"That was the unique thing about GOIPA," McPhee says. "They developed a special expertise in mitigating the health effects of industrial processes. Now it's called industrial hygiene. They'd run all kinds of tests at members' plants, including a test for carbon monoxide." The data was never made public, unless it could be used to a company's benefit. GOIPA used the data in scholarly papers, some of which actually advanced knowledge in the field. More often, these papers were aimed at lessening public fears about controversial occupational diseases like silicosis, asbestosis, and coal miners' pneumoconiosis. "They'd present selective data to show that the do-gooders' claims about the ill effects of breathing industrial dust and smoke had no basis in fact. It was a clever way of preempting emotional attacks by anti-smoke crusaders."

"At the Watts, the bosses always tell us breathing a little dust never hurt anyone with a good work ethic," Miravich says.

McPhee nods and adds, "Some of these papers remind me of those tobacco company ads...you know, claiming that smoking actually increases lung capacity and sexual potency."

In 1934, McPhee continues, an eruption of some sort took place inside GOIPA, and a new activist group came to power led by Robert DuBray, the chief of the industrial hygiene unit. Almost immediately the association turned into a malignant crusader against industrial unionism. It established branch offices throughout the mill valleys and staffed them with men whose primary duties seem to have been informing on union activists. The association conducted seminars for unionized firms on how to protect management rights from union incursion. With easy access to members' plants, the industrial hygiene activity came to serve a secondary purpose of antiunion spying, or worse. By some miracle of bribery and threat, DuBray managed to shroud his and GOIPA's activities from public scrutiny. His photograph has never appeared in a newspaper. Yet GOIPA has had enormous influence on the conduct of labor-management relations and pollution control—or lack of it.

"Who was this Robert DuBray," Bonner asks, "and how did he become such a... what's the name for it...?"

"There are several names for it, but 'psychopath' is a good one," McPhee says. He tells of searching old newspaper files and interviewing company executives who dealt with DuBray as well as retired board members of GOIPA. What set him on the right path was Miravich's story about the towboat *J.T. Buck*. Consulting old corporate directories, McPhee found a Jedidiah T. Buck, owner of a barge and towing company until his death by suicide in 1934. Buck, it turned out, was a founder of GOIPA and served as board chairman until his death. According to his obituary, McPhee adds, the poor man suffered from an extreme form of degenerative bone disease. McPhee reads aloud from the obit: "'...he was found dead in his palatial home, his body floating in a bathing pool next to an indoor sauna.' It was obvious, the coroner said, that he had committed suicide."

Bonner is the first to break free of rapt attention. "But if Mr. Buck died in 1934..." He pauses and restates the question. "Is that the end of the story?"

"Not quite," McPhee says, extracting a document from his briefcase. It is a copy of Jedidiah Buck's will, which he obtained in probate court. Buck's estate amounted to a substantial fortune, which Buck split between two people. A spinster sister named Zelda Buck, who lived with and cared for her unmarried brother, surprisingly received only a quarter of the estate. The remaining three-quarters, at least a quarter-million dollars, went to... McPhee reads from the document, "'...my loyal and beloved assistant, Robert E. DuBray who also shall be executor of the estate.'" Why did DuBray deserve so much more than poor old Zelda, who had devoted her life to her brother?

The final step in his research odyssey, which he took only yesterday,

McPhee says, was to interview a reluctant Zelda Buck. Now in her late eighties, she lives alone in an apartment in Shadyside, a high-income Pittsburgh neighborhood. Unfortunately, he learned almost nothing from the poor old woman, whose response to McPhee's questions alternated between unfocused confusion and lucid fury. Her fury she vented on a man she called "Bobby Bray," whom McPhee finally perceived with great surprise was the young Robert DuBray before he renamed himself.

The story came out piece by piece, McPhee says. In about 1920, Jeddy Buck was beginning to suffer from the bone disease and hired a live-in valet-secretary. Somewhere he found this Bobby Bray, a young man who possessed magnetic charm as well as a curious combination of intellect and obsequiousness. Zelda detested Bray from the first, partly because he supplanted her as Jeddy's caretaker but also because he was an "arrogant and devious young man," as might be expected, Zelda told McPhee, of one who came from "hard circumstances." Concerned about his effect on Jeddy, Zelda asked a lawyer friend to look into Bray's background. His father, it turned out, was a Pittsburgh mill worker who died in 1911 of acute alcoholism. Bray himself often spoke of his father in the harshest terms, calling him a "stupid mill man."

While living in the Bucks' home, Bray studied at the University of Pittsburgh at Jeddy's expense and acquired a master's degree in public health. After working in a GOIPA staff position created for him by Jeddy, Bray revealed his true, deceitful nature. He suddenly disappeared, walked away from everything. His mystifying and heartless departure, Zelda said, hurt Jeddy terribly. A year or two later Bray just as suddenly returned, now calling himself Dr. Robert DuBray, a self-proclaimed expert in the new field of industrial hygiene. ("Du," McPhee says parenthetically, is a French prefix indicating royalty.) Still under his influence, Jeddy gave DuBray a high-level position at the association, brought him back into the Buck home, and put him in charge of the family's financial affairs. A few years later, as helpless as a baby, Buck drowned in the pool beside the sauna.

It took an hour for McPhee to elicit this much from Zelda. She refused to answer questions about why Jedidiah Buck bequeathed the bulk of his fortune to DuBray. She had been "warned," she said, but would not say by whom or about what. "You know," McPhee says, projecting an air of puzzlement, "I think she didn't trust me."

"So," Miravich says, trying his hand at historical theorizing, "Bobby Bray's hate for his stupid, working-class father led him to create the phony Robert DuBray who hates workers and unions. But how was he connected to Mr. Buck, the murderer?"

"I'll need more time on that," McPhee says.

But there is no more time. Later in the day, Miravich receives a call from a man who identifies himself as Finley Cruikshank, assistant to Dr. Robert DuBray. DuBray has been informed, the caller says, that Miravich and a Peter Bonner have been making inquiries about him and his organization. DuBray offers to meet with them and answer any questions they might have. He proposes meeting at the association's branch office in McKeesport. Miravich agrees on an evening in mid-December and informs Bonner.

∎

Before the meeting, Miravich makes his own attempt to discover what Zelda Buck is concealing and why. Getting her address from Jim McPhee, he goes alone to her apartment.

A frail old woman cracks open the door. "Who's there? Are you the knife sharpener?"

"I'm a friend, ma'am, and I brought you a gift." He removes a pot of African violets from a shopping bag. "Can I come in and talk?"

Seemingly delighted, she forgets her caution, takes the pot and propels herself with a cane through the apartment, leaving the door wide open. Although she may once have been medium-tall, she has shrunk to about five linear feet under a severely humped back. She goes through the living room and into a front alcove, where she places the pot of violets among hanging baskets of spidery greens and colorful flowers. In the living room, oil paintings stretch in a band around three walls at eye level. There are throw rugs on a polished wood floor and ceramic figurines on bookcase shelves and end tables. Everything in the room speaks of money, probably ill-gotten money lavished on the comfort of this little old lady born to riches, Miravich thinks, feeling blood pumping angrily through his carotid artery as it always does when he comes face to face with wealth gained at the expense of others.

Five minutes elapse as she takes infinite care in rearranging pots so that symmetry prevails. She bends lower to seize and dispose of a tiny foreign object in the potted dirt. This done, she tries to straighten up but gets stuck halfway.

Miravich is by her side in an instant. He gently supports her under one elbow. She shuffles along on his gallant arm. "Thank you," she says, with a sidelong glance of infinite gratitude. She is a lonely woman.

Miravich clears his throat and says, "My ma used to grow violets like that. Every morning she'd put her pots in the east window of our shack... our home, and carry them to the west window in the afternoon. About ten pots, two by two. I made her a little cart with wheels so she could push them around."

"What a nice son you are. But she shouldn't give them too much sunlight."

"You should have a maid to help you," he says, guiding her to a chair.

"He promised to hire someone." She looks up at him from her stooped position. "Are you the one? You must take care of the garden, as well as drive and cook."

"Sorry, ma'am, I'm not the one." He introduces himself and says he has come to ask a few questions about her late brother. Finally she sits down, resting both hands on the cane, listening intently. Miravich gazes around the living room and exclaims about her remarkable art and ceramic collections. Her eyes lighting up, she begins to describe the paintings, naming the artists and telling how she acquired their work. After several memory lapses, her attention wanes. Abruptly she rises and leaves him alone, returning after a few minutes with a tray bearing two small cups and a pot of tea.

Miravich has never seen much good in tea, but he sips with tiny, appreciative slurps. Sitting across from him, cup and saucer rattling in her hand, she smiles with infinite, if momentary, pleasure.

"You've made a wonderful place for yourself, Miz Buck," Miravich says, his eyes once again sweeping the room. "So I want to make sure you have all the help you need. Who was it that promised to hire someone to help you? Dr. DuBray?"

"That may be, yes. Who is he?"

Miravich tries a new approach. "Do you remember what happened before your brother... passed on? He had a secretary named Robert Bray who suddenly disappeared for a year or two. Remember him?" Zelda Buck says nothing. "When he came back," Miravich continues, "his name was Dr. Robert DuBray. Your brother gave him a good job at that industrial association, the Greater Ohio something or other."

Now she is ahead of him. "Of course, Jeddy's association. The main purpose is to promote the open shop." Her voice quavers, but now she is the historian instructing a neophyte. "We are against unions, you see. Unions will be the ruination of the country." Her confidence deserts her. "Well, that's what Jeddy says. Is he right?"

"There's kind of a dispute about that. But this man Robert DuBray—it seems strange that he assumed so much influence over the Buck estate."

Her gaze has become a fixed stare. She seems to be taking in everything he says, examining it, analyzing it.

"And in the end your brother left most of the family fortune to this Du-Bray. He inherited the money that...well, that really should have been yours." Miravich throws up his hands in confusion. "So," he concludes, "what happened back there when your brother died?" As soon as the words are out, he realizes he has pushed it too far, too fast.

She begins to cry. "I don't know. Was something supposed to happen?"

"Oh, Miz Buck!" He rushes from his chair and squats in front of her. "Everything is okay, no reason to weep." He takes one of her hands between his horny paws. Fragile, pulsing faintly, like a dying wren. "Just some stupid questions, nothing to waste tears on." He looks into her rheumy eyes. "And we're all finished now. All finished, see." He pulls out a handkerchief, not soiled thank God, and tenderly wipes away the pain running down her cheeks.

He stands over her. "I've got to go now." Taking her gently by the elbow, he leads her into the front hallway. "Now, I want you to lock the door when I go out." As she nods, he takes a last look at the small head under a cascade of white hair. The story is locked up inside, probably for good. He pulls the door behind him. But it will not shut all the way. He looks back.

She has intruded a tiny foot, and says through the crack, "He murdered Jeddy, you know."

"Who, ma'am, who?"

"That man you were asking about."

"Bray?"

"The other one."

"DuBray?"

"Made him sign the will, then pushed his head under water in the sauna pool. Jeddy couldn't fight back. I told them but nobody would believe me." She softly closes the door.

CHAPTER 10: December 1949

Snow blows every which way, swirling out of heavy darkness on angry gusts. Moon and stars have scuttled out of sight, and the city lies entombed in extraordinary blackness. Wind blasts through the streets, ripping off loose roof shingles and rocking Bonner's sturdy Lincoln-Continental. This is no passive nightfall but an active, satanic presence that envelops and throttles.

Bonner pulls up at the curb and turns off headlights and engine. Fred's Barber Shop is a block up the street, dark now, two hours after closing. No light shows in the second floor office. Bonner and Miravich sit quietly, watching the street ahead and behind. Arriving early, they twice drove slowly around the block, studying parked cars and the few people hurrying along windswept sidewalks. Now they wait.

Bonner stares ahead, trying to identify shifting shadows in the streetlight's murky glow. Nearsighted eyes protest and pull back to focus trancelike on snowflakes whipping furiously across the windshield. He feels weak and drained of energy. Instead of sitting in the cramped car seat, he seems to be floating toward a final destination, hellward most likely. He is sinking, sinking, his eyes closing, his breathing labored.

Someone is shaking his shoulder. "Pete! Pete!"

He opens his eyes.

Miravich leans toward him, that hard dark face under the brim of his Fedora. "Where've you been?" Jocular voice. He presses closer. "You don't look so good."

"I'm okay." Bonner reaches impulsively for a cigarette, but he stops himself, determined to stick with his curtailment plan, only three a day. He will save the night smoke for later. His doctor has advised him to give up cigarettes, drink and sex and to "stop working so hard." This is what it comes to in the end: stop living in order to live.

Now his heart begins fluttering. It's part of the pattern, a period of weakness, almost blacking out, followed by an irregular heartbeat. Fingers fumbling in the dim light, he swallows a small tablet, known to him only as a powerful pep pill given him by a pharmacist friend. Anticipating a surge of energy, the tightness in his chest contracts into a tiny bearable knot just below the gullet. His doctor warned him about taking anything that might overstimulate the heart. He would rather take this risk than give up.

"What's that for?"

"Hay fever," Bonner says. "Look!"

Headlights approach from the other end of the street. A car pulls to the curb across from the barber shop. The lights go out, but no one emerges. Bonner starts his car and turns on the windshield wipers to get a clearer view. Separated by thirty yards, the two cars face one another on opposite sides of the street.

Minutes pass. The front doors of the other car open. Two figures cross the street, bending forward against the wind. They disappear into the building, and soon a light goes on in the upstairs office.

"Only two," Miravich whispers over Bonner's rapid breathing. "Are you sure you're up to this?" he asks. "I could get some boys from the local."

"To do what?" Bonner says. "It's *my* dream." He opens the car door and slides out. He doesn't know if he is up to it, but he does know that they have taken every precaution. Before coming, he even checked on Sal Grotto's whereabouts. "Gone on a trip," Louie Grotto told him. Wind and fast-driving snow bite at his face as he walks around the front of the car and continues on the sidewalk. He feels dizzy. Miravich, he sees, took off his overcoat and left it in the car.

They enter the cramped vestibule. The second floor landing is lit by a glow from the office. Bonner starts up the stairs but halts and leans against the wall, gasping for breath. He waves Miravich on, impatiently. Miravich climbs sideways past him in the stairwell, seeing the pain on a face that is pale even in this dim light.

Miravich pauses in the open doorway. Two men in overcoats, one half-sitting on the edge of the desk, arms folded, and the other—more colorful, wearing a gray bowler hat and camel's hair Chesterfield coat belted around the middle—stands at the window looking out. The familiar grubby office, a desk and ratty chair on casters, a flimsy wooden ladderback chair in front of the desk, filing cabinets along the wall with drawers hanging open, trash on the floor. An overhead bulb inside a dusty glass cover casts an indifferent light on the unheated room.

The man at the window turns to the visitors. "I am Dr. Robert DuBray." Beneath the overcoat he wears a dark pin-striped suit with a red tie. Lean and professional-looking, he has an angular face that might have been formed by glueing together paper cutouts with sharp edges—tiny ears, long nose, thin lips above a receding chin. He seems to stare sideways, like a disdainful bird of prey. His assistant is a tall, lanky man with a flat nose crushed against a pale face. Miravich recalls that blast-furnace workers described such a man as leader of the air sampling crew.

Miravich says, "I got a carload of boys right around the corner, but just in case…" He approaches the second man, who pushes off the desk, rising confidently to his six-one or two. "You must be Cruikshank. Spread that overcoat, bud."

Miravich circles the man, feeling for lumps. Love handles bulge above the hips, but no weapons. Miravich then goes through the same treatment, and DuBray and Bonner, though clearly not muscle men, submit to a cursory patting down.

DuBray sits in the ersatz leather desk chair with stuffing oozing out. He removes his hat and smoothes back thinning amber hair with a gloved hand. "So," he says, "why have you been harassing our employees?"

"Harassing!" Miravich says. "You've been trying to kill us."

Bonner sits heavily on the chair in front of the desk. His heart beats wildly, the pill only beginning to draw at his nerve ends. The others' voices sound liquid and remote. Their faces approach and recede, first one and then another, appearing at the podium, giving a brief opening statement, retreating. DuBray protesting that his visitors have been "prying into my personal affairs"; Miravich charging that "you guys tried to kill us." Bonner, the spectator, can only observe with numbed eyes for an undefined period of time. Finally the spinning room slows, the carousel music winds down with a drawn-out groan, and DuBray emerges from the whirl, staring at him with deadly intent. Did foolish hope and blind anger draw them into some sort of trap? Miravich, apparently coming to the same conclusion, tries to stay a step behind Cruikshank who keeps edging to the rear.

Bonner rouses himself to ask a question. "I just want to know," he says to DuBray, "why you scared off my investors. What kind of business association discourages new business?"

"Your plan was stupid to begin with, Bonner. We produce steel in the Monongahela Valley, not metal stampings or airplanes."

"We can't sell steel without customers."

"That's Chamber of Commerce thinking. Bring in a thousand small businesses to buy a ton of steel each. Absurd! They'd compete with the mills for manpower. We'd have to pay higher wages and dole out pensions and socialized medicine. You'd turn this region into a union-dominated wasteland."

"It'll be a wasteland all right," Bonner says. "The companies that belong to your association, did they approve this policy?"

"It's enough to say that they approve of my philosophy, a commitment to industrial capitalism." DuBray leans back, swinging a little this way and that in the swivel chair. "We act as their economic conscience, we enforce that conscience—"

"You're against everything they say they're for. Free markets...competition."

This brings a disdainful "Ha!" and a backward toss of his head. "You had your competition here, Bonner. Seventy years ago. The iron and steel industry won that race, won the right to exploit the coal and iron deposits and the river and its shorelines. Since then your precious Monongahela Valley and all its people have been dedicated to the making of steel. I call it 'industrial dedication.'"

Miravich and Bonner listen.

"Every drop of water," DuBray continues, eyeing them scornfully, "every speck of coal dust, every pebble, every wildflower on every hill is dedicated to steel. And all man-made things—transportation systems, small manufacturing, retail business, governments, religion... and, yes, even Sal Grotto and the numbers. Every business, every institution, every person in this hideous valley exists for one purpose only, and that is to make steel. To disrupt one element would be to disrupt all."

"Enough of this bullshit," Miravich says, stepping forward a few paces. "Let's get to it. Who's Mr. Buck?"

"Who?"

"The Mr. Buck who tried to kill Phil Murray. The Mr. Buck who's been dogging Bonner and me for twelve years."

DuBray laughs. "Hallucinations of a trade unionist!"

Miravich studies those evil eyes, tiny dark circles piercing fields of dirty white, like piss holes in snow. "You're no French aristocrat, DuBray. You're the son of a drunken mill man, one of those dumb brutes who couldn't do anything but carry pig iron in a labor gang. Your real name is Robert Bray, and you wormed your way into the home of this rich cripple, Jedidiah Buck—"

"What is this shit?" Cruikshank says. He stirs threateningly but can't decide which way to move. Miravich's remarks obviously are a revelation to him.

"You changed your name to 'DuBray,'" Miravich continues, "and drowned poor old Buck and stole his money and took over this association. We figure you even used his name to hire murderers and assassins. You're Mr. Buck!"

There is a long moment of silence. DuBray's lips curl disdainfully. "You puny little people!" He closes his eyes, and everybody waits to see what will emerge this time. "Robert Bray," he says in a calmer tone, re-entering their world, "had no father." Placing fingertips on the desk, he pushes himself up and moves around to the back of the chair, taking a surreptitious peek at his watch.

"Yes, I'm Mr. Buck," DuBray says. He smiles at stupefied Cruikshank. "My one mistake. In a stressful moment, I used the name as a front. But a pug named Whitey blurted it out at the jail in Charleston. Am I correct?"

He waves away their confirming nods. "I couldn't have the police searching for a Mr. Buck and reviewing old man Buck's death. They wouldn't have understood. It was justifiable homicide." He smiles. "Oh, yes! On grounds of political necessity. His money and power were desperately needed in the struggle to save society."

"From what?" says Miravich.

"From the likes of you. Radical unionist and disruptive entrepreneur. Enemies of authority and stability." DuBray looks again at his watch. "Yes, yes, yes," he says impatiently, "the assassination attempts, the frameup that sent Bonner to prison, the communist accusations...and by the way, your Father Strunka is a wonderful patriot."

"That's right!" Miravich says. "You were with him at the convention in Boston. And the Donora smog—you called it an 'act of God'?"

"Yes, yes, all of that," DuBray says. "But knowing that won't help you now." He turns to the assistant. "What time is it, Finley?"

"Eight o'clock. Check out time for our friends." Cruikshank backs toward the door and opens it.

Miravich clutches Bonner's arm and begins pulling him out of the chair as the sound of heavy footsteps resounds in the stairwell. Within a minute, three men enter in single file, bulky in overcoats, hats pulled low over their eyes.

"You're right on time, Pixie," Cruikshank says. His tone changes. "Who're these other guys?"

The three men crowd into the office. Pixie lays a hand on Cruikshank's shoulder. His companions advance on Miravich and Bonner. Miravich backs away and throws up a parrying arm. But a pistol thrust into his gut makes surrender the wiser course.

Miravich is chagrined. "Stupid!" he mutters. "Why didn't we think of this?"

Cruikshank, meanwhile, is squirming in Pixie's tightening grasp. "Not me, for Chrissake. Them!" He nods over his shoulder at Bonner and Miravich.

"There's been a change," Pixie says.

Comprehension dawns. "Hey, these are Johnny Mio's men. What's happening here? Where's Grotto?"

"Someplace," Pixie says.

"You double-crossed him," Cruikshank says, incredulity fading from his waxen face. He looks at DuBray, who is belting up his coat. "And you double-crossed *me*. The two of you are in it with Mio."

"Right for the first time," DuBray says. "If it hadn't been for the bungling of you and your operatives over the years, Bonner and Miravich wouldn't be here tonight. I made an arrangement with Johnny Mio and induced Pixie to join us. A more secure future. Right, Pixie?"

Ignoring Pixie's deadpan look, DuBray places the bowler hat on his head and turns to Bonner and Miravich. "We have come to the end of a long journey—"

"Enough talk," interrupts the man holding Miravich. He appears to be in charge of the thugs. His hat fell off in a brief tussle with Miravich, exposing a high, greasy pompadour. He stoops, picks up the hat and jams it back on his head. "Time to go." He gives Miravich a push toward the door.

"No," DuBray says. "I go first. That's the plan."

"Get going, then," Slick says.

As DuBray moves to the door, Cruikshank lunges toward him, shouting in fury. DuBray shies sideways, like a surprised bird on stiff legs. Pixie smashes his gun barrel against Cruikshank's head, and he falls unconscious. DuBray rushes through the open doorway, the wings of his overcoat flapping against the door frame. Down the stairs he goes—*thud, thud, thud*—two or three stairs at a time, like a hopping vulture. The bottom door slams.

"We're not supposed to kill them here, for Chrissake," Slick says, chiding Pixie. He kicks the inert body. "Now we got to carry him out. You stay and watch these birds till we get back."

Slick throws his arms around Cruikshank's legs while the third gunman grapples with the torso. They waddle toward the door, lanky Cruikshank's buttocks spragging along the floor.

During the struggle, Bonner has edged toward the window. He raises a corner of the blind and sees DuBray cross the street and get into his car. Another car, a large dark Cadillac, is parked behind. DuBray starts his car and pulls out from the curb with squealing tires. The thickening snowfall creates an illusion of tail lights rising and soaring into the night, carrying away Robert Bray (a.k.a. Robert DuBray, a.k.a. Mr. Buck), valet, industrial hygienist, propagandist, and murderer. He will alight again wherever the carrion poor lay to be picked clean; wherever the ruling class needs a justifying philosophy; wherever racial and ethnic divisions may be exploited to keep people in servitude; wherever mechanical concepts rule human actions; wherever common people allow the rich and powerful to make fools of them.

Bonner turns to Pixie. "You're letting him get away?"

Pixie smiles. "He may think that, but he don't know Johnny." Standing in the center of the room, he motions with the pistol. "Get away from the window. And you!" he says to Miravich. "Get over there with your pal."

Bonner feels a deep chill. Now he knows with certainty. There is no room for Rooseveltian optimism here tonight. Death will come much faster than he supposed. Feelings of self-pity overwhelm him. He has accepted the proximity of death, but not this kind of death. He has not invited violence into his life, but it has come anyway, looming far larger than he had expected. Out in the stairwell, Slick and his companion are cursing, bumping down the steps with their awkward package, a step at a time.

"C'mon!" Pixie says, again waving the gun.

They move slowly, trying to stay on opposite sides of their guard. Bonner sees that Miravich is grinning a little, a familiar goodbye glint in his eyes, ready to leap on the wings of circumstance. One hand is near the top rung of the ladderback chair.

"Okay, okay," Bonner says to Pixie. He holds up his hands, as if in final surrender. "Just tell me this..." One final request to an old adversary. "...where are they taking us, Pixie?"

Pixie's gun hand drops almost imperceptibly. "To the riv—"

The chair, whipped in a backhand motion by Miravich, shatters across his shoulder and head. The big man goes down in a rain of kindling. Stunned, he curls up, instinctively sheltering the pistol between elbows and knees.

Miravich pushes Bonner toward the rear room. "In there...the window."

Bonner flings the door open on a room full of trash. Miravich gropes along the wall and switches on the light. They close the door, shove an empty filing cabinet against it, and fling empty boxes and other debris out of their path. Newspapers, receipts and canceled checks flutter in the air. Miravich turns the window latch and heaves. The window flies open, revealing the dim outline of a fire escape platform. Bonner tries to climb over the waist-high sill but falls back, dizzy again.

Miravich slides a case of empty beer bottles under the window for Bonner to stand on. He gets his back under Bonner's thighs and levers up the lower part of his body. Pixie is yelling and throwing himself against the door. Revived by the cold air, Bonner begins scrambling, pulling himself through the window opening. They hear a screeching noise as the filing cabinet is pushed back inch by inch. Looking to his rear, Miravich sees Pixie's head sticking through the opening. He reaches for the wooden case at his feet, his experienced beer man's hand unerringly finding the hand notch at one end. Fear pumping up his strength, he snatches up the case and hurls it, bottles and all, back toward the door just as Pixie bursts into the room. Bottles hit the floor, popping like firecrackers, and the big man yelps and falls forward in a pile of debris. Bonner now is crouching on the fire escape platform, extending a hand back through the window. Miravich seizes it and puts one foot on the window sill. Looking over his shoulder, he sees Pixie raise the pistol.

Miravich wants to duck but instead hauls himself up until he fills the opening, a large target silouetted in the room's pale light, shielding Bonner. In this split second he is aware of the contrariness of the reflexive action, flinging himself suicidally into the capitalists' machinery to save one of them. He hears the shot, *splat!* sounding curiously muffled, but it had been coming at him for twenty years or more.

Bonner clutches Miravich's arms and pulls him over the sill. Both men fall on the platform. Bonner rolls Miravich to one side and squirms out from under. He catches a glimpse of Pixie trying to rise but slipping and sliding, arms windmilling, on newspapers and file folders that litter the floor. Buster Keaton running on banana peels.

"Joe!" Bonner shakes him. "You've got to try."

Miravich grasps the railing and tries to pull himself up. He falls back. "You go, down the ladder. Get out of here."

"You're coming with me." Bonner swings his legs over the edge of the platform, feels for a rung, descends until his head is below the platform. "Put your foot on my shoulder." A foot lands heavily on his head, slips off, raking the side of his face. He wraps one arm around the calf and pulls Miravich down. He manages another rung, slides past two or three more. A loud gasp from Miravich and he comes hurtling down, his foot slipping off Bonner's shoulder. Bonner lets go, giving up, figuring they may as well fall together. His rear end hits first, something hard and metallic, and Miravich on top of him. A clanging noise and metal grating against concrete. And then another drop of a few feet, and the two roll off a garbage can and land entwined on a wet pavement.

They lie stunned. Bonner feels weak and bruised all over, his breathing rapid and shallow. He cannot do much more of this. Pursuers are at the window, talking in hoarse whispers. He sees that he fell about five feet from the bottom rung of the ladder. He kicks the empty can, sending it rolling and clanging out from under the ladder.

Miravich groans heavily. "Alley...get to the alley."

Bonner grasps his coat collar and hauls him along, stumbling down a paved walk. They fall, get up, fall again. The pavement is damp, but the dry snow hasn't stuck.

Slick's voice at the window: "C'mon, get down there! What the fuck you doing?"

"Can't see shit down there," says Pixie on the ladder.

"Jump, asshole!" Animosity: Pixie apparently is not welcome in the new gang.

Bonner pushes open a heavy gate in a solid wooden fence about five feet high. They slide through and halt, panting, on the other side. From the direction of the fire escape comes a thudding noise, followed immediately by a rasping "Christ almighty!"

"What's wrong now?"

"Sprained my ankle. Watch that drop."

Forewarned, Slick apparently lands solidly and starts down the rear path.

Behind the fence, Miravich and Bonner sit with their backs against the wooden slats, gulping air. Bonner leans close to Miravich. "We should get out of here." His hand comes away wet—bloody, he guesses, but he doesn't know from what part of the body.

Miravich weakly shakes his head. With great effort he rolls to his knees behind the gate, which hangs open into the alley. A large shadowy form is coming across the back lawn, bent double, like a doughboy, as if someone might fire at him over the fence top. The jerk has seen too many war movies. Crouching behind the gate, Miravich makes a hand signal, which may have meant something to steelworkers or coal miners but is meaningless to Bonner. Yet he knows what Miravich has in mind, linked as they are through a sympathetic membrane stretching back through the years to Route 40. He mobilizes his weight behind the hinged end of the gate and watches Miravich who, one arm dangling useless, is peering around the open end.

When Miravich whispers "Now!" and slams his good shoulder into the gate, Bonner also throws his shoulder against it and drives forward on his toes. Both feel the solid impact as it smacks the big man, knocking him back into the yard.

Bonner is exhausted, breathing heavily again, ready to pass out. Somehow he gets Miravich moving on one foot and one knee. Across the alley they go and down a dim walkway alongside a garage. Miravich collapses.

No one seems to be coming after them. Snow is pouring down again, thick and heavy, but the wind has died to a weak blow. Another thud under the fire escape resonates clearly in the shrinking universe of a snowy night. The third man must have dropped down. Loud whispers. "Where's Slick?"

Pixie says, "Out cold. His face is stove in."

Bonner hears a new voice, a voice of authority, coming from the fire escape window. "Hey, you guys! What's going on?"

"Bastards got away. They can't be far."

"Let them go. They're nothing to me. Get back to the car."

Bonner cautiously crosses the alley and peers over the fence. Amid groans and curses, Pixie and the third man are dragging Slick around the building and along a walk beside Fred's Barber Shop, heading toward the street. A gate opens on squealing hinges. Lights in the upstairs office wink off. Bonner wants to stay here, safe behind the fence, but Miravich needs help. He creeps into the yard and follows the path to the gate he'd heard squealing. Two Cadillacs are now parked under the street light. In the first car, a driver guns the engine, jets of exhaust scattering snow. A blind is drawn on the rear window, and Bonner guesses that Cruikshank is inside. Front and back doors slam shut on the other side of the car—and the blind snaps up.

A face is peering out, not just peering but beseeching, pleading for help, the eyes bulging but the mouth stuffed with a gag. The eyes seem to confront Bonner, who recognizes that face, distorted as it is, and he knows the man. Sal Grotto.

The cars pull out together and move very fast down the street. Bonner can't see the driver of the second car. Probably Johnny Mio himself, the voice of authority.

When the cars have disappeared, two men come out of a nearby apartment building. Bonner steps out of the shadows and tells them to call for an ambulance and send it around to the alley, a matter of life and death. He stumbles back up the side path.

Miravich has crawled into the alley and passed out again, half-sitting against a garage door, one shoulder slumped sideways to the ground. Bonner slides down to a sitting position next to Miravich in the snow. He squirms a knee under Miravich's head and wipes away snow-water beading on his upturned cheek. His hat lies upside down in the middle of the alley with snow pouring into it. Bonner tries to stay conscious by guessing when the hat will be filled. He dozes, looks, dozes again. Each time he awakes, he expects to see white stuff flowing over the brim. But no, it's a bottomless pit.

CHAPTER 11:
December 1949–June 1950

In late afternoon, yearning for a cigarette, Bonner steps outside his beer store to escape the temptation, or perhaps to gratify it by inhaling mill smoke. The sun has sunk over the river bluff, leaving the city hostage to a winter freeze. He turns up his coat collar, breathes deeply, and coughs, gagging on sulfur and soot. Dusk in a milltown: the best time, commerce grinding to a halt and all objects sharply etched in the fading light—buildings, storefronts, cars, phone poles, mill stacks, all momentarily caught in a montage of straight lines and acute angles that reveal true shapes rescued from daylight's soft-focus haziness. Looking uptown, he sees a conglomerate reddish-green glow of dozens of neon signs, mounted high and low on brick buildings that line the winding Fifth Avenue canyon. Proprietors in all the grubby little storefronts and shops are adding the day's receipts, preparing to close for the night. Soon the stores will stay open late for last-minute Christmas shopping. But tonight the sidewalks teem with shoppers hurrying home, men from the day turn hurrying out of saloons to run for the bus. A man bursts laughing out of Saboulovich's, and the hubbub of a packed saloon floats out with him. "Ho, Pete," he says, raising a hand. A touch of pleasure tingles in Bonner's chest.

He goes back inside to his account books. Since leaving the hospital on the day after the escape from Johnny Mio's men, Bonner has worked longer and harder than ever. He is determined not to leave Mae saddled with debt. determined to satisfy the bank note and especially to repay the loan from Gas Stowe, not because Gas would have to give up his cars and mistresses without the $3,000. He would merely write it off as bad debt, and Bonner does not want to go into perpetuity as a name on somebody's income tax filing. Bonner kept his interest in the foundry to generate cash to pay off the bank and Gas Stowe. He may yet lose all if he defaults on the loan, but beer, he has decided, will be the last to go. When his heart flutters, he pops a pep pill (if Mae isn't in sight). Energy is what he needs, energy and time. He will not be defeated this way.

As promised, Bonner tells Mae the full story, one chapter at a time, like a serialized novel in a newspaper, leaving out details of some of the more violent happenings. Mae weeps a little at the climax of each episode, and she is disturbed and appalled and angry at Pete for not telling her before. But she comes to understand that moral turpitude did not lead him by the nose into his difficulties, although his affinity for risk-taking and rye-drinking undoubtedly smoothed the way. By the end of the tale, Mae's suspicions about her husband have dwindled to a precious few. Her one lingering concern is his susceptibility to unsavory characters who want something from him. If she ever runs into Max Trippitt, the manufacturing expert, she'll drop him from that stupid bluff over the Monongahela and see if he can reassemble his own smashed parts.

The Bonners celebrate Christmas in their new home. They put up and decorate a ten-foot tall spruce, and they sit around Christmas Eve drinking egg nog with a touch of rum. Bonner studies his sons with deep appreciation, amazed that they grew into young men while he was looking the other way. He feels a curious pride in knowing that his sons, so unaware now of life's complications, will nonetheless go beyond him.

In early January, Bonner visits Miravich at his home. The small livingroom appears empty despite an abundance of neatly-arranged chairs, couches, end tables, and painted handcarvings perched on every available flat surface. Miravich sits in a worn leather easy chair with his right arm in a sling. He is recovering from two bullet wounds, a through-hole in the right shoulder and an almost-healed furrow on the side of his head.

Bonner draws a small chair next to Miravich. He has brought three newspaper clippings and hands them over one by one. A few days after their run-in with Mio's men, according to the first story, the remains of Finley Cruikshank and a Tony Piccioletto ("our Pixie," Miravich refers to him with mock fondness) were discovered in the trunk of an abandoned car on a rural road. These were the only two thugs that Miravich and Bonner could identify when shown mug shots by the police. They never saw Johnny Mio in person.

The second clipping is a story from yesterday's *Daily News*, reporting that Sal Grotto's body was found snagged on a barge mooring line in the Monongahela. "Johnny sure spreads them around," Miravich says.

Finally, a small business item from a Pittsburgh newspaper published the day before Christmas. It notes that the Greater Ohio Industrial Propagation Association has ceased operations, leaving a half-dozen employees without a final paycheck. DuBray has disappeared.

"We beat them, you know," Bonner says in an effort to cheer him up.

"Do *they* know that?" Miravich asks. "It looks like DuBray got away."

"But remember Pixie told us Johnny Mio doesn't leave loose ends?"

"Yeah, but Pixie didn't turn out to be much of an expert on Johnny Mio's intentions, did he? Besides, I have this feeling, DuBray doesn't die. He's like an evil idea, maybe disappears for a while but pops up again somewhere else." Miravich swirls coffee in his cup.

"But we drove him out of town." Bonner's gaze, shifting to the left, settles on a blue statuette, a half-woman, half-ostrich, standing on one clawed foot under a lamp on an end table. He leans over, picks it up, thoughtfully runs a forefinger over the exaggerated rump. "Good work," says Bonner, the statuary expert. "Joe," he says softly, still studying the carving, "go get Mitzie. Bring her back."

"Back to what? There's no room to move around here." Miravich pauses, then goes on. "It's like spending a lifetime in low-seam coal. Mills, streetcars, and bosses jumping down my back. You got to walk with your arms pressed up against your ribs and your back arched for the next blow." He adds after more thought, "My trouble was, I wanted to change things, but I never had a plan. They called me a radical. Huh! Mitzie was the real radical."

Bonner prefers the old, cocky, irreverent, anticapitalist Miravich.

Driving slowly homeward, Bonner impulsively pulls off the street to park on a vacant strip of land overlooking the city cemetery, the Watts Works, and the business district. He walks to the edge of a cliff and studies the scene, feeling a strange need to commit it to memory. Two orange glows are subsiding in the west, one near and one distant, the far sunset splashing a deep rust-red color across the horizon, stealing attention from the man-made Bessemer blow over the city. Staring into the setting sun, Bonner sees the plains of Oklahoma glimmering in the torturous heat of late afternoon and beyond them the snow-bound crags of the Rockies jutting above the midafternoon haze and, far, far to the west the same sun rising over surf pounding the Hawaiian shoreline.

He is amazed that he can see so far and yet so near merely by adjusting his focus. Gazing at that faraway molten pool is hypnotic, very much like... like staring into the blazing interior of the reheating furnace in his foundry. Now an inspired idea leaps out of the fiery vision: he could install a second furnace at the foundry to start a new product line. Walking back to the car, he examines the idea. With some capital, he could make it work. He throws a final glance across the valley and sees that the Bessemer's drifting blob is creeping up the sunset, displacing the Hawaiian shoreline. Within five minutes, the Rockies and the Oklahoma plains also will be blotted out, leaving only the near horizon and the here and now. But that can yield its own radiant images to those who look hard enough, he thinks. And besides, it is all that remains.

■

After the dinner dishes have been cleared away, Mitzie and Joe go outside to get some air on this June evening. They sit on the front steps.

"You've kept the place up nice," Mitzie says. The five square feet of front lawn is neatly edged with bricks shaved to a point, and a hydrangea bush is beginning to blossom.

"It doesn't take much. Maybe five minutes of mowing, front and back."

It is their last night in this house where Mitzie grew up. She returned from California when the real estate agent found a buyer, and today she closed the deal. Tomorrow, the movers will come. She didn't want to force Miravich out, but he insisted that she sell the house. It is too big for one man, has too many empty rooms that cry out in anguish. He can't bear to sleep in their bedroom or enter her studio with its mingled odors of airplane glue and essence of Mitzie. He will move downtown to a two-room apartment close to the Watts's main gate.

"You look a lot better than when I saw you in the hospital," Mitzie says.

He feels her tightly clad thighs next to his. He leans forward and pokes at a crack in the sidewalk with a stick. "I don't think I'd have made it if you hadn't come." His shoulder wound healed quickly, but his head feels "sort of funny," he tells Mitzie. It is as if he still hears the shot that grazed his head—hears it *inside his head. Barrrrooong!* Partly for this reason, he has decided to leave union politics and return to a full-time job in the mill. He is associated with too many bad things: the communist accusations, the stories of his violent past, the race issue, and now the rumors that he was shot in a tussle with numbers thugs. He doesn't want to taint his friends on the Unity Team. Fran Luptak will run for president and Len Mrvos for grievance chairman. Rudy Semchek, who in Miravich's estimation has the best heart for a leader, will seek the vice-presidency and, Miravich hopes, move up when Luptak serves the term or two that he thinks he deserves. Some day Miravich may again run for office, or apply for a staff job. In the meantime, he will work and send money to Mitzie.

"You had so many good ideas for changing things," she says.

"Yeah, the great reformer," he says sarcastically. "A little bang on the head didn't kill the ideas. But, see…" He leans back on his elbows. "A reformer has to be more than angry. He's got to be strong in the heart and strong in the head to pull people with him."

She nods and says, "I've never understood what was between you and Pete Bonner. He sort of acted like your older brother."

Miravich smiles. "From another family, maybe. And we disagreed about a lot of things. But when it really mattered, he was closer than a blood brother." He pokes again at the crack in the pavement. "Pete died in April, and Mae asked me to be a pallbearer at his funeral."

Dolly's laughter tinkles merrily in the living room. Anna and her younger children came over for dinner, and now they are playing with Dolly. The thought of his daughter has swelled up in Miravich's heart, making him dizzy with love all over again. First the mother, then the daughter, and now mother and daughter together. He moves closer to Mitzie on the step, and she stays there, calf pressed tightly against his.

He would like to talk about what comes next for him and Mitzie but postpones raising the question, afraid of what the answer will be. When he drives them to the airport next morning, Mitzie herself raises it. "Maybe I wasn't understanding enough, Joe. Maybe I was too stiff."

"You're not long on patience, that's for sure. But I made a lot of mistakes, and now I have to figure out how to make good."

Dolly speaks up from the back. "Are you coming home with us, Daddy?"

He looks over his shoulder. She is standing in the narrow space between back and front seats, her chin resting on the top of Mitzie's seat. Wistful child with pigtails. "Honey," he says gently, "please sit back in the seat so you won't get hurt if we hit a bump."

"She misses you an awful lot." Mitzie is watching the road ahead.

He senses that she wants to say something, and he wants to say something. But he fears that they want to say different things. He tells himself that this is not like negotiating with management, where you lose an edge if you offer too much too soon. But he is not altogether sure. Pap told him about a lot of things, often with the back of his hand, but nothing about love.

He blurts out, "I'd sure like to be around Dolly growing up." He turns into the airport drive. "Maybe I can visit Dolly in a few months."

They leave it this way and kiss goodbye. Feeling better than he has felt in a long time, he is in no hurry to spend his first night in the stuffy little apartment over a used furniture store on Fifth Avenue. He turns south after leaving the airport. The pleasant afternoon draws him toward the open highway, down through the west end of Clairton and across the Monongahela at Elizabeth. Up and out of the valley, then through miles of open fields on Route 51's flat straightaway. A hawk soars far ahead, luring him on. In Uniontown, he begins the long ascent of Chestnut Ridge on Route 40. He wonders if he is retracing this path because, as Pap used to say, when you are lost at birth you need to find yourself over and over. Shifting the grumbling Ford into second, he runs into upslope fog, just as Bonner did on that day in 1937. The bump in the ass that changed history.

He slows down, intending to stop and somehow memorialize the place. But the sound of his tires crunching on roadside gravel irritates him, and he suddenly knows that it is time to seal off all those rooms to the past. He drives on and tops the rise in a forbidding tree-shadowed stretch of highway. There is open sky over the next ridge, and he keeps going. He now understands one thing he did not learn from his father: when the way ahead is not clear, always move from shadow to light.

John Hoerr grew up in McKeesport, Pennsylvania, the setting for *Monongahela Dusk*. He worked for several news organizations, including United Press International, a daily newspaper, *Business Week*, and WQED-TV, in Pittsburgh, Chicago, Detroit, and New York. From 1960 on, Hoerr specialized in national labor reporting in the days when the steel, auto, coal mining and other unions were strong enough to conduct nationwide strikes in support of wage demands. Out of this experience, he wrote three nonfiction books, *And the Wolf Finally Came: The Decline of the American Steel Industry; We Can't Eat Prestige: The Women Who Organized Harvard;* and *Harry, Tom, and Father Rice: Accusation and Betrayal in America's Cold War.* He and his wife live in Teaneck, NJ.

The Autumn House Fiction Series

Sharon Dilworth, Editor

New World Order, by Derek Green
Drift and Swerve, by Samuel Ligon
 ■ 2008
Monogahela Dusk, by John Hoerr

 ■ Winner of the annual Autumn
   House Fiction Prize

Design and Production

Cover and text design
by Kathy Boykowycz

Cover and text illustrations
by Bill Yund

Text set in Stone Serif, designed in 1987
by Sumner Stone

Titles set in Boton, designed in 1986
by Albert Boton

Printed by Thomson-Shore of Dexter,
Michigan, on Natures Natural, a 30%
recycled paper